BOOKS *by* TANIS RIDEOUT

FICTION
Above All Things (2012)
The Sea Between Two Shores (2022)

POETRY
Arguments with the Lake (2013)

THE SEA

BETWEEN

TWO

SHORES

TANIS RIDEOUT

McCLELLAND & STEWART

This paperback published 2023
M&S hardcover published 2022

McClelland & Stewart and colophon are registered trademarks of
Penguin Random House Canada Limited.

This is a work of fiction. Any and all places, characters, and events
are either works of imagination or used fictitiously.

LIBRARY AND ARCHIVES CANADA CATALOGUING IN PUBLICATION
Title: The sea between two shores : a novel / Tanis Rideout.
Names: Rideout, Tanis, author.
Description: Previously published: Toronto: McClelland & Stewart, 2022.
Identifiers: Canadiana 20220192901 | ISBN 9780771076404 (softcover)
Classification: LCC PS8635.I364 S43 2023 | DDC C813/.6—dc23

Cover and interior design by Lisa Jager
Cover art: Khanh Bui; helivideo, both from Getty Images
Interior art: British Library / GRANGER

Printed in the United States of America

McClelland & Stewart,
a division of Penguin Random House Canada Limited,
a Penguin Random House company

www.penguinrandomhouse.ca

1 2 3 4 5   27 26 25 24 23

Penguin
Random House
McCLELLAND & STEWART

For Sheetal and Elizabeth,
to whom I am very much obliged

This is a work of fiction.
It is inspired by true events.

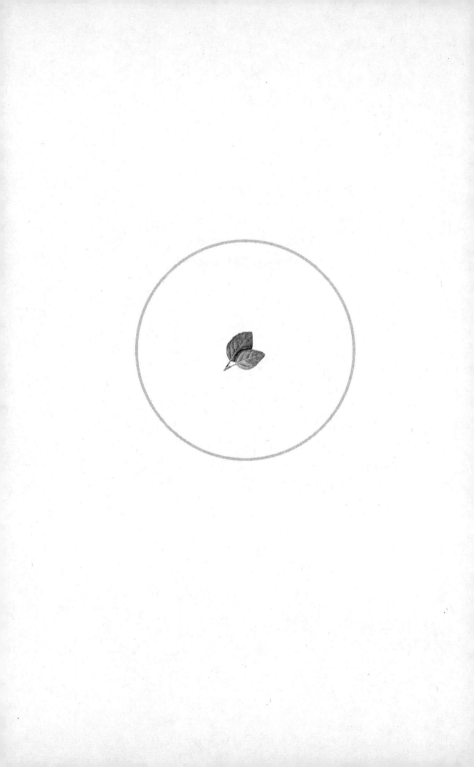

You row forward looking back, and telling this history
is part of helping people navigate toward the future.
We need a litany, a rosary, a sutra, a mantra, a war chant of
our victories. The past is set in daylight, and it can become
a torch we can carry into the night that is the future.

REBECCA SOLNIT, *Hope in the Dark*

Each time we tackle something with joy, each time
we open our eyes toward a yet untouched distance,
we transform not only this and the next moment, but
we also rearrange and gradually absorb the past inside us.

RAINER MARIA RILKE, *The Dark Interval*

Everything that happened made sense to someone.

CHRISTINA THOMPSON, *Sea People*

I

Rebecca

They were warned. For days, voices crackled from the solar-powered radio, and texts came in flurried bursts as officials and family in Vila tracked the churn of the massive March storm. Speed, direction, intent. Rebecca prayed for the cyclone to turn. She prayed for it to slow. She simply prayed.

In preparation, their neighbours and friends harvested not-quite-ready taro, yams, kumala, manioc, and peanuts from gardens strung throughout the bush. Harvest was usually a time of celebration, the exhaustion of good work staved off with song and laughter, but today there was only the toll of the church bell from the next village as each family harvested what they could from their own small plots before offering help to anyone who needed it, any longstanding squabbles set aside for a time. Rebecca worked with the baby napping nearby and her five-year-old daughter, Anaei, at her side, doing her best to help. They buried their meagre bounty of root crops deep underground, in pits lined with woven mats and banana leaves. Her husband, David, marked the place with a twisted bend of cane, as his grandfathers had and theirs before them whenever storms roared across their island from the sea.

Now, as the wind and rain howl outside, Rebecca paces the interior of her home. Even in the murky half-light of waning solar lamps, she can clearly see the twenty people huddled in tight clutches of family, children crying or nervously giggling. Prayers are lost in the wash of wind. Rebecca counts who is not here, pictures their fragile homes tucked under banyans and palm trees and grasping tangles of creepers, and prays they are safe. Her house is the strongest in the village, but even its concrete walls seem liable to crumble in the storm. The sound is unbearable, an angry squall scraped up from the bottom of the ocean, something ancient that echoes in her blood, uncannily familiar. She feels rather than hears the wails of her thirteen-month-old son, Ouben, as she cradles him against her, knowing that his head and sinuses ache just as hers do. She whispers her breath into the shell of his head, hoping, even if he cannot hear her voice, that the smell and feel of her will calm him. Her pulse throbs across her body, meets his with a chop, the way the waves rushing the shore meet those returning to the sea.

It must be midday by now, she thinks, as she stands at the louvred window covered over with plywood to prevent it from shattering. The banana trees will have been long torn down, and she can picture the palm trees being whipped into a frenzy and bending, penitent, until their trunks snap with cracks of thunder, shaking the ground as they fall. The gusts have been growing angrier since the storm picked up in the gloom of dawn.

Overhead, the corrugated roof twists as the wind pulls at it, and the rain is a battering of noise, louder than thought.

Worry churns in her stomach.

When the door bursts open, water sluices across the floor as David and his brother, Tomas, charge through, children in arms, trailed by Tomas's wife. David deposits his niece on a cot near the back of the room, into a cluster of other children, and then comes to take Ouben from Rebecca, holding him to his face, inhaling the baby's scent, as though he has just surfaced from the sea and needs his son to breathe. David puts his other arm around her, Anaei squirming in between them, and Rebecca leans heavily against her husband despite the wet of him soaking her T-shirt. For a moment they hold still while the storm orbits around them. Then she pulls away, takes their son in her arms again, and hands David a thin towel.

Taking in what he can see of this and the next room, he rubs the towel across his face and over his close-cropped hair, the back of his neck. "Where is Grandfather Moses?" He yells to make himself heard above the scream of wind. "And Marami?"

"I went to fetch them earlier," Rebecca says, "but couldn't find them."

"They could be with Moses's brother—he and his family aren't here either," Tomas offers, his words becoming silent shapes under a renewed battering of wind.

"Maybe," David says. "We need to find them."

Tomas shakes his head, still out of breath from their rescue, and Rebecca feels her own breath return with his answer. "We need to wait until the storm ends. If we're hurt, who will help tomorrow?"

David opens his mouth as if to speak but holds his tongue, nods to his brother, and then lifts his daughter into his arms.

Anaei flinches as the wind tears away a piece of plywood from the window. Outside, the world is bruised and wounded. The storm gathers the light to itself and makes a nightfall of the day. What little illumination is left has a yellow glow, unnatural and malevolent. Rain claws between the slats and mud oozes beneath the door. The entire building shakes.

David's mother, Numalin, leaves off her prayers and cries out to return to her home. "God, what have we done to deserve this? Help us! We will all die here when this building falls down on our heads."

"It won't fall," Rebecca whispers into the storm. "It won't." Her voice is an invocation, a calm she does not feel. *Please God*, she adds silently.

Children whimper under the growl of the wind that throws palm fronds, leaves, vines—anything it can hurl against the building. The roof lifts at one corner and threatens to leave them exposed to the storm's sublime ferocity. The air smells like fear, rot, and a current of fire all at once. Around their ankles a mire of mud and water rises, carrying small rocks and twigs that cut and scratch at their skin. Anaei's knobby-kneed legs dangle from David's arms, while Ouben is hot in hers, nestling into sleep. They hold their children close.

———

Nearly six months later, the stony August sky over the island is so low Rebecca could reach out and touch it from where she sits, silent in the doorway of her home, staring at what is left of their village. The place is different now. To her right, there used to be a line of bushes and trees that protected their homes from the brunt of cyclones like the one that destroyed this place. They were torn away by the storm, and the temporary shelters that have been built are exposed to the vastness of the ocean.

She turns her gaze inland, to the bush, where many of the fallen palm trees lie scattered on the ground like toothpicks.

The once-buried roots of larger trees now form ragged, muddy walls at the edge of the nasara, the ceremonial hillock of ground under the still-standing banyan trees. This is where the men gather at the end of each day to talk and drink kava; where the villagers have held so many celebrations and exchanges, so many funerals.

She closes her eyes.

Her arms are empty.

Her son is dead.

Her son is dead, and the hard rain is a weight on everything, bullying every new budding leaf downwards. Even the earth is sinking into itself. Her son is dead, and the paths are still flooded. Rain and seawater have made a turbulent pool of their village, and miniature rivers continue to carry bits of paper and plastic towards the small sand cove tucked between the rocks and coral, where they will be swept out to sea and away from here.

Her son is dead, and her feet are muddy in her broken flip-flops, her T-shirt wet across her shoulders and breasts, her milk gone now, her nipples healed. Such a betrayal—even that trace of him on her body is gone.

"It is always raining when it should be dry, and dry when it should rain," David says from behind her. She can feel the weight of him, imagine his shape in the dimness of their home. "Come eat," he says.

She should say something, but she has no words. She hasn't for months now. She roots for them in her stomach, in her heart, and even when she finds a simple word like *yes* or *no*, she cannot force it to her lips. She should have made dinner, but there is little to eat, their emergency stores long depleted, and so there is only the lately arrived aid rice and fermented breadfruit. Today there is rainwater collecting in the rusty drums and in the cooking pots, so there will be something to drink, and the rain will help the harvest. It could be dry again tomorrow. It should be. But then, Iparei has not been what it should be since well before the storm.

For six months, there have been stuttering starts at repairs and rebuilding, and the men have bickered about water and food and land, about where they should rebuild and how. They argue about why they suffered worse damage in the storm than other villages, other islands. There are rumours that less-affected islands have received more aid, and the men have argued even about that. It has been endless, this arguing over everything. What, they ask, have they done to deserve this? How have they angered their ancestors? God? They insist there must be a reason, that there must be something they can do.

Rebecca fingers the woven loop around her throat as she reaches her other hand out the door to the rain. There is no reason that anyone would deserve what has happened to her, to her son. God does not work like that.

The thickness of the air holds the scent of the dirt and the sea, and of the blossoms bursting from the tangled creepers that grow so fast in the rain she can almost see the stretch and reach of them. This chaotic multitude of green thrives on so very little; it could easily overwhelm what work has been done since the cyclone, curling around the temporary shelters, erasing paths that have only just been re-established.

David reaches into the rain for her hand, cups his other one around the back of her arm, and lifts her to her feet and away from the door. He leads her to the table where Anaei eats the rice that he has cooked, and slides a bowl in front of her as she sits. Ouben loved this bowl. The shiny red plastic of it recalling the bright buckets in the tourism photographs that advertise these islands as paradise escapes. She stares hard at it.

From the other room, Jacob emerges. "I'm going to see Robson," he says. Anaei springs to her feet and goes to stand next to her half-brother, gazing up into his face. He has returned to them an adult from his time in the capital city, Vila, where he has been working construction on the ever-expanding dock for the ever-larger cruise ships that Rebecca and Anaei occasionally spot on the horizon. Jacob palms the back of Anaei's head, and her face brightens and breaks into a smile. The love reflected in their faces as he scoops her up and returns her to her chair momentarily eases Rebecca's sadness.

"Right now?" David asks his son in their language, so different from the language Rebecca grew up with, so different from the Bislama that she and David use with each other. "It's raining."

Jacob shrugs. "He asked me to come see him."

"He can wait." David tries to soften his tone. "We are about to eat. Please. Eat with us."

Jacob's nose wrinkles some at the scarcity on their table. "You go ahead. I'll be back later."

David turns away from his departing son. "I worry that Robson is filling his head," he says.

Rebecca watches as Jacob disappears into the rain and prays Robson is filling him with hope.

Later, Rebecca sits alone in the dark while Anaei sings herself to sleep on her cot. Her voice is low and sweet, and she sings a song Rebecca used to sing to her when she was a baby, which Anaei in turn sang to Ouben. Rebecca's own mother had sung it to her and her brothers and sisters, as her own mother had to her. It sounds like the sea on the beach near her home, pulsing in and out.

When David returns, his phone is in his hand. He flips it open and closed, open and closed, the rhythmic snap of it itching Rebecca's nerves. He turns on the dim solar lamp and sets the phone on the table. The battery is full. So, he too has been to Robson's village. She wonders if Robson asked for payment for the use of his generator, as she's heard he asks others. She cannot imagine that even Robson would ask David for such a thing now.

Her husband sits and puts his head in his hands. She can see how everything weighs on him. Not just all the decisions to be made about their future, but everything that has already happened. He needs an answer, a direction. She wants to reassure him he is a good man, that it isn't his fault that God has forgotten them, but even if she could speak, he would not hear her. Instead, she reaches across the table to touch his wrist where his pulse throbs under the delicate skin. She leaves her fingers there until his heart steadies. He puts his hand on hers and gives it a soft squeeze.

He picks up his phone again. "There are things that must be put to rest if we want to move forward," he says.

She thinks of her own father, always worrying about giving his forefathers offence. "It never hurts," he used to say, "to try to make amends." As the sun sets, David and the other men have been retelling old stories over kava and then listening for its whisper, for their ancestors to speak to them. There is something to be resolved—that much is clear to all of them.

There is a hum in Rebecca's throat, a pressure pushing up against the top of her mouth, and she makes a soft noise. It is barely audible, but David stops clacking his phone and turns to look at her as though he's heard what she wishes she could say.

"I'm going to call them," he says.

She doesn't know if it will do any good, but it is a gesture towards the future. Her mouth shapes the word, but still no sound comes. So she nods, speaks a silent *yes*.

David stands and pulls her to him, puts his arm around her shoulders, and squeezes her gently. She allows herself to press into him, to feel his body along the length of her.

The sky is clearing, revealing the soft deep colour of night, so that it feels later than it is. This is a colour she has seen often in the past year, first walking with Ouben in her arms when he wouldn't sleep, and then without him when she couldn't. Her fingers are at her throat, worrying the neat length of braided vine tied there, a physical memory of him that she feels with every breath. This colour will always be his.

Michelle

It's Scott's idea: a long weekend barbecue in the backyard before the start of the new school year.

They used to have barbecues all the time—impromptu affairs that began with a shout over the fence to the Fraziers next door or quick texts to whoever sprang to mind, chaotic gatherings of families and burgers, kids and hotdogs. They haven't had that kind of gathering for the past two summers. Michelle has barely been in the backyard in over a year.

"It'll be great," Scott said to her when he came back from his Sunday run. "A fun break for all of us"—he stopped, corrected himself—"the four of us, before things get crazy with school and work. Do what we used to. Mark the end of summer."

"I can't," she said, casting about for a reason he would accept. "Astrid needs a new backpack and Zach—"

"Come on. I think what they really need is some family time. A little fun."

"Right, I'm sure Zach will think it's fun."

"They need this, Michelle. *We* need it." She's noticed a new tone in his voice recently, an exasperation maybe, or an urgency, similar to the one she's overheard him using on the phone when he thinks she is in her office or in Dylan's room. A tone that says something has got to give.

"Fine, I'll go pick up some things."

At the grocery and liquor stores she buys pop and beer and more than one bottle of cheap rosé, chips and hamburgers and, in a burst of hopefulness, the ice cream pops Zach likes. She stands in front of the bright boxes of cereal and tells herself they don't need any. Still, she picks up the one that's Dylan's favourite. In the car she opens it, inhaling the smell, and swallows a handful, then another. On the way into the house, she buries the box at the bottom of the recycling bin.

The water in the backyard pool fractures the sunlight into sharp, painful spears. It is just the three of them—Michelle and Scott and Astrid. Zach should be here, but as usual they have no idea where he is.

And Dylan. Dylan should be here.

With her chair angled away from the shattered shine of the pool, Michelle stabs a text message into her phone. *Where are you?* She watches for the dots to bounce in response. When they don't, she puts her phone face down and casts her gaze over the far end of the yard. The plants and flowers she used to love and tend have withered and browned along with the foolishly ambitious attempt at a vegetable garden; even Astrid's small "medicine" garden has gone to seed.

The sun is warm in the end-of-summer air, the wine in her glass is crisp and bright, and her stomach is even growling at the smell of the burgers drifting from the barbecue. She is almost relaxed—or thinks she could be if Zach would show up—when the phone inside rings. The landline never rings unless it's a call from school or her mother.

"Leave it," Scott says too casually from the barbecue. She tries to discern why, staring at him. He doesn't look away, only leans towards her to top up her wine.

"Leave it," Astrid chirps from behind her father. She is sitting on the ground with markers, colouring her toenails. Michelle would have objected to that, before. Now she can't think why she would have thought the colour of her daughter's toenails mattered.

The phone rings again and Scott moves closer, puts his hand on hers. She wills her own hand to turn over and take his, but can't. There is a new barrier between them—she sees more than feels him holding her there. She could let the phone ring in the empty house. She could hold her husband's hand. But instead she thinks of his hushed phone calls and suddenly she needs to know who is on the other end. "It might be Zach," she says, slipping her hand out from under his, pushing herself up from the chair, and heading for the sliding door. As she picks up the phone, she hopes it is Zach, hopes it isn't.

In the weeks after Dylan drowned, she was certain that every ringing phone was him, her younger son reaching out to her. Each time she answered to someone else's voice on the line another layer of her was flayed away, exposing a raw anger at the caller's inevitable sympathy if they knew what had happened, or their ignorance if they did not. The hope that it was him, the faith, was almost unbearable. She was convinced she must still be able to reach him. He couldn't just be gone. He had to be out there somewhere, just on the other side of where she waited.

There is a crackle of static through the receiver. "Hello?" Dylan's name is a prayer she repeats in her thoughts, even as she prepares herself for disappointment—or worse, someone whom only Scott knows.

"Hallo?"

A lightly accented voice, a beat late from long-distance delay, reminding her of when she was little and her mother would call her uncle on Christmas Eve; neither wanted to be the first to call, but they had to call before midnight, so each would try to wait the other out. Michelle never really understood the rules. Once there was the magic of them saying hello to each other without the phone ringing on either end. The wonder of that connection.

"Is this Michelle Stewart?" A tinny sound, a trill to the *r* that makes her name feel French and exotic. A man's voice. She exhales a breath she didn't know she was holding.

"Michelle Stewart-Petit. Yes." She leans into the phone, presses it hard against her ear so she can hear him better. "Who is this?"

"Mrs. Stewart, my name is David Tabé."

"How can I help you, Mr. Tabé?" She tries to pronounce the name the way he does, with a slight swallowing of the vowels, a lifting *eh* at the end. This is something she teaches in her workshops: names are powerful. People like to be addressed by name; it makes them feel heard. She glances out the sliding door. In the backyard Scott is bent over Astrid, examining something she holds in her hand; both of them look serious, deep in discussion, though she cannot hear them.

"I am calling from Iparei," the man says, then pauses, as though waiting for her to acknowledge something. "We are an island in Vanuatu," he continues, and this name rings a bell, echoing from somewhere so deep in her mind she doesn't bother to reach for it. "Your people came here a long time ago. The Reverend and Mrs. Stewart."

Clammy cold washes over her and Michelle slumps to the floor, her back pressed against the cupboards. "Mr. Tabé," she repeats, her voice the only thing steady about her. "Of course. But how can I help you? It's true, my great-great-grandparents went to your island. Sorry, I can never remember the right number of *great*s. But that was, as you say, a very long time ago."

He continues to speak, calm and instructive, as though he were not making a request, but offering her something. And how strange it is, she thinks, for this man who is a link to some long-distant moment in her family's past to be calling her on a sunny afternoon in early September.

All at once, time and space telescope for her and there is a breath on her neck, a voice in her ear. She is reminded of the time she visited the church in Dartmouth where these same grandparents were married almost two hundred years ago, where their names are inscribed over an empty grave, no bones to be interred, and where for an instant her body felt as if it wasn't her own but was occupied by someone else, held someone else's memories. The church grew colder and her consciousness suddenly flared to the infinite—it wasn't an obliteration, but rather an inclusion. She had never been more aware of herself as a link between the past and the future, and certain of her place, her connection to her ancestors, to her children. And then, as quickly as it came, the sensation was gone.

She never told anyone about that experience, but she begins to explain it to the man on the phone—how she feels that way now, like everything is aligned, the past and the present, her and Dylan, her blood, stretching all the way back through those generations.

But even as she tries to find the words, the feeling dissolves. The world collapses to the hard fact of her kitchen and she is left with only the emptiness of where Dylan used to be.

After Michelle hangs up the phone, she looks out the sliding door to see Zach has finally shown up, his fifteen-year-old body all angles and broken skin, slumped in the chair that she vacated. He throws balled-up leaves into the pool. His eyes are so shadowed they could be bruised. It almost hurts her to look at him. She's read the statistics. Families fall apart after losing a child. Husbands leave, wives have affairs, children lash out. But she doesn't know how to fight the almost inevitable.

She tops up her wine glass from the unopened bottle in the fridge, gulps it down, and returns to the backyard. Scott is joking with Zach, trying to call him back from wherever he always seems to be these days, lost in his phone or staring into space.

"Where were you?" she asks, and her voice is too harsh, but she cannot control how it comes out of her anymore. He shrugs, cuts his eyes away from her, stares hard at the swimming pool. There is a frisson around him, a charged energy that feels unpredictable. He could hug her, or throw her into the pool—either seems equally possible.

Instead, he asks, "Why did you get these?" He holds up an ice cream pop over his shoulder, melting in its unopened envelope.

"You like them."

"Nope. Dylan liked them."

His tone is hard, and she recoils from it slightly. Then she sees the bright logo of the ice pop in Dylan's hand, the stain of blue on his tongue, and how he would threaten to lick Astrid with it.

Zach tosses the packet back on the table and it sits between them.

She is about to say something when Scott interrupts. "Who was on the phone?" His tone is neutral.

She tries to conjure the way she felt only a few minutes ago, the warmth of belonging, of connection, but she can't. She is scraped raw again. She thinks of all the times she has asked Scott that same question in the past few months, the answers he has given her.

"No one, just a wrong number."

A few nights later, Michelle is in her office, too exhausted to sleep, having just coaxed Astrid back to bed after another of her night terrors. At least once a week, her daughter cries out, sounding smothered in her sleep, and Michelle, panicked, goes to her. There are shadows watching her, Astrid says, the shades of people, and they want something. She clings to a stone she took from Dylan's room, which she whispers to sometimes. At first Michelle thought the nightmares were because of Dylan, but if that were the case why had they only started five months ago? Why not when he drowned, almost a year and a half ago?

Michelle slumps into her office chair, peers at the dim room around her, takes in the neat stacks of paper, the organized bookshelves. Everything in its place. She presses her palms to the desk in an attempt to anchor herself. There are moments when it feels like Dylan drowned yesterday, and moments when she feels like she's crossed an ocean of time, only to find more water ahead. There are moments when she is sure he is right here next to her, and moments when it feels like he has disappeared completely.

Everything is a marker of his absence. Even the financial statement in the folder centred in front of her. Dylan's trust. Each of the children has one. She and Scott started them as soon as each child was born, and they were bolstered later by her father's will. These are their nest eggs for the future—for school, or travel, a house when they are ready. She is surprised by the substantial amount of money in Dylan's, passed down through generations, always with an eye to the future.

Scott wants to dissolve the trust. "Then we can decide what we want to do with the money later. Split it between A and Z, or, I don't know, whatever. But we might as well invest it—put it to work for us."

She doesn't understand why he insists it must be done now. Doesn't understand why he keeps picking at it, asking her if she has signed the document yet.

Why do they have to end the trust—and with it all of Dylan's possibilities, when there had once been so many?

She fingers the papers. She should just sign them. Would that help her move on, help them get back to normal, like Scott is always saying? She stares hard at that awful date on the form: *May 26, 2012.* One year, three months, ten days ago. She slams the folder closed and picks up the post-it note on its cover with David Tabé's phone number.

At first, she had tossed it away. After all, the idea that they would fly halfway around the world to a tiny island for some kind of reconciliation ceremony is absurd. She remembers her father telling her the story, and then later listening as he told it to her sons. The story goes that her distant ancestor, the not-quite Reverend William Stewart, was looking for absolution after a Road to Damascus–style epiphany. He hadn't been a good or a kind man, but then he found Jesus and was certain he'd been called to share his transformation with other unfortunates. In the 1830s, long before any authorized missions to the area, he and his wife, Josephine, travelled to what is now Vanuatu.

Almost everything that happened after they arrived is a mystery. All that is left of them are a couple of drawings that Josephine herself made of each of them before they departed and some loose pages from what was presumed to be a diary recovered years later and eventually returned to the family by a church group. The unnumbered pages are a confusion of superstition and fear, moments of connection, and vivid descriptions of the people who lived alongside them before their story ended abruptly. William and Josephine Stewart were killed on the island, and while there are theories, no one really knows why.

What can she and her family do about events that happened centuries ago? The past is the past. There is nothing to reconcile.

But then yesterday, when she came into her office, there was the notepad that normally sat beside the phone in the kitchen. The top page was missing, but she could still see the impression of the phone number. As she traced the indentations with her finger, she remembered making rubbings of gravestones with Zach and Dylan on school field trips. She picked up a pencil and rubbed the lead across the page. The figures appeared in relief.

She touches the number now and feels Dylan beside her. *You should totally go.*

And as she hears him say it, she pulls her feet up and spins herself in her chair, the way Dylan used to, the way Astrid still does—she grips the desk and winds up, then pushes herself around and around. She closes her eyes against the movement and imagines the swirling around her is a tropical wind, imagines Dylan in her lap, imagines dialling the number, the long plane journey, the heat of the sun and the wild spread of the ocean. She can almost smell the salt.

But what good would it do?

She spins faster and faster, and when she opens her eyes, she is dizzy and slightly nauseous. As the backyard flashes by, something—someone—flickers in the murky light refracting off the swimming pool.

She slams to a stop, her feet thump to the floor.

Her head and stomach still spinning, Michelle stumbles to the kitchen, where she stops in front of the sliding door that leads to the backyard. A shadow separates itself from the hedge along the fence, then stops and crouches by the pool, dips its hand in, and splashes water over its face.

The way he holds himself, the even line of his shoulders—it's Dylan. She's certain of it. She reaches out, the glass a hard surprise when her hand meets it. Dylan glances at the door, then stands and lopes towards the side of the house. She moves to the laundry room and stands frozen, just out of sight of the side door. It's impossible. Her heart is beating loudly and soaring out of her body as if to meet him, to bring him home. The door handle clicks itself loose and she waits for the familiar screech of the outer screen door when it closes.

She feels the shift in the house, another presence.

He's there, a shadow pinned against the door. He's grown during his time away. Not a surprise—he'd been growing so quickly it had cost them a small fortune to keep him in hockey gear.

She shapes his name with her lips but is too terrified to speak it in case he disappears.

"Mom?"

His voice pierces her.

Zach. It's only Zach. And how she burns with shame at the thought of that word—*only*.

She exhales deeply, with relief and anger at once. "For god's sake, Zach, it's the middle of the night. Where have you been?"

He says nothing, only shakes his head and goes to move past her. As he does, she can feel the heat of the outdoors radiate off him in the air-conditioned dark. She lifts her hand to touch him, and he jerks away as though burned.

"Nowhere. Just out."

Her heart thuds in her throat. She hadn't even realized he wasn't at home.

He starts up the stairs and she wants to stop him. He was such a tactile child, always touching and hugging her, using her to climb over or on top of things. She used to joke that she was his favourite piece of furniture and for a while he called her that jokingly—*Hi chair! Hey table!*—before collapsing into giggles. She cannot remember the last time she touched him, this body that used to be hers to cuddle and hold.

"You can't do that, just take off. It's not safe." In the half-light, Zach's features seem to flicker some and she finds anger rearing up in her, a black and red thing that sits at the edge of her vision. "Anything could happen to you. You can't just—"

Zach pauses on the third step. "As if you even care."

There is silence, the sense of the house breathing. They stand in the gloom, neither of them moving. She's about to say of course she cares, when there's a loud thump as the air conditioner kicks on, circulating a low hum.

"You told him you'd get it fixed," Zach says. His voice is low, like his father's. It breaks constantly now, moving between childhood and adulthood. She wonders what Dylan would have sounded like as a man.

"Get what fixed?"

"The air conditioner. Dylan hated it. Remember?" Zach laughs a little. How can he laugh? "It woke him up and he'd show up at my door terrified. I don't know what he thought it was. Maybe he just wanted the attention. It worked."

He steps up a stair and, before she can stop herself, she is reaching for him, wanting to pull him to her, wanting to throttle him. She misses his arm but catches his shirttail, and as he turns to shake her off, it rides up. She is surprised by the shape of him, the leanness of his waist, the cut of muscles emerging from the skinniness that has always been there. Then she sees the stain of a violent bruise rising up from his hip bone and spreading across his stomach, the angriness of it evident even in the dim light.

"What happened?" She tries to lift his shirt higher, but he is already retreating up the stairs, moving stealthily into the darkness before she can say anything more, before she can demand—what? An explanation? An apology?

She doesn't follow. She remains standing at the base of the stairs, her hands empty of both her sons.

Then, somehow, she is back in her office. For the past year she has found herself arriving at places without quite knowing how she got there.

The backyard is empty now, the ink of the pool like the wound on Zach's side. She wants to scream, to rip the world apart. It is three a.m., her son's body is bruised and broken, and she didn't even know he was gone. She tears at the neat lines of books on her shelves, throws them to the floor. She sweeps everything from her desk, papers snow-falling around her.

She collapses against the wall, knocks photographs of Zach and Dylan and Astrid askew, slides to the floor. Her pulse pounds in her ears, repetitive and strong, and she wishes it would stop. Her breath and her heart, the concussive sound of her own body. She has to do something. She has to do more.

She picks up her cellphone and dials the number, then waits for the voice on the other end.

Faina

Faina walked the stretch of coral, its jagged surface pricking the soles of her feet. The sun was high in the sky, and the ocean had pulled back into itself, leaving tide pools filled with stranded fish and sea stars, miniatures of the larger sea. Perfect for hunting eels. The small ones liked to search for prey up on the coral at low tide, slipping from pond to pond, chasing trapped fish. With one hand Faina gripped a smooth forked pole, and with the other she adjusted the basket slung low against her hip that would hold her bounty. Her feet sent a skitter of tiny crabs towards the sea.

The surf hushed her, moving languidly in and around the dark blue holes that had been punched into the reef by the first heroes who occupied the island, in the time before people grew here. As she watched for the muscled curve of eel, she kept an eye to the horizon line as well, anxious for the sight of more immense canoes. Nearer the shore was the familiar shape of one of her people's fishing canoes, its single woven sail pulled tight against a gentle wind. Were they using the new fishing tools that

Louvu, who spoke for her people, had traded with the missi for? It was said that the fish couldn't wait to be caught on them, almost leapt themselves into the canoes.

The missi were a whisper that had arrived with the onshore wind. Before the last new moon, knowledge of them had slipped from lip to ear to lip—what they looked like, how they spoke and moved, what they ate, so that all of these were simply things that Faina now knew, in the way that it was always known whose baby was whose, which roads between places and people were open and which were closed. The way it was known when a storm would turn the village to mud and tear the fruit from the trees and the trees from the earth, or when it would only clean the air of all the heaviness it held. Some things you just knew. But she had yet to see the missi with her own eyes.

Faina returned to scanning the coral ahead of her. The sea was turning, climbing back onto the island. If she didn't find an eel soon, she wouldn't at all. She stared hard into shadowed crevices, her breath keeping pace with the lift and fall of the sea. There was a soft bulge of something in the water, too large for an eel. A turtle. She watched the dark roundness of it distend the surface as he bobbed and moved just below the water, then lifted his face into the air to peer at her. She was glad to see him. Turtles were even older than the land itself, and venerated. Only the Turtle people down the coast had the right to hunt them. At certain times of the year, they would boil the turtle's head for their powerful men and sorcerers, then send the soft meat along their allied roads in exchange for the oysters that Faina's own people collected. She loved the rich taste of turtle flesh, but she hoped that this old man would find his way back to the sea.

As she turned away, she saw the muscled flash that she had been waiting for slip below a ledge. She gripped her pole even tighter, imagining the heft of a spear. Masai had fired the branch in the coals for her, and it was as hard as the coral she walked on. Faina stepped near where she had seen the creature. It wasn't a large eel, but it was spotted and wide, its belly pale and the fin wafting like a sea fan.

Then he was up on a ridge of coral and shimmying sideways, almost as quick on land as in water. Faina got herself above him and slammed the crook of her stick down, trapping the eel against the sharp rock. With a quick flick she struck its head against the rocks and the creature shuddered and died. She stood still a long moment, panting hard from the excited rush of the hunt and, once she was sure the eel was dead, she curled its body into her basket.

"Well caught!"

Masai stepped out of the brush where the road to the village met the shore, and Faina's body warmed inside, even as the sun slipped behind a high run of cloud. She settled the weight of the eel in the basket against her body and lifted a hand to him. She was about to speak when the rhythmic toll from the missi's cove rolled along the shore towards them. In the many days since the missi arrived on the island, Faina had grown used to the sharp sound that called up the hill with the first breaking of dawn and then at what seemed like regular intervals, cutting up the shape of the day until the sun set over the far sea.

"Do you think the missi is calling his spirits?" she asked Masai as she joined him on a shaded patch of sand. Sometimes their people struck special stones or shells to call on their ancestors. Who was the missi calling down?

"He must be," Masai said. "The man swings his hollow stone and it makes that noise." Masai leapt up and swung his own arm up and down, contorting his face in mock exertion. "Then he and the other missi stand, bow their heads, clasp their hands together like this, and speak for a long time." He murmured meaningless sounds and looked up at the sky, imploring.

Faina laughed, covering her teeth with her hand. "What do they ask?"

Masai only shook his head, then closed his eyes and sat back down against the coconut tree. The light danced on his skin, and the onshore breeze plucked at the vines and feathers woven into his hair. He crossed his long legs at the ankle, the muscle under the skin reminding her of the eel sliding below the surface of the water. Flustered, she tossed her skirt of pandanus leaves gently to dry the bottom in the breeze. The shells around her wrist chattered.

"Father's Father says the missi have built an unusual house, and they cut down trees the Hotwater people claim as theirs."

Masai shrugged at this. "But the missi made an exchange, with an axe that is made from a material that is harder even than our stone ones."

"But those trees would have given fruit for years and years. The axe will break—they always do."

"Maybe not this one. Maybe it was a good exchange."

Masai still hadn't opened his eyes, so Faina edged closer to him. He was a couple of harvests older than her but still had yet to marry. She liked to imagine that they could be married, even though it would never happen. She was already betrothed to a man from the Uplanders—a people that her own, the Middle Grove, had been at war with for a long time. They were trying to renew an old peace, and her marriage would be a part of that.

"The missi must be powerful if the bad spirits haven't driven them off the land."

The land that the Middle Grove people and the Hotwater people had agreed to let the missi use was tabu, a powerful place where long-gone ancestors had been buried after they fell in battle. The ancestors' spirits still battled on that land at night, and it was well avoided by the people of the island after dark.

Faina tugged her basket towards her, and the eel glistened in the shadow of it. "Father loves eel," she said. "I could bring this to him for lunch."

"At the missi cove?" Masai asked, curling one side of his mouth into a smirk.

"Oh, is that where he is?"

"You'll get in trouble." Masai opened his eyes to meet her gaze.

"Not if you go with me."

———

The night the missi arrived, torches shuddered in the wind, tossing sparks up into the clouded sky. There were no stars, only the night creeping close to dancing circles of firelight. The surf rang in measured booms against the beach, reminding Faina of her heartbeat pounding in her head when she swam in the sea.

She should have been watching the sand under Mother's torch, eyes sharp for the quick scurry of crabs as the ocean retreated. Instead, Faina watched the embers from the burning palm frond Mother held overhead float skyward. If Faina stared hard at the flicker and shine of sparks before turning her head towards the invisible horizon, their patterns duplicated themselves, making a spatter of stars where there should be none, like spirit images only she could see.

There were crabs everywhere; the ancestors must have been well pleased with their people to send the creatures in such bounty, and so the hunt was a kind of celebration. All around Faina, women and children sang and watched for the crabs, waiting for the sea to recede and then grabbing them when they were exposed in the backwash of sand. She loved the crabs' season. The people of Middle Grove would feast on them, and when they'd had their fill they would trade them Upland in exchange for the bald pigs that were their tabu animal, and in this way they maintained the fragile yet blossoming peace between the Uplanders and Middle Grove.

"Faina," Mother said, shaking the flaming frond in her hand so the sparks showered over her. "Pay attention."

As the water pulled back from her ankles with the familiar tug of the deep, Faina's fingers seized the shell of a crab who raised his pinchers in anger. The basket Faina had woven that morning while watching over her younger brother and sister was almost full with the snap of claws. She added the new crab and watched as the creatures scrambled over each other, fighting to climb to freedom. Then she stared at the rising string of sparks again before turning back to look at the sea. This time, the stars the sparks made did not fade from her vision. She rubbed at her eyes. The stars remained on the horizon.

What were those lights? They were not true stars; the night was too dark, too solid for that. The torches and the white foam at the reef that marked the farthest boundary of their territory were the only brightness. No star Faina knew was the colour of those in the distance, which were the colour of hearth fires, and sat just as low to the horizon. As she raised her arm to point at the lights, an ember landed on her wrist and burned her flesh, marking her. She grimaced in pain, but still she shouted through the intricate harmonies of the song being sung around her.

"Look!"

———

The cove had changed in the days since the missi's arrival. Much of the land had been cleared of the scraggly trees that once grew there. Faina stood at the edge of what was now a clearing, exposed to the sea. The lingering spirits had not harmed the missi at all.

When she looked over her shoulder for Masai, he had already slipped off to join the group of warriors sitting on an outcrop of stone, watching over others who were working. A small clutch of girls sat close by, waiting to fetch them water or fruit, waiting for kind words.

Not far from where Masai and the younger men were gathered, Louvu, Kaipar, and the older men, including Father and Father's Father, lounged and observed what went on. There had been much discussion among the men those first few days after the missi's landing. Should they send them immediately away on their strange canoe, or should they send them to the other peoples to seek permission to stay on their lands? It was decided, with Louvu making the last argument before a consensus was reached, that it was best to keep the missi on Middle Grove land, so that they might make an alliance with them. The strangers might be powerful. It was best to keep them close.

Faina didn't spot the missi at first, and wondered if maybe Masai and the others had exaggerated their difference, their height, the colour of their skin, their costumes. Some older boys from Hotwater and Middle Grove moved through the clearing, picking up strange objects, heads bending together to discuss them and to weigh them in their hands, before tossing them down and moving on to the next. A few other men from both villages were levelling an area of ground in front of the curious structure that Masai had described. The flat wood walls of it, the peaked roof, seemed unlikely to stand up to the storms that would come in the next season. It looked fragile and alien there. Faina shook her head.

On the other side of the clearing, a short way up the shore, men from Hotwater were gathered with clubs in their hands, dressed not quite for battle though they gave the impression of fortitude and strength, their hair dressed with fresh vines and feathers. She couldn't make out what the Hotwater men yelled, but Masai must have. He charged towards them with some of the other young men, before stopping short and hurling his own words at them. Faina's blood surged. Would there be a fight? She had never seen one this close, had seen only the results.

Then there he was! One of the missi moved down the beach with arms outstretched to stand in the empty space between the two groups. After the missi spoke, several of the Hotwater men spat on the ground and then backed away, retreating to the thrusts of coral that sheltered this curl of beach. Masai and the others withdrew to the shade of the palm trees on the far side of the clearing, weapons loose in their hands.

The missi remained where he stood for a long moment, his chest heaving. He was red-faced and sweaty, dressed head to toe in a fluttering material that draped around him, obscuring his body. She could make out the *V* of skin on his chest where the cloth on his torso flapped open and then tucked into black coverings over each of his legs, ending in bulky black feet. The man's skin was blotchy—pink and red and pale, like some of the pigs her father kept, the least valuable ones, not like the black-bristled ones. His head was bald, with only a fringe of hair more like thin feathers than the thick textured sculptures her people wore. He had a short scruff of beard that was an orangey colour, very different than the storm-cloud colour that dropped from his brow.

His shoulders drooped and he turned to sit on the trunk of a felled tree. He pressed his hands together and whispered into them as if conjuring, before casting dark looks at the people gathered around. Then he lifted his clasped hands to his face, murmuring into them, all the while scanning the clearing. The missi drank from something and then hauled himself back to his feet and returned to his work, some of the men from Hotwater and from her own village turning with him. The missi towered over the others, but they moved efficiently in their work while he was clumsy.

But there were meant to be two of them. Faina scanned the beach and clearing and spotted the other one bent over and digging through a great pile of what appeared to be wooden containers, their edges sharp and straight. Was it a woman? There was the slight shape of breasts, the slope of hips. Faina inched closer. The basket with the eel moved heavy against her own hip and tugged at her shoulder.

At Faina's approach the woman stood to her full height and Faina looked up at her shape, backlit by the brightness of the sky. The missi woman glanced quickly over her shoulder at the missi man who was watching them, before turning back towards Faina. "Hello," the woman said with a tight smile.

Faina faltered, but then smiled back—a welcome, an invitation. "Good morning," Faina greeted her in her own language.

This missi was tall too, taller even than the other one, and her hair hung long and dark down her back, tied together at the nape of her neck. She was dressed differently than her partner. The coverings on her upper body were tighter than the man's, outlining her arms and her breasts beneath, but at the waist the material dropped to the ground, like the pandanus skirt that Faina wore. It appeared to be of one long woven sheet, though, and was dull as a mid-afternoon cloud. The skirt made a soft noise as the missi crouched down so that she could meet Faina's eyes.

Her face was striking in its sharpness, the bones evident beneath the blotchy, scabbed skin. Her lips were cracked and dry. There were lines at the corners of her eyes, and her nose was long and keen as an adze.

"Hello," the woman said again. Like a question. She nodded an encouragement, a spark of something in her eyes.

Faina mimicked the sounds—"Ell. O."—and the woman clapped her hands together and smiled even wider, revealing small, yellowed teeth. Even though the woman's reaction irked her and made her feel like a child, Faina felt the frisson of connecting the meaning of her words with the woman's. The same thrill she felt when her mother's people came for the annual exchange and traded Faina their words for hers. "*Ello*," she said again. "What else can you say?" Faina asked the missi, but the woman stood up and walked towards where the other one had called to her. Father's Father whistled to Faina, and she repeated the missi's greeting in her head as she made her way to where he sat with the other men.

"You shouldn't be here," he said to her. "There might be trouble. You were told to stay away, no? You don't have work to do?"

She wanted to ask why it was okay for others to stay and not her. Why should she be kept away?

"I was hunting," she said instead, lifting the basket off her hip. "The eel led me on a chase, until Masai found me close to here," she lied easily. "And it made more sense to go home this way. I could cook it for you?"

Father's Father looked at her a moment. He sighed, indulgent, and placed his hand on her cheek before nodding. "Fine, make us a good meal, then." He turned back to the other men.

Faina kindled a small fire to life, then cut the eel into strips that she cooked on the hot stones, the smell of it wafting on the breeze. These missi were not the first strangers to come to their island. Father's Father often told his story of having met visitors who had come many harvests ago, about how brave he was as a child in standing up to them. He had a weapon that was given to him by their leader, Kap Kuke, and also the N-glish word for it—*knife*. It was from him that she knew the word for what the missi wore was *cloth*. Perhaps Father's Father had more words than even these.

There were stories even older than Father's Father, of people who had left the islands on their canoes to find faraway lands and who eventually would return. Was Kap Kuke descended from these long-ago ancestors? What about these missi?

Even Faina had seen canoes like the one that had deposited the missi and their smaller boat in the island's waters, but they always drifted by on their way to distant islands. None had ever come so close to here as to land.

When the eel was cooked, with her head down she delivered it to Father, Father's Father, and the other men.

"May I bring some to the missi?" she asked Louvu, nodding towards the newcomers. She glanced quickly at Father's Father behind him to watch his reaction: a short nod of the head that this offer of hospitality was the right thing to do. Louvu shrugged and gave a half-nod of indifference.

Close up, the missi was unattractive, paler than his woman. His nose was flat and webbed with red across the skin. He grimaced at what she offered and shook his head, said something harsh to her, and then turned back to the area he was clearing.

The other missi tended her own small cooking fire. On it was a type of hard basket that was not burned by the fire. It looked as though it was made from the same material as the head of the axe a man nearby used to chop at logs, and inside the basket, water boiled. Faina imagined cooking with it, so much faster than boiling water with hot stones. The woman too grimaced at the eel meat.

"It's delicious," Faina told her and smiled, picking up and eating one of the pieces. The fat of it melted on her tongue. It tasted of the sea. She made a small sound of contentment.

The woman bent to one of her hard baskets and removed something, and then gestured for Faina to follow her back to where her husband worked. She handed the man a flat circle and then one to Faina, then picked up the pieces of eel with a sharp tool and placed them on each of the hard, round surfaces. The woman and the man dropped to their knees, their food set on the ground in front of them. The woman urged Faina down beside her and then she and her husband pressed their hands together, as though they held something invisible between them. He bent his head forward and spoke to his hands. It sounded like an incantation, a spell, and reminded her of the way that Sero sometimes spoke to those who could not be seen on this side. The man looked up at the sky; Faina followed his gaze but saw nothing except the blues reaching higher and higher.

He must be their tabu man, then, Faina thought. Their sorcerer. Was he as strong as Sero?

The woman began to speak along with her husband. They spoke the same words with the same rhythm, but she spoke quietly, closely, while he proclaimed to the sky. Faina wondered at the meaning. Did they think she had cursed the food? Were they putting their own magic on it?

When the man finished speaking, he and his wife sat side by side on a nearby fallen log. They held their flat round objects in their hands. The woman swallowed down a bite of eel and turned to face Faina. She spoke words that had the tone of gratitude.

Then the woman spoke again and touched her chest. Two short sounds. She repeated them, tapping her chest.

Faina did the same. "Faina."

The woman smiled. "Thank you, Faina."

The man muttered something and shook his head, scraping the eel onto the dirt before getting up and taking the rest of his meal a short distance away.

The woman sighed. "Thank you, Faina," she repeated.

Faina glanced sidelong at the other missi where he watched the two of them, then down at the eel he had dropped in the dirt, that he wouldn't eat. She looked back at the woman.

"You're welcome," Faina said in her own language, "Jos-fine."

II

David

David stands under the hot weight of the morning sun, listening to the chatter and whoops of the children fading into the bush as they move down the green path towards the school in Robson's village. He tries to catch the squeak of Anaei's laughter or the sting of her tongue when she scolds a boy who thinks he is smarter or braver than her, but he cannot find her there. For a moment he wants to race down the road and catch up with her, to reassure himself that she is safe. Instead he closes his eyes, curls his hands into fists, and digs his nails into his palms. When he opens his eyes again, the spread of the ocean fills them with all its shades of blue, sparking to the distant line that splits the sky from the sea. He breathes it in—the smell, the depth, the colours—until he feels the ocean in his lungs and his gut, the wash of it slipping into his blood, holding him fast to the land. The village is bright and shining in the wet of last night's rain. It is beautiful and he wishes he could stay and enjoy this morning, but he will have to leave soon. The road to the airport will be pitted with potholes made worse by the downpour.

He turns to the threshold of his house and strains to hear if Rebecca is humming. She used to hum all the time. Or sing under her breath while working or walking the narrow foot roads between gardens and villages. She would sing with Anaei when they walked together to the next village—Anaei to school, Rebecca to clean the church—their voices tangled together so closely it was as if they sang with one voice. He yearns to hear her sing again, but it has been many months since she has. Even now she doesn't join the other women as they rehearse for the ceremony, though he has caught her staring in the direction of the voices that drift on the breeze. At least now she is speaking again. That is something.

But she is silent as he steps through the door.

"I have to go," he says. "The plane is due in an hour." He flips open his phone to check the time, clacks it closed. She turns to him but doesn't say anything. Her face has been drawn into sharper lines, the round softness of her youth now gone. He misses her old face and hates himself for it. "I know," he continues with a shrug, "the plane will be late, but the road will be washed out. I don't want them to have to wait. You know what white people are like."

Rebecca only nods.

There are fresh flowers on the table, their stems woven together to make a ring. They glow bright yellow in the cool dimness of the room swept clean and smelling of bleach. The flood line just above the floor is almost invisible now. Rebecca spent days scrubbing on her knees to remove it.

"The place looks nice," he goes on. A pause before he adds, "Thank you." She nods again. "Have you seen Jacob? He said he wanted to go with me, but I'll have to go on my own if he doesn't show up soon."

She presses her lips together, then points along the road that Anaei and the children have taken into the bush and says, "To Robson." Was her voice always this quiet? Even in these simple words he can hear her accent, the stutter of his language, the way she sounded when she first came to Iparei to marry him all those years ago. She was so young and beautiful then, her eyes clear and deep like a hidden place in the forest, or the pool below a waterfall. She is still beautiful.

"Why has he gone to see him?" He switches to Bislama when she doesn't answer, trying to make it easier for her to find the words, to speak them. "Robson is always full of such big talk and plans. I wish Jacob wouldn't listen to him." He sits in one of the chairs, still damp from Rebecca's cloth. "I think Jacob wants to go back to Vila soon. He is always talking about money, and how much he can make there. And the cinema, the kava bars." He grits his teeth. "But he needs cash to get back there. I don't think even Robson will be able to help him now, though."

Her fingers roll the length of woven vine tied around her neck, and not for the first time David wishes he had accepted her offer to twist one for him, as she did for Anaei. It is how her people grieve, but it is not his father's way. Still, he yearns for the small comfort she seems to draw from her kastom, wishes he too could mark his grief on his own body in some way.

David aches to hear his wife's voice, the hope running deep through him, and he fiddles with the flowers on the table until a stem comes untwined. He tries to repair it, but Rebecca places her hand on his for a brief second and then deftly weaves the flowers back together.

Her silence is total as she moves away from him and around the room, tidying what is already neat. She straightens the crucifix and the pictures on the wall—her parents, him as a young man in the city, and an old, faded photo of a group of people, including two men in traditional pandanus skirts, standing in front of the old mission house. His grandfather had told him it was a photo of his own father and one of Robson's great-grandfathers when they had just become men, taken before Robson's forefather left the island and never returned. There is the framed photo of Jacob graduating from secondary school, and tucked into the corner is the single photo they have of Ouben. He would have grown to look like Rebecca, the way Jacob carries his mother's look.

David flips open his phone, flips it closed.

"The Stewarts," he continues, "have a small girl about Anaei's age. Did I tell you? They can play together."

Rebecca holds herself still and inhales deeply before straightening the curtain, the light haloing her profile, her short hair, the bridge of her nose. When the phone rings in his hand, Rebecca startles like a dove from a branch.

He opens the phone, still staring at his wife.

"Hello? Where are you? I'm waiting." His voice is much too loud.

His son says he is on his way, and after David stands to leave, he kisses Rebecca, her lips soft and yielding. "This is good." He means their home, their village, the strangers coming to them. "Everything is good." She stares at him and he tries to read her look; he wants her to believe him. "I mean, it will be." As he turns to go, he isn't sure who he is trying to convince.

"Your son," Rebecca says, and her voice stops David at the threshold.

He turns to her. "Yes? What about him?" She chews her lip, but doesn't say anything else. Gives him a smile that is both loss and hope. He steps back towards her, but then glances briefly at the phone in his hand. "I have to go." It is a plea for her reassurance, her confidence in him. He kisses her cheek, the new lines that have formed at the corner of her eye. "It will be okay."

Sitting in the cab of his truck, David squeezes the steering wheel, wondering what Rebecca was going to say about Jacob. He suspects Rebecca knows more than she is telling him, because Jacob shares more with her than he does with his own father. There is a small flare of annoyance that his son has come between them, but then she and Jacob have long shared secrets. It was Rebecca who knew he wanted to stay in Vila after graduation, Rebecca who knew about the girl from one of the islands in the north. Most days, she is their bridge; on other days, she is their wall.

David watches for Jacob across the nasara, where the women have laid down woven mats for everyone to sit and eat after they welcome the Stewarts to the hastily rebuilt village. Looking beyond their dancing ground, he is still not used to seeing the open spread of the ocean. There used to be a thicket of trees and bushes that separated the village from the sea, but it was swept clean by flood waters, leaving only a blank scar. In the months since the cyclone there has been much regrowth on the island, the flowering of lianas, the bursting red of the croton leaves, the blazing of so many greens they are impossible to name, and yet this stretch of shore remains exposed. The straggling trees that still stand have not returned to their full growth, and the sway of palm trees is missing overhead.

Of course, that is not all that is missing.

Three dead. Ouben, yes. But also Moses and Marami, the village elders. He feels the weight of all the losses, the question of what he could have done differently. He tried. He wanted to go to them during the storm, and he went as soon as he could afterwards. He and Moses's brother lifted their bodies from their broken home, from the plywood and corrugated metal, twisted and all but buried in the mud. Their own sons and daughter were not on the island, and did not learn they had died until ten days later. They were buried without their children there to say goodbye.

Flipping his phone open, he checks the time again. David is just about to start the truck when his son raises a lazy hand and calls to him from across the nasara. He is raising his own hand in return when he sees Robson step out from behind Jacob. David feels a sting of irritation along his spine. He should have known that Robson would never let him fetch the visitors without him.

"An auspicious day!" Robson says loudly, climbing into the cab.

David makes a low noise in response, starts the truck, and turns onto the road.

They drive in uncomfortable silence until Jacob nudges Robson and says, "Tell him what you were telling me."

"It's nothing." Robson waves him away.

"I'm sure it is not," David says, "if my son is so interested."

"I had a call from my uncle, my mother's brother, in Vila." His tone is patient, condescending, as if he cannot understand why David doesn't already agree with what he has not yet said. "He knows many people in the government, you know, on the Trade Board. He is saying it will finally happen. The Chinese have agreed to build the ring road. Because we have to rebuild so much anyway, now is definitely the time."

Jacob chokes a little on his laugh as the truck is jolted through a particularly bad patch of mud, bouncing him hard in the back seat. "Imagine—a paved road linking the whole of the island."

Robson nods. "It makes sense. There will be more aid money coming from the NGOs, to help with the rebuilding. But we don't need more rice, or tents, or mosquito nets. We need machines to clear the land, and my uncle says the big men in town are already planning on sending them to Iparei to help rebuild the wharf at the north head of the island. When they arrive, we will not let them go, and we will build the road. Good news, yes?"

David shakes his head. "We need new homes and water cisterns more than we need a single road." He sucks his teeth. "There is always a new plan. For years they have been talking about this road. You think it will happen today?"

"This time my uncle says it will happen for sure. It's our turn. This is the way God works, yes? We serve Him, and He rewards us." Robson sounds pleased. "There is money, from the NGOs and the Chinese," he repeats.

"And what do you think they want in return?" David asks, but Robson doesn't answer. "You know it isn't just about money. There are so many disagreements over land. Some people will want to take the money, because they know they have no claim to the land they live on; others know that their place is worth more than anything they will be offered by the government. Once the land is covered by the road, it will not feed them anymore, will not nurture them." He shakes his head again, already hearing arguing voices in his head. "No. There will never be agreement."

"They will have to sell the land if the government says."

"But then there will be many people unhappy about it."

"Bah, you are always so gloomy and suspicious."

"Think of the money and jobs it would bring to the island," Jacob says. "Young men can clear the way for the road. Women can cook for the Chinese workers who will need to have somewhere to eat, to sleep. People will not have to go to Vila for work."

And for a moment, David can see it—his son staying on Iparei to work construction on the road, getting married, starting a family. He would be able to stay, at least for the short term, and it almost seems worth it: the giving over of land and water rights, the burying of the ancient roads that have connected their communities since the beginning of time for a single ring road. One instead of many.

Almost.

"Would you stay then?" David tries to catch his son's eye in the rear-view mirror, but Jacob looks away.

Robson slaps David on the arm and he cranks the wheel to avoid a pothole. When the truck is steadied again, Robson laughs. "We must think of what is best for everyone, not just for each individual. Not everyone will be happy, but most might be happier."

As they pull onto the short-paved curve to the airport, they hear the plane overhead. A blue tarp emblazoned with a white UN logo covers the gaping hole where the cyclone tore away the roof. Men sit on the grass in front of the small building while children chase each other or stand watching the plane circle. There is only one other vehicle parked on the dry patch of packed dirt, the truck from the village in the north of the island. The white doctor who drives it stands in the shade of the small building.

Robson goes off to join him, his hands spread wide, his voice booming. David and Jacob climb from the truck and watch the plane turn and make its landing, bouncing some as the wheels hit the earth.

"You can get agreement from disagreement," David's father used to tell him, "as long as people are talking." He wants to tell his son this now, to find a way to talk to him. He opens his mouth to begin, but Jacob gestures at him, then points to a small man, his hair a pale cloud around his head. Jacob says something about knowing him from town and calls out a greeting as he walks across the open lawn in front of the airport.

David watches his son's back and wishes he knew what was in his mind. He has always been drawn to the city, and David can feel it all the more as his son walks away.

When the plane empties, the Stewarts are easy to spot. Five of them climbing down the small steps—two men, two women, and a little girl—the only white people besides the doctor, sweaty, red-faced, and out of place. On closer inspection, they are not two men, but a man and his son, a few years younger than Jacob. All of them look uneasy, casting about for someone to claim them. What must his forefathers have felt, David wonders, when the Stewarts' forefathers stumbled onto this shore in a ship no less astounding to them than the first airplane that landed on this island had been to him when he was a boy. An impossible machine that lifts people into the air, lets them fly.

What did his grandfathers' grandfathers see?

A man and a woman, hopeful and desperate. Exhausted from their journey around the world, from beyond the horizon.

He sends a quick prayer to his grandfathers' grandfather that he is doing the right thing.

Zach

He didn't know the world could look like this. Iparei doesn't resemble anywhere Zach has seen in his fifteen years. It doesn't look like his Toronto neighbourhood, or even like the few foreign places he has visited—resorts in Cuba, Mexico.

From the window of the tiny nineteen-passenger propeller plane, the island had appeared stripped bare. The fallen trunks of palm trees lay across large bare swaths of land like the pickup sticks that he and Dylan used to play with on rainy weekends at their grandparents' cottage. But here on the ground, the jungle is a living green wall at the edge of the field that serves as a runway—towering palms entangled in vines, leaves like canopies, a riot of flowers. This place is huge and alive in a way that he can't quite describe. The way the lake-filled wilderness of Algonquin Park can feel in the middle of the night, when you've portaged to a quiet shore and there is only the crackle of campfire and the spread of the Milky Way.

It's unsettling and glorious. Anything could be out there. Anything is possible.

He turns slowly, panning the camera on his phone, before stopping the video and holding his phone up, searching for a signal. To his surprise, it beeps to life, though he isn't surprised by the series of texts from Chelsea.

Did you make it?

Don't rmbr how long flight is.

Miss ya, kiss ya.

He thumbs a quick emoji in response before his grandmother steps down from the plane behind him. "Wow," she says. "Your brother would have loved this, don't you think?"

It's such a relief to hear his brother invoked so casually that Zach has to press at the fresh bruise on his ribs to stop himself from laughing. It's not like he doesn't love his brother. Doesn't miss him. Doesn't wish for him back every fucking day. But his mother flinches whenever Dylan's name is mentioned, and his father only speaks of Dylan in reverent tones. It's exhausting.

He sways in the heat and heaviness of the air. He can taste the smells of the plane fuel, of sweet florals and something earthy. What *would* Dylan say about all of this?

Dylan was a good kid, probably better than Zach will ever be. Kinder, funnier. And mostly he was a good brother. But Jesus, he could be annoying as fuck.

When Zach was in grade one, Dylan would take Zach's dinky cars or his *Star Wars* figures, stand at the top of the stairs, and dump them out of their cases, watching the chaos of them spinning out and down the steps, ricocheting around the corner and under the sofa in the living room, where Zach would search them out later. Then Dylan would gather up what he could find and do it again.

"You have to share with your brother, Zach," his mom said whenever he complained. "Besides, you're not even home when he plays with them."

"But they're mine. Tell him to leave my stuff alone."

"Let him play with them," she'd say. "You'll be sorry when he's gone."

She hadn't meant dead, of course. Still, her words surface in his mind all the time now. *You'll be sorry when he's gone.* It was a curse, a jinx. He should have knocked on wood. Sometimes he wonders, if he had done just one thing differently, then maybe Dylan would still be here. The problem was figuring out which one thing. And when he thinks of all the mean stuff he did to his brother, all the things he'll never be able to take back, his mind seems to swell and double back on itself, and his skin gets tight across his body and his chest, until it feels as though he might burst open.

He concentrates on the sun beating down on him. There's not a flicker of breeze. It is hot and sticky and the air here is thicker than on even the most humid day at home. The chop of the plane propeller finally dies, and he tries to make sense of the burble of language around him—some English, some French, maybe the local language—but he can't discern any meaning. Beyond the babble of noise, he can just hear the wash of the ocean. He lifts his phone and starts filming again.

The airport is a tumble of a one-room building with part of its roof missing, and the runway a strip of packed-down earth that ends abruptly at the ocean, which tosses white foam on shades of blue as far as the eye can see. There is a jumble of luggage on a table in front of the building, though their suitcases, shiny newish hard-shells in five distinct colours, are set together on the ground. Other passengers heave up their own bags—some plastic, others old duffle bags, or even woven baskets—and sling them on their hips or over their shoulders and head off down the single muddy road that leads away from the airport. Most are greeted with great yells and hugs, many with tears as though they haven't been seen in years. Two pickup trucks wait nearby. A white man waves from one and loads up the bed with people, before driving off up the road in a shower of waves and laughter.

Near the table, now almost empty of luggage, he sees Astrid bent over a cardboard box, her gaze moving back and forth between it and a woman standing beside her.

"What is it?" he asks his sister, kneeling next to her. The earth is warm and damp under his knees.

She looks at him and then to the woman above them, who nods slightly. "A chicken," Astrid whispers to him, her eyes and smile wide. "He was on the plane. On her lap." The box leaps a little, a scrabbling sound from inside it, and Zach starts back, while Astrid and the woman giggle. It's so rare to hear his sister laugh out loud these days. It is a lifting trill, like some kind of birdsong, bright and musical, and it unlocks something in him so that he joins in, then leans close to the box a second time to see if he can get the chicken to scramble about again. When it does, he fakes being scared, and Astrid shrieks louder this time.

"Zach! Astrid!"

He ignores his dad so he can pretend to be scared of what's in the box one more time. Astrid is already tiring of the game, but still she smiles at him and then presses her face to a hole torn in the box, where she whispers something and then glances up at the woman indulging the two of them.

"Thank you," Astrid says quietly, before taking off towards their parents.

Left alone with the woman, Zach rises to his feet. He stoops his shoulders a little when he realizes he is taller than her.

"You are the missionary's family," she says, and it takes him a second to register her quiet words through her accent. It is not a question.

"Yeah," he answers, even though he doesn't feel any connection to the people who are just fading sketches in an old photo album.

The woman considers him closely, as if deciding something, then nods. "God bless you," she says, picking up her box and walking away.

"Yeah, um . . . you too. See ya."

He knows he's supposed to feel something because his ancestors came here a long time ago. Because they died here. But he doesn't. Ms. Pal, his guidance counsellor, told him to remember how lucky he was, to get such an amazing opportunity to truly understand his family's past, his place in it. That he was reckoning with history. But he isn't sure that anything monumental is happening, or that there will be a reckoning. All he feels is hot and tired.

"Zach, put down the phone," his dad says.

He grits his teeth and then heads towards his family, who are standing with two men. His parents are closer together than he has seen them in months; they're still not touching, but at least they're not pinging away from each other like magnets.

The two men seem younger than his parents. One is more compact than his dad and not much taller than Zach himself, though his muscles are evident through the soccer shirt whose team Dylan would definitely know. Zach is merely happy to recognize it as a soccer shirt. The man's skin is richly brown, his face lined with concern. He smiles as Zach joins the group, but there is something withheld there—genuine, but also guarded. It is a smile Zach recognizes, has become good at himself.

He has missed the introductions, but the man extends his hand to Zach, even as his mother says, "This is Mr. Tabé, our host."

"David, please. Welcome," the man says.

"Yeah, thanks," Zach says, the words just an empty sound in his mouth.

David waits for them all to settle, then makes eye contact with each of them in turn as he speaks. "Welcome to Iparei," he says, spreading his hands wide to take in the airport, the people drifting off down the road, the people watching them, the wall of green that seems to hide the rest of the island from sight. "We are very glad you have come." There is a formality to David's speech that makes Zach shift uncomfortably.

"Yes, yes! Welcome. God bless you!" says the other man, with a rounder face, a balding head, a wider, easier smile. He is dressed in a bright white button-down that painfully reflects the fierce sun. "I am Robson Kapere, the pastor of our church and our people, and we are so very glad you are here. We have so much work to do together." He pumps each of their hands more vigorously than David did, and grasps Zach and his dad by the shoulder as he does so.

David waves over a young man who is leaning against the truck. He is a few years older than Zach, and pulls himself up tall as he comes towards them. His hair is a cloud of tight curls, and there is a resemblance between him and David, something about the mouth, the set of his jaw beneath the beginnings of a beard. Zach tries to affect a posture of cool, one that comes so easily at home.

"This is my son," David explains, "Jacob."

Jacob smiles a thin smile as he lifts the bags to carry them back to the truck. Zach feels a new wash of embarrassment at the amount of luggage they have brought for their ten-day trip, only five of which they'll even spend on this island. He slides his phone into his pocket.

Zach sits in the truck bed, leaning against its metal side. It is too loud to talk with the wind and the rotted roar of the muffler. The place seems wild, the greenery impenetrable. Every so often there is a fist-sized shadow hanging between the trees, and he feels rather than knows that they are enormous spiders. After a few minutes, Jacob stands and leans on the front of the cab, where David and Robson, as well as Zach's mom, grandmother, and sister, sit. As they round a bend, Jacob takes a single step to the side of the truck as the massive bough of a giant tree sweeps across where he was just standing.

Zach wants to laugh, the movement of the truck as it bounces down the dirt road driving anger from his body. He would never be allowed to ride in the back of a truck like this at home. The wind smells of sea and green, the floral perfume so thick he can feel it coat his skin and lungs. Branches whip close to him and he leans back out of the truck to grab at passing leaves. A vine stings his hand as it is pulled through his grip, leaving a red mark the length of his palm. A lifeline, red and angry.

He stumbles to his feet and inches his way towards the front to stand beside Jacob. They aren't going fast—the road won't allow it. Still the truck moves unexpectedly, like a living thing trying to buck them off.

There are huge trees up ahead, making a cathedral of the roadway. "What kind of trees are those?" he asks Jacob, for something to say, though he cringes inwardly at having asked such a stupid question. He's not sure Jacob has heard him, and hopes his words have been carried away by the wind.

Then Jacob glances over at him. "Banyan trees," he says. "Each village has one at its centre. If you have a pig, a kava root, and a banyan tree, you've got everything you need for a party."

"Amazing," Zach says, though the word isn't enough to capture what he is feeling. The banyans seem alive to him in a way no tree ever has before, as though they are more animal than tree. Their leaves make great latticed canopies, and their massive boughs sprout enormous roots reaching for the ground, so that a single tree appears to make an entire forest.

Zach tries to hold himself the way Jacob does, so still and easy. He keeps his joints loose to anticipate changes of direction before they happen, his hips absorbing the movements of the truck. Dylan would be good at this. If he were here, he'd stand in the middle of the truck bed, arms out at his sides, pretending he was flying or surfing, waggling his hips or dancing.

Zach reaches into his back pocket for his phone and starts to film the lashes of green coming at him, sunlight spearing the road through the lace of foliage overhead. But even with the glare on the screen Zach can tell the images aren't what he wants them to be. It is a blurred smear of colour, a slice of sky so bright it looks white. He begins shooting again, using both hands to steady his phone, squinting hard at it and waiting for the light to fall in columns through the foliage, for a sliver of ocean to be visible through the trees.

He feels Jacob's hand on his arm, just as the truck drops to the right from beneath him and then slams back up against him. Zach falls hard into the bed of the truck, his phone skittering to the feet of his father, who is reaching towards him and yelling his name.

Before Zach can register what is happening, Jacob is crouched above him, pulling him up to sitting and then leaning him against the side of the truck.

"Jesus, Zach!" His father's voice is panicked. "What the hell? You've got to be more careful!"

His face burns in humiliation. For falling, for the way his father is yelling at him. For everything.

He looks away from his father's panicked face. Through the back window of the cab, Astrid's mouth is a worried *O*. Beside her, his mom has craned around with an expression that transforms from terror to relief. He smiles at her despite the pain in his shoulder, gives a short shrug and rolls his eyes, then puts on his sunglasses again.

The relief on her face hardens, and she glares at him, gestures that he is to stay sitting, then turns away.

He stares at the back of his mom's head as Jacob motions to Zach's dad to hand him the phone. Then he sits beside Zach and examines it briefly—the newest model, shiny and still unscarred, even from this drop—before handing it back to him.

"Thanks," Zach says, sliding the phone into his pocket without checking it.

Jacob nods. "We're almost there."

Zach rubs his shoulder where he hit the truck bed, wondering if it will bruise. It still surprises him: what bruises and what doesn't. It's not always the thing that hurts the most that leaves a mark.

Eventually, the air shifts and the truck slows, then rocks to a stop and there is the sea—the immense spill of it all the way to a horizon that is farther than anything he has ever seen. There are a few palm trees swaying overhead, and the rustle of wind through vines and leaves. A few buildings of corrugated metal or woven leaves blend into the edge of the bush, and there is a narrow cove of beach surrounded by high craggy black coral, the tide line demarcated with seagrass and detritus. The air tastes thick, the flavour of the ocean. He breathes in deep and holds it in his lungs, like he's smoking up. It fills him the same way. Then he stands and turns slowly in the bed of the truck to take it all in, even as his father leaps down and Jacob starts to hand down bags to other men who approach. Some reach up to shake hands with Zach. They all shake hands with his mother, his father, his grandmother.

He rubs at his shoulder again, the pain and embarrassment fading. He jumps down from the truck and stumbles some.

Astrid's eyes are clouded with concern. "Did it hurt?"

"Nah, of course not," he lies.

Jacob leaps down beside him, using Zach's shoulder to steady himself. Zach squints against the pain and Jacob squeezes slightly, a reassurance of sorts.

Zach is about to say something when his phone rings. Service! He pulls his phone out but its face is dark. Jacob flips open the phone in his hand and talks quickly as he begins to walk away.

"Where ya goin'?" Zach calls after him.

"Don't worry," Jacob replies. "I'll be back in time to go see your grandparents."

Zach stands a minute, alone by the truck. A crowd of people has gathered by his family. David is saying something and gesturing with his hands, but the ocean and the wind are in Zach's ears.

He waits for his mom to turn to him, wills her to, staring hard at her from behind his sunglasses. He keeps waiting.

Rebecca

The story begins on the shore, where so many stories begin.

Rebecca stands a short distance away and so can't hear what David is saying over the sound of the surf. But she knows the story—it is one of the many he has told her over the seven years of their marriage.

Overhead, the sun is hidden behind scrubby grey clouds that, despite stretching for miles, will be swept to sea by the time they return from David's planned trek. Right now, he is standing next to a stone just above the waterline on the beach. Thrust up from the surrounding coral, the rock is a dark volcanic thing, sharp and pocked, that comes to David's waist. The perfect height to place a hand. It is not a welcoming stone, not one to sit on to stare out to sea, to bask in the sun. It is said that the Reverend William Stewart placed his hand on this rock before he collapsed and died after running from his attackers, his blood staining the island forever. David touches the spot now, a smooth discolouration, perhaps worn from years of hands grazing it for luck as people go in and out of the water.

The Stewarts stand, listening conspicuously, like a group of schoolchildren before they break into song. Their eyes are hidden behind sunglasses, and their lips are set in serious lines, except for the little girl, who gazes around, an astounded smile on her face. The boy aims his unusual phone not at David, but at David's hand against the rock, and something twitches in her throat. His mother, Michelle, puts her hand on her son's arm, but he shrugs her off, steps away from her, continues peering through his phone. To cover her embarrassment, she asks a question that Rebecca doesn't hear. David shakes his head and Robson jumps in to say that there is no such mark where Josephine died.

Neither are there marks for where so many died of the illness that sparked the violence. Or perhaps there are, but the weight of that part of the story was too much for David to share.

He turns and leads them up the slope, past the bungalow and the nasara, which he explains is the heart of the village. The stamped-down space serves as a ceremonial ground, a dancing ground, a space for discussion and debate, exchange and chat. Then he leads them into the bush, where the path narrows quickly. The land is their history. Everything is written on it. They walk the story across the landscape.

They are not what she expected, the Stewarts. Although, she is not sure what she expected. Loud, gregarious people, she supposes, full of smiles and handshakes, like the family she worked for, years ago, in Vila. Forever taking up more space than anyone else she'd ever met, always certain of themselves, their words, their place. There is nothing easy about the Stewarts, not just with her and David, but with each other. They are careful and distant with one another—a flicker of resentment, of frustration, sparks among them. But the way the boy bends now to check on his sister stirs up a bittersweet memory of Anaei sitting with Ouben on her lap while he stuffed soft bites of banana into her mouth. Rebecca holds her arms in a tight circle close to her chest and tries to feel his weight there. She breathes in deep—earth and the spice of blooming ginger.

Michelle's face is taut angles and lines, her shoulders narrow blades in the long sleeves of her shirt; her mother, Joyce, is smaller than Michelle, and often glances anxiously towards her daughter. Scott is a big man, one of the largest Rebecca has ever seen. He towers over everyone, lumbering on the path. Zach, though he is taller than Jacob and still has years to lengthen, will not grow as big as his father; he has his mother's shape. The little girl too is taller than Anaei, though they are close to the same age.

It is still in the shelter of the shrubs and trees; no breeze reaches here from the ocean. Mosquitos buzz in the shadows, and green pigeons flit through the leaves. There is a hum of life to the bush that she cannot hear at the moment, though she knows it's there below the trample of feet, the murmur of conversation. The Stewarts bicker about something, tones barbed even when the words are not, and Rebecca looks away from where they climb ahead of her. David and Robson are both so sure that they must make some kind of peace with these people, though their reasons are different. Robson says he wants forgiveness, while David wants to fulfill an old obligation created by his ancestors. She wants David to be right, but as the Stewarts stumble along this path, she worries that his attempts will be futile.

The clouds have already skittered away, and the sun flickers through the shifting canopy overhead, lush with cascading tones of green. If she didn't know what to look for, it would be easy to imagine the bush is unchanged. But there are the towering upturned roots of a tree torn down in the cyclone, and the empty space where it used to stand. Here they must climb over a fallen limb that was never an impediment before. Even the shape of the path has changed, diverting around another fallen tree, skirting where a mudslide has remade the hill.

She is surprised by how strong her body feels, pushing up the slope. She cursed her own strength in the days after her son's death; it wouldn't let her slip away to follow Ouben home to God. But now she is grateful for her strength. She is still here for her daughter, who is so bursting with life. Anaei is in front of her now, and Rebecca reaches out and touches the halo of her daughter's hair, tugs a curl straight and lets it go. Anaei glances back at her mother and Rebecca smiles, opens and closes her hand, like an eye blinking. The girl returns the signal. It is a gesture Rebecca used to make on her children's tummies when they were babies. She can still feel the warmth of them in her palm.

Ahead of them, David leads the Stewarts along the footpath— the road to the old place, where his ancestors' village once stood and which will soon be their home again. Jacob brings up the rear just behind her, swinging his machete at the tangle of creepers and branches always reaching to reclaim the path.

She inhales, whispers Ouben's name into the air. This path has not been trodden much in recent years; she never carried him up this way to soothe him to sleep. Even so, he is all around her. In the rhythm of her footsteps, her breath. *Ouben, Ouben, Ouben.* She cannot sing, but she can chant his name, and it brings him to her. She feels his presence, and others now, move alongside her in the bush, making the trek with them.

Behind her, Jacob's footsteps sound Ouben's name too.

Jacob was twelve when Rebecca arrived on Iparei to marry his father. He was already spending the school terms in Vila, returning home for holidays. They had only a few days together before David sent him to school, along with several other village boys, in the leaky cargo boat that delivered people and goods to and from Vila every two weeks.

As far as she could tell, during his time at home Jacob ran wild in the bush with his friends. They ranged across the territory between villages, crisscrossing many of these same paths and finding some of their own, as boys do. Jacob often took a bow slung across his chest and his swim mask with him, tied up in a bag that had been his mother's. He would disappear for the entire day, then return with pigeons or reef fish, offering them for dinner.

When he was home, he prowled the edges of the cooking hut or the old shelter they used to sleep in, watching her. He picked at the food she made and glared at her sideways. He huffed and sighed. *Had he been like that with his mother?* she wondered at the time. Or was this disdain and exasperation aimed solely at her? She would come to learn that he was more complicated than that either/or, that he wore every feeling on his face.

She didn't know what to say to him then. His mother had been dead for more than a year. What could she say? Instead, she made sure everything was ready for him to go to school. She gave him the names and phone numbers of everyone she knew in the city—distant cousins and former employers. She washed his uniform and hemmed second-hand shorts, so that the fray at the bottom didn't show. She polished his shoes and hoped that they would last for more than the first term.

The day before he left, she returned from the church in Robson's village, where she had taken on scrubbing the wooden pews and sweeping the floors twice a week in exchange for a small payment, to find Jacob trying on his school uniform. He had his mother's old mirror tilted down so that he could see his full length. He fingered the hem she had turned.

"You look handsome," she said, finding the words in his language. He started, then looked straight at her, maybe for the first time. She stood still, let him examine her, while she did the same to him. His body was long like his father's, and he was already taller than most men in the village, but his skin was cast a little fairer, his hair with a hint of red that David didn't have. His mother in him, clearly. His eyes were wide and bright, and his mouth turned down at the corners, even when he was happy. But she didn't know that then. Perhaps his early sadness had bent his mouth this way permanently. She hopes Anaei will not suffer the same.

"You sing," he said to her.

"What do you mean?" She thought she might have misunderstood his words.

"When you are cooking, or walking. No matter what you are doing, you sing. All the time." He put the mirror back carefully in a basket that hung from the rafters. His mother's things. Rebecca hadn't looked in that basket, understanding it was sacred to him. "Why do you always sing?"

"It reminds me of home." She switched to Bislama to make herself better understood. "Makes me think of my mother and father, my sisters. I think maybe they are singing the same song too, and I don't feel so far away." She paused. "Sometimes, I sing on purpose. Sometimes, I don't even notice I am doing it. You could try it."

He told her later that he did. That it made being away from home a little easier. She imagined him in his room in Vila, finding moments alone and then thinking of her and beginning to sing under his breath.

He heaves another sigh and she wishes she could bring herself to sing now, to draw him out perhaps, get him to sing along with her. Instead she asks, "What's wrong?"

"If I tell you, you'll only tell him." When she looks at him, Jacob is staring past her at his father.

"I've always kept your secrets."

"Not true," he says, but with a laugh.

"No, you are right. I did tell him about the time you stole your teacher's canoe and hid it in another cove."

"It was a joke."

"Your father didn't think so," she says firmly.

David had yelled at Jacob for his disrespect, but later David confided in her about stealing his own uncle's canoe at a similar age. She then shared this story with Jacob, exchanging one secret for another.

"He is worried that I am going to leave," Jacob says, serious now.

The understanding settles on Rebecca. Of course it is time for Jacob to go off into the world—that is what they have been preparing him for—and of course David is terrified of this. "That's because you will leave," she says.

"How do you know? Can you read the future now?" He is teasing, but somehow the question cuts at her. How can she explain to him that some things are inevitable? "Robson says he can get me a job in New Zealand. On the vineyards. Or a farm. It is mine when I am ready to go, he just has to make a call. It would be a lot of money and I could send some back to help with Anaei's school, or . . . with whatever. I would." She nods. Jacob has sent money home since he started working in the city. "What does he expect?" Jacob goes on, defending against an argument not yet made. "That I can stay here forever? And do what?"

She doesn't respond. Their footsteps are soft sounds as they continue to walk. She can hear Robson's voice calling from up ahead, the story still unwinding along the trail. Here is where the sick men were found, he tells the Stewarts. Here is where a peace was made. Every hillock is a verse.

"He's different now," Jacob adds after a few minutes. "He worries for the worst. All the time."

She doesn't tell him the worst has already happened but there is still so much to dread. How can a son understand a father's fear?

As if reading her thoughts, Jacob exhales loudly into the canopy overhead. "My staying will not bring him back."

It is true. Everything has changed and nothing has changed. There is no more here for Jacob than there was before Ouben died. Perhaps there is actually less.

"Look. I found this," he says. Jacob's arm is extended before her, his cellphone open in his hand. She stops on the path, the rest of the group moving forward while the two of them fall behind. On the tiny, cracked screen of his flip phone is an image of her. She is holding Ouben, though he cannot be seen, only she can, exhausted and smiling. She has never seen this picture before.

"He was just born," she says, and her body remembers this moment she didn't know she'd forgotten. She can feel the pain of labour already fading from her body, dulled by her searing love for her son. The love was so strong, so true, that for a flash she had felt guilty that it was a different love than what she had for Jacob.

Voices drift from ahead of them, bodiless. "I knew you'd want to see it, even if you can't see Ouben really."

His name lights on her, soft and gentle, a balm, and she is glad Jacob has said his brother's name. She smiles, closes the phone, and clutches it to her chest before giving it back to her stepson.

It is a beautiful spot.

Near what was once one of the entrances to their forefathers' village, there is a clearing cut into the hill, high enough so that on most days the leaves are rustled and lifted by the sea breeze. And while there is no view of the ocean, Rebecca can still some-how sense the swells and breath of it. Farther along the path are overgrown tangles of long-abandoned gardens slowly being cultivated, replanted, and nursed back to health. The sounds of hammering, of hoes cutting into the earth and machetes into trunks drift towards her.

Robson's wife, Serah, is waiting for them in the clearing, lit by shafts of sun that shift and move across her body so she appears to be underwater. Her coconut broom leans against the low worn wall that has only recently been exposed at the clear-ing's edge. The wall was said to be built in the shape of a turtle, invoking the creature, but Rebecca does not see it. Serah is neat in her flowered dress, and Rebecca wishes she had dressed her-self and Anaei in their church clothes too, but they each have only one good dress, which will be worn for the ceremony. Serah has several.

"How are you?" Serah asks, her tone low, intimate, as Rebecca comes to stand next to her. Serah's children are all healthy and well, two already returned to school in Vila. It is true that their plantation has faltered, as David is always quick to point out, and they will have no crop to sell, but she and Robson have their family.

"The flowers are beautiful," Rebecca says, to avoid the woman's searching eyes. Serah has placed an intricately woven ring of blossoms and vines on the weathered stone that sits in the shadow of this younger banyan tree. Red flames of crotons mark the space as sacred. "You look very nice too." Serah makes a pleased noise and coyly dips her head.

Serah begins to talk quietly but incessantly about what needs to be done before the ceremony in three days. The church needs to be cleaned, she says. Will Rebecca be coming to help them? She has not been in some time, and she is missed. Rebecca used to go to the church at least twice a week, but she no longer feels any peace there. It is not that she has given up prayer, but her prayers have changed, and she is less certain who hears them now.

Robson is ushering the Stewarts forward to where a white stone lies flat on the ground, rising from the earth by a finger-breadth or so. It is worn and soft at the edges and spotted with lichen, as though it has been dredged up from the bottom of the sea. "This marks the spot," Robson is saying, standing with his feet apart and talking with his hands, the way he does during his sermons, "where the grandfathers brought the Reverend William after he was killed."

Michelle and her mother walk to the stone and kneel before it, and then Astrid leans against her mother. Next to Rebecca, Anaei does the same, and she is glad for her daughter's weight, glad to be standing in this quiet spot.

"But this stone is not from the Reverend Stewart's time," Robson continues. "It was placed later, when we became Christian, to remember those who tried to first bring us the Word. There is a plaque too, in our church, that you will come and see. A photograph. You can see how long we have remembered what happened here."

If the Stewarts' ancestors had not come here, Rebecca thinks, the Stewarts would not be here now. There would be no stones, no plaque. No need to remember such a story.

"He wasn't a reverend," Michelle says as she reaches out to trace the names on the stone. "Not really. He wasn't ordained, he didn't have any training, just . . . a lot of faith, I guess. He thought he had a mission, that he was called to leave home, or at least that's what I was told. But he wasn't a reverend." She sounds embarrassed.

"More like a zealot," Zach says from a short distance away.

"Zach," his father warns, "watch your tone." He gestures towards her and Serah, and Rebecca wonders if she should be offended by the word *zealot*. But it was not aimed at her.

"What? Wasn't he? Look what happened with the missionaries back home. With the residential schools and all of that. How they stole kids from their families and took their land. They just did whatever they wanted. How was this guy any different?" Zach waves dismissively at the stone in the ground. "Maybe he got what he deserved."

Scott lifts his palm. "Now's not the time."

"Are you kidding?" Zach spreads his arms to take in the whole of the ancient nasara, the entire island, everything that has gone on before now and will spool out from this place and this time. "Isn't that exactly why we're here? To, quote, 'face our past'? To tell the truth?"

"We're here because we were invited here," Scott says. His jaw is tense, his face controlled, but flushing red.

"'Cause they came here uninvited." Zach thrusts his hand towards the stone. "And then—"

"Enough!"

"Stop it!"

Both parents snap at Zach, who recoils in a grumble of protest.

The grandmother turns to Robson and David, who are looking away from the argument. "I'm sorry," the old woman says. "He's sorry. We don't want to cause offence."

Scott looks pleadingly at his wife as Zach withdraws to stand near Jacob, but Michelle won't meet his eye. The two young men hold themselves apart from their families. They would both rather be anywhere else. There is a slippery energy around Zach, who mimics the way Jacob slouches against the tree, arms folded, head cocked to the side, watching. Jacob taps the back of his machete blade against the bottom of his flip-flop; Zach pulls out his phone and jabs at it, aims the lens at the blade. After a moment, and seemingly without saying a word, they exchange what they are holding, Zach showing Jacob how the phone works, before turning to hack at the wall of green behind him with the sharp blade. Jacob films the boy's fast, angry movements, the sweat staining his back and armpits. Michelle turns away from Scott and the air crackles.

"Is this their graves, then?" Astrid asks and again leans her body into her mother. Rebecca feels her daughter do the same, mimicking the other girl's actions, and now it scrapes at Rebecca. She wants to tell Anaei not to do that, but when Michelle pulls away slightly from Astrid, Rebecca pulls her own daughter closer.

"No, honey," Michelle says, "this is just so we remember them. It's important to remember the people who came before us."

"Do we? I don't remember them. Not like I remember Dylan."

"I know, sweetie," says Scott, who bends to the little girl and pulls her away from her mother and to him. "But that's why your mom told you the story before we came. It's your story too."

Astrid grimaces before she turns in Anaei's direction and says, "Sometimes, we go to visit Dylan's stone. His says, *Whisper and I'll be there.*"

"Hush, Astrid," Michelle says quietly, her face pinched.

"Who's Dylan?" Anaei asks.

"My brother. He's in heaven." She points at the stone. "With them probably."

And now Rebecca can sense another boy here with them, though she cannot see him, doesn't know his age or what he looks like. She stares at Michelle and tries to read Dylan there. But the woman is hidden beneath the hat she pulls low over eyes hidden by dark glasses.

Later, Rebecca begins the long preparation for the Stewarts' dinner in the shelter of the cooking hut while David and Jacob sit a short distance away. Jacob smokes with one hand, texts on his phone with the other, and David works at twisting and repairing some wire, hoping to return electricity to the bungalow. Anaei sits on a mat close by, singing to herself and giggling while running the small plastic truck that Jacob bought for Ouben over her arms and legs. The tune is one Rebecca doesn't recognize. The words are silly, about one of the old demons in Mwatikitiki's time being slain by a baby boy. Anaei has a gift for receiving songs and stories.

"What is this song?" Rebecca asks as she sits beside her.

"It's for Ouben. It's about how he is a strong hero now," Anaei explains, and runs the truck's wheels up her mother's arm. "It came in my head and I wanted to sing it for him."

"He loves when you sing to him," Rebecca says. "Remember?"

"No! He used to laugh at me." Anaei frowns, which makes Rebecca smile; she pats her daughter's hand.

"No, that's good! Not everyone is so good at making their baby brother laugh. Babies like to cry so much, it's a gift to make them laugh." Rebecca thinks of the gurgle of sound, of what she would give to hear it again. "Do you remember his laugh?" she asks and Anaei nods. "Show me?"

Her daughter scrunches up her face and laughs a burble that almost sounds like Ouben's. Almost.

"No," says David, who has put down the wire he was working with. "It was like this." And he makes a sound more like a cow than a baby's laugh and it sends Anaei into even greater hysterics.

"You do it," she says, and flings herself into Jacob's lap. Jacob sounds the most like his half-brother.

Soon they are all laughing his laugh.

Zach

In the heavy dark of the bungalow, Zach wakes to the sound of Astrid mewling in the other room. Her cries are strangled, like she wants to yell but can't. Another one of her nightmares. As he slips into the flip-flops he left beside his cot, he hears someone move in the dark and murmur to his sister. The bungalow's two rooms are connected by an open threshold, and the private sounds of sleep and the smells of his family through travel and exhaustion are far too intimate for him. He stands frozen a moment, the moon whispering to him, buzzing outside the slatted window. His own body buzzes in response, itches to move, and he is slipping out the door before he realizes he is moving.

Outside, the whole world seems to stretch in front of him, and his muscles are already easing some. The ocean pounds its rhythm against the shore, ushering in a breeze that rustles the bushes and the palm fronds far behind him. Overhead, stars glisten, bright and piercing. He lifts his phone to capture the scene, but the screen is too bright, so he turns the camera on himself instead, bares his teeth at the lens before he breaks into an exaggerated smile. Then he pans down to his hand and focuses on the thumb he pressed to the blade of Jacob's machete, pretending the cut was an accident, the fresh scab of it a line of dried blood. "From a machete," he says to the camera in a bad Australian accent. "Actually, it's not much, more like a cat scratch."

His body hums with jet lag and the tug in his gut that has been with him for months—the thing he is always trying to escape or block out. He sets off towards the ocean, and his feet stumble over unseen rocks. His mind is foggy and slow, as though he is wading through water, while everything around him is too sharply in focus. The feeling is so familiar he stops and laughs at the sea.

Earlier in the evening the men had gathered in a loose circle under the banyan tree. They sat cross-legged on woven mats—his dad, David, Robson, Jacob, and a half-dozen others whose names he had forgotten, along with one white guy with blond white-guy dreads matted down his back. Noah taught at the church or was a missionary or something. Dim solar lamps made pockets of light around and inside the circle.

In front of David was a large plastic bowl and several scooped-out coconut shells. He dipped the shells into the bowl and handed them to Jacob, who in turn passed them to each of the other men before ending with Zach.

"That's a high tide," Jacob said, referring to how full Zach's shell was with muddy grey liquid. "Go easy."

His dad had already downed his serving, as had the rest of the men, so Zach tossed his shell back. It tasted like earth and pepper, and it was the exact temperature of the world around him, so that swallowing it was like taking in a part of this place.

Jacob and the white guy next to him laughed while Zach sputtered, making his face burn some.

"The kava on Iparei is the strongest anywhere," said the white dude, reminding Zach of the way Conner liked to brag about the shitty weed he got from his older brother that left them more headachy and anxious than anything else.

His dad was watching him, but Zach wouldn't meet his eye as he was handed another cup and chased the first. "Bet old Bill Stewart never did that," Zach said with a short laugh, his lips and tongue tingling.

David explained that the men drank kava at the end of every day. It whispered to them and allowed them to listen to their ancestors, to talk with them. They used the time for discussion and debate. After Zach gulped down another half-shell—low tide, Jacob explained—he ran his tongue over his teeth, floated on a mellow wave.

Now, back on the beach, Zach stares at the stars, the kava in his blood still loosening his limbs as he walks towards the black outcroppings of coral that drop off into the ocean. He picks his way across the uneven surface, feeling the serrated press of it through his flip-flops. He moves slower than usual, but he is glad to be moving.

He walks all the time these days—to and from school, refusing rides or the bus. He walks the hallways or around the portables between classes. It's better in the cold, which first pains and then dulls him. When Chelsea asks him to sit with her at lunch, most of the time he makes up excuses—he has to go to the art room, or check in with his math teacher or his guidance counsellor—leaving her to just stand there as he walks away.

The best walks are at night, when there is the possibility of something unexpected happening in the dark, something he both wants and dreads. It's that tension that draws him on.

He stares down at the ocean as it beats against the island and then falls back into swirls of white foam on the inky surface. He imagines the sharks below, swimming and never stopping, because if they stop moving they'll die. So will he. Whenever he is still, lying in bed or sitting in class, he feels as though he is being swallowed up, disappearing.

The wind carries whispers to him as he walks the edge of the island, the edge of the ocean, and it sounds like someone is calling to him. He can't tell where the whispering is coming from. It might be the ocean or the air. It might be, as David said, the kava, or his ancestors speaking to him. It might be all in his head.

Zach yells Dylan's name at the sea, but he can barely hear himself amid the wash and boom of the ocean surrounding him.

He keeps listening. How like his brother not to answer.

Eventually, he finds himself back on their beach; the bungalow and the small temporary shelters beyond are shadows before him. He knows there are people there, but still he feels utterly alone—a castaway. He turns to the water and stares hard at the rock that David showed them earlier, picked out from the moving sea by the glint of moonlight. It seems to swell and shrink with the waves that lap at its base. Zach approaches the weight of it, crouching down so his eyes are level with the place David said William had placed his hands. He can't make out the spot supposedly discoloured by William's blood.

Zach reaches across the tideline, puts his hand to where he imagines the mark might be. It still holds the heat of the day. He wonders what he carries of his great-great-grandfather inside him, apples not falling far from the tree and all that. He's peered at the sketches of them and tried to see himself or his mom in their faces, and there is maybe something around Josephine's eyes, but really they look like strangers.

"Don't you feel bad for them?" Chelsea asked him once. "Imagine what they must have gone through. The pain."

But hadn't they brought it on themselves? Not that anybody deserved a death like that.

Still, he thinks it was wrong of them to come here, to try to change things. But isn't that why his family has come now too? To change things? Maybe everything you do changes things, whether you mean for it to or not. Zach laughs a little at his own stoned thoughts.

"What about Josephine?" his mom asked earlier, as they stood near this stone.

But David said there was only a mark where William had died. He said it marked the curse William put on those who killed him, calling to his God.

Doesn't mean there isn't a mark for Josephine somewhere, Zach supposes. He moves over the up-thrust coral, searching for a mark that might be hers, for something he can offer his mom that might make things okay.

He is still examining the coral, which scratches into his palms and knees, when his phone buzzes in his pocket and he knows without checking that it's Chelsea. It's yesterday where she is. Or tomorrow. He can't remember which. They aren't even in the same hemisphere anymore.

He sent her pictures when they first arrived—the variegated blue of the ocean, the little bunker they are sleeping in, Astrid standing in front of it. He promised he'd text more, and he meant it, but he can't seem to find the words or the images. It's as though he lost something as they travelled from YYZ>LAX>SYD>VLI>IPA, as he posted on social media; he feels untethered somehow from where he started, from the people back there. He's ghosted her without meaning to. He's become a ghost.

She's sent him a small close-up photo of just her lips in red lipstick, curled into a smile.

I miss u.

He doesn't want to be missed. Real missing hurts too much.

U don't really know what it means to miss some1, he types.

He hits send. It tries and fails, tries and fails, and tries to send once more. Somehow the text wings its way around the world and immediately there is a stab of guilt in his guts. She didn't deserve that. She was only trying to make him feel better. She is always trying to make him feel better. But all he wants is to pull his own skin off.

Still, Chelsea has been there for him.

She held his hand all through the funeral. He didn't ask his parents if she could sit at the front with them, he just brought her up there. Not that asking his mom would have done any good. During those first few weeks his mom seemed to disappear; she barely spoke, barely moved, only sat in Dylan's room wanting to be alone. And his dad was busy taking care of Astrid. Chelsea listened to him talk about Dylan; she let him cry and she cried with him, even though she didn't really know Dylan.

"I'll always remember he brought me cereal," she told him once. And she meant it. He knew she could conjure up that bowl, the cold sugary milk, the half crunch. She was like that.

He hadn't gone back to school after the funeral. By then, it was close to the end of term, and his grades were good, or at least they were good enough that the principal said he didn't have to finish the year.

When he walked into school for the first day of grade eleven he felt like some kind of morbid superstar. A group of younger girls watched him as he opened his locker, whispering. The stoners who often hung out in the cafeteria hallway, where his locker was, skulked away when they saw him, looking startled and paranoid. Even Mr. Simms, the biology teacher, said something behind his hand to the student teacher.

"Zach?" His guidance counsellor pounced on him in the hall. "If you need a break, or anything, you know where to find me. If you want to talk—"

He wanted to turn around and run, but then Chelsea was beside him, holding his hand.

"We're good, Ms. Pal," she said, squeezing his hand until it hurt, keeping the pressure there, and the discomfort was like a hook in him, was something to hold on to. He focused on the pain. Most of the time he felt trapped in his head, with all his thoughts and anger and desperation, and yet the pain kept all of the noise away. For a few minutes anyway. "Zach's fine," Chelsea said. "Just, you know, overwhelmed."

So he let Chelsea speak for him. It was just easier.

But what he really wanted was for her to hurt him.

He moves over the scuttle of rock like a crab, or some other creature that might creep across the landscape at night, and feels a small burn of shame that he knows nothing about this place. Jacob has asked him about Toronto and Canada, and already knows so much more about Zach's home than he does about Jacob's. The ocean is high on the rocks and coming in higher. He stands still for a few minutes and thinks again of home, of missing Chelsea, which surprises him. He's an asshole for texting what he did. He taps in the passcode on his phone and thinks about texting *sorry*, but can't bring himself to do it. *Miss u 2.*

He watches for her response, but he can't even imagine where or when she is right now. He wishes he could talk to her. It's not like he can talk to Josh or Conner, not really. He still hangs out with them—they play video games, talk about the music that Conner's older, cooler brother recommends—but they don't talk about Dylan.

These days, though, it's like Chelsea talks about Dylan too much. And not just with him, but with everyone at school and out in the rest of the world. Just a couple of weeks ago, she told Conner that Zach didn't want to hang out and play the new *Grand Theft Auto* because it was almost Dylan's birthday and some days it was hard for Zach to do the things he used to do with his brother. Conner shot him a look, but Zach ignored it and quietly wondered how she knew. He played the game anyway.

Sometimes he thinks about breaking up with her. He wonders what that would feel like, what kind of hurt that would be.

The first time he hurt himself, he hadn't really meant to.

He was making himself and Astrid dinner, hot dogs boiling on the stove. It was a rainy afternoon, and the streetlights made the road, the sidewalks, the dirty piles of melting snow appear oil-slick. It had been eleven months, and already spring was creeping back into the neighbourhood, magnolia blossoms like bloody fists set to unfurl on the trees. He no longer expected to hear the commotion of Dylan leaving for early-morning hockey practice, no longer hid the last soda in the fridge so he wouldn't take it. Overhead, his mother was moving around in his brother's room again. Astrid was downstairs, playing some pink video game and waiting for this meagre meal. He wasn't sure where his dad was. He'd been coming home later and later, though Zach hadn't said anything, worried if he did say something it would turn his suspicions into facts, and his family would rupture even more.

He put the buns on a plate and grabbed the peanut butter instead of the ketchup, smeared it on thick, then added the hot dogs on top. He was watching the peanut butter melt when his mom came into the kitchen.

"What are you doing?" she asked.

"Making dinner."

She didn't say anything more. He wasn't sure she was still in the kitchen until he glanced over his shoulder and saw her standing there, unmoving, her face frozen. She looked terrified. "You shouldn't eat them like that," she said, her voice oddly flat and distant.

It was so unnerving he almost scraped his plate into the garbage. Instead he said, "Dylan always did," and for a minute he felt a surge of warmth, thinking of the way his brother used to shove a peanut butter hot dog at him, or chew it up and open his mouth, trying to gross him out.

"Don't laugh," Dylan had said to him one time over a backyard lunch of hot dogs. They were wet from the pool, and Dylan was goofing around, dancing, holding his hot dog like a microphone or, when their mom wasn't looking, pretending it was a penis. And Zach kept giggling. "Don't laugh," Dylan said again and again, and for some reason it made Zach howl all the more. He couldn't stop himself and eventually soda surged out of his nose, burning his nostrils and making him sputter, which made them laugh even harder. Their mom stood up at the table, shaking her head, until Dylan started in on her. "Don't laugh, Mom. Don't do it." When she hid her breaking smile with her hands and began to run to the house, shoulders convulsing, Zach and Dylan collapsed into paroxysms, the sound loud in the backyard, until Michelle's own laughter rose to greet theirs.

"He loved eating them this way," Zach said to his mom. He'd always thought it was disgusting, but lately he found himself doing things like this—mucking about with Dylan's hockey sticks, pulling on one of his T-shirts—with a kind of compulsion. It made him feel closer to his brother. His mom had to understand that, didn't she? She was always holding something of Dylan's or sitting in his room. They both just wanted to bring him close.

"Don't," she said, still not moving.

"He was always after me to try it, so I wanted . . . I don't know, to—"

And then she was reaching past him and grabbing his plate and dumping the hot dogs into the compost bin under the sink. "You can't just take things that were his."

"I'm not," he said. "I just . . . It makes me feel close to him."

She shook her head, her expression strange, her jaw set against him. He didn't understand. What had he done?

"I could make you one?" A peace offering.

Her face tightened even more and she stared hard at him, as if she didn't recognize him. "Clean up your mess." And then she was gone.

He doesn't know how long he stood alone in the kitchen, staring at the empty plate before he picked it up and hurled it back into the sink. Maybe he meant to break it—the satisfaction of its shatter—but he didn't mean to cut himself. Or he doesn't think so. He watched, curious, as the bead of blood on his palm turned into a small seam in his skin. It surprised him, how quickly the wound went from painless to a vicious flame, and how the anger in him suddenly evaporated. He held his hand, squeezing the cut, blood dripping into the sink. It was horrifying and soothing at the same time. He began to worry Astrid or his dad would find him, so he collected the shards and threw them into the garbage, covering them with some rolled-up paper towel. But he kept a single broken fragment.

That was how it began. His mom stopped talking about Dylan, visibly cringing and leaving the room whenever he was mentioned. And Zach started wanting to bleed the pain out.

u alright?

Chelsea's text brings him back to himself, as he steps out of his flip-flops and grinds his bare foot against the cut of coral. He can tell he hasn't broken the skin. He stands on an outcrop over the sea. He has wandered a fair distance from William's rock, unable to find anything that might mark the place where Josephine died. The bungalow is a remote smudge. The moon casts itself upon the water. There is no other land visible.

Zach: *Ur up?*

Chelsea: *On the way 2 school*

Zach: *What time is it?*

There is a long delay between texts.

Chelsea: *8:30. There?*

Zach: *middle of the night*

Chelsea: *U should b asleep*

Zach: *Can't*

Chelsea: *A?*

Zach: *Not this time. mayb jetlag?*

Zach: *Miss u*

Chelsea: *Miss u 2*

What else is there to say?

Chelsea: *sure ur ok?*

Zach: *just need sleep*

He sends a winking emoji, a sleeping one. He doesn't want her to worry.

She sends a heart with wings.

He stares at the sea. Not for the first time he thinks of what it would be like to drown. He slowly lifts one foot, and the coral grips him, his weight hard on the rough surface. The salt of the sea is on his lips. He leans against the wind, and all the tiny muscles in his ankle fire, so even as he wobbles slightly, he maintains his balance. He stretches out his other foot ahead of him, as though to take a huge step, walk the plank into the ocean. He spreads his arms to steady himself.

Below him the sea batters into the rock, as it has since the beginning of time, scooping it away. Someday this whole out-cropping will plunge into the ocean, be subsumed by it and washed out to sea.

He could just jump off, like he has jumped from the wall of rock near the cottage. He knows what it's like to hit the hard slap of the water. He's a good swimmer, even if he quit the swim team last year. He could jump off and swim back to shore. He could. No one would ever know.

Unless . . .

He imagines a riptide grabbing him, pulling him out and away from this island. The ocean seals over his head and he is clawing, sinking in its depths, fighting a losing battle with the sea.

He keeps balancing on one foot, ready to step out. The wind buffets him, the stone under his foot shakes. The kava whispers in his veins.

Michelle

In the dark there are others leaning in close and their whispering pulls Michelle from sleep. She doesn't know where she is, or when, and the fraction of forgetting is bliss, before the grief sets in. She forces herself to sitting.

The moonlight is a blur through the slatted window, the thin curtains drawn open to let in just enough light for her to make out the vaguest shape of Scott in his own cot, and Astrid across the room, then the deeper shadow of the doorway to the other room, where her mother and Zach sleep.

They are staying in David and Rebecca's home, though it has been scrubbed of anything personal, leaving only simple furniture. In the dimness she can't see the line on the wall a couple of inches off the floor that David pointed out with apologies. The waterline from when the cyclone flooded the building, he explained. She wishes she could sleep, deeply and blankly, but there is the noise again.

Astrid.

The cot creaks as Michelle pushes herself up and across the poured concrete floor, imagining having to wade through ankle-deep mud to reach her daughter.

"Everything okay?" Scott's whisper startles her.

"Go back to sleep," she says as she lifts Astrid into her arms and heads out the door.

Outside the air is crisp and clear, the sky a vast dome of stars like she has never seen before, even on the clearest nights camping in Northern Ontario. The ocean unfurls towards the distant line of horizon, where a ship is lit up brighter than the stars. There is a shush of wind in the trees and vines, and the endless waves that are the white noise of her own dreams. There are no other sounds.

She stands still, the air soft on her skin, and feels, what? *Small* isn't the right word, nor *peaceful*; rather there is a reassuring tension, something unseen tethering her in this place, in this moment. She tries to hold on to it, but Astrid is heavy in her arms, legs wrapped around her waist, arms around her neck. Her daughter is sticky and damp from sleep, and the salt from the sea she swam in earlier has made her skin tacky. Michelle lowers them both into a cheap plastic chair, ubiquitous on these islands it seems, and hopes it will hold.

Astrid's voice is low against Michelle's ear: "Are they gone?" She lifts her head a little to cast about in the blue gloom, the partial moon catching her blonde hair. She is panting slightly, and Michelle feels her daughter's heart pounding against her own.

"There's no one here. Just you and me." But she remembers the feeling she had when she awoke, of there being others in the room besides her family. "Were they there again?"

A nod. The dream—if it can be called that—is always the same, as Astrid tells it. "The people. At the bottom of the bed. How did they find me here?"

"They're not real, sweetie. They're only your imagination working so hard." Astrid shivers slightly and holds fast to Michelle, who wishes she could move Astrid where she sticks to her, but also wants to keep her daughter pressed against her forever. "Shhhh. It's okay. It's okay. They've gone."

She tries not to imagine the figures Astrid conjures or the fear that they instill, the same way she tries not to imagine Dylan's fear at the end. It will do neither of them any good. And she knows fear. She can comfort her daughter without sharing it.

"How do you know they're scary?" she asks. "Maybe they're just watching out for you. Maybe if you tell me what you're scared of it won't be so scary anymore. Sometimes saying things takes away their power." She wants this to be true, but knows it isn't. Sometimes saying a thing makes it real. Words only make things worse, never better.

Astrid moves against her. "I just know. I feel it in my belly. They want to hurt me. They want to eat me up."

"It's okay, sweetie. It's okay." A mantra Michelle repeats as she rubs her hand on her daughter's back.

Eventually, Astrid's legs and arms drop and her muscles go slack, pinning Michelle to the plastic chair. Her daughter will sleep now—the dreams happen once a night, never more, or at least not so far—but Michelle doesn't want to risk waking her even though she's uncomfortable, the chair hard, her legs falling asleep.

She glances around at the slumbering village, the jungle, the sea. She had expected more. She'd expected to arrive on Iparei and find some deep connection, some profound understanding. But she listened to the story and stared at the stones, and felt it was all a mistake. This isn't going to fix anything. She's come all this way and she's still her. She's still here.

Michelle leans her head back to take in the sky, the swirl of alien stars. She searches for the Southern Cross. Once, she stood on the stepladder for what felt like hours, arms over her head, hands going numb from lack of circulation, placing glow-in-the-dark stars on Dylan's bedroom ceiling. He'd become obsessed with constellations. She'd noticed him laying out pieces of cereal on the breakfast table in strange configurations. He explained it was Orion, or Cassiopeia, and he drew their maps and lines on pages that he stuck to his bedroom wall with Blu-Tack.

She'd found the stickers at an airport gift shop and brought them home to him. He laid them out on the floor and across his bed, in a reflection of what he wanted on his ceiling, handing them up to her one at a time, directing her and cringing when she almost put them in the wrong place. A few hours later, she lay in the dark beside him as he held her hand and traced stellar lines, recited their names.

She feels him pad up to her now, the weight of him leaning against her as they gaze up at the stars together. "Your great-great-grandmother wrote about those stars, Dyl. Look at them."

They're like a blanket, the stars, he says and points, his small finger moving in an arc. *They're so thick it's almost impossible to see any sky.*

She would like to hold Dylan, but for a moment it is almost enough that he is here beside her.

But then there is a sound in the night and Dylan disappears. The interruption ignites a flare of irritation in her and she squints at shadows upon shadows.

"Is she all right?" There is a slight movement a short distance away, on the path that leads to the cooking hut, and Michelle watches as a shape separates from the dark. It's David's wife, Rebecca.

Michelle tenses slightly, trying to ignore her irritation. "Yes. Yes. Sorry, we're fine. We didn't mean to wake you." She nods at Astrid. "She has nightmares."

"You didn't wake me." Rebecca's voice is quiet and creaky, as though unused. She shifts her weight on her bare feet, holds her hands clasped together. In the half-light of the moon Michelle can see her pretty face is marred by the hard set of her jaw, the press of her lips. Rebecca gestures at the chair near Michelle's own, and Michelle nods as though it is hers to offer. "What does she dream, your daughter?"

"That there are strangers who want to hurt her. She sees them at the foot of her bed when she wakes up."

"Sometimes David has nightmares, about Ouben." Rebecca's fingers go to her throat, to a thin cord tied there. "Our son. I dream of him too, but they're good dreams."

Michelle leans slightly towards Rebecca, like an animal scenting the wind. How did she not see it before? It is so obvious now, in Rebecca's quiet, in how she holds her shoulders, the tension in her jaw. The loss. The way Michelle feels it on herself, on her own skin, the mark of it so apparent she's certain everyone can tell just by looking at her that she has lost a child. That she has been through the unimaginable. Still, she isn't sure she is ready to hear what she knows is coming.

"I noticed this earlier," she says instead, gesturing at her own throat. "It's very pretty." And it is—an intricate weave, the light straw colour set off by Rebecca's skin.

The woman smiles, her teeth bright in the moonlight. The smile surprises Michelle, reminding her of the laughter she heard spilling out from the small, corrugated structure where

Rebecca's family are sleeping during their visit. Her son was dead. How could she laugh?

"It is something people from my place do when a loved one dies," Rebecca says. "A fasting cord, to remind us of our promise." Her voice catches and Michelle can see the wet on her cheeks. "We make a promise not to do something that we shared with the one who has gone. It is a powerful thing. I'll wear it for one year, and then, when the year is up, he will have gone on and I will have to go on too."

"Ouben?" Michelle says. The name is soft and round in her mouth, and she imagines a soft, round boy to go with it.

Rebecca smiles at the sound of her son's name and slips a phone out of the pocket of her skirt, flips it open, and hands it to Michelle. There is a grainy photograph of Rebecca smiling, holding a blur of bundle.

"That is when Ouben was born," she says. Michelle can almost feel the child there with them, the way she often feels Dylan beside her.

Rebecca looks out to the ocean. "He was more than a baby, but not yet a little boy."

"A toddler."

"Yes. A toddler."

"Ouben." Michelle feels the power in the name, as she does with Dylan's. She has all but stopped speaking his name, not wanting to lose its power to conjure him, not wanting him to slip away altogether. In the beginning, all Michelle wanted was to speak his name, to make everyone hear it. *Dylan. Dylan. Dylan.* It was a refrain. Like during the initial crush of love, when there is magic to be invoked in the simple syllables of a name. But then a year passed, and things began to fade—one day she couldn't remember the song he liked to sing as he brushed his teeth, humming along with his electric toothbrush. Why couldn't she remember it?

On the anniversary, Scott said his name first thing in the morning, and it didn't freeze her in her tracks, or catch her breath in her throat.

How had his name lost its ability to stop everything? How could she have grown used to his absence? The realization brought a whole new pain, and so she stopped saying his name out loud. She would keep his name for herself.

Now, though, sitting here with Rebecca and their memories of their sons between them, she feels his name pressing on her lips, her tongue, wanting to be spoken, wanting to be heard.

"My son died too."

"Dylan," Rebecca says.

His name draws him closer; he has been here with them all along. "What happened to Ouben?"

Rebecca seems to assess her, and Michelle straightens her shoulders, draws herself taller.

"When he died, after the cyclone, my voice went away with him. I was singing, holding him in my arms and singing to him a song that he loved. And when he went, so did the song. We all lived through the storm except for Moses and Marami. We had all lived, but everything was gone when we came out—the cistern, the food we buried to keep safe, most of the homes and gardens. Only our home, and the school and the church in the next village, were still standing. There were no airplanes from Vila for days. On the radio we heard that help was coming, that our island was hit the worst, that there would be aid from Australia, from churches. Even the white doctors in the highlands said that help would be here soon. But it didn't come.

"Soon, there was no good food left, no clean water, and so the old people and the little ones became ill. Ouben . . . " Her voice founders on his name. "He got very sick. By the time the doctors came to see him and gave him some of their medicine, it was too late."

Rebecca grows silent again and this time Michelle leaves the silence between them. Astrid shifts a little in her arms but stays asleep. Rebecca reaches over and puts a hand on Astrid's head, tucks a curl behind her ear. "The spirits, our ancestors, they speak to us in dreams. That's when our worlds are closest to each other. They tell us things if we listen—some are good, some bad. Sometimes it's the voices of those who have not left yet, not found their way to the sacred dancing grounds. David says Ouben is trying to tell him something in his dreams, but he doesn't know what. Ouben can't even speak yet, only *Mama* and *Papa*. And this is what he says in David's dreams. We must do something so that Ouben can go. I want him to find his way, to be with his family who are waiting for him. Not trapped here. Maybe we are a part of that."

Perhaps Rebecca is right. Maybe there is something for both of them here. She feels Dylan next to her, his name pressing through her lips; maybe it is time to share him, maybe Rebecca can help her. But the woman stands, and Dylan recedes into the night again.

"You should sleep. The next days are busy ones."

Rebecca walks away, her arms wrapped around herself as though cradling her child. Michelle watches until she can't make out the shape of her anymore.

Faina

Faina was already sitting when the sound of the slit drum ceased. Her skin felt skittery on her body. Even though she kept her head bent, she still managed to scan the faces of the men sitting across the nasara. Would she even recognize the man she was to marry? They had met only once, when they were still children. She hoped he would be as handsome as Masai.

She shot a quick glance at him now, sitting with the young warriors from the village. He had fresh vines woven into his hair, and the sunlight painted his skin. Overhead, the banyan tree spread its branches, its new roots reaching down to the earth. It was said that men were like the roots of the tree, connected to the earth, part of it. Women were like the birds that fluttered in its branches, moving to new homes and villages as they married, travelling to maintain the ties between places and peoples. She was to be a bird herself soon.

Faina felt the women of her family behind her—her mother, her uncles' wives, her cousins—and she drew support from their closeness. Other girls sat nearby watching the negotiations, anticipating the day when it was their turn to become the bride-to-be.

The men murmured, chewed, and spat outside the circle. Birds sang in the green bush that surrounded the nasara. Faina put her palm flat to the ground and felt its hum. She thought of all the feet that had stamped this ground in their dances, packing it firm; all the gifts exchanged upon it; all it had witnessed and absorbed. She thought of those gone, who now existed just out of sight, in the spirit world, holding their own dances at night and paying close attention to their descendants, blessing or cursing those who deserved it. She was certain she felt breath on her neck.

When she married she would move to the Upland. What would their place be like? What would Albi be like? Would he be a kind husband? Would he let her still visit the missi? She breathed deep, closed her eyes against the men, and thought about the words that she had learned, turned them over and over in her mind. *Bell*: the thing that sounded like a slit drum to gather people together to pray. *Pray*: the way the missi spoke to their father who lived in the sky.

Her mouth moved over the N-glish words without her realizing until Masai caught her eyes and mimicked her, moving his mouth silently and then shaking his head at her. She lifted her hand to cover her smile before looking away. He would take his own wife soon. She imagined a girl her age, one day sitting here in her village, in her nasara, Faina's ground becoming hers.

It was Masai she'd miss most. And the *mission*: the place the missi lived.

Faina glanced around again as Louvu stood to walk across the open nasara to welcome the Uplanders. As he spoke, the younger men shot glances at a shorter man who kept his face down, so that Faina could not see his features. Was it him? Albi?

At the end of his welcome Louvu returned to his place, and as Faina watched, the young Uplander handed a woven bag to an older man who carried it to a spot in the middle of the nasara. Faina couldn't hear his words for how the ocean swam in them, but knew he was offering his thanks for the welcome they had received, and for the exchange that was to come. Inside the bag would be a coconut seedling—a gift of new life.

"That is Narinam," Mother murmured to Faina. "Your to-be's father."

Faina eyed him, hoping for a glimpse of who her husband would someday become, but she could not make out the young man he might have once been. Mother reached over and squeezed Faina's hand. She squeezed back.

This was only the first in the series of exchanges that were to lead up to her marriage ceremony, to her leaving home. Already there were a number of mats that she and Mother and her uncles' wives had spent days and days weaving and dying, stored up high in the rafters of her sleeping hut. There were many more to make.

Narinam stalked the perimeter of the nasara, praising the neatness of the village, the paths that led to and away from it, saying he hoped this would be a reflection of his new daughter.

"After the next harvest," Narinam said, his shell anklet chattering as he walked, "we will be ready to make the marriage exchange. Will such a time work for you?"

She pulled her hand from Mother's, lifted it to hide her relief. She would have two more seasons to stay in her village, to travel to the mission.

Her first encounter at the mission had left her curious to return, but she'd been kept busy with dowry preparations and caring for her siblings. Finally, she'd been able to return when the people of Middle Grove were invited to the mission for one of the missi's ceremonies.

They gathered on what she now knew was *sunday*, the day their father favoured. People from all the nearby villages crowded under the shade of waving coconut palms and the towering bush on the inland side of the mission while the two missi stood in the full blare of the sun. Josephine rang the bell and William clapped his hands together, then held them out and pressed them downwards. A murmur went through the crowd that they should be quiet. The missi was going to do something. When the crowd had been quiet for a long time, William looked up to the sky and started to speak.

Faina couldn't understand his words at all. Even Father's Father seemed unable to make any sense of them. At first, William spoke calmly, loud enough to be heard over the surf and the rustle of leaves, but as the crowd grew restless, his voice grew louder, more erratic. His face went red, his clothing grew wet under his arms and across his chest and back. Next to him, Josephine seemed to wilt under the midday sun.

Some of the people began to drift away and William grew angry. His words were obscure, but his meaning was clear. He was hurling curses at them, berating them.

Faina's friend touched her arm. "Come on," Telau said, rolling her eyes.

Telau was the daughter of Kaipar, one of Middle Grove's most respected warriors, and carried herself with his pride, her chin always up. Faina tried to hold herself like Telau but forgot when they were not together. Her chin drifted down, even while she took in everything from below lowered lids.

"I want to watch," Faina told Telau.

"What is there to see?"

To Faina there was a great deal. The way the two missi seemed to droop in their overwhelming clothes, the way they were planting an unusual garden around their home, everything bordered by straight lines—a line here separating this patch of ground from that, a fence separating the land they had been allowed to use from the rest of the island. It was all so curious.

Telau left to join some of the other young women and men at the water, where they swam and played, while Faina remained and watched until William finally exhausted himself and collapsed on what Faina now knew was a *chair* in the shadow of his house. He mopped at his brow, drank deeply from a cup of water.

From a short distance away, Josephine called her by name, though it was stilted and foreign on her tongue. Faina pronounced it again as she approached her, tapping her chest as she had before. Josephine frowned and shook her head, before waving her hand in a gesture of dismissal.

Still, that day, Josephine led Faina around a small section of the mission, picking up or pointing at things and exchanging words. *Water. Tree. Coconut. Eye. Mouth. Nose.* Both of them shaping new sounds.

As Faina offered words, Josephine used a strange tool to make marks on what looked like thin white leaves sewn together. Faina asked what it was Josephine held. *Paper. Pencil. Words.*

Words captured there.

"It is about the missi, Will-am."

It was the sound of William's name being spoken that drew Faina's attention back to the negotiations. Narinam said the name with a swallow, as though he might conjure the blotchy figure to this place. Faina wouldn't have been surprised to see him arriving with a flicker just outside the gathering. William was often seen on the roads between villages these days, grow-ing assured of himself and his place on the island as the moon waxed and waned. He met with people on their way to or from their gardens or the sea, always with handfuls of fish hooks and tobacco, which some of the men had taken to chewing and some to smoking as William showed them how, coughing hard into open hands or spitting into the bush.

It was not only fish hooks and tobacco. Faina saw evidence of exchanges with the mission everywhere. There were the scraps of cloth that a few men now wore around their waist to hold up the nambas that covered their manhood. Nails held trouble spots together on old yam barns, or the posts in some of the sleeping houses. There was a hoe that was shared among the men's gar-dens, and a saw that made cutting wood for fire so much easier.

Narinam began to complain about the trees that William had cut down, claiming that he had cut down the young ones that were yet to fruit, only to set the wood aside, unused.

"Faina will ask them for us."

She startled to hear her name come from Louvu's mouth, though he didn't glance in her direction. None of the men did. Mother reached for her hand again, and Telau's titter floated to Faina from where she sat.

"The girl you are making a marriage exchange for has been learning their language, along with those we have sent to watch and protect them." He must be speaking of Marakai and Talawan, who at this very moment were at work at the mission. They were an older childless couple without any relations left in the village. They had not been sent to the mission so much as they seemed drawn to William's stories and gifts. Louvu went on, "When she comes to you, she will be able to help you in your own alliance with them." She hadn't realized that Louvu knew about her learning, or her time spent at the mission, but of course he knew everything that went on.

Her soon-to-be-father sprang up from his place to challenge Louvu. "We do not need this girl to speak for us!" He spat the words as he stomped back to the middle of the nasara, his feet pounding with his words. "We can speak for ourselves, we will learn their language." He stood silent, not returning to his place even when Louvu stood again and walked partway into the circle. Narinam continued, "We only ask for what is ours. They destroyed trees that fed our people for many seasons. They must offer something in exchange, or we will take it."

The two men argued back and forth about the mission, Louvu declaring that any attack on William and Josephine would be seen as an attack on Middle Grove. They were Middle Grove's guests.

Narinam seemed to concede, at least for the time being, and the men retreated to beyond the fence that separated their house from the rest of the village.

As Faina got up to follow Mother to the cooking hut, Telau grabbed her hand and pulled her down the path towards the curve in the stream. "I'll get in trouble!" Faina giggled as they collapsed on the bank. Telau was smiling broadly at her, her eyes squinting with glee.

Telau looked like her father, Kaipar—the bright eyes that flashed between joy and anger, the deep dimple in her right cheek, the high forehead under a crown of tight curls shot through with red threads. And she was impetuous like him, quick to act when necessary. Faina felt brave with her. Who cared if she was to get into trouble? The men would spend a long time listening to their kava this evening with the Uplanders. They would want to hear what it had to whisper to them about what they had discussed.

She wished she could sip kava, wondered at the taste of it, what its whispers sounded like, but it was forbidden to women.

"Well?" Telau prodded. "What did you think?" Faina feigned ignorance, shrugging one shoulder, while she slipped her feet into the stream. The water was cool and clear where it ran across her feet. "Come on!"

"I couldn't really see him," Faina confessed. "Could you? What did he look like?"

"More handsome than Masai," Telau teased.

"Really?"

"No!" Telau laughed. "But it seems as though they would be ready to go to war for you!"

"Not me." Faina grimaced. "Against the missi."

"But you're a part of that now."

Faina leaned back against the bank and watched the sky's sunset glow through the leaves overhead. She was a part of it, the story that was being told. Maybe her sons' sons would talk of her. The thought made her nervous and excited. But first she would have to marry. Albi. She turned his name silently in her mouth, tried to imagine what he might be like, but Telau caught her mouth moving and laughed at her again.

A few days later, while Faina waited for Telau at the start of the path that led to the beach and to the missi's house, she sang one of Josephine's songs. The tune of it climbed high and then swooped down like a bird plunging to the sea. The song was about a stone and a building upon it. The missi too believed in the power of stones. Maybe they weren't so different.

The boundary of the village was a liminal space and she stood so that her body was a bridge between the village and the forest.

Here, the tangles of vines and the reach of the branches were cut back to the dense impassable bush. Out of sight, birds and other creatures rustled leaves before they fell silent, announcing someone's presence.

"Going to the mission again?" Masai asked, using William's word. Had he heard her singing? She was proud of her voice, the low tone of it.

She nodded. "Where's Nako?" Masai and his friend were so often together they were generally referred to in the same breath.

"Hunting with his uncle."

"So, come with us. You could get a fish hook from missi." She crooked her finger into the shape of the metal that William gave to the men who came to the mission to work or listen to his stories.

"I don't want to be beholden to him for his gifts. It's enough that as a people we are in exchange with them," Masai said. "You are careful when you are there, yes?"

"Careful," she scoffed. "There isn't anything to be afraid of," she teased, trying to make him smile.

Instead his lips turned down. "Maybe the Uplanders are right, that we are too eager to try their ways when we should stay on our forefathers' roads."

"We can learn new ways without losing old ones. How could we forget who we are?"

"Already they've cut down trees without offering anything, changing the land without asking who has the right to them. The fruit from those trees would have fed people for generations, and he builds what with them? A house that is already falling apart." Masai sucked his teeth. "The Uplanders say he has a very powerful weapon."

"Will-am," she said and he frowned at her. "His name is Will-am." Masai didn't reply. "I know about the weapon." At this

Masai looked at her, a question in his eyes. "It is the same as the one in Father's Father's stories. It makes a loud noise like thunder and then it smokes and men bleed to death because it is so loud. *Gun.*" The word was like a lump at the back of her throat.

"*Gun,*" Masai repeated, and something flickered behind his eyes.

"What would you exchange for that?"

He stepped closer to her. He smelled of fresh earth and of the greenery and flowers twisted around his forearms. "It does not matter what I want." She was certain he was about to say more.

"What are we planning?" Telau chirped at them, appearing as if from nowhere and watching Masai as he stepped back from Faina. The air cooled on Faina's skin. "Careful, Masai. Even if some things have changed, your little friend is spoken for."

Faina flushed. How long had Telau been listening to them? She grabbed her friend by the wrist. "Come on. Jos-fine will wonder where we are."

"Not *we,*" Telau said, falling into step behind her. "Just you."

While they waited for Josephine to appear at the mission, Faina tried to see the changes the missi had made to the landscape as Masai might. All manner of trees had been cleared, and their large, hardwood sleeping house had been built on the cleared land, back from the sea but close enough to still hear the ring of the ocean as it struck the shore. One corner of the house had been peeled back by the wind and had since been replaced by woven mats made by Marakai, which held much better.

The structure was more than a sleeping house to William and Josephine. Inside, they slept and cooked and ate and did all of the living that was meant to be done in different places. They had strange flaps on the windows that opened and closed, and a banging door that announced entrances and exits.

From its steps ran a path marked out by broken coral bleached white from the sun. Lines of dead sea life also marked out their flat gardens, where they grew plants that Faina did not recognize but was learning to name. *Corn. Lettuce.* They looked malnourished and weak. She wondered how long it would be until Josephine and William harvested them. Their gardens were nothing like the islanders'—terraces sculpted into the island, fed by streams and small trenches dug for irrigation. Instead, William looked for water beneath the earth and, not having found any, charged those who had come to stay at the mission, particularly Marakai and Talawan, with hauling *buckets* of water from a distant stream.

Set back against the shelter of the bush was Marakai and Talawan's sleeping and cooking huts. The older couple had always lived at the fringes of Middle Grove. It was said there was an old curse about them. Their gardens rarely flourished, and each of their three children had died young, so the villagers had always kept them at a distance, even while supporting them on the common lands. Beyond their home was the foul-smelling hut that William and Josephine used for their body waste. It was foolish of them to leave their waste exposed like this, liable to attract any dark magician who wanted to curse them. When the wind shifted the smell reached into the cove.

Marakai and Talawan were bent over one of the garden patches. Marakai worked with one of William's tools, digging at the earth, while Talawan knelt and pulled at invasive plants, encouraging Josephine's to grow. They looked happier here than at Middle Grove. Talawan smiled easier, even at her husband. Before, he had often been heard berating her from their hut, but now he no longer raised his voice to her, and she, in turn, appeared happier to cook for him, and her food pleased him more. They reminded Faina now of Mother and Father—kind to each other.

Faina found it odd that leaving their place could make Talawan happy. "They don't know about our curse," Talawan had explained when she and Marakai first brought their sleeping mats to the cove and erected their own home. "Perhaps they can help us lift it. Sero hasn't been able to. Nothing has worked." Her face was creased deep with grief and exhaustion.

Faina lifted a hand to them now and they called a greeting in Josephine's N-glish.

Talawan now dressed the way Josephine did, in a long skirt of calico, a loose blouse. All the women and girls were to cover their bodies with similar items if they wanted to learn to sew, to read, to speak N-glish. They were sewing their own clothes that they left in a box at the mission when they departed. Talawan wore hers all the time now. The cloth was hot and sticky, suffocating in the heat. Faina hated it.

Telau fidgeted beside her. "I want one of those sharp things," she said, "and some of the soft mats they have to make a skirt." Faina frowned at her friend and offered her the N-glish words— needle, cloth (like the one Kap Kuke had left). Telau only shrugged.

They waited. The sea shushed on the shore, the palms overhead waved in a wind that swept the harshest of the heat away. Faina picked up the tune she had been humming when Masai found her on the path. Talawan came and joined them, wiping sweat from her brow and humming along with her. Still, there was no sign of Josephine.

"Maybe she's sick?" Telau asked. "Maybe someone has used some dark magic to bewitch her."

"I'll go see," Faina said.

She stepped up onto the long wooden platform that ran the length of the front of the house, facing out towards the ocean. From here she could see places where the wood had begun to pull apart at its joints, swelling and cracking from the humidity and the heat. The structure was all brutal angles, not like their curved buildings, shaped to the world around them. The wood creaked as she crossed the porch and slipped in through the open door.

She hadn't entered the house before. Inside, her eyes adjusted quickly to the dim light. The floor was covered in mats like in Faina's own sleeping hut, though she knew Josephine didn't sleep on them. On the wall were more mats, dyed the colours of the coastal tribes, and two arrows crossed against each other, which was a strange place for arrows and mats to be. Surely they would lose their potency here, where anyone could see them, touch them.

Josephine was silhouetted against a window, slatted coverings pushed back so the ocean was visible. She was bent over something Faina couldn't make out, a pencil in her hand. Josephine glanced back and forth between the thing in front of her and something just to her side. Her shoulders were tight around her neck, sweat darkening the back of her dress. She murmured to herself.

Was she making a curse? Sweat slipped across Faina's skin too, and she could smell the fear on herself. There was great magic everywhere on the island; they all called on it—to assist with crops, to stop an enemy, to heal, and to ensure healthy babies. But what if this was more dangerous magic? She wanted to creep away, but her feet held her fast against her will.

Josephine glanced up, surprised, as though she had flown far away and only just returned to this place. "Oh, hello. Is it time? I forgot myself, I was . . ."

Faina pointed at where Josephine had been focusing her attention. Pointing had become a question between them: *What is it? What is the word?* Josephine waved at her to come forward, and after a brief hesitation, Faina walked towards her.

Before Josephine, on a leaf of her paper, was a drawing. Faina's mother's people used sand drawings to tell stories, each line representing a particular part of the narrative, a character, until a shape was finally revealed. This was different. Josephine's drawing was of a child's face.

On the small shelf past Josephine was another drawing, hatch marks of lines making a picture of a boy's face, younger than the one Josephine sketched at. Faina reached for the boy but Josephine slapped at her hand. Faina recoiled but still stared at the image of the small boy trapped behind a hard surface, like water gone still. Josephine's face was crimped with anger. She pressed her eyes closed, inhaled deeply, and then looked at Faina as if from far away.

"Sorry," Josephine said. "I'm sorry." Faina grimaced in confusion and Josephine slowed down. "I'm"—she pointed at herself— "sorry. This is my son." She held out the image with its shiny surface, the little boy trapped there, but didn't let Faina take it. She hoped the little boy was all right, stuck there as he was. The new drawing resembled this one, but the boy's face was narrower, the eyes sadder. Still uncertain what to do, Faina nodded, a gesture Josephine and William both appeared to like from her people.

Josephine mimicked being pregnant with a bulge of cloth at her stomach, mimicked rocking a baby, nursing. "My son," she said again, and held her arms as though cradling a baby. Faina knew she meant the little boy. Josephine made a motion like waving goodbye, hugging, and crying. "I had to leave him behind," she said, "in Canada. I didn't want to come here." Her voice was little more than a whisper. "His father . . ." Josephine paused, and in the silence that followed Faina thought of the father in the sky, she thought of William.

"William," Josephine said at last, "isn't his father."

Josephine was sad and angry. The acrid feel of the air around her made Faina want to be back outside, where the breeze whispered against her skin. She didn't want to be in this house anymore.

Josephine's face changed suddenly, like too-bright sun through clouds. She smiled widely, held out her hand to Faina, and when Faina didn't lift her own, grasped it.

"I'll draw you." Josephine's voice was happy now, like the birds that woke them in the morning—happy, but forcefully so. She picked up her papers and pencil. "All of you."

The women settled and Josephine gestured for Faina to sit in front of her. Faina thought of the image of the boy. How did it feel to be trapped there like that? Her skin flushed. She felt on the cusp of something. Like standing on an outcropping of rock before plunging into the sea—anticipation and a frisson of fear. She declined and instead sat down a short distance away, next to Telau, who fiddled with the neckline of her cloth dress, adjusting her many necklaces to lay overtop of it.

Talawan sat herself in front of Josephine.

Josephine studied her, tilting her head back and forth like a pelican about to swallow down prey, then reached out and adjusted Talawan's shoulders, her hair. After long minutes of silence, Josephine bent to her page and with quick movements drew Talawan's image on the paper. Talawan sat up straighter the longer Josephine's attention was on her, a smile beginning to play at her lips when Josephine handed her the picture. She laughed out loud and Telau reached over Talawan's shoulder to take the paper from her, glancing at it quickly before passing it on to Faina. There Talawan was—her low brow, her long chin, the softness in the wrinkles around her eyes. It was magic. Telau stood and plonked herself in front of Josephine, her chin thrust forward. "Me next."

They each took their turn and giggled as their images were conjured before them. There was Telau's elegant nose, the squint of Leisa's eyes, the twist of feathers in Nafatu's hair. It was so easy to recognize each of them there on this paper. They laughed at the drawings, and chattered and played, touched the images, touched each other.

"Word," Faina asked, pointing at the image Josephine had made of Talawan, dressed in her strange clothing.

"*Picture*," Josephine said. "Picture."

Faina repeated the sounds and waited for her own picture to come.

When it did, Faina touched her hair and the echo of it on the page, ran her fingers over her eyebrows and watched the image of them smudge on the paper. She drew a line down the slope of her nose. On the page her lips turned down, but now her own curled up at what she saw. She was beautiful.

"What is this?"

William was suddenly there and standing over them, his shape casting a shadow across them. "Idleness," he said. His words were hissed at Josephine, who stood and spoke to him in the tone she had used with Faina in the house. Pleading, Faina realized. Apologizing. Behind William was Masai and his friend Nako. Beyond them was a clutch of other young men from neighbouring villages. They often hectored William as he made his way around the island telling his stories and bribing people to listen with his hooks and nails.

The air crackled. Turning her body away from Masai, Faina slid her image into the woven bag she kept slung across her body, then draped her blouse over it.

Masai took the paper from Talawan's hand, stared hard at it, and then passed it on to the other men, who each took their turn examining it, glancing from the page to Talawan and back again.

"What will they do with this?" Masai asked. Talawan cowered away from him. Masai had grown broad through the chest and shoulders in the past months. His new tattoo rippled on his shoulder. "Is it to make some kind of sorcery?"

"It was only a distraction," said Josephine.

The two conversations ran in parallel. Masai and Talawan; William and Josephine. Faina stood back from them all, trying to work through who had done what wrong. Masai grabbed the rest of the papers from various hands, though Nafatu tried to hide hers behind her back. Then he tore at them until they were mere shreds and walked to the small fire that smouldered near Talawan's cooking hut. Faina made to stand, but Telau put her hand on Faina's arm and shook her head slightly. Masai could do as he wanted. The other men urged him on, smiling and laughing. Faina clutched her bag tighter as Masai breathed the flame to life and then fed the scraps of paper to it; they curled to black then to ash, the flames burning bright in the shade.

Deep in the night Faina was awoken by whispering. It might be devils, or perhaps someone speaking to her from the other side. It spoke N-glish, and she strained to make out the words. It was not Josephine's voice. Not William's.

She sat up carefully on her sleeping mat. Mother breathed heavily nearby, and Father and Father's Father slept on the other side of the sleeping hut. The whispering was inside, close at hand, but no one else stirred. Her bag was hung from the beam overhead. She reached for it. At the threshold, one of Father's piglets snorted to itself in sleep. She would hush it, but the voice pressed her on.

Faina slipped from the sleeping hut. She had never walked out in the night by herself. The air was cool on her skin after the shelter of the hut. It was said that the spirit world was closest at night. She thought of her own world, the one she could see in daylight, and theirs, the one that came alive at night. The world is like one side of a leaf, Mother had explained to her. But the other side, and here she had flipped over the leaf she held, is always there, even if you cannot see it.

Could they see her?

When she slid her hand into the bag, the paper tucked itself against her palm and the whispering stopped. She pulled the paper out and it glowed a white blue, like the surf at night, so that it almost hurt her eyes.

Faina took a leaf from one of the nearby trees, folded the image of herself into it, and then dug a small hole at the edge of her garden. She felt someone leaning over her, watching her, their breath on her neck, but they didn't stop her. "Is this right?" She spoke low into the dark. "To keep this?"

There was no answer, only the silence of the night.

After she returned, Faina stayed awake in the sleeping hut, watching for the creep of dawn. She hoped to hear the voice again, but she would have to decide for herself what to do.

III

Rebecca

Morning comes with washed light and the rising chatter of people, the calls of roosters and chickens, the gurgle of children as constant as a river. The ocean marks an easy tempo on the shore, dampened by clouds. It is not yet hot, but will be soon. In the cooking shelter, Rebecca finishes wrapping some of the leftovers for Anaei to take to school. The girl sits on the ground just outside the entrance, glancing back now and again at her mother as she doodles with her fingers in the earth. She draws maps of this place, the paths she makes of it.

"I can help cook and clean," Anaei says, looking sideways at her mother. "And sew."

Rebecca tries to hide her smile. "You are going to school."

"Astrid doesn't have to go to school." And when that doesn't work: "I'm sad and miss Ouben." Rebecca reaches to her daughter, who comes to her. She wishes she could keep Anaei beside her, not just today but always.

"I know," Rebecca says in her mother's language. "Me too, but he is watching us from Heaven and doesn't want us to be sad." She pulls back to peer at her daughter, her open face shining. "If he was here, he wouldn't be able to wait to go to school, to see and learn all the things that you are learning." She kisses Anaei's nose. "He would want to be like his big sister."

Anaei squirms some, her pleasure at the compliment mixed with sadness, but she stays close as Rebecca folds the last small square of laplap into a wide clean leaf and seals it in the old plastic paint bucket—which, thankfully, they have not needed for drinking water since the clearing of the stream at the old village site—then hangs it from a hook in the rafters.

With her hands now empty, Rebecca feels unmoored, as though she is floating between two shores, longing for land to light on. The world narrows. She is not here; she is somewhere else. The same place her voice went six months ago, when Ouben died. She begins to hum a tuneless phrase to stop herself from wanting to stay there, to remind herself of where she is.

She has hummed like this to soothe herself since she was a little girl. Traditional songs as well as church ones; it is not the words that buoy her, but the melodies. She was humming when Ouben died in her arms. He was fevered and sweating, and her lips vibrated as she hummed a lilting tune against his skull. He could hear her, and she could hear the tune in her head, but no one else could. He took the song with him when his breath stopped.

She didn't tell Michelle that. She is still uncertain of what she is willing to share with this woman, who immediately clung to her when she mentioned Ouben. Rebecca almost regrets sharing him with their guest, but she couldn't help herself in the dark. His name is so often what pulls her through from moment to moment.

"We will see you in the gardens?" Lehina is standing in the bright sun just outside the cooking shelter and her question startles Rebecca, who lifts her hand in acknowledgment. Lehina lingers briefly, before returning the gesture and continuing up the nearby path.

It has been seven months since the cyclone and life goes on, both inside and outside of the cooking hut. The bush and gardens are growing again, the vines are creeping up over the fallen trees, and the tree ferns are once more spreading themselves wide, elegant when they dance on the breeze. Already, the plot where Ouben's body is buried has begun to disappear.

Her arms can't remember his weight anymore. Perhaps because he grew so much in the short time that she had to hold him—the small weight of him growing heavier and heavier in the first thirteen months, and him growing stronger as he began to pull away from her, arching his back in her embrace to get down, to get away. But then the cyclone struck, and he became lighter and lighter as he shrank into himself and into her. She tried to hold him fast to her, to life. Sometimes she is so physically desperate for him she picks things up around the cooking hut, trying to conjure the weight of her son, but none of these things—the empty pots, the woven baskets, the mats they sit on—have the weight of life.

"Hallo miss!" Bridely's voice comes like a wave before her, and the woman is already talking before Rebecca has a chance to greet her. "They didn't like the laplap yesterday," Bridely says as she steps carefully across the wide threshold, putting her hand on Anaei's head as she enters. She moves slower now, as the impatient baby grows inside her. It's true, Rebecca thinks, each of the Stewarts moved the food around the plates they had been handed, pecked at small bites of it, before making a show of not being hungry. "Did they like breakfast at least? You gave them eggs and bread?" Rebecca nods. "That's what white people like. And fruit juice. Everyone likes fruit juice."

Bridely doesn't expect Rebecca to speak about mundane things, so she fills the space with her own words and thoughts. It used to irritate Rebecca, but now she is glad for the young woman's chatter.

"My mother told me that I wouldn't like white people's food. 'Food belongs in its place,' she said." Bridely affects an accent that Rebecca cannot place, and she wonders if this is really what Bridely's mother sounds like. "But then she eats rice and canned tuna!"

Anaei stares at Bridely, fascinated by the young woman, her good cheer and her swollen shape.

"Me," Bridely continues, as she lowers herself heavily to the ground and sits with her legs stretched out on the mat, "I like pizza." She puts her hands flat in front of her mouth as though she is eating, trying to make Rebecca and Anaei laugh. "Have you had it?" Bridely asks, then pats the space beside her on the mat for Anaei to sit. Anaei shakes her head. "I had it in Fiji when Willie's football team was in a tournament there. I would eat it every day if I could. Or McDonald's!" She throws back her head and laughs.

Rebecca likes Bridely's attitude towards the foreigners— astonishment and dismissal at once. She takes what she likes from them, but doesn't see them as particularly special. Bridely goes quiet and then, as if she can read Rebecca's thoughts, she says with a small chuckle, "How are they supposed to help us? I'm not sure they can help themselves!"

Rebecca shakes her head, though she thinks Bridely is right. Instead she says to Anaei, "That food would make you sick."

Bridely smiles wide again. "That's what all the mamas say." She runs her hand over the round of her belly as though satiated. Rebecca looks away.

Bridely is so young, only a year older than Rebecca was when she first came to this island. She is a slight, skinny girl, her hair tinted with a reddish gold. Bridely supported her through the days and weeks after Ouben's death, guiding her hands until they remembered what to do, placing a knife in her palm, or taro in front of her to grate, distracting Anaei. She told stories of Ouben, described him over and over again to Rebecca, reviving his laugh and the deep brown of his eyes, the curls of hair at the nape of his neck, the seashell of his tiny ears, the whorl of his fingerprints. She offered them as gifts, and they sustained Rebecca.

Bridely's belly presses out of her now, round as a coconut, though much bigger. But she is skin and bones behind it. She should eat more; the baby is taking all of the food. Her belly grows, but Bridely does not. Without a word, Rebecca slides a leaf of leftover rice and some cooked taro to her, and Bridely scoops it sloppily with her fingers. Rebecca hands her a metal fork she has already washed, which Bridely takes with a smile.

Outside there is the murmur of voices—women coming closer, men moving away, the chaotic babble of children, like birds taking to the sky. Lalim, David's brother's wife, ducks into the hut, followed by David's mother, Numalin, shuffling her feet forward. Bridely begins to press herself up to give the old woman her space near the door, but Numalin puts a hand on her shoulder, both keeping her in place and using Bridely to lower herself to the ground.

"Looking for Jacob?" Numalin teases Bridely, who drops her gaze to hide her smile. "All you young women are always watching for Jacob," she continues. "He's always hanging around waiting for you to cook him something."

"I'm a married woman," Bridely says.

Lalim sucks her teeth. "Doesn't mean you are not looking. It is nice to have a young man around to look at." Bridely blushes. "Will Jimmy make it back for the birth?" Lalim asks, naming Bridely's husband, who no one has heard from in some months. His absence makes them all worry. They have birthed babies before, but it would be good if Jimmy sent money in case they need a doctor.

Bridely deflects by asking about Lalim's nephew. "Is he coming home soon?"

"There is nothing here for him right now. He has found a woman in Vila he wants to marry, and has to make money so he can."

"Jacob must have a girlfriend," Bridely says, turning to Rebecca, who shrugs. She goes on: "Probably many. He is too handsome." She leans slightly into the centre of the group, and her voice drops. "I heard he was talking to a girl in the north. They met in Vila, and she returned to her place after the storm."

"Jacob is a good boy. He won't be talking with girls. Who told you that?" Numalin asks.

"Never you mind," Lalim says. "I heard the girl was still in Vila."

"You are all gossiping," Numalin says. "There is no such girl. His parents would know."

"She would be lucky," Bridely says.

Lalim stands and pulls down a basket full of cloth from the rafters. Each of the women reaches in, takes a piece, eyes it up, and then bends to sewing, their hands moving evenly while they talk. Anaei watches Bridely, her head cocked to the side, taking in every detail of how the young woman moves.

The gossip about Jacob unsettles Rebecca. These women are her friends, but to hear them talk about him in this way, as though there are no consequences attached to what they jabber about, unnerves her. "Jacob does have a job in New Zealand," Rebecca says eventually. She has not said the words aloud before, has barely acknowledged them to herself. But in front of her friends she tries to sound proud, the way that she knows Lalim would sound if her nephew had gotten honest work.

"Ah! That's good news," Lalim says now. "He will be able to help pay for Anaei's schooling. Maybe she can even go away to Vila when she is older."

"I'm never going away." Anaei shakes her head.

"Don't be silly," Numalin says to her. "Wives go with their husbands. That is how it is."

"Then I'll marry Jacob."

"Not if he is gone away!" Numalin laughs her croaking laugh that sounds older than she is. Anaei frowns, and Rebecca tries to pull her daughter to her, but the girl scooches closer to Bridely.

Numalin's laugh slips to a cough, and after she clears her throat, she adds, "David must be pleased. It is hard to find good work."

Rebecca holds her tongue because she hasn't told David that Jacob does want to go away. She knows it will hurt him, and he has already been so hurt. But her friends are right. It is hard to find work, especially here. Especially now. He will be proud of his son, won't he?

"They are not what I expected," Lalim says, continuing a conversation out loud that she has clearly been having in her head.

She is often like this, changing the stroke of their talk in strange ways. For once, Rebecca is grateful for it, a turning away from Jacob and David.

"What did you expect?" Rebecca asks.

Lalim tilts her head, thoughtful, having spoken before she knew what she wanted to say. "They are more quiet than I would have thought," she begins, "like they might break something." She gives a quick bark of a laugh. "Or like we might break them!"

Numalin and Bridely laugh with her. Rebecca nods tightly.

"They have so much luggage," Bridely adds. "More than I had when I came to live here. And do you think they are old? I think they look old."

"I was surprised they brought a grandmother with them," Numalin says. "White people don't respect their families the way we do."

Bridely giggles again at this, then adds, "They're very tall."

"Not Michelle."

"No. But even their little girl is taller than Anaei!"

"They had a boy who died," Rebecca says, recalling Michelle's voice in the night, the exchange of their sons' names.

Numalin clicks her tongue, and Lalim makes an empathetic sound as she reaches to stroke Anaei's back. "They are not so different then. Not so big," she says, using a word in her language that Rebecca knows. It means when a man thinks he is important, thinks he is brave. Sometimes the women use this word as a sly jab at Robson, and they all chuckle at it, even Rebecca.

"I think they are different," Bridely says. "People are like their places. They are cold and full of money, just like Toronto. I should have married someone from there." She laughs loudly, the gap in her teeth flashing.

"It is sad," Lalim says, "but it does not change the fact that we must cook for them and share with them." She pauses. "They have that look."

"They are our guests," Numalin scolds, "no matter what they look like."

"What look?" Bridely asks Lalim, who makes a face, bending her lips into a frown.

"That sadness. You know. Pity." She glances at Rebecca.

Rebecca knows the look. It was how the doctors looked at her when they finally came from the north and saw Ouben. They told her she should have come to them sooner. They said maybe then they might have been able to do something, as they squirted some bright-coloured antibiotics into his mouth. How was she supposed to get to them? The roads were impassable with uprooted trees and mudslides. Her baby was too sick for such a journey.

"Robson says that when we have their forgiveness, then things will change here," Bridely adds. "But how does that change things?"

"Not forgiveness," Numalin says, her voice a croak again. She clears her throat once more and spits into a square of cloth that she pulls from the pocket of her wide skirt, then folds and sets just outside the threshold of the hut. "We must come together, that is how our grandmothers would say it."

Rebecca wants to confide a thought that has been nagging at her, about these people being here, how maybe they carry too much need with them, too much grief. She worries they will take more than they give, and the people here can't afford to give any more.

She is about to say something when the church bell in the distance tolls and the women begin to shift themselves to leave, taking small wrapped packages of leftovers—some to eat in the gardens later, some to deliver to the men clearing grounds to build new homes.

Lalim rests her hand on top of Rebecca's head when she passes, and it is a soothing, soft scratching like a mother would offer a child. She misses the touch when Lalim moves on. "We will see you in the gardens, yes?"

Rebecca nods.

Soon it is just Rebecca, Bridely, and Anaei in the cooking hut once more.

"You should get ready," Rebecca tells Anaei, though she also means it for Bridely, who will walk with the children to the school in Robson's village. Anaei grabs her small flip-flops but then giggles at a growl from Bridely's belly. Bridely smiles with one hand over her mouth, hiding the pretty gap in her teeth, her other hand resting flat against her belly. "He is hungry today." Her belly rolls. "And angry."

"And what about you?" Rebecca does and doesn't want to talk about this baby.

Bridely shrugs. "I'm whatever he is."

Rebecca remembers the defeat and astonishment of this, feeling like her body was not her own. Feeling occupied by another being, by the future. Ouben made her happy and slow, where Anaei made her anxious and unable to sit down.

"I heard on the radio," Bridely is saying, "that Willie's team won in Fiji."

"This is good news," Rebecca says, handing Anaei her lunch, which the little girl slides into a small bag like the ones she has been learning to weave.

Bridely's brother is her one love. A football player with the national team, he travels much of the time and has not been home to see his family for over a year. He sends home money and shirts and scarves with the team logo on them, which Bridely wears with devotion. Rebecca lets her talk. She knows that Bridely doesn't get much chance to in her father-in-law's house, where she sleeps while her husband is away in Australia. He has been away since before Bridely discovered she was pregnant. Bridely is glad that he is gone and so is Rebecca. He was rough with his wife. When she was first married, Bridely was often seen with bruises on her body or cradling an injured arm. Rebecca and the other women didn't mention the injuries, but they would make sure she had food to serve him, and a place for herself among them. He sends home a little money to his father, but Bridely sees none of it.

"They are going to Australia for the playoffs, and I am going to go with them. I'm going to go, and I think never come back here. I'll find a job in Sydney and live in a big apartment away from the sea." She peers over Rebecca's shoulder at the sparkle and dance of the ocean. "You can come visit me."

"Everyone there wants to live by the sea," Rebecca says.

"Not me. I will never live by the sea again. It is always so loud and booming." She shivers. "Willie will introduce me to all the famous football players and—"

"Ouben was going to be a football player," Anaei says from the entrance of the shelter, shifting anxiously from foot to foot. Sometimes Rebecca worries that Anaei spends too much time with Bridely listening to the football games, too much time listening to Bridely. But her comment makes Rebecca smile.

"You think so?" she asks.

"Oh yes! Remember the way he kicked you in your belly, and even when he was out? Kick kick kick." She mimics the flailing of his soft round legs.

"He would have been a great one, I bet," Bridely enthuses.

"A great what?" Jacob appears in the threshold as a shadow.

"Football player—Ouben," Anaei explains, and kicks at the air around Jacob's ankles.

"I bet he would have."

As Anaei and Bridely set out for school, Rebecca tries to conjure Ouben as a young man, to see him at Jacob's age, at the cusp of a new life. Would he go away? Would she be able to find a way to keep him here? It is almost impossible for her to picture him. She can picture Jacob, and her own brother. She can imagine David as a young man. But her heart stutters at the empty space where Ouben should be.

"Are you ready?" David asks from where he has appeared behind Jacob, startling her.

She should tell David that his son is thinking of leaving, and she should tell Jacob to talk to his father. She wishes she could be the bridge that joins them, but for now their silences settle back upon her.

David

David stretches and cracks his back as the church bell sounds noon through the bush. It has been a long morning under the hot sun, scraping flat the earth that was left undisturbed for generations. His brother, Tomas, calls to David as he goes to eat his lunch in the shade of their grandfathers' banyan, where he is joined by Matthew and Naling, emerging from other plots along other paths. All of them sweat and groan themselves to the ground. David stands over them a minute.

"Sit," Tomas says. "Eat."

David declines. "I have to go find Jacob. There is still the pig to pick up for the feast."

"Hezekiah has sent the kava already and we'll prepare it tomorrow," Tomas says.

"Good, good." David nods. Everything is going smoothly. "Do you think we can start building soon? I'll ask Jacob to join us if we are."

"Maybe," Tomas says. "If the weather holds. It would be good to have some young blood to help us out, instead of just us old men." The four of them laugh.

"I thought Jacob was leaving right after the ceremony?" Naling asks.

"No," David says with a confidence he does not feel. "He isn't sure when he is heading back to Vila yet."

"I heard Robson say he is going to New Zealand."

David forces himself to laugh. "I think Robson is just talking. You know the way that he is. He always wants you to think he knows everything that goes on." He feels a small pang of guilt at saying this about his friend, even if it is true.

Naling shrugs.

"He does like to talk," Tomas admits, though he doesn't sound convinced.

David leaves the three of them chatting over their lunch as he heads towards his own gardens, where Jacob is helping Rebecca. Clouds scuttle low over the island; he hopes they will burn off. He knows the Stewarts expect a bright blue sky, the water to shine. A tropical paradise, as all white people do of this place. Overhead is the soft coo of a dove and David pauses briefly on the path to peer through the foliage, but its green feathers render it invisible. Today, the sounds of the place soothe him only slightly. The doves; the wind higher up rippling the trees; farther away, the chatter of voices in the gardens. Below it all the rhythmic harmonies of a building song.

He can't help but think about what Naling said, and he feels a rising anger that others are gossiping about his family, that his son has gone elsewhere for advice. David doesn't want Robson to lure his son away.

It is true that he and Robson were themselves nineteen when they went to New Zealand together to work farms and fields for a year. Only a few months older than Jacob is now, they were both already married with children. Every time David had news from home, his heart swelled and broke all at once. He longed to hold his son, to speak his name.

David pleaded with Robson to return to Iparei with him, but Robson wanted to stay. Another year, he said to David, and they would make big money. "Think of what we could take home to them. A generator. An outboard motor. We could buy concrete and build homes. We can do more by staying here. It will take years to make this kind of money at home."

But there was the draw of his wife and son, the hope of more children. David felt uprooted, the better part of himself missing. His feet were itchy, he explained, for the ground he grew up on.

Robson did stay another year, sending home money and letters. When he came back, he returned as a big man, with money and big talk and new connections in Vila and overseas. He took over in the church, having become involved with a congregation in New Zealand who had sent money back with him. He had a new bell cast to look exactly like the one Reverend William was said to have brought with him to Iparei, which had been lost or stolen in the decades since. He had a plaque carved for the church that told of its founding, and he hung a copy of the mission photo that included David's great-grandfather. Robson built a three-room home, the first concrete building at their end of the island aside from the church, and he paid for the new school building. He leased a large portion of land and planted coconuts that he processed into oil, and he started growing cash crops instead of subsistence ones, all the while urging David to as well.

He talked about constructing a hotel. He talked about building a yacht club for rich foreigners. He talked of establishing a ring road that would link all the places on the island together. Yes, he has done well—but his coconut palms were devastated by the cyclone, and it will be a lean year without the copra money. He will be looking for a new venture. And David is worried that Jacob is part of some new scheme.

When David enters the clearing, Jacob is bent over a shovel, scraping out the terraced hillside for the yam plants that he will mark with a twist of cane. Rebecca kneels where she has planted the taro that she loves from her island. It is reassuring to see the plants growing so well.

"You have done so much work," he calls out, and his wife and son stop what they are doing to look up at him. Nearby, in the surrounding bush, others pause to listen before picking up again. "You've done so much!" David says again, trying to keep the anxiety out of his voice.

"Thanks to Jacob," Rebecca says, her own voice pitched low in the midday air. A troubled shadow passes over his son's face. They both sweat in the glare of the sun.

"It's lunchtime," David says. "You didn't hear the bell?"

"We're just stopping," Rebecca says. "Your son is the one who wants to keep working."

"Are you trying to make up for something?" David asks, trying to make it a joke, but his wife and son exchange a quick glance before Rebecca goes to the small woven bag she has carried to her garden, to retrieve their lunch.

"Jacob," he says, ignoring the food that Rebecca holds out to him. "I'm going to the north to get the pig for the ceremony. Come with me. They haven't seen you in so long."

"I promised Rebecca I'd . . ." Jacob begins, lifting his shovel and then angling it down like a blade into the earth. "I should stay here."

"Perhaps you should," David says, and his stomach turns slightly. They are both avoiding looking at him. "Is something wrong?"

"No," Jacob says quickly. "No, I'll go with you," he adds and then glances at Rebecca. "Is that okay?"

She nods her encouragement and whispers something to Jacob as he goes to kiss her cheek and hand her his shovel. He wipes his face with his forearm and heads down the path towards the shore. David watches him go before turning back to Rebecca. She lifts a hand to wave him away without saying anything, and joins the others who are breaking to eat near their own gardens. David hurries after his son, catching up to him easily and falling into step behind him on the path.

Jacob and Rebecca have silence in common, though David wonders if Jacob sees it that way. As a child, whenever Jacob was angry, he would set his jaw the way it is now. He wouldn't speak, but would creep about as quietly as possible, as though he might be able to make himself disappear. But then his mother died, and it was as if he broke loose. He became a cyclone of noise and action that David didn't know how to control. He'd long worried about Jacob's withdrawals, which Jacob's mother said were just him thinking but which David read as simmering anger. He worried about how his son ran through the bush with slightly older boys, about the rumoured still they had built deep in the woods in one of the old tabu places.

He decided to send his son away to school in Vila, and when he told him, Jacob did disappear. He walked three hours across the island to his mother's family, his aunt sending word that he was safe with them. It was then David knew he must marry again. But he couldn't have known how much his son and Rebecca would come to love each other. He could not have known that sometimes they would form an alliance against him. Or how glad he would be for their bond.

"You don't really need my help," Jacob says over his shoulder to him as they walk.

He's right. "Maybe. But I would like it," David responds, watching his son's back.

Jacob makes a noncommittal noise. Their feet sound softly on the path. Around them the bush is alive with birdsong, the click and hum of insects. David thinks of Jacob as a boy, standing on a path like this, bow in his hand, and how he used to guide his son's eye.

"Do you remember," he says, "when I first taught you to hunt? How many bows did you go through? You made them so easily. More than I ever did."

"I had to. I lost them all the time."

"Yes! After you got a pigeon you always forgot it behind, you were so excited. I told you to go back and get it, but you said someone else would need it." His throat constricts, somewhere between laughing and crying.

"I just didn't want to go back and look for it."

David laughs into the humid air, remembering Jacob's long body, stretched out in a growth spurt, barefoot and scrambling up trunks that even now are still growing. In a flash he sees Ouben at the same age, at seven years or so, rounder than Jacob was, certainly, and a little less sure, a little less bold—and then he is gone.

"I bet he would have been a better hunter than me," Jacob says. That they are both thinking of Ouben comforts David, who reaches forward and squeezes his son's shoulder. Jacob stops under the touch and they stand together on the path. The air murmurs around them. The trees sing as their branches slide against each other. The ocean is a distant hum.

"Vila doesn't sound like this," Jacob says. He pats his father's hand on his shoulder and then walks out of his grip.

"Nowhere sounds like this."

Eventually, they step out into the open space of the nasara, and the few chickens scratching nearby disappear into the bush. The sky is bright and fierce now, cracking open as the sun cuts through the clouds overhead. The two of them stand side by side squinting into the bright of the ocean and the whole of the world laid out in front of them.

It is quiet; everyone is out on their land. David raises a hand to Joyce and Michelle, sitting on chairs angled towards the ocean under the banyan, drinking bottles of water, a plate of fresh fruit untouched between them. Two skinny cats sleep in the shade of their chairs. The women wave back. He takes his son's arm and steers him towards the pickup truck.

"I hear that you are leaving," David forces himself to say.

Jacob pulls up short and then bends to the back wheel of the truck, pretends to examine the shocks that David complained about the other day.

"Rebecca said she wouldn't tell you."

David feels as though he has been struck; Rebecca knew. "It's fine," he says, talking about the rear wheel. "Leave it."

Jacob stands but doesn't meet his father's eyes; instead he climbs into the back of the pickup and plucks fallen leaves out of the bed.

"Did Robson get you the job?"

Jacob only shrugs.

David inhales deeply. "Jacob, why didn't you come to me?"

"You have enough to worry about."

"You always come first," he says, but Jacob sucks his teeth, which irks his father. "Why do you have to go? Do you owe Robson something? Someone in Vila?"

"I owe *you* something. I *owe* my brother something." There is a sudden edge of desperation to Jacob's voice, as though he is searching for an escape.

David sees the silent child that Jacob once was and worries he will stop speaking and slink away, but his son continues.

"What happened two hundred years ago, the past, it doesn't matter. We need to be thinking of the future. They say this place will be swallowed by the ocean, will disappear entirely. Not because of anything we have done, but because of them." He gestures in the direction of the Stewarts, where they lounge in the shade. "If we want to be able to stay here, then we need money. You think I can just plant a little garden and live like that? It's not enough."

Maybe he is right. What is there to keep Jacob or any of the young people here, on the island? Most of them have already gone away. Iparei has become a place of children and the older generation. But all he wants is for his son to marry and have children who David can sit with on his knee. Who cares about what else they may not have?

Jacob stands in the bed of the truck and stares out at the sea. "I couldn't tell you because you wouldn't have heard it. You've changed . . ." He slows and chooses his words carefully. "Since Ouben." He lets the name sit between them. "I miss him too. He's my brother, my heart." Jacob stares up at the sky. "I didn't tell you, because I didn't want to hurt you. But I have to leave."

"You don't."

Jacob leaps down from the truck and walks around to open the passenger door, refusing to meet his father's eye. "What choice do I have?" he asks.

David stares at his son, before he turns away and squints at the light reflecting off the water. He tries to think of something to say, but for the first time he finds that any real answers escape him.

Scott

"No," Michelle says. "Absolutely not."

Scott takes a deep breath and wrings his damp bathing suit in his hands before he responds. "I don't want to argue. I just want to have some fun with the kids. David said that it's the safest snorkelling around. It's totally calm, like a swimming pool." He cringes as soon as he says it, then rushes past the words. "Zach will love it. And Astrid—she'll have on her floaty. We'll be together. Nothing will happen."

He wanted to go as soon as David suggested it, even though Scott got the feeling David was trying to get rid of him. He'd interrupted David and Jacob on their way somewhere, and when he offered to help out, David politely refused him.

"Is there anything else I can do?" Scott asked. "Tomas said you were rebuilding your homes in the woods. That you're moving? I'm good with a hammer."

"Thank you, no."

"Can I ask why you're leaving? It's just so gorgeous here." He gestured at the sea, the sky, the soft breeze.

"It is. But the storms that come now are so much worse, so much stronger than they used to be. We didn't always live here." And when Scott glanced at him, David explained, "Our ancestors lived inland. The beach was a place for gathering, for fishing and swimming and travel, but we lived up the hill, sheltered from the sea, and from what it brings." Scott knew he wasn't just talking about the storms, but about Michelle's ancestors, the garbage on the shore, them. As if to confirm his hunch, David continued, "It wasn't until your forefathers came, and they built the churches and the schools, that people gathered into new villages here by the ocean. The old places are part of us. It's time to return home."

Scott was about to confess that he had been thinking about moving too when David said, "I should go, but do you like to snorkel? There is a place where the reef makes a bowl in the sea. It is calm and protected, good snorkelling—so many fish, bêche-de-mer. You should take your son."

Now Michelle glares at him from where she sits under the banyan while Joyce pretends to ignore them, and he is embarrassed to be pleading with his wife in front of her mother.

"You know that, right? Nothing will happen. We used to snorkel with the boys all the time, at the cottage, in Mexico. They loved it. You loved it!" Her face has become unfamiliar to him. He tries to remember the last time he touched her cheek, the last time he kissed her. "Come with us! I bet there's another mask and snorkel somewhere. The more the merrier."

Michelle looks towards the sea and for a moment he actually believes she will relent. When she does, he'll sweep her up in his arms, thrilled to have her back, even for just a few minutes.

Instead she says, "Zach won't want to. He quit the swim team. He doesn't want to be in the water anymore."

"Well, I'll ask him. If he doesn't want to, fine, but I want to do this."

She doesn't meet his eye but says, "Not Astrid. She's too little. And if you let him out of your sight . . ."

The sting of the accusation is like a slap.

A short while later, Scott waits under the banyan tree for Zach. Michelle left as soon as he returned with Zach's agreement, taking Astrid inside for more sunscreen. Beside him, Joyce opens a soft cloth bag full of origami birds, and pulls out a square of paper to make another one. "I'm glad he's going with you," she says, and he gives a small grunt in response. "Yesterday, you really tore a strip off him. You should go easier on him."

Scott bristles at his mother-in-law's comment. What does she know about it?

"I dunno. Maybe I need to be harder on him," he says, watching Joyce's fingers turning and folding the piece of paper in her hand, pressing a nail along the seam until she holds another small bird in her palm. She sets it down on the ground, selects another sheet of paper, and begins again, her hands moving automatically as she stares at him over her chic sunglasses. He looks away and picks up one of her paper birds.

"When did you start this?" he asks.

"One of the women in my support group told me she folded hundreds of them after her son died. Each day she set herself the task of making just one bird. So she made one and then she made another and another. Something that small gave her a reason to get out of bed." The wind moves the branches over their heads, dappling the birds with light, giving them the appearance of movement. Scott imagines the lot of them taking flight, settling in the tree overhead. "It does me good, you know," Joyce says, "talking to people. Maybe Zach could try it?"

The phrasing almost makes him smile, remembering how Michelle used to complain that her mother phrased imperatives like questions, when she meant them like orders.

"He sees his guidance counsellor at school."

Joyce doesn't respond, only folds and folds. After a long pause, her fingernail scoring the paper, she says, "I caught Zach sneaking out the other night. At the motel in Vila. Or was that last night? It feels like we've been here forever, doesn't it? People say to do unusual things if you want time to slow down. It's when we live by routine that life seems to slide away from us."

There is nothing more unusual than your child dying, he thinks. "I thought he'd stopped doing that," he says. Guilt washes over him as Joyce turns to him, surprised. "It was about a year ago." Even to his own ears it sounds like an excuse.

Someone had been moving through the middle-of-the-night gloom of their house. The opening and closing of the side door was timed expertly, coinciding with the thump and rumble of the air conditioner. Scott pulled on a pair of sweatpants and a T-shirt, and slipped past Dylan's bedroom where Michelle was sleeping once again.

By the time he reached the front door, he just caught sight of Zach disappearing around the corner at the end of the street. He followed his son, worried he was going to buy drugs, or that he would be hit by a drunk driver racing home in the small hours. Zach simply wandered alone down the middle of the road, stopping occasionally to stare up at the dark windows of their neighbours' homes.

Scott kept to the sidewalks, unable to decide whether to call out to his son and walk with him in the quiet dark, or order him home and to bed. He did neither, just continued following him, hoping to keep him safe from a distance. They didn't see another soul, didn't hear a single dog bark. There was only the distant hum of late-night traffic over on Bayview. When they completed the loop of their neighbourhood, Scott watched Zach let himself in the side door, and then waited a few minutes before letting himself in the front door.

"What did Michelle say when you told her?" Joyce asks, jarring Scott back to himself. His wife is watching Astrid play on the narrow stretch of sand, but she stands apart from her. She used to play with the kids.

"I haven't told her. She doesn't have much to say about the kids these days."

Joyce's hands finally stop moving. "That's not fair," she says, "and it's not true. It's been torture on her, losing a child. I can't even imagine."

"Yeah, well, I can." And he moves to get up.

"Stop," she says, reaching towards him. "I'm sorry. That was . . . cruel. I didn't mean . . . You know I love you too. We're all heartbroken. I'm sure she's trying."

Scott sighs. "She needs help."

"She's grieving."

And again he's reminded that Joyce doesn't know he's the one who's been taking care of the kids, making sure they are fed, they have clean clothes, they get to school, while Michelle has been possessed by a grief that she seems incapable of surfacing from, even now. Joyce doesn't know Michelle has spent more nights sleeping in Dylan's bed than in theirs. That he can't even talk to her about their children, about their future, without her face clouding over and turning to stone. And he knows, of course he knows, that Joyce is only speaking from her own concern— for Zach, for her daughter, even for him. But god, he wishes someone was on his side.

He and Zach tread water at the surface. Around them, a sheer underwater ring of coral drops down twenty feet to a white circle of sand. Fish of all sizes flit and soar around them. Beside him, Zach's movements are easy and relaxed, his T-shirt billowing in the current. His son turns his way, snorkel in his mouth already, and forms his fingers to ask *OK?* the way he was taught. Scott returns the sign, waits for his son to dive, and then breathes deeply through the snorkel and dives beneath the surface of the choppy water.

Below is a cacophony. There is the white noise of the water itself, but also the ticking of parrotfish pecking at the coral, like the sound of Rice Krispies popping. With strong strokes he fights against the pull of the surface, forces himself deeper. Thermoclines race up his body, warm then cold, then colder still in the vastness of the ocean. Light plunges down in dappled columns, and fish move in and out of the gloom like bright shards of colour, blue and red, yellow and green, and a turquoise colour that seems more turquoise than the word can allow. When he reaches towards them, they scatter before re-forming their school elsewhere. He observes vicious-looking sea stars, the slither of a sea snake, the thick, dark bodies of the sea cucumbers David told him about, the spread of intricately woven coral fans moving back and forth with the waves, easing him sideways and then back again.

Suddenly, he is deeply happy to be here.

When Michelle first told him she had bought tickets for the five of them to travel to Iparei, it was a shock.

"You just decided unilaterally? To spend that kind of money? I thought we were in this together, Michelle. We're supposed to discuss decisions like this."

"How? How was I supposed to talk to you about this? I don't know how to talk to you at all anymore."

It was a relief to hear her admit it. After Dylan died, they had made promises in the dark of their bedroom. They promised each other over and over again that they would get through this together. They wouldn't let this tear them apart. They had already lost so much—they would do whatever it took to save what was left of their family. But Michelle had pulled away from him. In small ways at first, ways that almost made sense to him; then at some point in time, they stopped making sense.

But a part of him was relieved she had kept this trip and the call from David a secret. It made him feel less guilty about his own.

He hadn't intended to buy a new house. But then he saw a *for sale* sign one evening after he left church.

He'd started going to the church almost by accident, the autumn after Dylan's death. The church was a big old thing, by Toronto standards anyway—an imposing grey stone building, stark and severe, even on a summer evening. When they first moved into the neighbourhood, he'd imagined them going there to celebrate holidays, but they never did. He'd never imagined holding his son's funeral there. After that, he'd avoided passing by the building altogether, until one frigid November evening, when he took the shortest way home from the subway. He stopped when he realized where he was, and something compelled him inside.

That first time he stayed only a few minutes, hovering around the entrance of the church. But there was a calmness there in that vast cathedral of space, a power. It was like he was being held, cradled somehow. He didn't feel Dylan in that peace, but somehow that was okay.

He started going regularly—after work or on quiet weekends. Then one night after church he passed a house that caught his attention. It wasn't so different than the others in their neighbourhood, a little smaller maybe, tucked back farther from the road. But it was brightly lit and he could see figures moving inside, and for maybe the first time since his son died he didn't hate other people for their happiness or ease. He envied them. He wanted to be in there with them, in that warmth and chatter. There was a "for sale" sign on the front lawn.

He didn't put in an offer on that house, but he and the agent he met when he went to look at it started meeting at least once a week, whenever she was in the neighbourhood or near his office. She brought him beautifully printed listings of new houses, and they talked about all sorts of possibilities. He knew he should tell Michelle, but the time was never right.

The day they flew to Iparei, the agent sent him a listing, saying it would be public soon, but wasn't it perfect for him? He made a pre-emptive bid from the airport. The thought makes him giddy as he dives deeper into the sea, feeling the weight of the water push down on him. The ocean nudges him and everywhere there is the flit of fish, shadows moving just beyond the range of visibility.

The pressure is growing in his throat, a burning desire for air, but he stays submerged. After Dylan died, he researched what it felt like to drown, tortured himself with internet knowledge. He knows that when you feel like you've run out of air, there is still more, reserves held deep in the lungs that you never use, but most people just give in to the compulsion to breathe.

He closes his eyes under the water. The mask squeezes against his sinuses, while his lungs push against him from the inside. He lets loose a bubble of air, easing the discomfort, and remembers the sound of being underwater in their pool at home, the way the rumble of the neighbourhood traffic seemed to envelop him, the feeling there was always someone nearby. He wonders about the sounds at the new house, hedged off from the street, a new heating and cooling unit that won't thump in the night.

His lungs begin to burn. He sees the flash of Dylan's red sweater, the tendrils of hair floating at his temples. His hands on Dylan's narrow chest, the water running from his mouth.

Scott shoots to the surface in spite of himself, his body reaching for air. The waves bully him as he gasps and shudders, his palm slapping hard at the water. He pushes the mask up on his forehead and rubs at his eyes and glances around.

Zach.

Where's Zach?

The waves have turned Scott around so he is facing the chop and heave of the ocean. He spins himself quickly towards the shore, where Astrid plays in the shallows, Joyce and Michelle watching carefully nearby. But no Zach.

He twists around to search the horizon. His heart is high in his throat. He pulls the mask down over his eyes and dives into the water. The mask leaks, filling with salt water, stinging. "Zach!" he screams into the water, his voice a murmur coming from every direction at once, but his son isn't there. He breaks the surface again, gasping for breath.

And when he finally rubs the salt from his eyes, he spots Zach paddling easily towards the shore. Scott's head drops back and he sinks with relief for a beat before treading water. He can't breathe. He tries to calm himself. It's fine. Zach's fine.

Scott is still breathing hard when he reaches Zach in the shallows. The water is even warmer here, swelling up around his thighs and then pulling him back towards the ocean. He wants to yell at his son, shake him. Instead, he pretends nothing happened; pretends he isn't still terrified.

"How was that?" he asks, as they both sit in the shallows, the water moving against them.

"Yeah, cool," Zach says without much commitment.

"You should take that off." Scott gestures at the T-shirt, wet and clinging across Zach's narrow shoulders. "Get some sun."

"Nah, I'm good."

"Chelsea doesn't like a tan?" Zach doesn't answer, pushes towards the shore. Fuck, how is he always saying the wrong thing? "See anything good?" he asks, trying to draw his son back to him. "I saw this huge starfish. Red and white and covered with all these spines. Looked deadly."

"Don't lick it," Zach says, almost automatically, and they both freeze. It was something Dylan used to say whenever someone pointed out something gross or dangerous—dog shit or broken glass on the sidewalk, a spill of cleaning fluid. *Don't lick it.*

Scott stands too.

"Crown-of-thorns," Zach says.

"What?"

"The starfish. I read about them at the motel in Vila. They're an invasive species. They eat all the coral that other fish and stuff need. And they're super poisonous. If they sting you once it's really bad, but the poison builds up, so, like, by the second or third sting, it can kill you."

This astounds him about his son. Zach will read something once, and it lodges itself in his brain and then pops out days or weeks later. Scott always thought that kind of memory was a blessing; now, he isn't so sure.

"I guess you're right then," he says, with a smile. "Don't lick it." Zach turns to walk up the beach without responding. "Hey, wait a minute." His hand is on Zach's arm but when Zach looks at it, Scott lets go. Before he realizes it, the words are out of his mouth. "How would you feel if we moved?"

Zach shifts away from him. "Are you and Mom getting a divorce?"

The question stuns him. "What? No. Why would you think that?"

"She's . . . I don't know. She's different now."

Scott only nods. "Yeah. Maybe we all are. But no, I was just thinking that maybe . . . I don't know, I saw this great place. You could have a bigger room, not be stuck up there in the attic. It might . . . do some good?"

Zach is quiet for a long moment. Eventually he says, "I don't know." His voice is cautious.

"It's okay," Scott says. "Just thinking out loud. Forget it."

"I'll think about it," Zach says and strides away. He doesn't speak to his mother or sister; he just picks his phone up from where he left it and goes to sit in the shaded doorway of the bungalow.

Scott stands in the swell of water, the sand covering and uncovering his feet, and thinks of his son's body—how fragile it is, the bumps and bruises it has already suffered, how much more pain is likely still to come. The idea is almost impossible to live with. Scott lifts his face to the sky and closes his eyes and sends a silent prayer upwards.

Michelle

The dark comes on fast here—no long, lazy sunsets like she was expecting. Michelle crosses the dusk of the nasara, to where the women are gathered on woven mats under the canopy of trees. The glow of the few solar lamps casts strange shadows. Across the open space, the men are gathered in a group as well, as they did last night, laughing and chatting. She tries but fails to hear Zach or Scott among them.

Michelle hadn't felt left out last night; she was grateful for the cot and the hush of the ocean after the exhausting days of travel. But she felt a surge of relief this evening when Rebecca, who had come to clear away the dinner they'd eaten as a family, asked if Michelle and Joyce and Astrid might like to sit with her and some of the other women while Scott and Zach joined the men.

"They drink their kava," Rebecca said, "but it gives us time to talk too."

Now Michelle wipes at the mat and then sits awkwardly. "I've brought some things," she says and holds up a plastic bag for everyone to see, before she pours the contents out onto another mat in the middle of the loose circle of half a dozen women. Pens, notebooks, some cute flashlights shaped like the CN Tower, water bottles with maple leaves on them. She waits for the women to smile, to say thank you.

When no one speaks she reaches out and picks up one of the flashlights to illustrate its use, trying to flick it on and off. When it fails to light up, she shrugs. "It just needs batteries."

"Batteries," Rebecca repeats and catches the eye of the young pregnant woman, who holds one of the flashlights and clicks the switch on it uselessly. Michelle fishes for her name among the details she stored away when they met to help her remember—young, just married, a bride. Bridely.

"I'll just pick up batteries next time I'm shopping," Bridely says with a forced laugh, and the other women press their lips together.

Michelle simmers slightly. The guidebook said to bring gifts. She's only doing what she's supposed to.

"It's the CN Tower," Joyce says, holding one of the flashlights upright. "It used to be the tallest building in the world. It's not anymore though."

"How tall?"

Joyce laughs. "You know, I have no idea!"

Michelle resents her mother's ease, resents her for not having the sense to be embarrassed by the women's reactions. She tried. Her eyes brim a little in the dim light.

"Thank you," Rebecca says quickly and sweeps the gifts back into the bag. Michelle can't help but think of Dylan's clothes sitting in the closet at home, the trust in his name. She banishes the thoughts.

She'd been sure Rebecca understood. Last night, sitting with her in the moonlight, Michelle felt such an intimacy. She was certain that this woman might understand her, that she could help her. Why doesn't Rebecca sense that too? There must be a way to show her that Michelle isn't like her ancestors. She's different.

She clasps her hands, as if in prayer, and lands on it.

"There's something else."

"My husband told me the story on our second date," Joyce says, as Michelle unfolds the soft worn papers along with the two engravings that she has just retrieved from her suitcase. "He was so handsome, and I just wanted to listen to him talk. I think he thought the story made him seem exotic, worldly, but he was not a worldly man."

The word *exotic* makes Michelle stiffen. As does the way her mother moves her hands in the air around it. She should know better. Rebecca's eyebrows knit together for just a second before her face smooths itself again, while Bridely pushes her shoulders back, stares hard at Joyce. She should apologize for her mother, but she doesn't want to make the women uncomfortable.

"But I didn't see the pages until after we got married, didn't even know they existed. We lived in this little dinky house. A crackerbox house they called it, because it was tiny and shaped like a box. I'm not sure we'd even been living there for a month, and off he went to church on a Sunday like he always did. I didn't go, not after the wedding. But he never bothered me about it."

The men have quieted down across the nasara, and Joyce's words seems to carry in the evening air. Michelle tries not to study the women listening politely to her mother's story, which feels so irrelevant here. She tries to catch Rebecca's eye and smiles at her. Rebecca gives her a small nod back but doesn't return the smile. Michelle reddens in the dark.

"His mother, though. Oh, she was bothered. One day, he returned from church later than I expected, with this thin envelope of papers. From his mother, he said. I didn't even look at them. Just made him his Sunday lunch, like I would for years and years. I didn't want to read them. Didn't want to give that woman the satisfaction of it. But eventually I started reading them. And they were hers. Josephine. The woman he'd told me about on that second date.

"I'm pretty sure Mrs. Stewart was trying to tell me something. That I was some kind of sinner, I don't know. So I hid them away. For years. Until you said you wanted to read them." She puts her hand on Michelle's leg. "Do you remember that?"

She does. She was in university, taking her first women's studies class. The story her father had told for so long was about William; she wanted to know more about Josephine.

Michelle pats her mother's hand and begins to speak, but Joyce carries on, leaning across Michelle to say to Astrid, "Your granddad told Dylan the story, showed him the pages." Michelle's shoulders tense at the mention of her son's name. She avoids Rebecca's eyes, wonders if the woman has told everyone gathered here about her loss. "I think he even gave Dylan a stone he said came from this place, though it looked like the ones in the garden." She pauses and smiles at the thought of the two of them. "Those two, thick as thieves. He was so curious about everything that went on around him. It was like he was trying to understand it, figure out who he was. He'd sit and listen to your granddad talk forever, asking questions.

"He was a sweet boy," Joyce says, and Michelle nods despite herself. "Do you remember that time I came for dinner and I didn't have any cash? We were having takeout for some reason." It was after a hockey tournament, Michelle remembers. Dylan's team lost. They were supposed to win, and they had reservations at the local pizza place for a post-game celebration, but no one wanted to go. She doesn't say any of this, and instead shuffles the pages in her hands, top to bottom, bottom to top. "Anyway, I didn't have any cash, and I said I'd pay you back. But your brother"—Joyce smiles at Astrid—"Dylan went upstairs and got money from his piggybank because he was worried that I was stone broke."

"Were you?" Astrid asks.

"No," Michelle says, and her voice is tight in her throat. She forces the sound past her teeth, out into the air. "But he wanted to make sure Grandma was okay."

"Dylan is your son," says Lalim, Rebecca's sister-in-law.

"Yes," Michelle says. She feels the women's eyes on her and wants to hide. She wants to be staring at the stars with Dylan. She waves the thought away, squints through wet eyes at the pages she holds. "Here," she says, "I have these. They're like diary pages. From Josephine, William's wife, from when they were here."

The women pass the pages from hand to hand, the paper fragile in their fingers. They touch the edges like relics, run their fingers in the air above the inked lines. The writing is smudged in places, hard to read.

Michelle remembers looking at these pages with both Zach and Dylan, and making family trees when they were small. Astrid hasn't done a family tree yet; they don't do them in her school anymore. The boys were fascinated by them, in their different ways. Zach thrilled at the descriptions of the people, the drums that Josephine wrote of hearing, the strange men and women she described. Dylan wondered about William, who only appeared at the margins—domineering, angry, and, yes, Zach was right, fanatical.

Dylan said, "I don't think he really gets God."

Across the open space there is a burst of laughter from the men.

David's mother speaks, her voice creaky.

Bridely translates. "She asks, will you read them?"

Michelle doesn't want to, suddenly sure there are things written in the pages she doesn't want to share.

"Of course," Joyce says, and reaches her hands out for their return. She spends a minute shuffling them back into order and the women resettle themselves. There is a snuffling outside the ring of light that holds the women, and Anaei stretches behind her and drags a puppy onto her lap by its front paws. The thing is skinny, ribs showing through thin fur, and struggles a beat before settling its head on Anaei's knee. Astrid bends down and puts her nose to the puppy's.

Joyce starts to read and Michelle aches in her discomfort: "*I departed in hope—or reconciliation with my husband and with God. I came in Faith. With Faith. I came here to do His work in this place, as it is being done across the world. We are blessed to have been shown the light, even if I have sometimes stumbled in the dark, and as W. says we must bring it to all the corners. We do not keep blessings for ourselves. And they are much in need of light here.*"

Her mother blunders on, hesitating only when she wants to elide the spaces between entries, explaining the order where pages are missing, explaining family theories about what may have happened in between. As if this history doesn't belong to these women, as if they don't know what happened.

But for Michelle it is as though, in the company of these women, she is discovering these pages for the first time. Words seem to spit from her mother's mouth and land in the space between them: *savage, primitive, fallen, dark. Illness.* Why does she keep reading?

She wants to tell her mother to stop, to take the pages from her hands. But maybe the women don't notice the words, or they know that it isn't what she thinks. After all, it was a long time ago. Things are different now.

Her mother passes her each page as she finishes, but Michelle hands them on without looking at them. From across the circle, Rebecca avoids her pleading gaze and examines the words closely, searching for something in the writing, before she passes them on.

When Joyce finally finishes, she tuts slightly. "Imagine," she says, "what it must have been like for her."

"What what was like for who?" Bridely asks. In the shadows cast by the solar lamps, Michelle finds it hard to make out Bridely's expression.

"They were just so different," Joyce continues. "Imagine all the things they must have shared, must have learned from each other."

"I'm not sure that your Josephine learned much," Bridely says.

Lalim reaches a hand to Bridely to hush her, but the young woman shrugs her off.

"No?" Bridely asks of the circle. "It is sad that your people died here, but they did not learn much from our people. They never learned to grow food, or even how to speak our language,

beyond a few simple words. We died here too. From that illness."
She makes a dismissive noise, blowing out air. "They did share
some things, I guess."

"Of course, there were many things they didn't know," Lalim
says, "but they brought us God's words." She looks to Joyce. "We
are glad to know Him."

Bridely repeats the noise, then adds, "Both things can be true.
You can be hurt by someone and somehow be glad for what they
have given you." She cups her belly, gazes down at it. This time
Rebecca reaches over to squeeze Bridely's forearm.

"We are sorry for what happened," Michelle says, "but it was
so long ago."

"Yes," Joyce chimes in. "I don't think they meant it. It was a
different time. They didn't know any better."

Bridely sucks her teeth. "Maybe not so different."

Later, as she paces outside the bungalow, Michelle runs the conversation over again in her head. Tonight, she is the one who
can't sleep. She thinks of Josephine's diary pages and about what
Bridely said, and wonders if the other women feel the same way,
if Rebecca does. She brought the gifts she was supposed to, shared
the pages. What more can she do? She can't change the past.

Michelle continues to wait, hoping for Rebecca to appear,
hoping to hear another surprise burst of laughter from where she
and David are staying. She longs to talk to her again about their
sons, to hear about Ouben, to tell her about Dylan. His name is
bubbling up inside her.

She opens the star app on her phone. Dylan installed it, and
he would ask for her phone whenever they were out at night,
then turn on the spot, moving the phone up and down, pointing

out where some constellation would rise later on. She searches for the moon now, and finds it hiding, just below the horizon. Soon, it will emerge from the ocean.

If Rebecca comes, she will show the app to her, hold the phone up and point out the stars, the way Dylan used to.

She thinks of waking Scott and Zach from their kava dreams and bringing them out here. They could stand together and stare at the stars overhead, and just for a moment they could pretend that they are okay, that the past doesn't exist. Maybe, if she could go to them, they could finally move forward.

She stares at the horizon, and waits for the moon to rise.

Faina

The seasons kept circling. The missi's presence had become routine by the dry season, although there was the occasional scuffle or confrontation. As the wet season approached, so too did Faina's marriage ceremony.

The mission cove was now an entire place of its own, entangled in a network of paths leading to and away from other villages. It had its gardens that grew strange plants as well as exchange yams, which Marakai had insisted William should grow. He had explained the value yams had to all the peoples of the island—ceremonial and practical. A person who grew good yams and had many huge ones to give away was well respected, and would have much to offer at exchanges and ceremonies.

"Why on earth would we give away the fruits of our hard labour?" William had scoffed, but he'd allowed Marakai to plant them.

Several small wooden buildings now stood near William and Josephine's house. Some of the buildings were stores of the goods that William had brought for exchanges, making him a node in the vast web of roads that bonded the people of the island. Marakai and Talawan, along with three Hotwater men and their wives, now slept in huts nestled against the line of brush at the edge of the cove.

Faina stood outside the small white wooden fence and recalled the N-glish words she knew, as had become her practice: *bell, man, woman, house, church, sky, fence, pig, book, clothes, prayer, song.* She recited them silently, shaping the words with her tongue, pleased with herself. There were harder words—*god, soul, heaven.* Josephine had tried to explain their meanings to Faina.

Josephine said that *god* was like Faina's ancestors' spirits, was like a great father who made them all and would punish them if they misbehaved. Her *god* would only let good people into his dancing ground, called *heaven.* The bad people were sent to a place where they burned forever, and it reminded Faina of the stories of the volcano on the next island that spewed fire and heat and ash high into the air.

Faina tried to explain to Josephine, as Mother had to her, that the spirit world was just on the other side of this one and everyone went there after they died, good or bad. She'd held out a leaf to demonstrate how the sides were hidden from each other, but were part of the whole. Josephine shook her head and said, no, that *god* lived in the sky and decided who would sit by him. Faina looked but did not see him.

"Faina?" Josephine's voice pulled Faina back to herself.

Josephine stood near Marakai and Talawan's sleeping hut, beckoning. As Faina approached, the stench reached her nostrils— vomit and waste, something rotting inside. The air reeked of illness, of some curse at work. She halted, disgusted and afraid.

"Come," Josephine said, and beckoned again.

Faina wanted to retreat, to run away from whatever magic was at work here, but the plea in Josephine's voice forced her feet forward. Josephine's face was slick with sweat, her dress was wet with it, and she swiped at her forehead with a scrap of cloth. Faina wiped at her own forehead, which was dry and smooth.

The smell inside the hut was even stronger—the stench of fevered bodies, their excrement, and bile. Josephine seemed to pale further as she moved into one of the small rooms. Faina followed and stood at the threshold as Josephine sat beside one of the Hotwater men, his hair twisted, different from how any of the Middle Grove men wore their hair. Josephine wrung out a wet cloth and held it to the man's lips, then his forehead. She muttered to herself, or maybe to her god.

A moan came from behind her, and Faina turned to the other small room, where Marakai lay on a woven mat on the floor, Talawan bent over him. Both of them were pale and drawn, their lips cracked dry and caked at the corners.

"They've been cursed," Faina said. "Did you do this to them?"

Josephine didn't look up, but spoke loud enough for Faina to hear. "I don't know what illness this is."

Faina leaned to Marakai and spoke to him in the Middle Grove language. "Who is responsible for this?" Marakai only groaned and stared past Faina. He clutched at Talawan's hand, and her eyes glossed with tears. It hurt to even glance at her, the anticipation of her grief.

Faina crossed back to the Hotwater man Josephine was tending to. She had never spoken to a man from another place. "Who did this?" She said it in N-glish. She didn't know his language.

"No one did this," Josephine snapped. Then she exhaled slowly. "This is God's will. God is testing us and them, but He is the true healer." Josephine spoke slowly, using gestures in a way that had grown familiar. "Our Father has the power of life and death."

"You must make him stop," Faina said.

"I pray for them, but they must ask His forgiveness. If it is God's will that they suffer, then His will be done." She took the small cloth and dipped it in a bowl of water again, wrung it out, and handed it to Faina, who held it in her hand, uncertain. Josephine repeated the actions with another cloth, and then placed it on the man's forehead, then gestured for Faina to do the same to Marakai.

Next to him, Talawan sang a healing song, her voice quiet and cracking, and Faina picked up the tune with her. Marakai quieted and listened to them; even the Hotwater man seemed to listen to the words that pleaded for whatever curse this was to be lifted.

Josephine crossed the space between the two rooms quickly and grabbed Faina's shoulder, her fingers digging into flesh. Faina thought again of birds, this time the falcon that held with its claws and ripped with its beak. "Don't use your Devil's mumbo jumbo here." The song faltered on Faina's lips, and she was sure she felt the ancestors slip away. She glanced at Talawan, who still murmured to Marakai, this time with Josephine's prayers. Faina burned with anger and humiliation, feeling a slow simmer inside, like boiling stones in her belly.

Josephine returned to the other man and poured something into a bowl beside her, a powder that she stirred into a cloud in the liquid. Then she lifted the man's head so that he could drink from it. She handed Faina the bowl.

Would the liquid cure him? Maybe their magic *was* stronger, their god as powerful as they claimed. Faina stared at the water in her hand, milky and grainy, like how Masai had described kava to her. She wished she knew more leaf medicine. There might be a leaf magic that could help Marakai.

Talawan took the bowl from Faina's hands and looked up to the sky. "God, Father, please help him," she begged. Which father did she call for? Faina wondered. Talawan lifted Marakai's head to her lap, still murmuring to god in a mix of N-glish and Middle Grove, then poured the liquid into his mouth. He coughed and spluttered some of it before swallowing, groaning again.

Faina moved her lips; she hoped the ancestors might still hear her. She prayed to them until Talawan turned and shook her head at her. "Mumbo jumbo," she said, echoing Josephine, "won't work."

Faina felt struck, even more than when Josephine had insulted her. Talawan's eyes burned, with fever or something else. Faina slid away from them, then rose and slipped out the door.

Marakai and the Hotwater man died.

The people of Middle Grove gathered at the mission the next day. It was quiet except for the murmuring of conversation, a burble of languages—Uplander, Middle Grove, N-glish. There were no wails of grief, no drumming or stamping of feet in ceremonial dance, no song being sung.

Faina sat in the shelter of the bush. She wanted to watch but didn't want to be seen. She didn't know what to say, to Talawan, to Josephine. It was too hot, even with the low clouds, and the blouse she had finished making before the illness arrived at the mission stuck to her. She wanted to strip it off, but she knew if she did it would make Josephine angry. Next to her, Telau lounged comfortably against the trunk of a palm, the breeze teasing her pandanus skirt.

A short distance away a grave had been dug, straight down into the dark earth, exposing the damp of it. Beside it, Faina realized, was Marakai, hidden beneath a stretch of cloth, white as the foam at the edge of the sea. Her breath caught behind a lump in her throat. If Josephine and William hadn't come here, maybe Marakai would still be alive.

Louvu had sent word to the mission that Middle Grove would come and claim Marakai to bury him in their own way, but Talawan was the one to refuse. William had told her that if she wanted to meet Marakai again in heaven, she must let him be buried in their god's way and everyone should come to celebrate his life together.

The Hotwater people had come to claim their man and retreated from the mission. None of them remained now.

William and Josephine emerged from their sleeping house and moved to stand by the hole in the ground. The sky was grey and close overhead, as if it might begin to weep at any moment. The ocean shushed itself. Water dripped on William's head from a towering palm and he swatted at it again and again, as if it were a mosquito.

It was strange to see Josephine and William standing next to each other, as they so often kept their distance. They were thinner than when they had first arrived, their clothing hung loose from their shoulders, and lines were drawn deeply on their faces. They had seemed old in their paleness when they arrived, but in the moons that had since passed they had aged much more than anyone else.

"He looks weak," Telau scoffed beside her.

It was true, William looked frail. Perhaps he was ill too.

He draped a piece of cloth across the back of his neck. Faina remembered the cloth from her sewing lessons. Josephine had sewn patterns onto the rich cream of it with colourful threads she didn't let the other women use. She drew symbols with the thread, and it was beautiful where it lay draped across William.

"Please rise."

Faina stood at his words. So did Talawan, and a few of the Uplanders. Telau sucked her teeth and tried to pull Faina down, but she shook off her hand. The rest of the crowd watched William, who spoke again and lifted his hands in a sweep to the sky.

"He wants us to stand up," Faina said softly to those near her.

Nafatu, Louvu's youngest wife, who came often to the mission but was interested only in the goods that she could acquire, picked up Faina's instruction and relayed it loudly, as though she was the one who understood it.

There was a shuffling, and some stood, but others did not.

Faina stared at the grave, dug as a pit instead of an alcove to shelter the body. The earth was dark and lush, and smelled of freshly turned gardens, of the air after one of the great storms that swept across the island in the wet season.

William spoke at length, his voice rising in pitch, but there was no force to it. He was not a great speaker. Not like Louvu, who could make a sound argument from weak facts with his voice. Faina found William hard to believe now, even if she had wanted to.

Talawan wept next to the grave, her lips pressed closed against the traditional keening that had filled Middle Grove when news of Marakai's death arrived. Faina could feel her own grief in her throat, but she held it tight.

William talked about Marakai living again, and she wondered if this was another power of William's—to bring him back to life.

Many men on the island had the power to curse and kill, but no one could bring the dead back. She watched for movement under the cloth that covered Marakai's body, but there was none.

William sank to his knees. "Forgive us, Father, for we are all sinners." He used this word for them often. *Sinners*. She knew this meant that they were bad. *Evil* was another word that William and Josephine used. He said, "Those of us who have been baptized and born again in you will be born again in eternity."

Josephine and Talawan sank to their knees too, their hands pressed together. Everyone else stood and watched. Faina felt her knees weaken but stayed standing.

"We commit your beloved servant to the earth, knowing full well he will be reborn seated beside you in heaven."

William bent to Marakai and took his shoulders to lift him, while Josephine came to take his feet, and the two of them struggled to place his body into the hole, stumbling so that Marakai tumbled into the grave, haphazardly, falling feet first, instead of being tucked into the earth with respect. Louvu muttered and a few of the others gathered let out small sounds. The spirits would rise at such treatment. Masai spat to ward off the evil. Faina's hands curled into fists and she looked away across the sea. She wished she had never seen the lights there. She wished that William would stop, that they could carry Marakai up the hill to lay him to rest where all his ancestors had been laid before him. Her tears fell.

William jumped down into the grave and straightened Marakai's body in its hole. After William climbed out he dropped to his knees and began speaking again. Some of the words Faina already knew by heart, so often had she heard them repeated. Talawan and Josephine joined in. Faina kept her tongue still, refusing the taste of them.

When William finished, he picked up one of his metal tools, a *shovel*, and began to scoop the dirt into the hole. It seemed to be finished. Josephine knelt and began to pile the dirt into the hole with her hands. She reached up to brush at another tear and left a streak on her face.

There was no wailing. No feast. There was no food set aside for Marakai, to fortify him for his journey. Did they not care about Marakai? How would he know that he was mourned, that he was dead? Why would Marakai be willing to travel to the spirit dancing grounds if he did not hear their wailing? Every ghost wanted to be grieved. If he did not find his way to the dancing grounds, he would haunt them here. Likely, there would be more curses.

Faina wanted him to be reunited with his forefathers, not to be lost in Josephine's heaven, all alone. She would do what she could. She took a small length of creeping vine from a nearby tree as she watched the missionaries bury the body. She plaited two lengths of it, wound it around her throat, and tied it there. Masai caught her eye and gave her a sad smile.

She would have to forgo something that Marakai loved in order to honour him. That way he would stay in her memory whenever she longed for the thing. For a moment she thought of quitting the mission, the place where he had died, the place he was buried. He had seemed drawn to the place, to find some joy there before he died. But she still loved the words she gathered there. Could she give those up?

No. Instead, she would give up the mangoes that grew on the common land by the stream. He had often gathered those mangoes when his own trees had failed to fruit. The next morning, she gathered some before she went to the mission and hid them near his grave, so that he might have the strength to make his way.

A full moon after the burial, Faina returned to the mission and stood in the shadow of the bush, waiting for Josephine to appear. Tensions had sharpened after the illnesses, but Faina still hoped to understand the missi better—that in her way, she could help. And she craved more. She hoped that Josephine would tell more stories today. Not just the stories that came from her book, her *bible*, but of her home beyond the horizon. A place of cold, where rain fell white from the sky and gathered like feathers. *Canada. Halifax.* Faina wanted to know more about Josephine's son.

William was dozing on the porch of the house and Faina inched towards him. Anyone could strike him down, sleeping as he was. She could do it herself. She lifted her hand, imagined holding Father's club or Kap Kuke's knife. What would it feel like, bringing it down on his skull, the split of skin, the spill of blood? A frisson went through her. Her feet were silent on the path, as was the cloth of her skirt, quieter than the pandanus she had left tucked into the bush. Her power gave her a quick smile. She was near him now. He smelled of rotten fruit, of an acrid tang, his clothes mouldering, like something left on the forest floor. His face was sharp, bristles making dark shadows on his chin. She could slit his throat, if only.

"Good morning, Faina."

Josephine stepped out from the small building that sheltered their bodies' waste. She glanced from Faina's hand to her dozing husband, a flicker of understanding in her eyes, and gave a thin smile. "Come," she said, and turned towards the women waiting for her in the shade of the trees.

Faina stood still a moment, watching William. He gave a soft groan and then sat up straight in his chair. He gave a huff in her direction and his breath smelled strong and ugly. He poured a liquid from one of his metal baskets into the cup he drank from, and then looked at her, his eyes hard. She turned to follow Josephine, but he grabbed her wrist. She tried to jerk it away, but he held it tight in his fist and brought his face close to hers.

"You are better than her," he said. His words tumbled against each other like a mudslide, wet and broken. "At least you don't know what you do is wrong."

She backed away from him and went to Josephine.

A short time later, Faina sat among the gathering of women. Not as many as when the missi first arrived, but more than in the days after the deaths at the mission. Faina sat close to Josephine in the shade and kept her head down, moved the needle and thread in and out of the edge of the cloth. Josephine spread the book in her lap, closed her eyes, and *prayed*. Talking to Jesus.

The sounds Josephine made were repetitive. This wasn't the sorcery that Faina was waiting for; the recitation of stories and words were something she knew well. No, what she wanted was new stories, deciphered from the marks in the book Josephine held on her lap. *Reading.*

"If a man owns a hundred sheep, and one of them wanders away, will he not leave the ninety-nine on the hills and go to look for the one that wandered off? And if he finds it, truly I tell you, he is happier about that one sheep than about the ninety-nine that

did not wander off. In the same way your Father in Heaven is not willing that any of these little ones should perish." She left the book on her lap. "What do you think? What does it mean?"

No one spoke.

"The story," Josephine said, and then she sighed heavily. "Jesus told this story to his followers." She gestured, poking at the bible, waving her hands at all of them. The story was about them. "God is looking for you. You are his lost sheep."

"Sheep?" Faina said. "Word mean?"

"An animal. Like . . ." she cast around. "Like pigs."

Faina scoffed at the absurd idea. "We are not pigs," she said, first in her own language, and then to make it clear, in Josephine's N-glish.

"No," Josephine said, "it's a story, to teach us."

Faina was about to speak again, but Josephine ignored her and turned her face back to the book. She kept it close, treated it reverently, holding it tight, moving her palm carefully across the marks on the page, tiny and black. *Writing.*

Faina wanted to be able to read the marks there. The writing would tell her things. She turned back to her sewing.

Eventually Josephine stood, set the book on her chair, and went back to the stinking building. She had never left the book behind before. Faina looked around. Everyone's head was bent to their work, even as they began to chatter in Josephine's absence. Hurriedly, Faina discarded her sewing, her needle pricking deep into her finger and drawing blood. She reached for the book.

It was heavier than she had expected. It felt like what she imagined the tabu stones that Sero kept would feel like in her hands—heavier than they appeared and humming with possibility and energy. Before the start of each yam-planting season, Sero offered the growing stone a meal of yams from the previous season, so it would fill the ground with more yams to feed them. Then Sero would spend a moon in solitude with the stone, feeding and bathing it, oiling and singing to it. She did not know the songs, or what it was fed, what stories the stone was told—it was dangerous for her to know such things. That stone was one of the oldest things on the island, connected to the power deep within their world and the world in which the spirits of the ancestors walked and lived. Was this bible Josephine's tabu stone?

The pages inside were so thin as to be almost transparent.

"What are you doing?" Talawan hissed at her. "Put it down." Talawan's face was still drawn with grief and the remains of the illness that she had overcome. She had recommitted to the mission after Marakai's death and had not returned to Middle Grove once. Faina wondered if she missed her home. Still, she ignored the older woman now.

She sat in the chair, opened the book on her lap, sucked the blood to the surface of her finger, then turned to a blank page. With her blood she made her mark. A line of dots, a small curve below them like a wave that carries a canoe to sea. It made her smile. Her mark. Hers.

And then there was the hard sting against the side of Faina's head, and she fell from the chair, ears ringing. There was a cry that she could not make out. She squinted against the pain and scuttled backwards, a single leaf in her hand, a page torn from the book.

William stood over her, the bible now in his hand, held high and away from her. His other hand was clenched in a fist, and his face was a rictus of purple anger. William had struck her. For a moment he opened his mouth to speak then closed it again. He swayed slightly. Faina put her hand to the pain in her head; a small bump began to swell.

William was yelling, but then Josephine was there and there was a chaos of words and language. Faina tried to listen to them, but her ears sang like the water below the waves. There was no beginning or end to what they said. No word she could hold fast to.

Still stunned, Faina watched as William tore a weave of vines and flowers that Nafatu had made for Josephine from his wife's hair and threw it to the ground.

"You want to be like them?" he spat, and yanked the cloth covering her arms down to her wrists, hiding the red of her skin. "Go back to what you were before?"

Josephine cowered back from him and he turned again on Faina. He hurled words at her, she could feel the boil of disgust in them as he moved towards her. She stood her ground, holding her hand to the swollen place on her head. Before he reached her, Masai appeared as if by magic from the brush and put himself between Faina and the missi. Masai held his axe tight in his hand, his chin jutted upwards.

"Don't you dare strike her," he said in Middle Grove, and Faina could see the fear light up William's face even though he didn't understand Masai's words. It was clear what his body said. Faina had never seen Masai ready for battle. He was beautiful and strong, and she felt a surge of pride and love and gratitude for him.

"I didn't mean . . ." William said. "I'm sorry. It was a shock. We want to share His words, but they are precious. And to mark it this way, with unclean blood . . ." He gestured at Faina's hand, where the torn page flapped like a dying bird, and at the blood on her finger and in the book that he still held aloft. She put her hand behind her back. William frowned and moved on. "Everything in its time. Reading. Writing. After prayer. After obedience. We must show the Word respect."

She alighted on the words—*reading, writing.* These were their magic, but Masai didn't seem to hear them.

"Rispek." Masai spat the word back at the man, picking out one of the words they both could grab on to. William was puffed up, but still weak and shaking despite his red-faced anger. Masai pulled the book from William's hand and threw it to the ground, then spat next to it. "You have no rispek," Masai said and then switched back to Middle Grove. "You should go. We didn't come to you. You came here, to our place, and you don't respect the place, the ways. It is bigger than you. Than us. You are putting everything in danger."

Masai turned and grabbed Faina by the hand, hauling her from the ground. "Take it off," he said, gesturing to the dress she still wore. "You look ridiculous."

Her face burned at his rebuke, but she gathered her own skirt from where she had left it and slipped it on before stepping out of the dress. The air was cool on her skin, and she felt like herself again.

She knew she shouldn't go back to the mission. William had hit her, and while Josephine had spoken in her defence, it was Masai who had stopped him from doing it again. Still, she found herself drawn towards it, the way the ocean pushed at you underwater, so you moved fast and easy, its whole weight behind you.

Her feet found their way to the path. She was almost at the spot where she had fought with Masai.

At first, he had been tender with her when they left the mission. He turned to her in the cool gloom of the path, the branches and vines making a high tunnel around them, the light dappling their skin. "Are you all right?" He peered at her, his face soft with concern.

She touched her head then and looked at her fingers, but they came away clean, even as the bump swelled and throbbed. Masai reached and pressed his own fingers to her skull, beneath the tight halo of curls. "I'm all right," she said, and winced as he touched the bump. He winced in response.

She didn't thank him for helping her. Maybe she should have thanked him, because his face clouded over then and he stepped away from her.

"You can't go there anymore." She opened her mouth to object but he cut her off, slamming the butt of his spear into the ground. "No! They're dangerous. What would have happened if I wasn't there? You should be weaving your marriage mats for your new family. You can't run around doing whatever you like."

Anger turned her stomach. How dare he. "But you are not my husband. I don't answer to you."

She brushed past him up the path, felt his hand reach for her but fall short. She wished he would touch her again.

"I'll speak to your father then." His voice was almost inaudible. She didn't turn back, just pushed on towards Middle Grove.

But he hadn't spoken to her father. Or if he had, her father had not forbidden her to go. Not yet.

She hoped he might appear in front of her alone, without Nako. And what? If he did, she wouldn't turn back. What would that achieve? The wet season was halfway over. Soon she would be married, and then how long would it be before she saw Masai or the mission again?

She pressed on down the path, the earth damp but firm under her feet. She knew every turn and curve of this road, and suddenly there was an ache in her chest for all the familiar things— the roads around Middle Grove, her garden, the way she had terraced it to make the most of the rain and sun. The ache almost made her turn back, but then she thought of the marks on the pages of Josephine's book. She needed to know what was there.

She stepped onto the mission ground, and Josephine came down from the porch to meet her.

"I'm sorry about what happened," she said. "He didn't mean it."

Faina was used to this word from Josephine's mouth. *Sorry.* She said this word often, but it did not set things right.

Still, Faina nodded at her, then pointed at Josephine's bible. Josephine stepped back and clutched the book to her chest, then glanced around, looking for William, before turning her gaze back to Faina. A small sneer curled Josephine's lips, but she nodded before pointing to the trunk where the women's clothing was kept.

They stood facing each other. Faina didn't want to put on Josephine's clothes. She didn't want to give in, but she wanted the book, the power that was in it. She went to the trunk on the porch and lifted out a blouse. She stared hard at Josephine as she pulled it on. She left the tie at the throat unfastened, so the plaited necklaces that fell across her chest were still visible, as was the cord she wore to mark Marakai's death.

She returned to Josephine and held out her hand again for the book.

Josephine slowly handed it over.

Faina sat on Josephine's chair, opened the book, and put her finger to the marks there.

"What is word?" she asked in Josephine's N-glish.

"*Writing*," Josephine said. She held a finger up and moved it in the air as though casting a spell. "It is for reading," she explained.

The evening before, Faina had sat on a log, her brother and sister gazing up at her from the ground as she looked at the page from Josephine's bible. She'd peered at the marks, willing them to make sense.

"What is that?" her sister had asked, her fingers reaching for it. "Let me see."

"No! You can't understand it."

"Neither can you. You don't have the power to tell those stories."

She would though. She had made her mark in the book. And she would give Josephine all her words in exchange for the chance to do more.

"Reading?"

"Yes."

"Teach, please."

IV

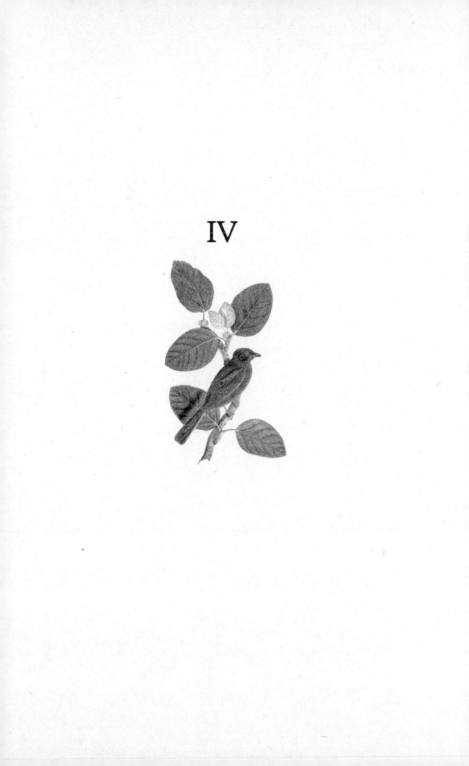

Rebecca

Rebecca wakes at dawn and the air is already starting to glow, even while the world is still cast in shades of grey and blue. She leaves Anaei and David sleeping, slips on her black skirt, the T-shirt David wore the day before, still smelling deeply of him, and grabs one of the woven baskets from the rafters.

The roosters caw the morning awake as Rebecca crosses the paths she used to walk with Ouben swaddled against her, to gather the eggs. She stoops to the first spot but finds it empty. She puts her hand to the ground, trying to feel for any remaining warmth, but can't tell if a chicken has laid here. She moves on. She tries a few more spots but doesn't find a single egg. Is it a sign of something to come? An earthquake? Another storm? Perhaps the birds can sense a change.

How will they feel when they are carted up the path to their new homes, she wonders, with new trees to roost in, new dirt to peck? What about the pigs, the dogs, the cat with her new family? How will they feel about being forced away from everything they have ever known? Will they try to find their way back here? Will she be bending to these same spots again in a week, in a month? Or maybe they will forget this place entirely. Maybe place means nothing to them. After all, they live on the land, but they are not a part of it, as the people are.

Rebecca continues searching out eggs, checking long-abandoned nests, and eventually finds one lone egg, but it is soft in her hand. A ghost egg, shell-less and inedible. She feels the delicate weight of this almost-egg, and something shifts inside her. She fights the urge to cry, to mourn this half-formed thing.

When she arrives back at the cooking hut, Anaei and David are up, and a basket of eggs stands next to the cooker. The sight of them causes the tears to creep from her eyes; the failed egg is still warm in her hand.

"What is it?" David asks. But Rebecca only points at the cottony glow of the eggs in the morning light. "Jacob collected them," he says, before telling Anaei to get ready for school. The girl stares at them a moment before dashing off.

"Here, sit," David says. But Rebecca can't.

"Breakfast," she says. She has to make breakfast for the Stewarts. She will scramble the eggs, or fry them. Robson has said that Serah will send bread, and it's true that Serah's bread is always delicious, though she must be running short of flour. There is fruit to cut and squeeze for juice. She should put the ghost egg down, but she doesn't know what to do with it. So she begins to pluck utensils and cooking pots from the rafters with one hand, the way she used to when Ouben needed soothing.

"Jacob is trying to make amends," David says, staring at the basket of eggs. "Because he's leaving." There is a tension in the air around his words.

Rebecca lights the cooker, sets a pot to boil. Tea. Coffee. Readies the skillet for frying. She is still holding the ghost egg, cracking the others one-handed into a bowl, setting aside the shells that she will turn into the garden later.

"You didn't tell me," David says, and his voice is barely audible. "I'm the only one who didn't know. He should have talked to me, or you should have. You know, as much as I do, Robson is always going to do what is best for Robson."

She beats the eggs to a pale froth, puts teabags into a small pot, coffee into a strainer. "He wants what is best for Jacob. Everyone does."

"I know what is best for him, I'm his father."

"He isn't a child," she says, and is surprised at herself. David seems surprised too. She doesn't often disagree with him; or when she does, she normally does so quietly, asking questions, waiting for him to come around, to change his mind, cajoling him. She cradles the ghost egg against her before turning to face him directly. "He's a young man, and he's thinking of the future, the same as you did when you were his age. As you are doing now. It's his time to go out into the world and see what is out there. You need to make sure he knows that this is his home, his place, and it always will be, even while he is gone from it."

She looks away from David now, exhausted from speaking.

The silence between them swells like the sea.

"What if he doesn't come back?"

She ponders the weight of the question. They both know what it means to have someone not come back.

"But what if he does? We can't be sure of the future." She has doubts, so many of them, they crawl across her skin and weave through her thoughts. Doubts about moving, doubts about her every decision that brought her here, but she won't voice them, not to David. This is what she can give him—her pretence of faith. She puts the ghost egg down in a small bowl and feels lighter for a moment.

"Jacob will go," she says. "That is the only thing we can be sure of. We can decide how he will depart, and what he will take with him."

That is the gift they are being given, this time.

Last time, she had no warning.

Her wailing pulled everyone from sleep. She was singing to Ouben when he left, her body curling around his, cooling quickly, the sweat drying at his temples. She wept until her throat ached raw. She was almost unaware of Anaei weeping beside her, of David crouched outside the door, his hands over his eyes.

David's mother, Numalin, was the first to arrive at the house. She sat across from Rebecca and moved her hand back and forth between Ouben's head and Rebecca's, who wished it was her own mother's hand. Rebecca didn't make a sound. Her voice had gone with Ouben.

How long did she lie on that cot? Her body pained her, clenched as it was, but she didn't care. Her baby was dead. Her breasts ached and leaked milk onto his skin.

As day broke, David came into the room with a bucket of water and she screamed at him. She couldn't form any words—there were none that could express her broken heart, her broken body, her anger at David for bringing her such pain. She wished she had never come to this island. She wished she had never married David. If she hadn't, she wouldn't have a dead baby.

She was only rage and pain. He left the bucket and slipped back out. She wouldn't let him near her son.

"Here." David's mother handed her a wet cloth. Rebecca pulled herself to sitting and stared at it, dripping water onto her lap, onto the floor. This rag. She would not wash her son's body with a rag like this.

She found the white tunic easily. Her mother had sent it with her years ago, when she first left her home to come to this island. It had sat in this basket for years, waiting for the time when her son would be christened.

The tunic glowed in the dim room. She brought it back to the cot, dipped it into the bucket, and then laid her baby on his back. She lifted first his small hand, and washed each finger that not so long ago had been creased with his baby fat but was now skinny and fragile in a way she had never thought of him when he was alive. She worried she would break him.

She washed the whole of him, memorizing him again as she went. As she had when she washed him that first day, first week, first month. The second. The sixth. His first birthday. Here was the mark on the bottom of his foot where it looked like his skin had been burned—a mark that she loved, and pressed her fingers to, her lips to. Here were the tiny curls at the nape of his neck, so like David's. The swoop of eyebrow, the curves of fingernails and toenails, one broken where he had stubbed it when he was just learning to walk.

She didn't want to finish cleaning him. If she finished, she would have to cover him. Then she would have to cut the strings for the fasting necklaces. Then they would have to measure him. Dig a grave. Put him in the ground. She could not finish washing him.

Eventually, someone took the garment from her hand, replaced it with a woven mat. She looked at it a long time, the weave of it, and thought of fingers intertwined. Thought of her own fingers weaving. Of Ouben twirling her hair when he nursed. She spread the mat across his tiny body.

They only sat with him a day. People came in, crying and wailing, and sat with her a while before departing again to sit outside. Anaei brought in food and left it beside Rebecca until the ants came for it, and then her daughter would fold up the leaf and take it away again and burn it in the cooking fire.

They dug a grave for him. David must have done it. Near the tree where Ouben would nap while they were in the garden nearby, the tree on a slight rise so they could see him from where they worked. She didn't remember David coming in, but he was sitting beside her, his hand on hers, hers resting on the mat that covered her baby's body. It was hot inside the bungalow with the crush of bodies surrounding Ouben. She wished them all away. She wished herself away, to wherever Ouben was.

Someone said it was time. She wanted to say no. She wanted to tell them to leave her alone, but her voice was gone. David wrapped Ouben in the mat and lifted him in his arms. She stumbled after him.

The sky was low and grey, the path muddy. Wet smoke hung in the air. She didn't want him to lie on the ground beside the grave. The grave that was so small because he was so small. She would crawl into it with him. Robson was there and spoke about God. David did his best to invoke the short life of their son. She could not cry. She could not move. She could not do anything. David's uncle came forward and swept the sides of the grave with a handful of leaves, chasing off the bad spirits. But the bad spirits had already done their worst.

She stayed by the grave. Long after it was filled in. Long after they slaughtered a young pig that Robson had provided for Ouben. She stayed, thinking of what she should have done for her son, what she should have said to him. She wouldn't leave her boy there alone. She stayed well into the night, always with someone by her side—a rotating cast of women taking their turns to be with her. Eventually David appeared. He pulled her to her feet and led her back down the path to their home.

She didn't speak again until David told her he had called the Stewarts.

Zach

Zach slumps in the plastic chair, revelling in the scorch of the sun and picking at a scrape on the inside of his arm. He rips the scab off and watches the blood bead out of the healing wound. He imagines the pain as sparks of light going off in his brain, which zap and fade until he's left with only the usual ache that is the shape Dylan left behind.

Zach stares at his phone on his knee, willing Chelsea to text back. He texted her what his dad said to him yesterday—*How would you feel if we moved?* Then: *Do u think he's gonna leave?* He tries to do the math of time zones again but keeps forgetting if it's yesterday or tomorrow there.

He looks at the footage he shot the day they arrived in Iparei, after the weird trip to the memorial stones—Jacob showing him how to swing the machete to cut through the vines in the forest. Or is it the jungle? Maybe he should ask Jacob which it is.

His phone vibrates slightly. Chelsea.

Chelsea: *Maybe it wld b good. fresh start. Not for him to leave.
for all of u*

Zach: *U dnt think he's gonna divorce her*

Chelsea: *Ur dad luvs ur mom so much it's gross :)*

He sends her an emoji back. What she says used to be true,
but maybe it isn't anymore.

Chelsea: *U ok? Miss u*

He presses into the bruise on his ribs, from the fight he picked
the day before they left. Chelsea saw it afterwards, blooming
fresh on his skin, in her bedroom. He flinched when her hand
grazed his ribs.

Zach: *Yeah.*

He tries to think of what else to write, something to reassure
her, but then he spots Jacob cutting across the nasara, in the
direction of the shore. Zach locks his phone before Chelsea has
a chance to respond, and hurries after him.

"Where you going?" he calls to Jacob when he's close enough.

Jacob looks over his shoulder; his jaw is set, anger in his face.
He glances past Zach to where David is watching them. "I have
to go check something," he says, and then continues on towards
where the island curves away and seems to end.

"Oh," Zach says, "yeah, cool. Can I come?"

Jacob squints back at him for a long moment; Zach pushes
his sunglasses up onto his forehead. "All right. But we have to go
quick, or the tide will change. Leave that." Jacob nods at Zach's
phone. "You'll ruin it."

Zach tucks his phone under his towel and follows Jacob
across the short clearing and south along the shore, over the jagged black rock. Before coming to Iparei, he'd only seen the gentle
lap of waves on all-inclusive beaches. Here, the ocean is constantly battering the shore, slamming against the island, loud

in its assault. The spray flies up and wets him and the rock, making it slippery.

Jacob moves easily while Zach slowly inches his way over and around tide pools. As he approaches one, the calm mirror of its surface becomes transparent, and the drowned space within it comes alive in the drift of current. Tiny fish slip into crevices, and the long strands of some alien creature reach out from a hidden recess. There is the deep blue of a starfish, the round body of a sea slug. He stares, imagines the gelatinous feel of the creatures. If Dylan were here, he'd climb in, pick up the sea slug, thrust it at Zach. He wasn't scared of stuff like that. Zach stands at the edge, wanting to reach in to touch something, but can't.

"Almost there," Jacob calls, and Zach turns to follow.

The tide is shifting, coming in, and what had been exposed coral is now submerged. He picks his way inland some. Ahead of him, Jacob turns towards an outcrop of rock and then disappears from view. Zach hurries after him, stumbling and cutting his knee, his hand. He holds his scraped palm to his mouth and licks at the sharp mix of blood and salt there.

When he spots Jacob again, he is standing in the ocean, the water surging around him, so it climbs up his body to his waist and then retreats, now at his knees, now at his waist again. He motions for Zach to join him. The salt water stings the cut on Zach's knee.

"We're going to go in there," Jacob says when Zach arrives at his side, gesturing at the rock wall that rises straight up into the air in front of them, black and jagged. There is nothing to see except the mass of it.

"We're climbing that?" A spike of fear, an anticipation of pain.

"No, we're going in." Jacob points at the waterline, and when the waves pull back there is the shadow of a hole in the rock that only just breaks the surface of the ocean.

Fear scrapes deliciously along Zach's spine.

The ocean pushes Zach back and forth, a nautical sway that makes him stumble as though he's stoned.

"How do we get in?"

"We swim through. It's a short tunnel, easy to swim, but you have to time it right so that the sea pushes you through."

Zach knows he can swim long distances underwater, no problem. He can make a whole length of the school swimming pool and then most of the way back before coming up for air, and even then, he's not gasping. But swimming while finding his way in the dark of an unfamiliar tunnel?

"That's the best time," Jacob continues, "so the water is pushing you in through the tunnel. But it's okay if you time it wrong. You'll see the opening as soon as you're underwater. I've done it since I was a boy. Here." Jacob takes a snorkelling mask from around his neck and hands it to Zach. "You'll be fine. Want me to go first? Or you?"

Zach doesn't know. If Jacob goes before him and gets stuck, then Zach will get stuck behind him and they won't be able to get out. But how will he know when to go without Jacob here to tell him?

"You go first?"

Jacob nods. "Count to thirty and then wait for the ocean to tug you out a little. And then"—he makes a diving movement with his hands—"you'll come out on the other side."

Jacob plunges into the water and Zach watches the shape of him move towards the hole. Suddenly he is alone, the colossal blank weight of the Pacific Ocean pushing and pulling at him.

If he slipped under right now, no one would ever know what happened to him. He could just disappear off the face of the earth. He looks back at the endless splay of horizon, the most emptiness he has ever seen. He could set off for it, the horizon. He's a strong swimmer. How far would he get? And then what?

Then he'd be the mystery. He'd be the wonder of it. He'd be the disappeared one.

The ocean never used to scare him.

Zach plunges his hand into the water, the salt stinging him back to himself. As he's done numerous times since Dylan drowned, he focuses on the pain, a way to keep the ache away, a way to keep going. He inhales deeply and holds his breath. Holds it until his head starts to spark, his vision begins to narrow. He tries to be with Dylan for those last moments his brother was alive, but he can never quite reach him. Because, despite everything, Zach knows he can just start breathing again.

He pulls on Jacob's mask. The tempered glass is foggy, spotted with salt and water. He swallows several quick gulps of air, filling his lungs, breathing deep into his diaphragm. He has to go. Jacob is waiting for him. The next push, the next swell of water, and he will.

And then he dives into the water, the sea pushing behind him, and he is in the tunnel careening towards the bright spray of light only a few metres ahead. He's almost reached it when the ocean grabs him and hauls him back into darkness. His body slams into the wall of the cave and he feels the skin on his back tear before he is somersaulted by a surge of water. He is turned around, the adrenaline metallic in his mouth. The water glows with daylight in both directions. Either way is safety, either way is air. He concentrates on the burn in his lungs, the salt-sting of his back, and he is fighting—his hands claw at the ocean, his feet kick against it, but he isn't moving. He's held in a tightening fist and is this what Dylan felt? This panic? This terror?

He can't breathe anymore—but just then the ocean lets him go and suddenly he's free, gulping lungfuls of air.

There is a yell, and he sees Jacob standing in a column of light shooting down from the roof of the cave fifty feet above him. Zach paddles himself in a circle. Barks a sound he realizes is a laugh.

"Holy fuck!" His voice bounces around the space, slides fast across the water.

"Holy fuck, indeed," Jacob echoes.

Unable to stop himself, Zach whoops. He's made it. Only a minute ago he thought he might actually die. And now, in spite of himself, he's still alive and he's high on a burst of adrenaline greater than any he's felt before. He could climb a mountain. He wants to swim through the tunnel again.

Instead, he pulls himself to a small arc of sand, lies back, and stares up at the dazzling sunlight streaming through a hole in the roof of the cave. Palm fronds slowly resolve themselves above him. The light makes the water glow blue, as if lit from below. The cavern feels untouched. Even on that one back-country camping trip his dad had insisted would be good for him, there were beer cans rusting in the woods, the flutter of plastic bags caught in the underbrush. There is none of that here. They might be the first people to ever see this place.

He is about to ask Jacob about the cave when he grabs the mask, takes a few long strides, and dives into the water.

Jacob stays down a long time and Zach sits up to watch for him, scanning for air bubbles. Nothing. The water is calm in here without the urgent push and pull of the sea, and despite the light there are depths that are too dark to peer into. Zach wishes he had his phone, so he could film this amazing space, film Jacob's plunge into the pool. But he just sits and waits, his pulse thrumming at his temples, his muscles tensing.

He is about to call out when Jacob finally reappears, and Zach exhales with him before Jacob dives back down once more, lifting his legs straight into the air to drive himself deeper into the water.

Eventually Jacob breaks the surface again, and swims one-armed towards where Zach waits. Jacob drops the T-shirt that he was wearing on the sand between them. When it falls open, there are two enormous sea urchins inside, their spines moving in the air, making a slight ticking sound as they knock against each other.

"Looks like you got slammed," Jacob says, pushing up the arm of Zach's T-shirt to examine his shoulder.

"Is it bad?" He can already imagine the blood weeping with the salt water.

"A scrape. It'll bruise, but you'll be fine." Jacob pats the tender spot and Zach relishes the pain.

"Got caught up, I guess."

"Never turn your back on the ocean."

"My dad told me that once."

Jacob makes a dismissive noise, and Zach isn't sure if it's aimed at him or at fathers.

The only sound is the lapping of the waves, their echoes marking a complicated rhythm against the stone walls. Zach focuses on the water, timing his breath with the movement of it, so he and the ocean breathe as one. The quiet stretches between them, and the need to say something is building up. The longer it goes, the worse it becomes. "Did you know," he begins before he really knows what he is going to say, "there are different types of drowning? There's wet drowning, when someone actually inhales water into their lungs. That's what we think of, mostly. But there's also dry drowning, where their lungs are dry. It means the water never got into their lungs, 'cause they choked, or maybe were even unconscious."

He hadn't meant to bring it up, and now Jacob is staring at him, waiting for him to say more.

Zach falls back on the sand, feels the grit of it on the scrape of his shoulder, and imagines bacteria climbing into his flesh, eating at him. "My brother drowned," he says to the hole in the sky. "That's how I know. About dry drowning, I mean." There had been an injury at Dylan's temple, and no water in his lungs.

Jacob stares ahead of him. "What happened?"

People always want to know, but few of them ask directly; there is some relief in Jacob's asking.

"He fell into our swimming pool, hit his head, and drowned." Zach goes quiet. "He shouldn't have been out there by himself." Zach should have been there.

Jacob leans back on his elbows. "My brother died too."

That Zach hadn't expected, and the confessions grow into another drawn-out silence as the water laps at the sand near their feet.

After a few moments, Jacob sits up and points at the urchins. "Want some?" And seeing Zach's face, he adds with a laugh, "They're delicious." He finds a sharp stone and whets it quickly against another, then flips one of the sea urchins over and begins to cut into its underside.

"What happened to your brother?" Zach asks.

"After the cyclone he got sick, from the water, or bad food." Jacob shrugs but doesn't look up from the urchins. He turns one over carefully and pours the liquid out of it, staining the sand dark, then does the same with the other. "It was impossible to take him to the doctors, and we didn't have that kind of medicine here. He was so little. He just couldn't fight anymore."

"I'm sorry."

Jacobs stands and takes the two urchin shells to the water, slips his hand into the creatures and scoops out the yellow globs, and then rinses them in the salt water. He brings them back, lays the lobes on his T-shirt, and pops one into his mouth. A small wave of pleasure crosses his face. "Have one," he urges.

Zach doesn't want to—they look strange and alive, the yellow blobs still pulsing—but he doesn't know how to say no. He presses a blob against the top of his mouth with his tongue, and it gives, softly, almost like a paste. It tastes of the ocean; not the ocean that grabbed him and held him in the dark, but the ocean when it's calm and there's a light wind and there's sand between his toes. It's wonderful.

"Good, right?" Jacob asks.

"So good." Zach takes another piece.

They eat in the soft sounds of the waves until, this time, Jacob breaks the quiet. "I forgot what it felt like to be here."

"How'd you find this place anyway?"

"My father used to bring me here when I was little, the way his father brought him. I would hold tight to his neck through the tunnel. I was so scared, but I knew as long as I could feel my father's shoulders in my hands, I would be okay. He would keep me safe. And when we surfaced in here . . . I couldn't believe it." Jacob smiles out into the space of the cave. "He told me this place is a road to the afterlife and I thought there would be a real road, but my dad said only the dead could see the road. I wouldn't see it for a long, long time. When I got older, my friends and I would come here, to mess around, or for these. Sometimes when I'm home now, I come on my own, just to think."

Zach wonders if he should apologize for intruding, then offers,

"I used to have a place like that. There's this ravine near my house, and near the river, there was this old concrete platform, from a building that used to be there, I think, but it's long gone. And I would go there so I could think. I could see the trail from where I was, behind this screen of bush, but no one could see me. It was mine, or it felt that way, like I was the only person in the world who knew about it. It used to be a place I could go and just be on my own."

"Used to?"

"I find it hard to sit still now." It's the first time he's said it out loud.

"What do you mean?"

"Like, just being in my skin. I'm always feeling I need to do something, go somewhere. If I can just do the right thing, go to the right place, I keep thinking I'll feel, I don't know, better? That's not it. I feel like there's something I should be doing. Something that will make things . . . right." He sounds stupid. He should have kept his mouth shut, but Jacob nods.

"I get it. I'm going to New Zealand soon. There are no jobs here, there's nothing I can do here, and like you said, I have to do something. At least there I can make some money. That will help." He scoops up a fistful of sand, lets it run slowly through his fingers.

"Do you want to go away?" Zach asks.

Jacob seems to think about it. "Yeah, I want to go everywhere," he says, with a small laugh. "I've been away from home since I went to school. It's not so bad. But it doesn't really matter if I want to go or not. There are no good jobs here. I want to travel, and make money. I want to see the world, like you are."

"I've never been away from home without my parents. Some school trips, camp, but not like, far away on my own. A lot of my friends want to go away for school, but I don't know. I can't really imagine leaving Toronto."

"What's it like?"

Zach tries to think of what might be interesting about his city. "It's just home. It's grey a lot," he says. "In the winter. It's grey and slushy and cold. The buildings and the parking lots, and dirty snow. But in the summer, it's pretty great. It feels different now, though. Since Dylan. Like it's not quite mine anymore. Or like, the real version of it is hidden somewhere that I can't quite reach." He wishes he could explain better, articulate something that he doesn't even know the shape of.

"Maybe I'll come visit and you can show me around."

Zach tries to picture it, what he could possibly show Jacob. All he can think of are dumb touristy things—the CN Tower, the Rogers Centre. "Yeah, for sure," he says. "Though I might go away to school. You could visit me there. Vancouver maybe. Or Montreal. They're cooler anyway. I think my mom would be glad if I was gone." The words surprise him, even if they're true.

"She's your mother," Jacob says, and there are so many things that could mean. It could mean that is what all mothers want, for their children to leave the nest. It could mean, she's your mother and she loves you. It could mean that Zach is right and she just wants him gone.

The column of light has moved, and it shines into the back of the cave now. The tide has risen up the small beach. "We should head back," Jacob says, hauling himself from the sand.

Zach doesn't want to go, doesn't want to leave this hidden place, doesn't want to face his parents. He casts about for a reason to remain, wonders if they will have to stay here longer if they miss the turn in the tide.

"My granddad said that there were cannibals here. I know that's dumb. I always used to tell Dylan that it was just stupid church people telling stories."

"My people wouldn't have eaten your people," Jacob says, and his tone is sharp. "This is the trouble. White people think they know about everything. They have opinions about everything. They don't think to ask, they don't think to listen, just always making assumptions."

Zach's face burns; he shouldn't have brought it up. He meant for Jacob to understand that he knows better, that he isn't like his ancestors, or even his parents. "It wasn't cool, my great-great-however-many-great-grandparents coming here." He keeps talking, even though he isn't sure what he wants to say. "I've read about missionaries and about residential schools, that kind of stuff, in history class, but I never really *thought* about them, as like, actual people, my great-great-grandparents, your great-great-grandparents. The whole story never felt like it was something real. That sounds stupid, right? But it was just this old story that had nothing to do with me."

Jacob frowns. "For us that history is still alive, everywhere—in our relationships, our land quarrels. We talk every day to our grandfathers. Robson and my dad think that this ceremony is going to set things right between our people. That it will somehow reconcile what happened back then. Robson thinks we need forgiveness, but my dad thinks that we need to repair the road that once existed between us. I don't know." Jacob stands and paces the edge of the water before turning back to Zach. "It wasn't just your ancestors that were killed here. So many of our people got sick and died after the missionaries came, the traders. You need to remember them too. There are many sides to the story, and I hope they will all be told tomorrow."

Jacob looks up at the sway of palm trees overhead, the light dancing over him. "What happened here, what is going to happen tomorrow, it isn't just a story," Jacob goes on. "Stories are important, they tell us things we need to know, remind us of things we might otherwise forget. This 'story' did not start with my forefathers or yours. It started before them, when the island was first pulled from the sea. And it keeps going too. The storm that killed my brother, more and more like that are coming. Our island is shrinking because of what your people are doing. People keep dying. There is no ending."

Zach's only ever thought about his ancestors in the story, even if he thought what they did was wrong. "You're right," he admits. "I didn't think of anyone else but them. Truthfully, I didn't even think of them that much. And I think I get what you're saying about tomorrow. Whatever happens, it isn't the end. But it's kinda cool that we were connected before we even met. By what happened here." The idea excites him, the idea of being connected, of being part of things. He looks back at the high arc of the roof, this place that feels underground, or like another world altogether. "I'm sorry for what they did. I really am. I wish . . . there was something I could do. But I'm glad I got to come here."

Zach stands and goes to join Jacob at the water's edge, lets it lap gently at his feet, in and out. "I'm sorry," he says, "for like, everything, but thanks for bringing me here. For the urchin, I can't believe I ate it. But it was fucking amazing. And just . . . thanks. It's incredible." He sounds like such a tourist. "Maybe we could come back here later? I'd love to try and film in here."

Jacob considers Zach for a long moment. "No," he says. "I don't think so." He drops the empty urchin husks into deep water. "We should go."

Scott

The church in Robson's village is beautiful—all bright white-washed lines and wooden benches worn soft from years of faithful attendees. It's more welcoming than the sombre heaviness of the one back home with all its gloomy Presbyterian stone. Scott closes his eyes and waits for the calm that sometimes comes to him when he sits in those pews. But the air is different here: the ozone smell of earth, the thick scent of the lush vegetation. The sounds are strange too: the coo of a hidden dove, the barking of a dog; a sudden burst of children's laughter from the school across the open space of the village, a tight knit of harmonies as women sing in the distance.

Back when she still spoke about Dylan, Michelle told him once that she could feel him near her—his hand in hers, his weight leaning against her. Scott has never felt that. Still, he tries: "Hey, buddy. Can you believe this place? It's wild, huh?" The air shifts around him, and Scott holds himself still, hopeful.

Is he here? Everything on this island is so alien to him that it feels possible. "Are you there, bud? I miss you."

There's no answer.

It was Michelle who wanted a house with a pool; Scott had just seen work, expense, an inability to sell the house down the road. They would never use it, he said. They'd find drowned raccoons floating in it. But Michelle described hosting pool parties and barbecues with tropical drinks. She imagined them at the centre of a small neighbourhood universe. And she was right. They strung lights across the backyard and had those parties, fruity drinks in hand, imagining island paradises that were nothing at all like Iparei; they even swam naked together more than once, when the kids were in bed.

Neither of them thought the pool was a danger. There was a fence around the backyard and motion-detecting lights. They made sure the gate to the yard was always latched, and taught the kids to check it as well. And there were plenty of rules: the kids weren't allowed to be out by the pool alone; they all took swimming lessons. They did everything they were supposed to.

Ten kids a day die by drowning in backyard swimming pools; that's three thousand deaths a year. He came across that statistic while trying to figure out how he had let it happen.

The weather was hot for May and the pool sparked, as Astrid would say. He'd been skimming the pool, even though Zach was supposed to come down and do it. It was just him and the boys at home.

Dylan leaned over the pool, already in his swim trunks and his hockey hoodie, his fingers dragging in the cold water, his legs goose-pimpled.

"How's the temperature?" Scott asked, putting the skimmer away.

"Cold. Really cold." Dylan shivered with pleasure.

Then the phone rang, and Scott thought about letting it go to voicemail. One of a million tiny, seemingly inconsequential decisions he made that morning. If only he'd let the machine pick it up. If only. If only.

"Come on, bud." Scott jokingly snapped his fingers, pointing at the sliding door to the kitchen, but Dylan ignored him. "Dylan!" he shouted, his tone sharper than he'd intended. "You can't be out here on your own. You know the rules."

Those were his last words to his son. *You know the rules.*

Dylan shot him an overly dramatic glare, all furrowed eyebrows and turned-down lips, but then followed him inside. Scott dawdled just long enough to see Dylan smile at the ridiculous face he pulled and then lean against the sliding door. It slid a little and he stumbled some before righting himself.

Scott answered the phone and walked with it into the living room. It was a telemarketer. Someone selling some damn credit card. He should have hung up as soon as he heard what they were selling, but he always tried to be polite. That was who he was talking to while his son drowned.

After he hung up, he went back to the kitchen, but Dylan wasn't there. He didn't think anything of it at the time; Dylan could have been in the bathroom or gone upstairs.

Scott stood in the doorway, looking into yard, squinting against the blinding light. He couldn't put it together. The red-and-black shape at the bottom of the pool. Why had Dylan thrown his hockey sweater in the water? Scott's brain ticked slowly. There was something he wasn't grasping. The way the sweater hung at the bottom of the pool—and then his body was jolted through with understanding.

He doesn't remember running to the edge of the pool, doesn't remember flinging himself into it. He only remembers being in the water with the heavy drag of his son's body in his arms, struggling to keep Dylan's head above the surface. He heaved them both onto the scrape of concrete that encircled the pool, and he was pumping his son's chest. He didn't care if he broke his ribs. He needed his son's heart to beat. He needed his lungs to fill with air.

Every second was an eternity, fracturing into fragments. Every one of them taking him further away from Dylan, and Dylan further from him. He yelled for Zach to call for help. He had to keep Dylan alive. Dylan couldn't die, not on a sunny day in his own backyard. It was impossible that Dylan's chest wasn't moving under his father's hands; impossible he wasn't sticking out his tongue and laughing.

There had been no splash. No shriek. Nothing. Scott opens his eyes and studies the heavy wooden cross hanging on the whitewashed wall. When he closes his eyes again, the cross hangs dark in his vision.

He doesn't know how long he has been sitting like that when he becomes aware of voices outside the church. They are speaking a language he doesn't recognize but the tone is irritated enough to make him uncomfortable. He hears Jacob's name just as Robson and David reach the threshold of the church, Robson trying to steer David inside.

Scott stands and is about to make his presence known when Robson spots him and calls out: "Hello, Scott Stewart!" His voice booms off the walls, and his hands are already grasping Scott's and pumping before Scott even has a chance to correct him that

Stewart is Michelle's name, not his. Robson pants heavily, his large chest heaving, his smile wide. There is sweat on his forehead. David looks away.

"Sorry, I didn't mean to intrude, I just wanted to . . ." Scott gestures around the church, meaning quiet, meaning sanctuary.

Robson smiles broadly. "Of course. You want to see our plaque! The photograph of our grandfathers." He moves to the wall to the right of the altar and beckons Scott to join him in front of a brass plaque, the kind found in churches everywhere, it seems.

In memory of Reverend and Mrs. William Stewart,
who died bringing God's light to these shores.
Commemorated on this day, August 26, 1999.

"I had it made when I became the rector of our church," Robson says. "And these are our great-grandfathers," he adds, singling out two men in the framed photograph next to the plaque.

It is a picture of a building not unlike the one they're in. Both are small, single-storey whitewashed structures, though the one in the photograph is made of wood. The setting in the photograph is different, the jungle pushing closer to the church, which looks out of place, as though it has been dropped from the sky, whole cloth, from a back road in Ontario.

"This photo was taken during the Second World War. You can see the first church we had on Iparei, built fifty years after your people were here," David says, speaking for the first time. "It was destroyed a long time ago, but our village was built where it once stood."

Now Scott can see the shape of the cove. A few narrow canoes rest on the shore. And in front of the building, the two men are in a small group of people, some wearing piecemeal

European clothing along with what must be traditional garb. Scott wonders who took the photograph, but David is pointing at one of the men.

"That is my great-grandfather," he says. "He worked very hard to bring the church to this place."

"And that is mine," says Robson, reaching across and pointing to the other man. Scott searches for resemblances, but the image is a faded blur, the soft texture of the paper making it difficult to pick out details. "We continue the work they started, to build the future they wanted for us, and we want for our children too." He spreads his arms to indicate all that has been accomplished, all that is yet to come.

"What must they think of us now?" David asks quietly, checking his phone. "I should go."

"I'll head back with you," Scott offers.

"No, no!" Robson pleads. "Let me show you around my place now."

Scott glances between the two men and then nods, uncertain who to refuse, who he might offend. He knows he interrupted something between them that can't be discussed now, not in his presence. Something to do with Jacob, he thinks, remembering the earlier conversation he had with David about the difficulties of sons.

"I'll see you later then," David says to him, and then pauses as though he's about to say more, before making his departure.

Robson gestures for Scott to sit.

Scott does as he is told, expecting Robson to sit as well; instead, he steps towards the front of the church and takes his place behind the pulpit. "This is what has grown from the seeds that your family first planted. They brought us the stories of

Jesus and His Father in Heaven, and we have cultivated them to become our own. And despite all the difficulties, for that we will always be grateful."

"They weren't my people," Scott says, clarifying, wanting to distance himself. "The Stewarts; they were my wife's family."

"Wives make us family," Robson says with a small shrug.

The wind moves through the eaves of the church.

"Are you married?" Scott asks.

"Of course. I've been married a long, long time." Robson exaggerates the words, making the word *long* sound comical. "We have three daughters and two sons, and we are waiting on a second grandchild."

"Congratulations." And then, after a beat: "It's not easy, huh? Being married as long as we have."

Robson laughs again, an open rolling sound that Scott finds comforting, finds himself joining in, despite everything. "No, it is not easy. She is always telling me that I talk too much and should listen more. She thinks I am too hard on my sons and not hard enough on my daughters. But what does it matter what we fight about? We are one, in the eyes of God. We made promises to each other. We love each other."

Scott grimaces slightly at this. "Sometimes it feels like other people made those promises. Things happen in a marriage, to people, that change them. For better or worse." He laughs bitterly. "Maybe sometimes *better* means going our separate ways."

Robson comes down from the pulpit and sits in the pew in front of Scott, angles his body towards him. "It's easy to make promises when we believe they won't be hard to keep."

The two men sit quietly. The singing in the distance has stopped. Scott is about to speak when the voices pick up again.

Robson wipes his brow. "They are rehearsing for the ceremony tomorrow."

"The ceremony," Scott repeats. "I have to admit, I'm not really sure I understand what the ceremony is about. It was ages ago, and if anyone was in the wrong, it was clearly Michélle's family. Maybe it's best to just let the past lie. Just move on."

Robson cocks his head, taking him in, and Scott feels his face redden. "The past is a road that connects us," Robson explains, drawing lines between them in the air. "Us to our ancestors, to our descendants. You and I. You to them." Robson must notice his confused expression. "The exchanges that were made between your ancestors and mine bonded them—the food they shared, the knowledge. Those obligations still bind us together now. We are stronger because we are bound together." Robson pauses. "Those bonds came at a cost. There was so much fear and anger, so little understanding. Many of our people died from the illness that came with your people, and yours were killed."

"But that's what I mean," Scott interrupts. "If William hadn't come, your people wouldn't have been killed. We're the ones who should be asking for forgiveness, not you."

Robson shakes his head again. "It is not about forgiveness. Jesus preaches forgiveness, and it is good to forgive. But forgiveness is only part of the work. We must repair the road that was broken. Then we can begin to move forward, together. When we honour our obligations we are stronger."

"It's so different than how we do things. We just want to assign the blame, and move on."

"Does that work?"

"Not really."

They grow quiet and listen to the distant sound of the women's voices until their complex harmony is suddenly submerged by the chaos of children's voices.

"School's out," Robson says, standing. Scott follows him out of the church.

Across the neat green lawn that sits in the centre of Robson's village, children of various ages stream from a small, corrugated building out into the sun, all wearing matching polo shirts. Among them is a lanky white man, dreaded hair bleached by the sun. He greets Robson with a word Scott doesn't recognize and Robson claps him on the shoulder.

"Ah, you remember Noah," he says to Scott. "He lives here and teaches in the school. Sometimes he speaks in the church, though I do not think you will have time to come to a sermon."

"No," Scott agrees, and shakes Noah's hand. "How long have you lived here?"

"Oh, not even a year." Noah has an Australian accent, his words flat as a becalmed sea. "I asked my church back home to send me, and pitched up here. Robson took me in, made me part of the family."

"See, it is like I was telling you," Robson explains. "Each person has a place in the web. My son is someone else's cousin, someone else's grandson." He interlaces his fingers, spreads them out, interlaces them differently. "Knowing how we are connected to each other tells us everything we need, determines who we are to each other. So when someone comes to live with us, to be a part of our community, we make them family, by adoption. Not like your adoption, though sometimes that happens too. Still, Noah is my son, as I am his father. I take care of him now, and later he will take care of me."

Robson moves his hand back and forth between himself and Scott. "We are like family, in a way. That is what the road between us means, and why it's important that we rebuild it. Tomorrow isn't an ending to what went on before—it's a new beginning."

The sun presses down on Scott's shoulders as he walks back to David's village. It makes him light-headed and sway slightly. He thinks about all that Robson has said, about repairing roads, making amends. About obligations. And family. He can't help but conclude that his is probably not the kind of family that Robson or David wants to be connected to.

He has tried, hasn't he? He's made sure that the kids are fed, that they get to school. But then he thinks of Astrid's nightmares, of Zach wandering the streets at night. Yes, he's made promises to Michelle; he has obligations to her, to use Robson's words, but what more does he owe Michelle? She's the one who hasn't met her obligations. He is hot and sweaty and daydreaming of the coolness of the ocean, of being held by it. He is thinking of the house, the offer he has put in. Something has to change. The kids have to come first.

He is thinking of the right words to tell Michelle this when he sees Joyce hustling towards him, Astrid in tow.

"Is Zach with you?"

"Zach ran away," Astrid says, bugging her eyes out at him. "And Mommy's really mad."

"He hasn't run away, he's just off . . . playing," Joyce says.

"I haven't seen Zach since this morning. I'm sure he's nearby, filming or something." But Scott is looking towards the ocean, scanning the waves, worried. "I just came from the other village."

"David says Jacob is gone too." Joyce tries to keep her tone calm, but there is an edge there. "I'm sure they're together."

"I'll look. You stay here with Astrid in case they come back."

He moves down to the black carved shore, scans the blue holes where they snorkelled, the farther horizon he knows is not as far away as it feels. The light on the water casts shadows like boys' bodies floating below the surface.

The rational part of his brain tells him his son is fine, exploring the island with Jacob, like Joyce said. Zach has wandered off before and he will again. But then Scott has already lived through the impossible. His throat aches and he wants to scream and cry for how powerless he feels.

And then there he is—one of a pair of figures coming around the curve of the island. The boys, they look almost like young men from here. Zach's laugh drifts towards Scott, boisterous and loose, and a rage rises up in him. *How dare he be so goddamned selfish.*

When Scott reaches his son, he pulls Zach to him, feels his body go rigid a moment in his arms before he returns the hug with a small bark of a laugh.

"Where the hell were you?" Scott asks, still clinging to his son. "You can't just take off like that."

Zach pulls away, his face clouded. "I was just hanging with Jacob."

"You didn't think to tell someone?"

"Why? It's not like you guys care where I am."

That's when Scott sees the blood on Zach's shirt, spreading across his shoulder. "What the hell happened?"

"It's nothing. A wave caught me. That's all."

Scott doesn't see it happen. It's only when he spins around to say something to Jacob that he realizes a small crowd has gathered behind them, and it's while he's looking at Rebecca and a couple of other women whose names he doesn't remember that he hears the sharp sting of it, flesh on flesh. When he turns back to Zach, Michelle is there, her hand in the air. Zach's hand is on his cheek, red and inflamed, his eyes glinting with tears. His face begins to crumble, but he fights against it.

Zach looks back and forth between his parents before his eyes land squarely on his mother. "I wish it had been me."

Faina

When Faina arrived at her garden she walked the boundaries of it. She climbed the terraces at one end, then paced the forty steps across the back of it, slipping from shade to sun.

The light shone hard on the variegated greens of her plants and she was sweating in the bright glare of it. Josephine talked of light when she painted while Faina drew letters in the dirt with a stick. Different light. Josephine murmured about capturing it and spread colour on rectangles of white paper, conjuring the ocean there, the sky. But Josephine didn't see it the way Faina did. Light was not still. Look where it caressed the twist of the yam's vines, curling with them around the stakes, bent and sculpted, to please the eye, to please the ground, to please. Look where it ran down the tree and then slipped into the undergrowth. Light could not be captured. It danced. Across the water, and the leaves. But she watched the light closely now, measuring its movement, and followed the slip of it to the ground that held the yams.

In places the earth looked sunken. Using a stick she shifted dirt carefully. It wasn't yet harvest time; she didn't want to disturb the yams. What she saw, though, was mushed and rotten. She turned to another plant to look. It was the same. Were they all ruined?

Telau had collapsed in the shade of one of her mango trees, and drank from the bamboo tube they had filled at the stream near the village. "Telau?" she called, and her friend raised a lazy head to her. "How are your yams?" Telau shrugged, but dragged herself to her feet. Faina crossed her own garden to join her friend. The plants here were healthy and strong, the vines reaching out across the ground where Telau had failed to tie them up properly. Faina bent now to correct one such vine. She glanced back at her own. "Are other gardens doing as well as yours?" she asked.

"I think so. Father said that our yams will be the largest at the exchange. Maybe even so large we will have to hold some back, so as not to embarrass the Uplanders."

Faina turned back to her plants, ashamed at the state of them. The women in Father's line were gifted in garden magic, and so were much sought after as wives. And yet, the more she looked the more she saw her failings. Even the fruit trees bore almost no fruit.

Faina moved to the centre of her plot, running her hands along the raised mounds of vines, to the small shrine set there. She peered inside to see the food, a few flowers, and the blue stone that she had found on the shore. She thought of what else she had buried at the corner of the shrine. Perhaps that had upset the ancestors.

She turned her back to Telau and then dug into the ground to retrieve the length of bamboo buried there. Inside was the image of her, blurred a little where the paper had gotten damp. From the woven basket she kept slung across her body, she took out the page torn from Josephine's bible. She could read some of the words now. *Jesus*: the name of the ancestor who spoke to their father in the sky on their behalf. *God*: who was that father. *Love*: which was all the good feeling in the world that made you warm and happy. She rolled the words into the bamboo tube and then buried it back in the ground. Over the troubled earth, she wrote one of her words with her finger, *love*, then wiped it away, the way she did on her slate. Maybe this magic would help.

When she stood up, she noticed that Telau had come closer and was staring at her. "I could use some help," Faina said, and bent to try to aerate the soil, hoping it wasn't too late for some of the crop. Telau watched for a moment and then Faina heard her turn to the work too.

After a few minutes of working in silence, Faina asked, "Do you think that we are in charge of the land?"

"What do you mean?"

"Will-am says that, as children of their father, the land is theirs and they must subdue it."

A hard word: *subdue*.

Telau laughed her dismissive laugh that Faina had known her whole life. She would miss that laugh. "No one controls the land. That is why Sero takes his fasts and feeds the stones, so that the old ones will make the gardens grow." Her friend paused a moment in her work to look hard at Faina. "Have you done something to upset them?"

She couldn't answer, and it occurred to her that she had never had secrets before Josephine and William came. It made her wonder if others had secrets too. She was about to ask Telau if she had any secrets when there was a sharp crack like thunder even though the sky overhead was clear and bright, presaging the drier days that were to come. The sound was so loud it felt as though it had emerged from inside her, as if something that had been drawn taut in Faina had snapped and echoed out into the world.

"What was that?" Telau asked. She looked ready to run to the village. In the distance, voices from other gardens called out.

The sound came from the direction of the mission, Faina was sure of it.

"We should go back," Telau said, already moving along the road to the village.

"You don't want to know what it is?"

"No! Louvu will send someone. They will let us know. Come on."

They stood, feeling the tension between them, as though they were tethered by a liana, both of them pulling in the direction they wanted to go.

"We won't go to the mission," Faina said, relenting some, "but let's go to the cliff where we can see?"

The space between them slackened a little. Telau nodded.

When they arrived at the cliff, Faina pushed through the last line of trees and the whole of the ocean spread out before her. The mission cove was hidden from where she stood, but floating beyond the reef was another of the great canoes! *Ship*—she called the word to mind.

"Look," she said as Telau appeared beside her.

"More of them?" Telau's voice was narrow with anger, and fear.

"Maybe."

"We should tell Louvu and my father."

She was right, but just as Faina turned to follow her friend she saw a small canoe round the thrust of the island, departing from the mission cove. She could just make out the flicker of blue that was Josephine's skirt. They were leaving.

William and Josephine were gone one night, then two, but the ship remained, bobbing and shifting on the waves.

On the third morning, William appeared at the edge of the village. He had finally learned to wait at the village border, where the namele leaf was posted, until he was welcomed into the nasara. Faina saw William gesture for his two companions to do the same.

Louvu stood to welcome them. When the new men refused to sit on the ground where he motioned, he scowled. "We welcome you and your companions to our village." He sounded exasperated as he sat down.

William cast about, and when he spotted Faina, bent over another of her marriage mats, he motioned her to come forward. She froze. It would be one thing for Louvu to give her a role in speaking to these men, but something else altogether for William to invite her into the conversation. When she didn't move, he motioned again, more emphatically. "Come here, girl."

She glanced at Louvu, who didn't nod, but didn't discourage her either. Faina stepped forward slightly, but kept her distance from William and the two men behind him. They were splotchy and red, their hair long and straggling like seaweed. Their clothing was the same shape as William's, but they wore their shirts open, revealing their sunken chests, and the colours of the cloth were different. From where she stood, several arm's lengths away, she could smell them—that rank smell of rotted fruit, of dirty bodies and clothing. She scrunched her nose against it.

William sat opposite Louvu and the other Middle Grove men who had gathered, while his companions remained standing. When William began to speak, Kaipar muttered that he was rude to not stand to say his piece. William ignored him.

"These men are traders and I told them about the sweet-smelling trees you have here—sandalwood." William seemed unsteady as he sounded the word out slowly. He didn't even glance in Faina's direction. "They will give you two axes to take them."

Louvu glanced at Faina. She shifted her weight from one foot to the other—she wanted to be certain to get the words right. She looked at the ground just in front of Louvu and explained.

Louvu frowned and scoffed some. He was about to reply, but one of William's companions had wandered away from the circle. There was a small clutch of women gathered near one of the cooking huts, watching and listening intently. The man stumbled some and then turned to his friend. He held his hands in front of his chest, miming breasts, and then cackled. The other man laughed too. William grimaced, but said nothing.

Masai, however, leapt to his feet, Nako quick behind him, but Kaipar spoke sharply from where he still sat beside Louvu. *Stop.*

Masai and Nako froze, their hands tight on their weapons, while the man nearest the women reached for something at his belt before his companion called him back. The man muttered as he returned, leering at Faina as he passed her. She recoiled from him. He stopped in front of William and spoke to him rapidly, gesturing over his shoulder at Louvu and Kaipar, his hand grasping an object held at his waist. William held up his hands to the man, urging him to calm down, and when the man stormed past him, William turned again to Louvu and this time was indignant.

"They're just trees, they're not worth anything to you. The san-dal-wood." He exaggerated the word in Faina's direction, as though she were stupid, even though she knew far more of his language than he did of hers. William had not gone beyond simple greetings, or naming things like a small child did when they first learned to speak.

"The sweet trees," he said and wafted his hands as though smelling something. "Up the slope?"

She explained to Louvu about the trees that the men wanted.

"Why is he asking us?" Kaipar asked. "Those trees are not ours to decide what to do with. He should go and speak with the Uplanders." He spat the words towards William. Behind him, Masai and Nako were still tense, watching not William but one of his companions as he strode towards the edge of the nasara, turned his back to them, and urinated into the bush. Faina looked away, disgusted.

"What did he say?" William barked.

"You ask the Uplanders."

He glanced at the man, who shook himself dry and adjusted himself as he walked back to the group.

"She comes too," William said, standing and pointing at Faina.

She didn't want to go with them. The new men scared her; they gave off a jittery, dangerous energy. She looked from Louvu to Masai, and when he stepped forward a small relief welled in her, but did little to swamp her dread.

Masai said, "We'll go with them," and Louvu grunted his assent.

Faina had never walked this road towards the Upland before, and she watched carefully to see if there was any great change as they moved out of Middle Grove territory. Masai led the group, with Faina close behind him. She was in turn followed by William, then Nako and the jittery men. Behind them, Kaipar and two others brought up the rear. All the men had their hands on their weapons and the air crackled around them. Masai moved quickly, and William huffed his stale breath against her neck. He was too close to her, but she was almost on Masai's heels and had nowhere to go.

William cleared his throat with a wet rattle and spat into the bushes.

To distract herself from William and the men who trailed behind him, she examined the path. It pressed steeply through the brush, so that occasionally she had to use a thick vine or slender trunk to pull herself upwards. She could hear a hidden waterfall not far from the road. Finally the ground levelled out ahead of her and Masai picked up the pace.

Was the earth a different colour here? Perhaps lighter, not quite as wet. That could be good for crops. She knew Albi had several gardens, and would receive more when they were married, some of which would be hers to care for.

"Are we almost there?" she asked Masai.

"A bit farther yet." His voice and breath came easy.

When she looked back, one of William's companions was bent over at the waist, the other leaned against the trunk of a tree. Masai stopped a short distance ahead.

"Almost there," Faina said to William, but he waved a hand to dismiss her.

Nako threaded his way between the men and joined Masai at the head of the line. Faina stepped nearer to him too, while Kaipar and the others kept a close eye on William.

"Why are we wasting our time?" Nako asked, careful to make sure Kaipar didn't hear him. "The Uplanders won't want to exchange with them." He wrinkled his nose at the men trying to recover their breath, trying to look relaxed and failing. They were scared. Faina could tell by the way they stayed close to each other, the way their heads snapped round at every sound, the way they clutched at the guns at their waists.

"Have you been to the Upland before?" Faina asked when Masai didn't answer.

"Sometimes we hunt pigeons near there and we share kava, if it is the end of the day." He shrugged.

"Will it make a good home, do you think?" She glanced back and forth between their faces, trying to read them. Eventually Masai nodded slowly.

"They'll be good to you."

When they finally reached the namele leaves that marked the boundary of the Upland village, Masai stopped the small group. "Hello?" Masai called into the close air and turned slowly around, as if searching for signs of men hidden in the trees, in the tangles of llanas. Faina was sure she felt eyes on her. She inched closer to Nako and Masai.

They waited a long time, the bush quiet around them. Just as one of William's companions went to brush by Masai and enter the village, two Uplander warriors appeared on the road without a sound. The man stumbled back, startled by their striking appearance—feathers were woven high into one of the men's hair, tendrils of soft vines cascading from them. Around taut biceps they each wore armbands made of shells traded from the Hotwater people, and their chests were marked for a ceremony or for battle. They had been prepared for people appearing on their outskirts.

Kaipar stepped forward and told them they would like to talk with the village.

The Uplanders beckoned for the group to follow them into the village. Ahead of Faina, Kaipar talked with their Uplander escorts. Their languages were not so different—a few unfamiliar words and names for things, a slightly different affect to some of the sounds, but they understood each other clearly.

The group stopped in the nasara. Faina took in the open space that was the heart of the village. It was wetter here, farther inland and higher up, and the smoke from damp fires hung close to the ground. The nasara was a thick layer of mud over hard-packed dirt. Overhead a pigeon cooed, and near the edge of the brush a few piglets snuffled.

At one end of the nasara, mats were spread on the wet ground, and their escort gestured for Kaipar and the others to sit, which they did. The traders stayed on their feet, shifting uncomfortably. Faina went to stand a short distance behind them and peered around. Like in her own village, paths led away from the nasara and into the bush. She tried to spy homes through the brush but couldn't make out anything. There was a low resonant pounding, perhaps of posts being worked into the ground, or a terrace being flattened, but she couldn't tell which.

One of the Uplander escorts picked up a stick and pounded out a short rhythm on a well-worn log, shined from use. He paused and then repeated the tattoo.

Eventually, a small group of men entered the nasara. Her father-to-be, Narinam, lifted a hand in greeting to Kaipar, who stood as the older man approached. Narinam waved Kaipar back to sitting. There was a quick flurry of activity as a young woman brought water and dried coconut cups that the men drank from.

Faina watched her closely. The girl was about her age, though taller. Would she still be here when Faina came to this place as a wife? Or would she be gone to another village too?

She had a brief idea of women circulating the exchange roads the same as goods did, moving from one village to the next, replacing each other, filling spaces left behind by another.

Albi was not among the men gathered. Where was he? Gardening, perhaps. Or hunting. She wondered if Masai had hunted with Albi. Why had she not asked him?

After Narinam and Kaipar finished their courtesies, Kaipar stood again and spoke quickly.

"These men are friends of our friend, William." He seemed to want to spit at William's name, at the word *friend*, but he did not. "They have a wish to exchange with you, something of your place."

Kaipar then paced back to his spot and returned to sitting again. He would do no more for William, no more for the new strangers from the ship.

Now Narinam stood and spoke. "We do not want to be in an exchange with these men," he began. His pace was languid; he moved a few steps and then stood and swayed some, not in weakness, but with an elegance, like the palm trees dancing in a slow wind. When he spoke again it was with a rigid formality that was different from the way that Louvu led a discussion.

"We didn't want you to let the missi stay on our island. We didn't know what they brought, for good or bad. We have a good life here in this place, living in the way of our bubu, as we have lived since the rocks first came from the sea. We asked you to join us in this decision, refusing to let the missi stay, as we stand together in so many decisions. Our alliance is fragile. The marriage exchanged between Albi and this girl was to clear the road between us, and yet you have changed the terms, and you have brought these men here. Perhaps we are mistaken in allying ourselves with you."

"You should keep an eye to which road you would prefer to keep open," Kaipar said.

There was a threat in his words, even Faina could sense that. Perhaps there was a time coming when sides would need to be chosen. Kaipar was convincing.

William's companion nearest Faina turned slightly towards her. "You," he said. "What do they say?" She shook her head slightly, scrunched her nose. She would not speak while the men spoke. The man grabbed her wrist. "Tell me." He twisted his hand and she pulled back.

Masai turned to them from where he sat, already rising to one knee. "Let her go."

That, the man understood.

Faina's heart beat hard in her chest, the slap of bird wings against the sky. She could still feel the man's hand at her wrist, hot where he had grabbed her, and see the wet of his sweat on her skin. She was glad that Albi was not here to see this man touch her in this way, glad that Masai had intervened. She stepped away from the stench of William's companion, out of his reach.

Narinam sighed; this time he did not stand. "What do they want?"

Kaipar gestured at William to stand and speak. When he did, William waved Faina towards him, but she hung back, shook her head again. None of Middle Grove men scolded her. She was certain Masai had even nodded slightly at her refusal.

She stood where she was and translated the request. The men from the ship wanted trees from the Uplanders' place.

Narinam's face clouded as she spoke, and the other men around him murmured among themselves. "We can't let them have the trees that they ask for," Narinam explained. "The trees are tabu. Our ancestors planted them when they came from the sea and divided this land from your land. That grove is the place they keep as their own and we are tasked with its care. The wood is tabu, it is used in ceremonies that only our tabu men know."

Faina explained Narinam's words, but William's companions argued with him. "We don't need to bargain. We'll just take it. What are they going to do about it with their bows and arrows?" And they stood with the guns in their hands.

Suddenly everyone was on their feet, weapons raised amid a chaos of sound and noise and words that sent Faina scurrying back, quick as a crab on the sand. There was a scuffle as Kaipar, Nako, and Masai put themselves between the Uplanders and William and his companions.

One of the strangers raised his weapon and Masai struck at the gun with his spear. The man careened back and the gun fired into the air, ripping a branch from the banyan overhead. Nako struck the man with his fists, and the weapon fell to the ground. Faina's ears were muffled, her breath heavy in her lungs. But the shot had silenced them all.

The man grumbled to his feet. His companion, who had retreated a short distance, held his own gun as the first man recovered his.

Other men, women, and children had appeared in the nasara, drawn by the noise. William and his companions cast around, backing away, their weapons up.

"Leave here," Narinam said and pointed towards the road. "Don't come back."

The three men backed towards the entrance to the village and disappeared, swallowed by the brush.

Kaipar bent and picked up the fallen bough of the banyan, then crossed the nasara with it to Narinam. He knew the strangers' violence had offended the Uplanders deeply. "I'm sorry we brought them here. Please don't break our peace because of them." He handed the branch over. With the branch in hand, Narinam turned and walked away.

Faina looked up as a hand reached down towards her and pulled her to her feet. The man's hand was dry in hers and he smiled slightly at her before squeezing her hand gently.

"Albi," Narinam called, and then Albi let go of her hand and turned to follow his father.

She watched her husband-to-be retreat, while Masai took her by the arm and drew her back towards the road. Her blood thundered through her body like the sea.

Michelle

"Jesus fucking Christ, Michelle."

Scott's voice cuts through the gloom of the bungalow. The air is cold after the oppressive heat outside and her skin prickles and tightens as though with a fever. Small mews come from under the cot against the opposite wall—the kittens the mother cat hid there last night. Michelle flexes her hand; it still stings, feels swollen and foreign. Her rings are too tight, and she wrenches at them, scraping at her fingers. But they won't budge.

Scott clutches at his hair, paces the concrete floor, the shape of him huge in the small space. "Jesus fucking Christ."

"I didn't . . ." she stammers and lets her words drop away. What can she possibly say? She struggles with her rings, her swollen knuckles ache.

It wasn't supposed to go like this. She tries to remember why she needed to come here. She was going to find—what? Peace? The idea is absurd, laughable. Magical thinking.

Outside a rooster crows. Always a rooster crowing here, no matter the hour.

Scott turns on her. "Don't you think he's been hurt enough? That we all have been?"

The cold leaves her in a rush. Her hands are in fists and she spits back at him, "Where were you?"

Scott goes still, a backlit shadow against the single square of window, grasping the concrete ledge. His head drops, then his shoulders. The rooster outside falls quiet. Michelle stares at those shoulders and then at her hands, remembers them holding on to him. Her hands are so empty.

It used to be so easy to reach out and touch them, her husband, her children. Now she finds it almost impossible. When was the last time she touched Zach? She holds Astrid after her nightmares, but Zach? It has been months, and now when her hand does reach out to him, it's to strike him. Who is she? She collapses to the cot, which sags beneath her.

If her son were in front of her now she would clutch Zach to her and hold him as long as possible. Because he'll be gone soon—off to university, a career, a life of his own, the way children are meant to. She wants to rise and go to him, but the grief swallows her as she remembers all the things that Dylan will never have, will never be.

And the future drops away from her, even while the rest of her family is setting out into it. She is being left behind.

Scott has turned back to her, stares down at her expectantly, waiting for her to answer a question she has not heard. His face shifts, from pleading to anger.

"Right," he says. "I wasn't there. You think I don't know that? You think I haven't relived every moment of that day? What I could have changed? But I can't! I wasn't there when

Dylan needed me. I'll live with that every day for the rest of my life." His voice drops to a whisper as though he is no longer talking to her. "Where was I? What was I doing? Don't answer the phone. Don't go inside. Just stand in the doorway and watch him, watch your son by the pool." A small smile plays across his face, like a quick dash of sunlight, and she can see Dylan there in front of them, they are standing at the door together watching their son, his limbs too long for his body, all angles and silly walks. Then Scott's face darkens again. He straightens up, pushes his shoulders back. "But I was there. *I* pulled our son out of the pool. *I* held him. *I tried* . . ." His voice catches, and his hands twitch slightly; she imagines them pumping on Dylan's chest. He closes them to fists. "And I'm here now, Michelle. Where the hell are you?"

Her mouth moves, but she isn't making any sound. *How dare he?*

He holds up his hand to silence what she isn't saying. "No. Not just today. We both fucked up today." He begins to pace again, returns to the louvred window, the world outside nothing but blurred shapes, and stares at it. The rooster starts up again. "Jesus, what was I thinking?" She can barely hear him. "If something happened to him . . ." He shakes the vision from his head, but she can't—she sees the vision he has conjured, of Zach, broken, floating in the sea.

"It's not my fault," she says, her own voice barely audible. She needs him to agree. She needs him to say it isn't her fault. *Please.*

"No? Of course not. Nothing is ever your fault. But it must be somebody's, right? So, whose fault is it? Say it. It must be mine. Or Zach's? He was there too, you know. He was the one who had to call the goddamned ambulance. There's enough blame to go around. Why not blame Astrid. Just anyone but you."

"I'm sorry," she manages at last. It is all she can say. She stares pleadingly at Scott, hoping he knows that she means it. "I'm sorry," she repeats.

"But are you really? You keep saying it. But what the fuck does it even mean? You act like *you're* the only one hurting here, and we all have to tiptoe around you, let *you* have your grief *your* way." He's examining her like she's a stranger, and his voice quiets. "Your face changes when someone brings him up, you know that? You disappear. And it's terrifying. What do you think that does to them? To me? Astrid's having nightmares, Zach is sneaking out at all hours—"

"You knew," she says, and the energy shifts in the room, like the tide has changed. "You knew that Zach was sneaking out. And you just let him keep doing it? How dare you blame me for this when you didn't do anything to stop him."

"Neither did you." He scoffs. "This is the problem. This . . ." He waves his hands back and forth between them. "We aren't even talking to each other, Michelle. I feel like I can't count on you."

"He could have died today!"

"Yes," Scott says, and he seems to have decided something. "He could have. Because you won't talk to him. Because we don't talk to each other. You have to stop punishing us. You can stay trapped in your grief, but I won't let you do that to them anymore." He looks around the room as if seeing it for the first time. "What are we even doing here?" he asks. "Seriously, Michelle. Why are we here?"

Why? It made some kind of sense to her, when she thought she saw Dylan in the backyard, when he said they should go. "I thought it would change things. Change me," she says.

"You told me you had to do something, remember? That you had to be able to make something right. Well, we're here now. What are you doing to make things right?"

"You didn't have to come."

He rears back. "I believed you. I would do anything to get you through this. I would have tried anything." And then he tosses it like a spear: "But I don't think I can do it anymore."

They are both panting, as though they have run a race, swum the channel. They are silent a long time. When he speaks again, Scott sounds sad. "Everyone used to want to be us."

She remembers that, remembers how smug she used to feel about their relationship. But now it feels like remembering someone else's life. An old friend she doesn't see anymore. "I know."

"I loved that, that we were better than everyone else. I was sure we laughed together more than anyone else did too. It was you and me against the world, remember?" He sighs. "Maybe it was too perfect. Maybe we should have known better."

"I can't just forget him."

"Do you think he'd be happy, if he could see us now?" Scott sits down across from her, on the other cot. "Dylan would hate knowing we're like this." He looks at her. "Maybe it's time," he says, hedging, "to think about trying something else—like selling the house, moving."

She stares at him. His face is side-lit, split in two, half in shadow, half in the light, hers must be too. She turns her face away from the window.

"A change might be good," he continues. "It would allow us to imagine a different future. It would be good for the kids. For us."

"You want to leave him behind. And what?" She gives a strange laugh. "And start fresh?"

"Yes. No." There is a choking sound from him and she glances sidelong at her husband, turned now towards the light of the window. He is crying, those shoulders shaking. She doesn't reach out to him. She stares at the shadow under the cot he sits on, hears the soft mewls of kittens, the tiny scrabble of claws.

"Moving house, moving forward isn't going to make either of us forget him. Nothing could do that."

"No. No way. I can't."

"Just think about it? Please. Just say you'll think about it. That you'll think about us. I can't do this alone anymore."

He comes to sit beside her on the cot. It creaks under him. The mother cat pushes open the door and sunlight splits the room, cutting across the cot between them. The cat slinks under the bed. Even from here, Michelle can hear the mother cat purr as the kittens nuzzle into her.

"Please," he says again. "Think about it."

She watches him walk out into the bright light, leaving her alone in the shadows.

She leans back against the concrete wall, which is damp and cool. She casts her eyes over the fresh flowers on the round plastic table in front of her. The five of them used to be a lopsided group at their own kitchen table, she and Scott at either end, the head and the foot, Zach and Dylan on one side of her, Astrid on the other. Now, without Dylan, they form a proper foursome. She came home one day to find only four chairs at the kitchen table. It was neat and even and it crushed her. She found Dylan's chair in the dining room they only ever use for special occasions, celebrations. She couldn't imagine ever using the dining room again.

Now there is always the empty space of Dylan. No matter how much time passes the space remains, all razored corners and endless depths. *Get through the first year*, her mother told her, *it will get easier*. And at first, she desperately wanted that. She wanted not to feel the horror of a world without her son. She kept his name in her mind, on her tongue. And her mother was right, the edges of the pain softened with time. But she needed the pain to stay fresh, constant, not worn smooth with familiarity. If it became too familiar, surely she would accept the loss, maybe even forget it. So one day she stopped speaking his name.

If only there was a way to keep her family frozen in the past, in a single, perfect, eternal moment: the five of them at their dinner table, loud and chaotic, Dylan talking about hockey with Scott, his mouth full, Zach eyeing his phone under the table, Astrid chattering about her garden or the medicine kit she was going to make. She'd insist Astrid take one more bite of vegetables before they could all have dessert. They would laugh at Dylan dancing in his seat to urge her on. Zach would hold up his phone to capture it all.

But they keep moving. Astrid has grown out of all her clothes, and Zach has become ever more sullen. Scott wants them to move. Only Dylan is stuck in time, stuck at who he was. This part of the loss still surprises her. She has pictured him graduate, met his first girlfriend, imagined all the things he could have been. He could have been anything.

She was never prone to nostalgia. She was always looking ahead. She had her life all planned out: university, then a career, marriage, and family. Still, despite her confidence, her plans, she could not have imagined the life of happiness and ease she would have. What has she ever wanted that she didn't get? She has a husband, a family, a successful career, and when it all happened for her it didn't surprise her, it just seemed her due. And there was always more to look forward to. There was always a brighter day to come, another spark in the future. For so much of her life, the opportunities for happiness just kept growing.

Michelle never used to think of herself as lucky because she didn't believe luck had anything to do with it. After all, she'd worked hard for everything she had. And yet she kept hearing it from people, from friends and acquaintances: *You're so lucky.* And she knew what her life looked like from the outside. She and Scott were good-looking and fit, and still in love. They never used to argue, not really. They had three children who were as well-behaved, as good as anyone else's and better than plenty; two boys and a girl, each their own person. A beautiful home where they hosted casual parties. Yearly vacations somewhere warm and safely adventurous.

She *was* lucky, she knows that now, and if she had thought about it more back then, it should have worried her. She should have known. Luck runs out.

Rebecca

When Rebecca enters the cooking hut with David and Jacob, Bridely is already there, though she draws back into the shadows, hoping not to be seen and sent away.

"He wasn't hurt," Jacob says, collapsing to the mat. "It's a scrape. It looks worse than it is because the salt water stopped it from clotting up. He's fine." He talks quickly, slipping between languages—his own, Bislama, English.

Rebecca nods and sits on the mat beside him, and leans against the post that holds the new plaited roof over them. These posts, pounded deep into the earth, were among the few things that weren't destroyed when the cyclone hit.

"If he was really hurt," Jacob continues, "I would have brought him back right away." He is still so much like a child, pleading when he thinks he is in trouble. David sits across from her.

Bridely slips forward and pours both Jacob and David half a cup of coconut water. Rebecca almost stops her—they need it for the laplap tomorrow—but she understands the girl's impulse to offer something, to smooth the way. David takes a sip from his and then hands it to Rebecca, who smiles at her husband's kind gesture and pretends to drink from the cup before handing it back. Bridely settles herself beside Jacob and watches as he drains his cup to the dregs.

They sit in silence, listening to the sounds of waves and wind, so much a part of her that Rebecca often fails to hear them. Above the hush of the ocean, children giggle and shout. Through the entrance of the cooking hut, she can see them playing under and around the banyan. Zach sits nearby on a large log, his hand reaching to probe at his jaw, staring at the phone in his other hand.

Perhaps this has all been a mistake—inviting the Stewarts to come, planning to return to the old place. She so wants to believe that this change will keep her children safe, but maybe there is nothing they can do. God has His plans and His ways. All she can hope for is to protect her family as long as she can. She thinks of Michelle striking her son. Rebecca might not understand much about Michelle, or the fragile, angry way she carries her grief, the brittleness of her family, but she understands the impulse Michelle had to strike her child. She has felt it herself—a fear gripping so tight that it becomes a need to strike out at something, anything. The anger that comes in the shatter of relief that the one you love is safe. But striking out isn't the solution. It only stokes the fear in the end.

"She was worried about him," Rebecca says, and finds herself believing it. "Someday you will understand."

Jacob sucks his teeth and David tenses; he hates this habit in his son. She is about to say something to defuse the tension between them when Bridely chirps in: "If you were my child, I'd smack you for that." The gap in her smile where one front tooth is missing gives her face a mischievous cast. "Rude." And she swats Jacob lightly on the arm.

He looks at the spot where Bridely's hand rests before it flutters away. Rebecca could hug Bridely for her joke, for this gift she has of lightening a conversation, for loving Jacob even though she is married and Jacob does not love her.

David puts his cup down too hard on the mat and coconut milk spatters out. Rebecca places a hand on his leg to steady him. He squeezes it but speaks anyway. "If you want to be treated like an adult, it is time you stopped acting like a child."

Jacob's face clouds a little, but his voice stays bright. "It's barely a scratch. I've had much worse." He turns his arm to show the scarred flesh on the back of it. She remembers holding him as the kleva called down from the next village pulled an arrow from Jacob's arm. He had been mistaken for quarry in the bush. "It didn't bother him at all," Jacob continues, still talking about Zach. "He's tough." Jacob presses his lips together, as though to keep himself from saying more.

"That is a dangerous place. You shouldn't have taken him there at all."

Jacob grimaces. "I've been going there since I was a child. I know that place, the sea around it. You think I would have taken him if it wasn't safe?"

"How am I supposed to know what you are doing these days?" David asks. "*You* know this place." David repeats himself, changing the emphasis: "You know *this* place."

Jacob's brow knits in confusion. "You told me to make friends with him. 'They are our guests, Jacob.'" His imitation of his father is uncanny, every resemblance from his mother's line dropped from his face and shoulders. "'No matter what you feel, you will welcome them.'"

Bridely giggles at the impression and this time Rebecca cuts her a quick look. The girl lifts a hand to her mouth, stifling the smile. Beyond them the world chatters, ever-present birdsong and the brush whispering to itself in the wind.

"Enough," David says and his voice is sharp as a new machete. It is the voice he uses to command attention at meetings and gatherings. The voice that makes it easy to believe that he knows what is right. Behind it, though, Rebecca sees the shiver of doubt in his eyes. He is trying to do what is best, but even David doesn't know what that is anymore.

"You think you are a man ready to go into the world and make his own way, but a man knows how to ask for what he needs. And you, you didn't ask me for help. Behind my back you went to Robson?" It is a question and an accusation all at once. Jacob opens his mouth, but David doesn't allow him to speak. "You want to be a Big Man, like him. You think his way is best? Robson's crops are all gone. Did you know that? All his big plans for copra and kava, for a plantation that would make more and more money, it worked for a little while. But he won't be able to feed his family this year without our help. And of course we will give it to him, despite how little we have. He's my brother, the meals we've shared and the time we've lived make us brothers. I will always help him and he will always help me. That is how it is. But he chased after money, and now he has filled your head with the same. He doesn't understand the value of the old ways— he has forgotten that, maybe, there are some ways that were better before, that there are reasons we honour our forefathers. He thinks he knows better, but he has lost everything."

David has never spoken of Robson this way before. They disagree over many things, she knows that, but she did not know it went as far as this. She thought that the two of them were in this together.

David continues, "Do you think he got you a job for your sake?" He clucks his tongue. "He will get paid for sending you to work in New Zealand, you know."

Jacob frowns. "He's your oldest friend. You always said—"

"He is and I love him," David says sadly, "but I also know who Robson is. I have always known, and I love him regardless. But I know what I can and cannot expect from him. Or I thought I did. I didn't expect that he would take you away from me for his profit." David pauses and looks over his shoulder into the bright light of the nasara, where they have sung so many songs, stomped so many dances. Where tomorrow they will try to make some kind of peace, make something new, between them and the Stewarts, them and their ancestors. David lets the quiet swell between them. "It breaks my heart that you want so much to be like him."

His disappointment sits heavily on all of them. Bridely fidgets, is about to speak, but Rebecca makes a small gesture—this is between father and son.

"I don't want to be like him." Jacob's voice is low, and edged with hurt and confusion.

"No? Then why did you go to him to find work? Why didn't you come to me?"

Jacob doesn't meet his father's eye as he speaks. "Because you are always looking backwards. You don't understand what it is like today, in Vila, for me. What am I supposed to do? You're returning to the old place that our people left. Perhaps they left for a reason. And you invite these people here"—he gestures angrily towards the nasara—"for what? To apologize to them? Why should we apologize for something that was not our doing? And how are they supposed to help us when they cannot even help themselves? They are no different than any of the others who came before. They will take what they can from us—our forgiveness, our obligations, whatever we offer—and leave us with nothing. They cannot help us."

"Of course I look to the past, but it is with one eye," David says, calmer than Jacob, though his voice is tight. "I honour our fathers' ways in order to find the best way forward. Maybe we have forgotten too many things, or maybe we haven't learned enough new things. There must be a middle road somewhere. There must be," he repeats. "And I didn't bring them here to help us. We are doing this for ourselves. Whether they are here or not, whether they take part or not, we must reckon with what brought us to here. The past must not be forgotten but reckoned with, if we are to do better."

David puts his hand on Jacob's knee.

"I understand the lure of the world, of making money and having adventures, I really do. I was drawn to it too when I was young. But that was before all the young people left, before all the young people had to leave. Who will we be when the rest of you go?"

"It won't be forever," Jacob says.

"We can't ever know that," Rebecca whispers. "We can't know when we won't see each other again."

Ouben sits with them, then each of them holds his weight in their lap, hears the small burble of him, a giggle, a chatter. He closes a fist around his mother's fingers.

"I wish I had known him more," Jacob says, looking at her, and his eyes are wet.

David stands and for a beat Rebecca worries he will walk away from his son's pleas, but instead he reaches down to him. Bridely nudges Jacob and he looks up to his father. They clasp hands and David pulls his son to his feet and then into his chest. Jacob, taller than David now, is briefly stiff in his father's embrace, but then they cling to each other.

"I wish there was a way that you could stay," David whispers, and Jacob nods against him.

Rebecca sends a silent prayer to her ancestors for the same.

A little while later, Rebecca is walking through the nasara when Anaei sprints towards her. "Mama, look!" she says, holding a tiny red-and-gold bird in her hand, made from shiny folded paper. Her fingers clasp its tail and the bird's wings flap. Rebecca's daughter beams up at her and it is impossible not to return the smile.

"Beautiful," Rebecca says, and she means her little girl, even though Anaei thinks she means the bird. Joyce sits in the banyan's shade. She pats a spot beside her and Rebecca sits. Anaei and Astrid fly their tiny birds around the nasara, holding them over their heads, chirping and laughing.

Zach holds his phone up and aims it at the girls, tracking them, dancing across the open space.

"He makes movies," Joyce says, with a touch of pride.

Rebecca thinks of what Jacob said about this family taking all that is offered to them and more, and she finds it discomfiting that this stranger will have this movie of her little girl. And that he will take it and all the others he has made away with him when he goes, and she will never see them again. That someone else will have her daughter recorded, and be able to look at her whenever they choose, if they ever think to, while she will have it only in her memory.

And still, she thinks of her little girl, playful and carefree, the ocean dancing behind her. She thinks of the sound of her laughter, her excited shrieking, thinks of it being held somewhere forever, even if Rebecca never hears it again, and there is a sad joy in that.

Rebecca nods at Joyce and watches Anaei play. She doesn't want Zach to stop.

Zach

The red-and-gold paper birds dip and rise, glinting on the screen of Zach's phone as they pursue each other, first against green bush, then the white-dotted sea. It's hard to see the details in the glare of the sun, but he's tracking Anaei's hand clutching one of the paper birds his grandmother is always making these days. The bird's sharp edges make Zach think of *Star Wars* and all those space battles he and Dylan re-enacted in the basement. His throat catches. Holding the phone steady, he reaches with his other hand to probe the pain where his mother hit him. His mother hit him, he thinks over and over. The ache offers no relief; it doesn't hurt nearly enough.

Squinting at the screen, Zach zooms out to follow the two little girls leaping across the empty space, the hard ground tamped down by generations of feet, seasons of rain and baking sun. He isn't sure what he is making, but there is something compelling in the movement captured on screen, something bright, like a memory of relief.

In a strange way he's glad his mother hit him. It makes more sense to him than the way she's been acting for the past year—glaring and withdrawn, silently avoiding him. Her hitting him is something he can point to—*see, that's how she feels about me.*

He zooms in on Anaei's smile, and when she slides out of the frame, he pans to focus on his sister until she too slips away. He does this over and over again. He'll cut the footage together into a loop of the two girls continually grinning.

He thinks of Dylan smiling up at him, his missing front tooth.

The day that Dylan died, Zach was annoyed, not just at Dylan but at everything, at life. This irritation was an ache in his body, a physical discomfort. Growing pains, his mom called them. Everything and everyone bothered him. He was annoyed that his mother was away for work, and annoyed that his brother and father were home. He was annoyed that Astrid was going to a friend's birthday party and would be a whiny brat when she came home hyped up on ice cream and cake.

That morning he'd gone to his room at the top of the house and pulled down the blind so that it was a dark cave. He turned up the Sex Pistols on his laptop and was pissed at the tinny sound of the shitty speakers. He looked at footage he'd shot on his phone, tried to find something interesting there. On the screen, he watched Dylan jump off the roof of the garage and into the pool, backwards and forwards.

Outside it was bright and hot, the kind of spring day when it's clear that summer is close and everyone is dressed in shorts. That annoyed him too. His computer beeped at him through the din of guitars. Chelsea. He ignored her, thrashed his head against the air, before turning to spot Dylan standing in the narrow doorway.

"What?" Dylan just shrugged. Zach strode to the door and stood in front of his brother, blocking him from entering the room. "Then buzz off."

"Lemme in."

"No."

He didn't hit Dylan or push him. He just stood there, shifting slightly to keep his brother from getting past him. He felt big next to Dylan, like he could hurt him if he wanted to, something Zach didn't feel around guys his own age.

"Come on, Zach!" Dylan whined, and he pushed against Zach with the whole of his weight. Zach stepped aside quickly and Dylan fell to the floor with a thud. Yet when he turned over onto his back, he smiled his gap-toothed smile at Zach like he had won.

"Dad says we can go swimming."

"So?" But the thought of the pool gave Zach a quick shiver of something almost like happiness. Swimming was something he was good at. It was in the water that Zach was faster than Dylan, always pulling him under and then zipping away when Dylan tried to retaliate. "Who cares."

"He said to come get you. You have to skim it. Check the balances."

"Forget it."

"You have to, or we can't swim." Dylan was still lying on the floor. He picked up one of Zach's dirty socks and tossed it at Zach, who kicked at it clumsily, landing a foot on Dylan's ribs instead. He hadn't meant to. Dylan began to wail before he even had a chance to apologize, which made Zach want to kick him again.

"Stop, Dill. Come on. Look, I'll come. I'll check the pool and we can go swimming, cool?" Dylan was still sobbing. "It was an accident. Jeez. You're fine."

Dylan got up then. He clutched at his side a little, but he'd stopped crying. "You'll come?"

"Yeah. Fine. Give me a minute."

Dylan flashed his smile again and then was gone.

Maybe it *was* Zach's fault. Maybe he'd hit Dylan harder than he thought and that was why he fell into the pool. Maybe Dylan really was hurt. Crazy things like that happened, didn't they? Freak injuries, that kind of thing. What if he hadn't kicked Dylan that day? What if he'd refused to do the pool chores? Then maybe . . .

"What are you shooting?"

His mom startles him and he thumbs his phone to black.

"Nothing." He starts to retreat into the shadow of the banyan tree whose leaves hang like lace over so much of this space, their dancing ground.

"Zach—"

"Look," he says, "whatever you're going to—"

"No," she interrupts. "Not whatever." She stretches towards him, and he steps back. Her hands stay suspended in the space between them, and her face begins to crumple. Zach looks out towards the sea.

How far could he swim before he was exhausted? How long would the sea hold him up? Not long enough to reach another shore.

"I don't know what came over me," she says. "I didn't mean to . . ." When she trails off, he turns back to her. She is staring at her hands, as though they don't belong to her, before dropping them to her sides. "It will never happen again."

"Right," he says.

Her shoulders tense, and so do his in response, but he sees her force them down. "What's that supposed to mean?" she asks.

"Nothing."

"Stop it, Zach. Stop shrugging and saying 'nothing' like that, it's maddening. I'm trying to talk to you."

"What am I supposed to say? Huh?" He reaches back to where he scraped his shoulder at the entrance of the cave, picks at it where the blood has dried, until he feels a sticky warmth. "I used to believe you, you know. If you said you'd do something, it was like a promise. You'd go on your trips, and every time you went, you'd say when you got home we would do something. Do you even remember that? You'd say, 'When I get home, we'll go for a bike ride to the Brickworks, you and me.' 'When I get home, we'll go to that movie you want to see.' 'When I get home, we'll go buy you that camera you've been saving up for.'" Her face blanches as he speaks, and the muscles tense, as though she is fighting against herself. "You promised we could when you got home from Banff, but it's like you never came home." He is breaking open now. He won't cry. Not here.

Over his mom's shoulder, he sees Jacob walking down to the shore, and a ripple of humiliation goes through him.

"I have to go," he says.

She reaches for him again and, as he wrenches away, his phone flies from his hand and lands with a crack against a scrape of rock that borders the nasara. They both stand stock-still, staring at the small glinting rectangle there on the ground. Zach bends to pick it up, doesn't look at it, only holds it in his palm.

"Zach, I'm trying to say I'm—" his mom starts.

"Forget it. You've already said enough," he says and walks away towards the shore.

———

He overheard her the first time he snuck out. It was early fall, a whole season after Dylan drowned, and sometime just before midnight he kicked through fallen leaves. He'd been surprised by how truly chilly the night was this early in the season, and his breath fogged in front of him as he turned for home. The upstairs windows of houses glowed warm on either side of the road; the air was scented with the occasional puff of woodsmoke. His own house was at the end of the street, and it both pulled and repulsed him. From the outside you'd never know something so terrible had happened there. He hated that everything in this neighbourhood felt safe when it wasn't.

He turned onto a side street that looped him around to his back gate.

In the yard, the winter cover sagged over the mostly empty pool. A small half-frozen swamp of leaves and rainwater collected in it near the diving board. You could drown in that much water.

He slipped into the mudroom, his bare hands and face burning against the sudden warmth. The house felt silent and empty, and he wondered if they'd finally left him. If they had just been waiting for him to leave so they could all disappear.

When he reached the top of the stairs, the door to Dylan's room was partially open and he could hear voices coming from inside. He paused, tensed in the dark of the hallway, to make sure he wouldn't be caught. As he began to creep past he caught his name, his mother's voice desperate.

"Where the hell was Zach? He should have been there!"

His body went numb. He waited for his father to say something. When he didn't, Zach slipped his hand into his pocket for the lighter he kept there. If he flicked it, they would hear. But so what? Maybe if they heard him, they'd have to talk to him.

He flicked the lighter, the sound and light sparking in the shadows, and he heard them freeze in Dylan's room.

He waited, but they didn't come out, didn't say anything more. Zach extinguished the light and slunk up to his bedroom where he blasted The Clash too loud in his headphones until his ears rang and he couldn't hear anything anymore.

———

The screen of his phone is cracked, but Zach plays back a video to make sure that his phone and camera still work. He scrolls through and picks one at random, and it's the scratchy music he recognizes first, the bright sound of it cutting through the shush and heave of the ocean. And then there is Dylan dancing to the stupid music from the video game he loved. But Zach didn't film this.

Dylan must have taken his phone and recorded this in the basement. A message in a bottle. He watches his brother dance, a smile on his face, no missing teeth so this is from the winter before the accident. When the song ends, he turns around and shakes his butt at the camera, slaps it once, twice, and then comes towards the lens, sticks his tongue out at his brother, and stops the recording. Zach stares at the frozen image of his brother.

"You all right?"

When Zach looks up, Jacob is there, a plastic paint bucket in his hand, one of the huge ones like they sell at Home Depot to store crap in.

"What's that?" Zach asks.

"Shit from the beach." Jacob shrugs. "All this crap gets washed up from other places. Mostly garbage, but once in a while there's something good." The bucket is full of six-pack rings and plastic bags and small unidentifiable bits of washed-out garbage tangled with seaweed. Zach can't imagine finding anything useful in there. "Sometimes there are those little toy bricks too—you know, Lego." Zach actually smiles at this. "Once, I found a watch. It didn't work, but I sold it in Vila when I was away at school."

"That's cool," Zach says as he slides his phone into his pocket and crouches down to start picking at the bright plastic at his feet, tossing it into the bucket. "What are you going to do with all this stuff?"

"I'd like to do something cool with it, like cut it up and tile a floor with it or something. I don't know. There's not much use for most of it, and nowhere to take it. It'll probably just get dumped in the bush somewhere."

Zach swallows, his throat tight. "The tile floor sounds cool, though. Like a mosaic."

"Yeah." They sort through the rubbish together, separating out colours. "You sure you're okay?" Jacob asks after a while. "I didn't mean to get you in trouble."

"Oh, no," Zach says, and his face feels hot, though maybe it is only the sun. He sits down on the sand. "My mom's just, I dunno, she's different now. She didn't use to be like that. Sorry. I mean, I wish it hadn't happened, you know? Maybe I shouldn't have gone, but I'm glad I did, really. It wasn't your fault. It's just a scratch."

"That's what I told them."

Zach wants to hold on to this connection between them. He needs to. "Wanna see a video of him? My brother." Jacob nods. Zach cues up the video and hands his phone to Jacob, who smiles when he watches it and then takes out his own phone and flips it open, taps at the keypad and hands it to Zach.

"Ouben?" Zach asks and Jacob nods again.

They sit on the shore and look at their brothers.

Michelle

Zach is walking away from her. She was trying to reach him, but her hands stretched out in front of her are empty.

"Mommy!" Astrid is suddenly at Michelle's hip, a sticky hand grasping hers. In her daughter's other hand, one of Joyce's folded birds is wilting. No number of birds will make what happened right. And yet Astrid is sunburned and sweaty and happier than she has been in months. Michelle can almost feel the ache in her daughter's cheeks from the width of her smile. Her own mouth twitches but doesn't break.

"Anaei said her mommy would take us to see a magic place. Can we go?"

A short distance away Rebecca is crouched in front of Anaei, who stares at the ground. It's a tableau familiar to Michelle from schoolyards and playgrounds—the little girl has spoken out of turn, the invitation came from the child, not from the mother. Michelle should say no, but her daughter is still smiling up at her and this is something she can give her child, isn't it? She tries to make her voice chipper. "Doesn't that sound like fun! Of course we can go."

Astrid makes a little skip and hop in place before spinning to run towards Anaei. Astrid's long legs are a surprise, the shorts riding up too high, her heels hanging over the backs of her flip-flops, as she smiles glowingly at Anaei, whose own face is bright and open in the sun. It is as if Michelle has skipped forward in time. She shuts her eyes a moment and then breathes deep and walks over to Joyce.

"Anaei wants to show Astrid something. She's excited," Michelle says to her mother by way of apology, to explain why she is going to disappear and leave her son behind again. She stares down at the beach where Zach is crouched with Jacob, imagines what he might be saying about her. "Can you keep an eye on him?" she asks. Joyce gives her a look, one Michelle has seen all her life—her mother's disappointment at whatever Michelle is choosing to do, but supporting her anyway. Joyce nods.

Michelle turns to Rebecca, but doesn't meet her eyes. "Shall we?" she says.

She presses upwards along a narrow path, the bush pushing in on them from all sides. Creepers grasp towards ankles to try to trip them, or tangle down from overhead. Hidden birds chirp and sing and make the occasional flutter of shadow out of the corner of Michelle's eye. She is following Rebecca, who follows Astrid and Anaei, who set the pace. The girls stop to stoop over thick lines of ants, or to look up at birds and the lacy overlay of trees. Michelle pants her breath to normal each time the girls pause.

Neither she nor Rebecca speak. There is just the sound of one foot in front of the other, the bush alive around them. The air is so close and heavy here, wet and thick. It smells of green and earth after rain. It smells of the sea. There is nothing in this place that reminds her of home, and Michelle doesn't know if she loves it or hates it for that. Nothing to remind her of any place she has ever been before, not even the tropical resorts they have visited in the Caribbean. Those were all neat and curated, the landscape domesticated by armies of hidden gardeners, the beaches and paths swept clean, the blooming plants dead-headed. Everything was safe and sanitized, she sees now—a Disney version of a tropical destination.

What was she thinking, dragging her family here? That somehow *she* would be different if she was *somewhere* different? That she would find some kind of peace here, or forgiveness?

Up ahead, Anaei and Astrid gather leaves, holding them like hands of cards, trading them back and forth over their shoulders. Michelle's own hand stings and throbs with the memory of her son's cheek. She wishes she could take it back, take everything back.

If Josephine had never come here, then what? Would Dylan still be alive? How far back do you have to go to undo the past?

Her legs burn as they climb, while Rebecca and the children seem to move so easily ahead of her. She leans into the discomfort, kneads her thumb into the palm that struck her child, refusing to let the throb of it fade. The trees open up overhead and Michelle leans back to watch a single airplane as it crosses the sky, whisking people like her around the world to places like this.

People like her.

But she isn't who she used to be. That's what Zach said. And she realizes he's right. She can barely remember who she was before Dylan died, but whoever she was, she never came home.

Or at least that's what it feels like. She left herself somewhere up in the air, on that airplane.

————

She was in Banff, flown there first-class by an equity firm facing a crisis after a string of misconduct allegations. She had led workshops for senior management and staff, mediated discussions between them. Some ground had been gained, but there was still so much work to do.

"We just might have to book you again, back in the city," the CEO had said to her the night before, as they sipped Manhattans in the bar and watched the sunset against the mountains. He was flirting and she liked it. Harmless, but flattering. She had one too many drinks and slipped back to her room alone.

Now she lounged in the slight sulphur smell of a hot spring and thought about nothing. Her head throbbed a little from the altitude and the bourbon, but she didn't mind. There was not a single demand on her. The workshops had been challenging, and she was exhausted but content. It wasn't a high peak of happiness, sure to plummet away, but a larger contentment.

Floating in the mineralled water, squinting at the bright blue of sky and the blinding white of the mountain tops, she thought about staying an extra day. She could change her flight, hold on to her room; she deserved it and Scott would understand. Everything could wait. Astrid and whatever plan she'd cooked up to make candles the way pioneers did could wait. Dylan's never-ending parade of hockey games could wait. Zach's video games, the latest movie he was shooting with his phone, all of it could wait. She would stay.

She has relived that moment over and over again—her lazy bliss, the casualness with which she selfishly thought her children could wait for her. Who was that woman floating there in that pool while her son drowned in another? She can't understand how she wasn't ripped apart right then and there, didn't feel his agony all those miles away. She had always felt their hurts as though they were her own. With each birth, her body became a sympathetic tool, some kind of machine to reflect and deflect all of their pain; but on that day it failed her, because she failed him.

She thought about not going home, and so her son drowned.

She chokes in the wet humid air of the Pacific, something rising in her. A longing—for her son, yes, but also for who she was, how easy everything once was.

A cab dropped her off back at her hotel. The world was sharp and clear in a way that it never was in Toronto, the mountains cut out from the sky, the trees from the mountains. She was planning what she would do with her free evening when she realized her name was being called, rupturing the quiet.

The young man behind the front desk said the word *emergency*. What crossed her mind then? All the gruesome, terrible imaginings that you learn to live with when you have a child. You cannot protect them from everything—strangers, car accidents, and with boys like Dylan, the belief in their own invincibility. Did she think of Zach or Astrid first? Did she think of the pool? No, it was too early in the season, and it was cold where she was. She didn't think of the pool.

She tried to calm herself, but Scott wouldn't call if it wasn't really an emergency.

Back in her room her phone showed dozens of missed calls. She imagined the sound of it echoing in the empty room, like some mad bird, while she floated in the stink of the hot spring. She hit Scott's number. No answer. Again and again. She saw his phone ringing on their kitchen counter, in his car, clasped in his lifeless hand, and her throat caught again. No. No. He had called her. It was his number.

She called her mother.

"Michelle." Her mother's voice was cracked, distant. Michelle's thumb moved to hang up. If she hung up now, she wouldn't know. If she didn't know, everything would be fine. Her thumb hovered over the red button.

She didn't speak.

Did she speak?

"Sweetheart," her mom said. She hadn't called her *sweetheart* in a long time.

"No."

"Sweetheart—"

No. No. No.

Looking back now, she must have known. She was already falling, the floor rushing up to her, she was screaming as her knees hit the thin carpet, the concrete underneath. She was screaming into the phone, into the void even as her mother spoke.

"It's Dylan."

She bargained.

If she got to the airport and there was no lineup at security, then Dylan would be alive. If she was sent to a line without the body scans, he'd be alive.

If her plane crashed . . .

In a pocket of turbulence she longed for the plane to ricochet out of control and kill them all, longed for her body to be tossed up to the ceiling the way she'd seen in movies, slammed about the cabin. If they all died, then Dylan could live. She would do it, kill them all so he would live.

She prayed for her own death.

Then Toronto was underneath them—the spread of the city butting up against the blank spill of the lake. She longed to plunge into that icy blackness, be consumed by it. The last-minute miracle of death.

They couldn't land. If they landed, he would be dead. In her mind the plane crashed over and over again. She saw flames and smoke and heard the screams.

They touched down safely and her heart stopped.

Walking through the airport, she stared at every little boy she passed, hoping she would see her son, pleading to trade their lives for his. How dare they live?

At the hospital, she held his body, small and cold and so fragile, in a room that must have been the morgue. She touched her fingers to his, held his palm to her chest, measured him against her. He smelled of the swimming pool, of a summer not yet arrived. A summer he would not see.

Dime-sized wounds on the knobs of his spine, the bowed lines of his ribs. She touched them gently.

She hadn't let herself think of his last moments, even while she imagined the violence of trying to hold Dylan fast to life, Scott thumping on his chest, his back scraping concrete. The feel of his ribs, an insubstantial cage, under the fat meat of a palm.

The trauma of trying to resuscitate him had been marked on his body, even while the drowning left no mark. She pitied Scott having to do it. God knows what she would have done herself.

In the days that followed she was a shell, scraped empty of everything but a howling pain that moved like a blizzard through her. She clung to Zach and Astrid and wept against them when they felt wrong in her arms. Zach was too long and awkward, his body already turning to a man's, filling out like his father. Astrid too delicate, and quiet.

Now, though, her arms long for Zach so much. Even Astrid is drifting from her.

All those dark first days, Dylan's name was on her tongue, as though she could incant him back to life. His name was the only thing that kept her afloat.

What happened? She asked the question over and over. Asked it into the darkness of their bedroom, standing in the doorway unable to sleep, hating Scott for finding peace in slumber, before dragging him back to her own waking hell.

"What happened?" she asked into her phone, leaving the question on his voicemail when he left the house. *Where were you?*

The most important moment of her life and she was not even there.

———

They come out on a high path that overlooks the ocean, white-caps flashing in a code Michelle can't decipher, all the way to the horizon. She stops and stares, her daughter's chirps drifting farther away, back into the shadow of the path. If she stares long enough, maybe she will know what to do. Or maybe she'll lose everything she still has left.

Dylan slips from the shadows and stands beside her, and her breath settles a little in her body. Together, they stare at the infinite sea.

How far to the other shore? he asks.

Far.

Yeah. Can't swim it.

No.

Imagine, he says, *being capsized out there.*

She does. She thinks of whalers, and of the earliest people who charted these islands in their dugout canoes—Polynesians, Melanesians, and Micronesians. How they sailed between distant shores, believing other places existed because the sea told them they did. Such faith in what lay ahead, what lay on a far shore.

She tries to imagine a new house with Scott, with Astrid and Zach. It's almost impossible. How could she live in any room that Dylan has never set foot in, never laughed in.

Never been hurt in.

How could she do it?

How could Scott ask her to?

"Mommy!" Astrid's voice brings her back, her daughter taking Dylan's place beside her. She is excited, bounces from one tiny foot to the other. "We're here, look!"

Michelle doesn't see anything to indicate that they are anywhere special. It is all just green, more greens than she knew existed. The soft first-spring green, deep emeralds, greens so dark they are blue.

She doesn't say anything as Anaei takes Astrid by the hand and slips behind a curtain of leaves.

Rebecca

Rebecca and Michelle sit in the mouth of the cave. The sun never reaches the back wall and coolness radiates from its depths. Nearby, Astrid and Anaei play in the shards of light cutting through the trees, their chatter quick and close. The bush makes the place feel sheltered, hidden.

Anaei has loosened over the last two days, excited by her new friend and by the ceremony tomorrow, her own part in it. She has helped with the weaving and the sewing without having to be nagged. She doesn't tangle her fingers in the cord Rebecca has tied around her throat but rather touches it absently, softly.

That's why Rebecca agreed to show Astrid this place. Anaei wanted to share this. Her daughter doesn't yet understand that there is a balance to be found between sharing and protecting.

"It's a place we go to," Anaei told Astrid on the walk, "when we are sad about Ouben." And while that is true, it is not the entirety of what this place is.

"People have come here for a very long time," Rebecca explains to Michelle. "Women, mostly. For us, it is a place of refuge. It is said a woman who didn't want to marry the man who was chosen for her ran away from him and her family and came here to hide."

"He was a mean man," Anaei interrupts.

Rebecca continues. "He already had a wife who he treated badly. She was often limping and bruised, so the girl who was to be his new wife ran away. He chased after her, but when he arrived here, he couldn't find her no matter how hard he searched. She knew this place better than anyone did. For a long time, the place was tabu and people were afraid of the dangerous spirits that lived here. But the girl loved someone so much that, even though she was scared, she came here, hoping to hear his voice through the crack deep in the wall of the cave. She came here and tended the plants nearby, and left food and gifts for the spirits who eventually began to whisper to her. When she ran from the man she was to marry, the cave swallowed her in its darkness and made her invisible. After two days, the man went away and left her alone in the cave. She was never seen again, but it is said that she lived here the rest of her life. Other women brought her food and water, and the spirits nourished her. She became a healer for them and this place became a place for women to find peace." As she finishes, Rebecca sets out a small packet of food, her own offering for the spirits here.

Michelle looks around her, and Rebecca wonders what she sees. Does she feel the power that still pulses, however weakly, from the earth? Does she notice the faint trace of handprints on the walls? There is fear and hope and peace embedded in the very walls of the cave. Rebecca has felt their spirits when she presses her own hands over the prints, divining the stories that brought each woman here, connecting her in an unending line to that first hero ancestor who recognized the power of this place. There is comfort in this connection, less an erasure of her own suffering, her own fear and hope, than an embrace.

"Maybe she came here," Michelle says, a slight plea in her voice. "Josephine." And Rebecca knows then that Michelle doesn't grasp the importance of the story. She simply sees a cave, something empty and dark, that is only meaningful because of how her own people might have marked it. "There is a cave mentioned in her papers. Are there others? Maybe she came here," she repeats, pressing her thumb into the meat of her opposite palm.

All the losses and loves that have been marked in this cave, the worries and dreams that have shaped this place, and yet Josephine is the one who is named. Even the first woman to come here, her name is lost. Her betrothed's name is remembered, but Rebecca won't think it in this place. If Josephine was brought here, she came as Michelle has done, to stare and scrutinize and to record it. She didn't understand, as Michelle doesn't. How has everything changed since that time and yet nothing? Irritation crawls up Rebecca's spine. She fidgets and thinks of leaving. Normally, she has to force herself away from the cave, but with Michelle here, she wishes they had never come.

Rebecca reaches for the cord at her throat, rolls it between her fingers. She will make a memorial to Ouben, so his name is spoken a hundred years from now, a thousand. She imagines his tiny handprint on the wall, his name handed down story by story, generation to generation, as they have always done. Anaei will carry his name in her heart; she will name her own son for him.

"There are a lot of caves on the island and a lot of women came here," Rebecca says, her voice strong in her throat, fully come back to her at last. "Some still do."

"Or course," Michelle says. "I didn't mean to . . ."

"What didn't you mean?" Rebecca asks when Michelle trails off.

"I'm sorry," Michelle says.

The woman is always apologizing, Rebecca thinks. The words come easy to her, but they're hollow.

The silence swells to fill the cave and Rebecca settles into it, familiar with the feel of the air here—open, anticipatory. The girls still play, the light making shadows of their bodies. They are digging a garden of some kind at the edge of the bush. But Michelle insists on cutting through the quiet. "Josephine left her child behind," she says, indignant, into the breath of the cave. "I can't even imagine that. Though there are stories that the child wasn't really William's son."

"Blood isn't the only thing that makes a family," Rebecca cuts in, thinking of Jacob, as much a part of her heart and body as Anaei and Ouben.

The woman's lips draw tight. "Maybe," she says. "Maybe his son just didn't want to be associated with him, with what he did. Coming here and . . ." She doesn't finish whatever it is she means to say.

Rebecca thinks about this, about Jacob trying to distance himself from his father. But Jacob would never deny David.

"But how could she have just left him?" Michelle asks. "She must have known she would never see him again. And if she had known, how could she ever let him out of her sight?" Rebecca understands this plea, would give almost anything for one more moment, one more glimpse of her own son. "It serves them right," Michelle says.

The woman stands and walks into the cave, dragging her fingers along its damp wall, and Rebecca flinches at her presumption.

It's true, Rebecca has done this too, but this is her place. It has become a new kind of church for her since Ouben's death. She has looked for the crack, the entrance to the other world where the first woman listened, and she has hoped to hear Ouben's voice. Michelle does not belong here.

Rebecca wants to tell her not to touch these walls. She wants to tell her to listen, to say that *sorry* is more than a word. Instead, she says firmly, "Please come and sit."

Michelle returns to the mouth of the cave, squints at Astrid and Anaei. "I couldn't do it. I can't." She squeezes the hand that struck her child into a fist, loosens it again.

Rebecca will never see Ouben as a young man the way Jacob is, growing away from her, from David.

"Ouben is always with me," she says. "I hear him, feel him. But this is where he is the closest." She whispers his name, as though calling him, repeats it to feel the shape. His name is a soft coo on her tongue, the way she soothed him, the way his mouth pursed into an *O* of surprise before he smiled, the way his laugh sounded, round like waves across the deep. "Ouben. Ouben. I brought him to this place. I told him I would keep him safe." She is crying now, can feel the wet on her face. She doesn't care if Michelle can see it in the shadow of the cave. Michelle's eyes flit away and return to her several times before she meets Rebecca's gaze. Then her eyes cloud with unshed tears. "Why?" Rebecca asks. "What did I do wrong?"

"It's not your fault," Michelle begins, and then barks a short sound that might be a laugh, might be a yelp. She inhales deeply and then continues. "At least, that's what people tell me. That it wasn't my fault. But it was my job, my only job, to protect him, and I didn't. I wasn't even there when it happened. I should have . . . but I decided to—" She stops. "I guess I'm the same as them."

Rebecca feels herself opening up, the way she only does in this place. This woman has lost her child too—they have that in common at least. It is a beginning. "When Ouben died, my voice went." Her hand flutters in the air, a restless bird taking flight.

"I don't understand," Michelle says.

"It was gone, my voice. He took it with him. I wanted to talk of him constantly, speak his name. I needed to feel like he was still alive, that we still shared him—David and I, Anaei and I. My father and mother never even met him." Pain upon pain. "I will never meet his children. *Ouben* is the only word I want to say." She repeats his name silently to herself, and her little boy's laugh echoes in her mind.

"Ouben is still alive in us. Anaei loves to tell stories about him; she giggles about him every night before she goes to sleep." Rebecca can feel herself smiling now. "And now that you know about him, he is alive in you. You will return home and he will go on and on and on. To stop saying his name would be another kind of death."

Michelle looks at Astrid and emotions flicker across her face—fear, anger. Sadness. She whispers, "He drowned in our backyard. Alone. No one was there."

Rebecca nods. She doesn't say anything. What is there to say? Only his name. "Dylan," she says.

Astrid glances over at her and smiles a little, then repeats her brother's name.

"You know, he would have loved it here. This cave," Michelle says, the words coming a bit faster. "He would have gone all the way to the back of it, tried to find a passage out. He was brave. Silly." She makes another strangled sound, then is quiet again.

Rebecca can almost feel the boy between them, the way she feels Ouben. She thinks of backyard pools like some white people have in Vila; she thinks of this mother flying away from her son. A heat flares inside her.

"My son would not have died if he was yours," Rebecca says and knows that this is true. She fumes at everything she cannot control. "The cyclone that shouldn't have come when it did. We weren't prepared for it, but why should we be? We are not the ones causing these changes. And yet these storms grow worse every year, causing more and more damage, because you refuse to see what you are doing to the rest of the world. Our islands are going to be swallowed by the sea." She lifts her hands to her lips. There are so many things that Michelle has that she does not. "Your son had every opportunity. Everything that could have been done for him. Your son would not have died like Ouben did. From lack of medicine, lack of attention."

Michelle's face goes red. She looks away and will not meet Rebecca's eyes. Rebecca doesn't care, imagines Ouben's ancestors, Anaei's, sitting opposite Josephine.

"William and Josephine. They didn't care about us. They came here to change things. They never wanted to understand, they never wanted to be part of this place." She is trying to find the words. "We are supposed to fit into your world, shape ourselves to your ways, but then we are left out of it, denied all the wonders that it has to offer—clean water, electricity, safe homes, medicine to save a child. We pay the cost, but receive what?" She says it again: "My son would not have died if he was yours. No one cares about my son's death."

Rebecca is surprised at herself, at the voice she has found. She waits for Michelle to say something.

They sit in silence for a long time.

Faina

The sound of wooden drums called across the forest, the tattoo of it sharp in the twilight. People came out from their cooking huts to gather at the nasara, where they sat in clusters, men in one circle, the women surrounding them. The wind rustled above them. Clouds sailed beyond, dancing across blossoming stars.

"Who saw them last?" Kaipar was already asking when Faina arrived with Father to the dancing grounds. It was unusual for anyone to speak before the drum had finished its call and everyone was assembled. As Faina and Father took their places, Masai's mother began clutching at her throat and wailing, and at her side her daughter echoed her. Nako's uncle sat staring at the ground. Faina's stomach churned and she swallowed against the acrid fear that coated the back of her tongue.

"Masai and Nako are gone," Telau said, squeezing Faina's hand. Telau's face was wet, her eyes glossy with tears. "No one has seen them since yesterday."

Voices flew. Where were they seen last? At their gardens, at the stream, on the shore fishing. All of the sightings were from yesterday or the day before.

Faina's eyes blurred the world with tears. She thought of Masai's hand on her arm, leading her away from the Uplanders, away from Albi. She added her wails to the others.

"Enough!" Louvu yelled over the din. "We don't even know yet if we should be mourning!"

"It must be the Uplanders," Sero said. "They accused us of betraying them with the missi, of wanting to injure them. They have struck us first, like the cowards they are." He shook his head, spat outside the circle. "They're afraid of the alliance we have made with the mission and so they killed our best and strongest."

"We should avenge them!" someone else called.

The voices moved fast in the gloom and confusion, echoing up into the trees. Voices Faina had known her whole life sounded like strangers, unanchored by the loss of Masai and Nako. She thought of the way the two of them tussled with each other, watched over her.

"No!" shouted another voice.

Faina didn't look to see who it was. What did she care who spoke? Masai was a dark, empty spot inside her. She scratched the letters of his name into the dirt, as though to conjure him. She should have shown him this magic, these symbols that meant him.

She wiped his name away and wrote it again, careful to keep her hand close to her thigh, where no one could see.

All the men were talking, the normal order of discussions giving way to fear and panic. "It is those new strangers who came to the mission. They have taken people before when they did not get what they wanted."

Father stood, drawing attention. He shifted his weight from foot to foot and pressed his lips together. "How could it be these new strangers?" Father asked, his voice calm in the tumult. "Their canoe sailed away. We watched it go. In the dawn the sea was empty. Maybe it was the Uplanders. They are angry at the change in the exchange value and don't want to honour their promise to us."

Another wail went up from Masai's mother, others joining her this time. Nako's mother had died two harvests ago and Faina was struck by her absence. She ground her teeth against the fear and anger and sadness that rose in her, but as she traced Masai's name and hers over each other into the dirt she felt a power rising up in her. He must still be nearby.

Kaipar stood, walked to the centre of the nasara, and waited for everyone to quiet. "What is more likely," he asked, his voice low, soothing, "that these strangers, who we do not know, who we have no quarrel with, would take our smartest, strongest? Or that the Uplanders, who are upset in the alteration in the marriage exchange, in the alteration of alliances, would?" He paused, letting them take this in. "The Uplanders are afraid of us! They fear our spirits and ancestors. That is why they want to be allied together with marriages and children. They skulk at the edges of our lands, wanting all that we have." There began to be murmurs of agreement. What he said was true.

He did not move to sit or to concede the floor to anyone else. "If Masai and Nako are alive, we will bring them home. And if they are dead, they will be avenged." There was a chorus of approval from the men. Kaipar smiled as he returned to his spot.

Louvu stood and lifted his hands for quiet. "We will go and speak first to Will-am. We will ask him what he knows of Masai and Nako." A muttering rose around him. "We will be certain. If they don't know anything, then we will take vengeance on those who would dare harm our men." He stood still, bringing calm; even the wind seemed to obey and allow for long moments of consideration, the ancestors doing their part.

Faina strained to hear what they whispered. She prayed that Masai and Nako were alive, for the Uplanders and Albi, for Josephine. For herself.

The next morning, the sky was shrouded in grey clouds stretching in every direction, as though they had been trapped by the high hills of the Upland. The sea was calm, reaching away to the horizon, which was close today. The air at the edge of the mission did not move. It felt as though a storm was coming.

Louvu drew the handful of men he had brought with him to a stop at the mission fence, just as Masai had stopped them at the Uplanders' boundary. Talawan hurried to usher them in, before retreating to her hut. William sat on his porch, and cowered at their approach as though he knew why they were there.

He recovered quickly, and stood on the porch so he towered over Louvu. "What do you want now?" he asked, and his eyes flitted across Faina before darting away again, looking anywhere but at the men in front of him.

"Two of our men have gone missing," Louvu said. "The ones who went with you to the Upland. Where are they?" He was measured as always and Faina was glad that he was the one who had come, not Kaipar.

William glanced about, nervous. Josephine came out of their hut. "What is going on?" she asked.

He scowled at her and she recoiled. "I don't know," he said to her, and then turned and repeated the same words to Louvu.

"I don't know. How should I know?" He sounded small, even as he puffed up his chest, tried to stand taller.

Josephine shifted her feet. She didn't look at Faina; instead she stared out to the sea, as though she would rather be anywhere than where she was, before glaring hard at her husband's back.

"How can you not know?" Louvu asked with a careful smile and Faina's help. "You say your great father in the sky sees everything, judges everything. You say he speaks to you, that he tells you everything." Louvu paused, but when William gave no answer, he continued. "Which is the lie?"

"The Lord works in mysterious ways!" William's voice boomed like a wave on shore as he thumped his hand on the railing of the porch.

The word, though, troubled Faina. She stopped William, then turned towards Josephine and tried to echo him. "Mis-ter-ous?"

"Strange," Josephine said as she stepped forward. "Things we cannot know." She pointed at her temple, waved her hands around. "Things He does not see fit for us to know."

William returned to his seat on the porch as though dismissing Louvu. "Perhaps your men are being punished for their evil ways," he said. "They are in God's hands now, and you must ask Him for mercy. You all must repent if they are to be saved. I will pray for your men too, ask Him to deliver them."

Faina hoped that William still had some power to wield, but she would not count on it. She would do what she could.

She entered the cave with a murmur of greeting.

She knew she shouldn't be alone on the roads, alone in this place, not when they didn't know what had happened to Masai and Nako. There was an uneasy energy on the island, hissing through the trees with the wind, vibrating the ground beneath her feet. Where were they? Who had taken them? She swallowed as she crossed the cave's threshold—she hoped they were still alive.

She sat in the cool shelter of the cave and listened. She could hear her blood in her ears, the voices of her foremothers. She could hear them whisper all around her, in the heavy stillness of the island.

After they had left the mission, some of the men talked of killing William, others of attacking the Upland village. She understood the urge. And if Masai's blood had been spilled, she would want some spilled in exchange—she wouldn't even care whose. But blood would not bring him back.

She unrolled the bible page from the bamboo she kept buried in the garden, and held it in her hand. William's stories told of people returning from the dead. Jesus. And someone else. There were so many stories. Maybe there was a way. Maybe she could ask Josephine how it was done.

No. Josephine wouldn't have the power. William might but he would not tell her such tabu things. But it could be done. She stood and walked the perimeter of the cave, her hand on the wall, tracing the stained handprints of all the women who had come here before.

There were places on the island where the spirits of the dead found the entrance to the hidden dancing grounds, where they would sing and feast for the rest of time. This was one of them. At the back of the cave was a crack that ran deep into the centre of the island, into the ancestors' world.

Faina stood in front of the crack, felt the breath of air beyond it. "Masai!" She shouted his name and it stayed close in the cave. "Come back! Please."

She waited to hear his voice. She strained for the smallest sound on the movement of air from that place, but there was nothing. And that brought a tiny sense of relief. If he were to return, perhaps he would be angry at being called back, at not being able to stay in the dancing grounds.

Still, she wanted his hand in hers. She wanted him to take her away. She was safe with him.

She returned to where she had left the page from Josephine's bible and peered at it. Some of the words made sense to her now, but there were still so many she did not know. Would she ever know them all? Were these all the words ever written? How could anyone know all of the words?

She bent to make a small fire, the wood spinning in her hands, warming them, and fed soft bits of dried leaves into the glowing spark. She would send all the power she had acquired to Masai and perhaps he would at least know that he was still loved here. They had no body to bury, no way to plant him in this place that had birthed him. He would no longer be a part of them.

When the fire was burning steadily, she sat back and watched it flicker. The smoke crept along the floor, towards the back of the cave. She watched where it slipped into the crack. She banked the fire to glowing coals, picked up the page and looked again at the words there, wondering when she might possess such a thing again. She touched the corner of the page to an ember. It curled as it burned, first glowing then darkening to black, the way leaves did. She set the page into an indentation of a nearby rock and watched it turn to black ash, the words disappearing, the story disappearing.

When the page was nothing but powdery ash, Faina pressed her hand to it, until the black seeped into every line of her palm.

She walked to the crack in the rock and spoke his name into the depths of the earth. She whispered her desire and pressed her blackened hand to the stone.

Faina stumbled away from the cave, exhausted and spent. She was nearing the village when she saw the spirits walking abroad in the daylight, silent and clinging to each other. They were unrecognizable in their weakness, in the way they leaned together, naked and bloodied, their faces wan and sharp. Were they in her world, or she in theirs? Had she slipped through to the other side? Was she dead? Her heart sounded in her chest, alive as the sea.

Faina's breath caught in her throat. "Please," she pleaded with the apparitions, "don't hurt me."

It was her fault. She had brought his spirit back here by scratching his name into the dirt, into the flesh on the inside of her arm, a temporary tattoo she had made again and again in the days he was gone. *Masai. Masai. Masai.* She should not have brought him back, not like this.

"Faina."

Her name was a gasp, barely any sound to it. Something heard in the night, in the voices of the spirits. Masai's face was a sickly shade, his lips split; the flesh was swollen and misshapen. She went to him, not caring what might happen, and touched first Masai, who flinched away from her, and then Nako, whose skin burned like fire.

And then the world crashed back down on her, like a rogue wave, as the sounds and yells of those behind her in the village called Masai and Nako's names. A new kind of wailing. They were not ghosts; they were here, returned to them.

There was a chaos of shouts and tears, the stamping of feet. Someone struck the slit drum so it called out to those who were still in the bush or at the gardens to hurry back. The light was already bleeding from the sky. Sero waved the crowd back, and instructed the men to help the returned to his own hut, one of the largest, where a fire was blazing bright against the encroaching sky.

The dark came and it began to rain.

Those who could not fit into Sero's home huddled outside in the wet and mud to hear what had happened. Faina wove her way into the hut unnoticed and tucked herself into a corner. She rubbed her thumb over Masai's name on her arm. She had done this. The inside of Masai's arm was scraped and raw in the same place.

Masai's mother brought food and Sero called for particular leaves and roots, then chanted over the wounds on the men's bodies, pressed his leaf medicine to their bruises, scrapes, cuts. Nako seemed to fall into a deep sleep, but Masai's eyes darted around at all of them, searching their faces.

"What happened?" Kaipar finally demanded, and the murmuring that had been present since the men's arrival ceased.

"They took us on their large canoe," Masai said. He looked as though he was uncertain of his words, his tongue clumsy in his mouth against his broken lips.

"Will-am?" a voice asked.

There was a shushing and another voice that chided, "He does not have one of the great canoes."

It took Masai a long time to tell his story. When he winced in pain, Faina did too. She could almost feel his agony. Sometimes he lapsed into extended silences, as though he might still be far-away on the sea. Nako occasionally surfaced to consciousness, but did not speak.

Faina wished she could cradle Masai's head, sing to him, as she had to Marakai almost two seasons ago.

The men who wanted the Uplanders' tabu trees had approached Masai and Nako when they were fishing.

"They asked us to come with them to their ship. They said they wanted to make amends for their violence. I thought I understood them." Masai shook his head, a cloud crossing his features, as though what was to come was his own fault. The cloud blew away quickly, and his jaw set as he continued. "They promised us they would give us the weapon that William has. We talked"—he put his hand on Nako, who flinched under the touch, making Masai pull away—"and we thought it would be good to have their weapon."

She could picture them rowing their double-hulled canoe alongside the massive cliff of the ship. Masai would have been excited, while Nako would have been nervous, perhaps urged him to turn back.

There were so many men on board, Masai explained, but one was clearly in charge of all the others. He barked and gave orders and did not appear to spend any time listening to those around him. Masai and Nako were given food and drink that he said smelled sharp and burned their throats, that made their thoughts thick and slow. Not like the quiet whisper of kava, but a swamping that made the men around them louder and more chaotic.

"And then I woke and couldn't see anything and wondered if I was dead."

There was a clicking of tongues, another shushing. A drip of rainwater slid down Faina's back. She closed her eyes so she could see Masai's story, and felt the move of the ocean under her feet making her dizzy and nauseous, felt the darkness creep up on her.

He described the next two days, waking to a blinding stench, caught up in strong ropes. There were others in the place with them who coughed and vomited and shat on the ground. They didn't want whatever curse these men were under to take them too, so they tried to keep their distance. Why would the men on the ship want to curse them like this? Why did they leave their own men alone and without care? Then Nako grew weaker and began to shake.

"When one of the men came in, I grabbed him, and even though Nako was weak, he struck the man about the head and ears. His screams brought more of his fellows, and we told them to just let us go. We would swim back to our place. We could find the way.

"They laughed and then hauled us up to the air and beat us hard for holding their man and injuring him. They had their weapons so we couldn't fight them. They left us on the deck with nothing to eat, until we began to feel very sick."

Faina opened her eyes when Masai stopped talking. He shook his head as though to forget what he had told them.

They were dumped on a rocky, barren stretch of shore. It was not their land, but despite how ill they were, and dehydrated, and sore from the blows they had taken, they made their way back to their own village.

"We're glad you're returned to us," Louvu said.

At that, Masai collapsed into unconsciousness, and Sero chewed some of his leaves, ground them with a small paste, and spread it over Nako's forehead and Masai's too.

"They have a dangerous curse," he said. "But they are strong and are good fighters. The magic will work on them."

V

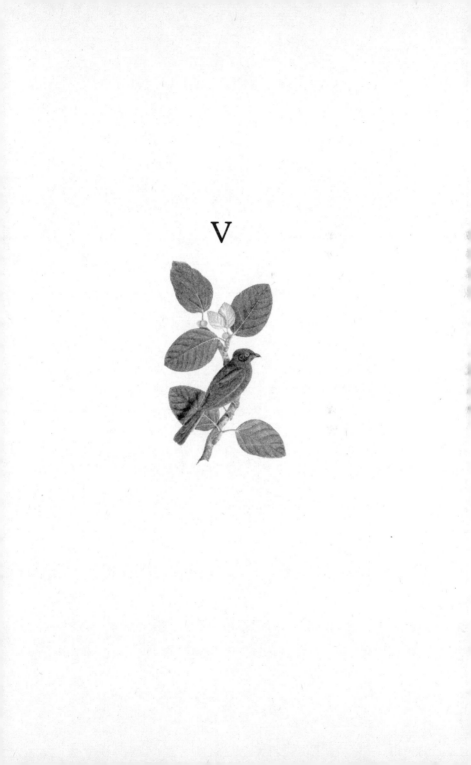

Michelle

The next morning perhaps a hundred people encircle the nasara, presumably from neighbouring villages. The adults are dressed up in brightly coloured floral dresses and shirts, the children in slightly mismatched school uniforms. There is a festive feel to the day, the energy of celebration, all chatter and anticipation, but to Michelle the world is too brilliant, too hot, too humid, the thick air clinging to her skin. She has barely slept. She tossed herself from semi-sleep and stared into the dark, picturing Zach's face crumpling as she struck him, his back as he walked away, until she remembered Rebecca's rebuke: *No one cares about my son's death.* She thought of Astrid's nightmares, and of Zach wandering the streets at night. She thought of Ouben, and what might have been done to save him. To save any of them.

Now, Michelle sits on a plastic chair in the nasara, feeling foggy and slightly dizzy. The full force of the dazzling southern sunlight is heavy on her shoulders, and she shifts uncomfortably in the colourful Mother Hubbard dress that Rebecca presented her with earlier—three matching ones, for herself, her mother, and Astrid. The dresses are the same style that most of the women are wearing so well, but Michelle is certain that she and her mother look ridiculous, the dresses with their puffed sleeves and loose waists both hiding their bodies and making them fat and bulging at the same time. Still, they are beautifully hand-made, the stitches neat and precise, the leaves and flowers on the fabric perfectly aligned at the seams. Zach and Scott wear wide-collared shirts of the same material. It pains her how handsome they look, how much work must have gone into preparing their clothing for the ceremony. How has she earned this kind of care?

David had tried to explain to her that first time they spoke that there would be a ceremony, that it would be about putting the past behind them, repairing a long-fractured relationship. It was their kastom way to make a public exchange, he said, to put an end to any conflicts and disagreements. Robson has spoken of the ceremony differently, describing it as a chance to ask for and offer forgiveness, but Michelle wonders if she *can* be forgiven, and whether she has anything worthy to offer in exchange.

In her lap Michelle holds a folder containing documents she scooped up from her desk at home in Toronto, along with the remnants of Josephine's papers. Since being here she has begun to wonder what is missing from Josephine's story. What didn't she write down? Or what might she have recorded that never made it back across the sea or down to Michelle? Maybe there is something more here, something she has missed. She grabbed the folder on her way out of the bungalow—something to occupy her hands, something to look at when she can't look at her son, her husband. She opens one of the envelopes now and there is the form for Dylan's trust. She glances quickly at Scott beside her, thinks of the house he is threatening to buy. Is that why he has been urging her to dissolve the trust? She stuffs the form back into its envelope and slides it to the bottom of the pile.

Except for Astrid, the rest of her family sit beside her on plastic chairs angled towards the centre of the nasara. Scott suggested last night that maybe it would be better if Astrid wasn't present for the ceremony. It was the only thing he had said to her since their argument.

"Of course," she agreed, glad for any word from him, and hopeful he might soften towards her. "Of course." But he only nodded and walked away to arrange for Astrid's care.

To Michelle's right is Joyce, then Zach studying his phone in the seat farthest from her. Scott is on her left, then David and Robson and a couple of men whose names she has already forgotten. Robson is the only man not wearing a floral shirt, dressed instead in a white button-down with a dark tie. He holds a well-worn bible on his lap.

There is the sense of a breath held and about to be released. They are all waiting for something to happen, for someone to begin. She scans for Dylan among the faces—there are flickers of colour in the brush beyond the crowd. He is here somewhere, she knows it.

At some invisible signal, a tall man dressed in what Michelle assumes is traditional clothing—a short mat woven from some plant fibres wrapped around his waist, leaves wreathed around his biceps and ankles and woven through his hair—bends over a hollowed-out log so massive it looks as though it could be a small canoe. He scoops out a few handfuls of water from inside it, raining droplets over the top and sides of the log and the ground around him, staining both the wood and the earth dark, and then he rubs the water into the trunk. With a thick smooth stick, he beats against the hollowed log and a complicated rhythm rises and falls in the air, cresting over the trees. The sharp high sound echoes across the clearing and the small cove, reaching out across the sea.

Josephine wrote about these drums, the way they called across the islands. *One wakes to them, falls asleep to them. Sometimes they sing the rhythm of a racing heart, or the staccato of a complex dance step that I will never learn. The men make the drums speak in dozens of ways, so that the rhythms can rally, or send mournful cries. They announce battles and rituals. They argue with each other and send on greetings and good news.* Michelle imagines this place alive with the music of them and tries to understand who the drums are calling now, when it seems so many are already here. All around the nasara, the people begin to settle.

The man continues to pound the drum in the unfamiliar rhythm, looping and urgent, and from down the row David leans forward to speak to her family. "The drums call our ancestors and anyone who hears them to join us here," he says, and she wonders if that includes Josephine and William. Would they even know to come? Surely it includes Ouben, but what about Dylan? She casts around for her son again. In the light breeze the trees make a dance around the nasara; the sky is clear as far as she can see. The ocean marches at the island, an army of small whitecaps. When the drummer finally stops, the muscles in his arms and back are tense and shaking, his sweat dripping to the ground. The silence seems stronger than it was before, taut— even the birds and trees are quiet. Anticipatory. The hair on Michelle's arms rises in the oppressive heat, the sun fiercer here than on even the most scorching day in a Toronto summer.

Michelle glances at her family on either side of her. Zach watches through his screen, and she has an urge to reach over and press his phone down, but resists. Scott doesn't even look at her. As the birds begin to sing again, Astrid's voice sounds from the nearby trees, mixing with those of a few other children. She thinks about calling to her daughter, about going to her, but she cannot move, pinned by the sun, by the anticipation that crackles across the nasara.

Robson stands and walks with Noah, the young schoolteacher, to join a group of women who have gathered under the wide spread of the banyan tree. Robson's wife, Serah, who they met on their first day on the island, stands in front of the group, and when she lifts her hand, they begin to sing. It is a stunning sound, some voices soaring to high notes that ring against rumbling lows, and her mother is suddenly holding Michelle's hand, grabbing it in amazement. Michelle squeezes back, glad for the touch. She wishes she could reach for her husband and son, but she's scared they would only pull away.

Some of the women close their eyes as they sing and tilt their heads back so the fullness of the sun shines on their faces; some stare directly at her. She tries to hold each gaze in turn. The voices in the air are clear and open, their harmonies sounding chords that echo deep within her. The lyrics are not in English, but she thinks she hears her name, or rather William's name. Stew-art—long and drawn out. An incantation. Michelle finds herself longing for something—the feeling of time telescoping, the surety that she belongs somewhere.

After the singers return to their places, David stands, walks to the middle of the clearing, and turns slowly in a circle before he speaks. He makes eye contact with each member of her family, and Michelle fights the urge to hide her face, to flinch away. He then casts his gaze to include everyone gathered, to take in the jungle behind them, the ocean ahead, and the whole vast world beyond it. She could grab that imaginary line of horizon and either push it farther away or pull it nearer, so that it encroaches on this place the way Josephine and William did. The way history does.

"We welcome you all to our place on Iparei," David begins, and she senses that he's speaking not just to those who are physically present, but also to those who cannot be seen. There is someone behind Michelle, perhaps the figures from Astrid's dreams or Dylan pressing close. She does not look over her shoulder, just feels the breath on her neck, heat radiating towards her. This place feels sacred and hushed. Even the ocean is only whispering.

"This is our fathers' island and their fathers', and on and on, all the way back to when the first people arrived here from the sea. Today, we come from our own dancing grounds, our own gardens, our own homes, to be here together. We thank those who offer food for our feast and those who offer songs, those who offer dance. We are indebted to you. We thank those who have left us and returned. We thank the Stewart family for travelling so far, in order that we may repair the road between us that was abandoned a long time ago."

While he speaks, David continues to turn slowly, his hands wide and gesturing, and his voice surges and fades.

"We welcome our ancestors, who teach us and provide for us, and whose work we continue today. We hope that we make them proud, and they will continue to whisper their wisdom in our ears. They planted gardens that we might harvest them, they built roads that we might be connected. It is our duty to ensure the same is true for our children, and their children, and theirs. We are the road that connects the past to the future and that is why we must keep it safe."

David pauses for a long moment, his eyes closed, as though he is listening to something only he can hear. Nearby, Robson clears his throat, shifts in his seat, pats the bible in his lap.

"That is why we gather here, why we dance and sing songs and prayers, why we tell the story again. We gather together to declare our intentions in ceremony, and in this way, we make sacred our promises to our ancestors and to our descendants. Because we make such declarations publicly, we are all obligated to assist in their fulfillment."

David backs up until he has returned to his place in the circle.

"There are many roads that connect us. Some of them are the actual paths that link village to village, ally to ally. But we also build sacred roads through marriages and exchanges, through children and adoptions, until there is a web that connects us all, reminding us who we are charged to take care of, who takes care of us. The roads never disappear, but they may grow over, or be forgotten. We gather here to remember."

Here David begins an invocation of those who have gone before them. Initially, Michelle thinks it is a prayer of sorts in a language she cannot understand, but then individual names emerge, including some that she recognizes from Josephine's papers, becoming a story of their own. She shivers involuntarily. It is a long litany of the dead, and Michelle understands for perhaps the first time the scope of the loss that occurred here. She feels it swelling inside of her. It is not just her dead that they are gathered here to remember. How did she not understand that before?

The names call the past to them now, and the whole of that history presses against her. David walks to the middle of the open space again, invoking the power of this place, the spirits who live here. He names Josephine and William; Moses and

283

Marami. He names Ouben. She is surprised and flushes with gratitude and grief when he names Dylan.

Robson stands and there is another hymn, this time sung by children who gather together in front of Noah, who waves his hands about and points as though conducting them. The children don't watch him, but rather fidget as they enthusiastically sing, tugging at collars and shirtsleeves, grinding toes into the ground, jostling each other.

When they finish Robson begins to pray, almost to himself at first, and then his voice lifts to an ending: "*God of all glory, on this first day you began creation, bringing light out of darkness. On this Lord's Day grant that we, the people you create by water and the Spirit, may be joined with all your works.*

"We thank you for your servants, we thank you for the opportunity you offer us, to begin this day in a new spirit of friendship so that our past may not haunt us anymore."

David takes over again. "When William Stewart and his wife arrived on our island, our people and yours were strangers to each other. How can we know what they thought of each other? Perhaps our grandfathers thought the strangers were the ancestors who had left here generations before, returned from across the sea, though they seemed to have forgotten their home, their kastom, and their obligations to us. They forgot that we are all connected."

Michelle finds it unbelievable that this is the same man whose words she had to strain to make out when they first arrived, he spoke so quietly. He is commanding now, taller and broader, entirely in control. Next to her, her mother smiles. They are all smiling stiffly. She can feel the tightness of the grin that she plasters on her own face whenever someone catches her eye. The back of her neck is burning in the spots of sun that cut like lasers through the leaves of the banyan. She forgot to put sunscreen on the skin above her collar as she always does, distracted by trying to get Astrid covered. Her skin is hot under her hand where she touches it. She shrugs into the wide neckline of her dress.

"A road was opened when the strangers arrived here," David continues. "Gifts were given and received, and with those exchanges our people and yours were bound together by reciprocity. Today, we meet each other on the road that our people built long ago, with words and gifts and ceremony. The road that was broken and forgotten. To find the road we must first tell the story of what happened, and each must have their voice."

David steps to the edge of the nasara. The circle of people opens to expose the clearing to the ocean. It beats against the island.

From somewhere behind Michelle, a group of people in traditional clothing come to the centre—men, women, a few older children. Their skin gleams in the harsh sun. The men's hair is marked with feathers and vines, leaves and twigs, all dyed red and yellow and white, and their faces are painted with oranges and reds. They wear the same style of mats around their waists as the drummer, and shells chatter on their ankles. The women and children wear skirts made of long dried leaves, with vines woven in their hair, shells and bright stones chiming around their ankles. The group gathers behind two men, the most decorated of them all. Tusks from great tusker pigs curve and wrap around their biceps, and they carry large heavy-looking spears that they plant into the ground. They stand tall and ready, their hands loose on their weapons.

Then all the men cluster together, and the women and children form a ring around them. Slowly, a man's voice rises, and more rise to greet it. As they sing, they begin to stamp their feet on the ground, pounding out a new rhythm, the men moving in one direction, the women in the opposite with lighter footsteps, almost skipping. The song is traded back and forth between them.

David, who has returned to his seat, leans over and explains, "This is the song that is sung when the yams are harvested. It is part of the exchange ceremony." The men continue to stomp hard on the ground, making a hollow sound, and the women circle and circle, so Michelle grows dizzy watching them. And then a small girl shouts and points out to sea. The dancing stops and everyone turns towards the dazzling water.

A small boat Michelle hadn't noticed before bobs offshore, just inside the break. There are two figures inside, swaying with the ocean; one pulls on the oars and the craft lifts and falls as he drives it towards the shore. The two climb awkwardly from the boat and fall to their knees, lifting their hands to the sky in prayer. The performers play up their exhortations and there is some laughter from the audience as the two continue making their gestures to god.

A man and a woman. She is dressed in a long calico skirt and a T-shirt; he wears dark pants, and a white shirt like the one Robson wears. He gestures heavenwards with his bible and thanks the lord for their safe deliverance. William and Josephine.

William points at the other performers dressed in traditional clothing, and Josephine draws back. The women and children retreat to the treeline, while the men arrange themselves along the high-tide line, fierce warriors armed with spears and clubs and bows. Each of them is tensed, ready to spring into action. On her knees at the water's edge, Josephine cowers.

A shiver runs through Michelle, something like memory. She's told this story to each of her children, as she was told it by her father, and he by his father before him. It is hers, and yet not hers—she feels both compelled to be a part of this, and as though it has nothing to do with her at all.

The warriors approach William and Josephine, and one of them gives a command. A younger man dashes to the trees and returns with a fistful of leaves that he quickly twists together. The man who has spoken bends to the ground and, with his hand, he blades a line in the sand, slowly and deliberately, moving from the hard-packed sand of the tideline up to the dry sand, perpendicular to the shore. His men stand on one side of the line, Josephine and William on the other.

The young man passes him the leaves he has collected, along with one of the spears, and the man who Michelle assumes is their chief jams the spear into the ground. She resists the urge to look at Josephine's pages to see if she named him. He winds the leaves around the top of the spear and, gesturing to it, announces something that Michelle doesn't understand. Or rather, she doesn't understand the words, but she understands the line in the sand, senses the prohibition he makes with the spear and the leaves, with his hands and his words.

William, however, doesn't seem to, or does not care. He stands and steps unabashedly towards the men, and a kind of dance occurs. Josephine, still kneeling, watches while her husband approaches the line. The men on the other side bristle and speak words sharp and low, clutching at their weapons; they seem to grow larger and William retreats. Once and then twice more this happens, before each group settles on the sand, eyeing each other.

William and Josephine retrieve woven bags and a plastic bucket from their boat and pull items from them, conferring close together, all the while casting glances at the men on the other side of the line. This goes on for some time. The audience shifts. Michelle looks at Zach but he doesn't look at her. She glances down at the ground as if expecting to see a line drawn between them.

Finally, the man who drew the line takes a coconut shell from a warrior behind him and walks to the line. He stretches an arm across and William stands, accepts the cup, and drinks. He makes a face but swallows, then offers something of his own to eat, miming it for the man, who takes it and likewise grimaces. Then the man ushers William and Josephine up the beach, each keeping to their side of the line.

They are still wary of each other, careful, but another man brings forward a small pig tethered with a length of vine and offers it to William, who takes it and hands over in exchange a small metal axe. They regard each other. William approaches the line again, hands spread wide. The chief once again steps forward, this time with his own arms open, a clear welcome that William shies away from, his hand stuck out in front of him. The chief speaks in his language, one of the more than thirty Michelle has been told are still spoken on the island. She strains for a familiar word, anything to hold on to.

And then William speaks, and she clings to the English. He praises the lord loudly to the skies, he assures those he addresses that their time of darkness is at an end. She cringes, thinking of Josephine's notes, of the words that she feels she is finally starting to understand. Josephine comes to stand behind William, and the two parties exchange more gifts: cloth for breadfruit, iron nails for yams. They each stay to their side of the line; they each communicate as much with signs as with words. Josephine and William turn to the goods they have brought, the goods they have received. The men settle in the shade of a tree nearby to do the same.

This was the beginning then. Peaceful, if apprehensive. A feeling-out. A hoping.

Suddenly she senses Dylan is beside her, and he is whispering to her, pulling at her to come away. He doesn't want her to see what is going to happen, but for once she cannot will herself to look away.

In the space between them and the villagers, Josephine and William act out planting, they act out preaching, they act out building a home, a church. The performers are fine mimics. Their movements are like dance steps, specific and stylized, but it is truly Josephine and William before her. How many times have they danced this story? How many times have they watched it being re-enacted, like a Christmas or Easter pageant? A history lesson in which their own ancestors are the characters.

As the two missionaries go about their work all the others watch them, sometimes sitting on the rocks or ground nearby, sometimes from a farther distance, from their village. William begins to step over the line, travelling farther and farther, until he meets the people in their villages to mime his sermons. When William finishes his preaching, a few of the villagers follow him back to the mission. Josephine offers them clothing, and, slowly, they begin to look like William and Josephine.

Michelle's palms sweat. She knows what is coming.

But then two men skulk in the bushes. She hasn't seen them before, but they are dressed like William in pants and button-down shirts. They hold sticks like guns at their shoulders, hats cocked over their eyes. From behind they grab two warriors, who fight back but are frightened by the guns. The young men are hauled away to the boat that brought Josephine and William to the island.

There was no mention of other westerners in Josephine's papers. Her stomach turns. Who are they? Where did they come from? She wants to ask David, but the villagers begin to call out for their lost men. A small girl goes to Josephine and William and asks if they know where the warriors have gone. But they have no answer.

The villagers continue to wail, but then the small girl points again to where the two captured warriors are returning, stumbling, clutching at their stomachs, miming illness. Their families hold them, try to nurse them with poultices and songs. It does not work.

The illness sweeps up the beach until, one by one, others in the village falter and fall down sick. Some crawl to Josephine and William, who offer them cups of something that seems to have no effect.

The wailing stops. In the silence, the man who drew the line in the sand points at two children lying on the ground. The children are sick. Michelle looks away.

Faina

The days that followed Masai and Nako's return were murky with rain; mud caked Faina's feet and ankles as she carried water from one sleeping hut to the next. Voices moaned, in this world and the next. She felt she was being stalked by the same dangerous magic that had seized the village, the same that stalked all the villages on the island, allies and enemies alike.

The island was rife with rumours—of illness and the curses that caused it. Men and women disappearing and reappearing. No one knew what to believe anymore.

Masai and Nako still muttered with thick tongues at the spirits that threatened them. Faina couldn't see them, but she could feel them. They were unfamiliar to her. Perhaps they had come with Masai when he was returned.

A deathly smell came from many of the sleeping huts, from the bodies themselves, as well as the fouled mats they lay on. The ill sweated and shat and vomited, so that they were quickly worn down to bone, the insides of them becoming more visible. Boils and pustules appeared on bodies, weeping and then hardening. Those like Faina, who were well, were scared and unsure what to do.

When she went to fetch water, Faina found Telau slouched against a tree, her chin on her chest, her watertight basket spilled next to her. Panicked, Faina crouched next to her friend and shook her, whispering her name. Telau slowly opened her eyes and waved Faina away. "I'm fine, I'm fine." Her voice was impatient. "Just tired." Though she looked pale and her hands shook some.

Faina nodded, not wanting to argue, not wanting Telau to be ill. She refilled Telau's basket for her and then filled her own before joining Telau against the tree.

"Why would they do this to us?" Telau asked. Faina didn't have an answer. "Will-am brought them here, he helped them."

"Maybe he could help us now," Faina said. "Maybe he knows what curse this is. Do you think I should go to the mission?"

Telau shot her a look. "All they have done since they arrived is insult our ancestors and our ways. If they didn't curse us, surely our ancestors are insulted by how we have let the missi behave in their place." She shook her head. "No. They can't help us."

Telau hauled herself to her feet and led Faina back through the brush.

Faina felt strong, even while the village was suffering with the illness. Why did she feel strong? Why didn't she get sick? Was Josephine protecting her? If so, then why not the people she loved? Her mind tumbled with questions as she tended on her cousin and his wife, on Father's Brother, on Louvu's twins who seemed to wither particularly quickly. She wished to sit with Masai, but he had finally recovered some after long nights of shaking and stuttering. He and Nako had been taken to the men's house, behind the fence, when others started to become ill, Sero following with his leaf medicine. For days there were chants and the stamping of feet, singing and the rising of smoke from fires.

"How is he?" Faina asked when Father appeared after two days. At first Father only shrugged, but she grabbed his forearm and so he turned to her.

"He is in a powerful battle, but he is strong and will win. Nako thought . . ." Her father shook his head. "They're fighting hard, we all are. But this is powerful magic. Sero has never heard of a curse like this. Even Father is bewildered."

"I want to help."

"Take water to those who need it. Do as you're told." She was about to speak, but he cut her off as though he knew what she was going to say. "Stay away from the mission until this is past."

She meant to do as she was told.

She fetched water and some fruit and went to Louvu's sleeping hut. She choked on the air as she stepped inside. She put her hand to her mouth and peered into the gloom. The two boys lay still on their sleeping mats, curled around each other. She waited and exhaled a breath she didn't know she was holding when their small chests finally moved. Beyond them, their mother lay on her own mat. She tried to lift herself to sitting. "No, no," Faina whispered. "I'll take care of them."

She sat beside one of the boys and eased his head into her lap. They were two of a kind, exactly alike, born at the same time, the same hour. Some peoples, she knew, saw twins as dark sorcery, but not here. Here, they were much loved by everyone in the village; the boys smiled easily and rarely fussed.

She tipped water into his mouth and he coughed against it. She shushed him as he moaned, and when he finally stilled, she moved to nurse his brother. He would not swallow, the water ran from his mouth, and his eyes stared past her. Faina couldn't look at their mother.

She had to do something. She had brought Masai back. Perhaps there was more that she could do, more that she could learn from Josephine.

Faina stood watching the mission, trying to remember what it had looked like that first time she came with the eel she had caught. She tried to recall the sunshine on the sea, the flurry of activity, the excitement of the new. Now the cove was still, the clouds pressed down, everything sagged in the rain.

She slipped in through the gate. The garden had wilted to rot where a short time before it had been bleached and drying. Their plants didn't belong here. Maybe Telau was right—the missi did not either. Faina moved first to Talawan's sleeping hut. As she neared, she heard the moaning and murmuring that came with the illness. So the curse had reached here too. If William wasn't to blame, who was? He was allies with the men of the ship, had spoken on their behalf, had walked the exchange roads with them. But what if the curse had stung the missi too?

Faina climbed up to the threshold of their house. The door was open. She stepped in. The shutters were closed and the air was stale and smelled so foul she could taste it as she breathed through her mouth. The sleeping platform was a tangle of soiled clothes, and more dirty clothing was piled on the floor. She turned slowly in place. This was only the second time she had been in this room. The little boy. Was he still there? Josephine's son.

She moved to the wooden plank that stood on one side of the room. Beside the picture of the boy that looked as if he'd been captured behind the shining surface, there were now others where he appeared older. She slid one, quickly, unthinking, into her bag. In front of her were other pieces of Josephine's paper. Faina leafed through them—there was another drawing of her and several sketches of other women from her village. She picked up the pencil on the desk and on the back of the drawings she wrote each woman's name. The way she had written Masai's in the dirt, on her body. She was here. They were here.

"What are you doing?"

Josephine was a shadow in the doorway.

"Are you sick?" Faina asked, her voice a lilt of false concern. She turned the page over, hid her name.

"I haven't seen you in some time," Josephine said, stepping towards Faina, her hand out to her. Faina backed away until she was pressed against the wall. Josephine dropped her hand. "I heard your men were returned. Are they . . . Are they well?" Faina shook her head. "Oh, of course."

Faina searched for the words, her mind tangled up with a growing anger. "You knew Masai was taken? Did you do this to him?"

Josephine looked skyward and sighed wearily, but didn't say anything.

"You did." Faina didn't ask this time. Kaipar was right; the missi were to blame. She felt the sharp stab where her grief became fury.

"All they wanted was some wood." Josephine sat down heavily in a chair. "Why didn't you just let them have it. It wasn't so much to ask. Now it is all in God's hands. All we can do is ask for His blessing."

Faina shook her head. "No. Those men. They can't just take what they want. No."

She had so many words, but not the ones to tell Josephine how wrong she was. She and William had become part of their roads; they had exchanged the use of the land for their tools, they had exchanged food, they had exchanged words, and still the missi wanted more, without meeting the obligations they had made. How could they just continue to take and take as though they were infinitely empty inside?

Josephine knelt, her knees making hollow sounds on the wooden floor. She grabbed Faina's hands and pulled her down with her. Josephine's eyes were wild, but she was not sick; she sweated in the close air as she always did. "We have to pray." Faina tried to pull away, but Josephine held her hands tight, pressed together between hers, and began to call to her god. Her voice scratched at the air, asking for their father's help.

Faina thought of the twins, of Masai and Father's Brother. She would do anything to help them. Would their pleas to the missi's god work? If he had caused this curse to come, he could cure it. Josephine and William, the men from the ship, they were god's people. What if they could cure the illness?

She had to try, didn't she?

She stood up, pulling her hands away from Josephine just as William appeared in the doorway. Faina pointed from one to the other. "Make your god help."

When Faina and the missi arrived at the village, Faina's father sounded the slit drum to call the others.

"Why have you brought them here?" Kaipar asked.

Faina was about to explain that she would try anything to lift the curse, but William spoke instead. "We are here to help. We are only God's messengers, but we have medicine, and prayers are the best medicine of all. Let us speak to the sick, and if they will accept Him, then perhaps they will be saved. If not in this world, then in the next."

Kaipar frowned. "So you admit that this is your god's curse?"

William spread his hands. "He decides who lives and dies, His will be done."

The men retreated to discuss the missi's offer of help, leaving William behind with Josephine and Faina. The three of them shifted uncomfortably. Finally Kaipar and Louvu stood together.

"Let them try. But if they fail, they will have to go. You will take your canoe and leave this place."

For two days they served the sick.

Faina shadowed and helped William and Josephine offer strange fluids and powders to those who were lying ill, the way she had so long ago when Marakai was dying. She hoped this time it would work; she hoped that this magic was strong enough.

A few mornings later, men from the Upland and Hotwater arrived at the village to discuss what must be done. They gathered in the nasara in groups, making a circle around the open space, talking about the number of people who were ill, that the new strangers' ship still lay in wait in a nearby cove. Louvu sat, his head in his hands, while Kaipar stood and held his high to bring them to quiet. Even with the crowd it was easy to see that there were those who were missing. Faina noticed that Albi was absent, but she didn't send a whisper along the line to ask about her betrothed. She did not want to know. Josephine stood a short distance away; she was drawn and pale.

A murmur drew her attention away from Josephine. Masai entered the nasara, with William trailing behind him. Faina's throat ached with relief and happiness, tears prickled at her eyes. She had not known he was so much better. Though he still appeared weak and shaky, he held himself upright and stared straight ahead, his steps careful and measured. Her relief was dampened by his refusal to look around; she wanted him to see her, she wanted him to know that she had been trying to save them all.

"Nako has died," Masai said. He swayed but stayed on his feet.

Kaipar whirled around and stalked towards William, who was glancing around in panic.

"Your hand is in this," Kaipar said. "Such things didn't happen until you came here, and you refuse to put an end to this darkness. We will let you know what we decide." Kaipar looked past Faina and she wished that she had never brought William here, never laid eyes on him or Josephine.

"Take him back to the mission," Kaipar told her, and then he turned away and, without waiting for the group to dissipate, disappeared down the road towards the men's house.

Later that night, Father came to her. The men from the villages had been talking late in the nakamal, the men's enclosure. They had drunk kava, and listened deeply to it; they had talked with the delegates from the other tribes. They had decided what must be done.

"Will-am and Jos-fine must leave this place," Father told her, waking her up from her sleep. Her heart stuttered some. She pictured them climbing into their canoe, rowing towards the ship that still stalked the nearby sea. "They will go on their own, or we will deliver them ourselves. We tried to make them welcome here, but they have done this to us, or they have insulted our ways and for that we are being punished. It does not matter, but they have to go." He was silent for a long moment. "Albi," he said eventually. "He died from this curse."

Her heart seized again. What would this mean? She would not marry so soon, perhaps. Or—

Father interrupted her thoughts. "The people of the Upland will be our ally in this, in insisting the missi leave. They will be our ally." He paused. "And you will be the wife of Yakeh in that place."

They were right. The missi needed to go, but somehow she wanted to plead for Josephine the way she wished someone might plead for her.

"We will go to them tomorrow and tell them what has been decided. They could have been a part of these conversations, but they refused their obligations."

"Will I go with you?" Her voice finally cracked the dark as the sun was rising, a spear of it piercing the corner of the hut.

Father nodded.

The next morning, Faina travelled with Kaipar and Father and men from Hotwater and Upland to the mission. She stood behind them and watched as William came to greet them, with Josephine behind him. She was like Faina's own strange reflection. They were afraid, Faina realized. They all were. Fear lay everywhere on the island.

There were so many dead, and there seemed to be no way to end it. Even here she could smell the acrid scent of fires that had been lit as different tabu men tried to break the curses that swept the roads. There were whispers and voices everywhere.

"We tried to make you part of us," Kaipar said, and marked the place as restricted with the namele leaf, "but you have brought only death and division. We sent word to the ship. It waits for you around the head of the island. You can paddle your own canoe, or we will take you."

Faina shaped the words as best she could, wanting William and Josephine to understand, wondering when she would be able to speak this language again, or if she would be like Father's Father, with sounds and meanings trapped inside her that she would repeat as stories that no one else would truly understand.

William looked at her with disgust, as though she had somehow betrayed them, when all she had done was try to make them understand each other, tried to understand them. William and Josephine were the ones who had betrayed those they had promised to be allies with.

"We will not leave," William said, and his voice was desperate. Faina was too stunned to speak. "God sent me here. He came to me, in my darkest winter, and told me if I served Him in a lost place like this then I would be loved, I would be blessed. I am God's messenger. I obey Him, I follow Him. He wants me in this place so you cannot send us away. This is God's dominion and He will have it. I will not leave." He grabbed on to Josephine's wrist. "We will not leave."

Faina tried to explain his words, but Kaipar shook his head. He understood enough. "You have until the morning after tomorrow's night."

The men turned to walk away, and Faina followed them. William yelled after them, his voice catching in the wind. "God will punish you! And He will protect us. You will burn in Hell."

William and Josephine had been told to go. There was nothing left for Faina to do.

But they refused and even still remained at the mission, and the whispers, the murmurs on the island, stirred to a wind that whipped the trees, a wind that blew hard in the night and brought with it a new wailing as the morning came. She had thought she had grown used to the mourning wails.

In the nasara, Faina ran into Masai and Telau.

"It is Louvu's sons," Masai said. "Both of them."

Telau sent her voice into the air too, and Faina's face grew wet, with tears and with the rain that had begun to fall, beating the earth, sending small splatters of mud onto her feet and ankles where the drops exploded.

She stood there a long time. She felt the weight of the boy's small head in her lap, his brother's weak smile. That they were gone pulled at her, yes, but it was as if all of the grief was building up on her shoulders and in her head. A pressure, pushing outwards, that reminded her of when she dove deep into the punched blue holes of the ocean, pulling herself down and down and down to grab the spiny creatures that hid under the rocks, and how her skull filled with an ache until she swallowed it down. She stood swallowing and swallowing—grief and aches and guilt and pain—until she could not deny the truth anymore.

She knew what was going to happen. She knew what had to happen.

Faina ran her hand along the perimeter of the cave.

She stretched to reach the one spot that caught a ray of sun late in the day, where there were the handprints of all the women who had come before her. It was said that one of the handprints belonged to the first woman to come to this cave, that she had lived in its depths rather than live with a man. Faina held her hand against them, hoping that she might hear a whisper of their wisdom.

She thought of being here after Masai was taken and how she had brought him back. She touched her palm to the print she had made. She pressed as hard as she could so she could feel it pressing back against her, the whole island holding her up. She stayed that way until she could not tell where she ended, where the stone began. She imagined melting into it, part of her left here forever.

When she let go, her body was warmed and hummed from the rock. Then she moved to the back of the cave, to the crack where she had pleaded for Masai's return.

She thought of his name, marked on the dirt, on the wall, on her body; of how he came back to her. Outside, the storm lashed sideways at the cave, the bushes and trees bending as though trying to see what she was doing, what she would do. The wind whirled, but she was safe and dry here. She pictured the bodies of Louvu's twin boys. She imagined her marriage exchange and having to leave behind everything she knew. What could she do?

Slowly, she wrote William's name into the dirt at the crack of stone leading into darkness. Then, hesitating, she wrote

Josephine's. They had come to the island uninvited. She had tried to help them, to learn from them. They all had. Kaipar and Louvu had protected them, made them part of the web that encapsulated the island, and yet William and Josephine had failed to honour their place in it, to recognize the role that they had elected to play.

She wrote the names of others—Albi, who had taken her hand in his and helped her up, who might have been kind to her; Marakai all those months ago; Nako. She still looked for the shadow of him just behind Masai. Telau's mother was gone, and Father's Brother. She wrote their names over and over and hoped they were dancing.

She bent her back to the storm and her face close to the earth, the smell of it thick in her nostrils, relieving some of the pressure there.

The wind came up behind her as she pursed her lips, as though all her ancestors breathed with her. She blew, and the storm blew with her, wiping the words away and carrying them into the darkness, down into the earth.

She waited for the storm to pass.

It grew wild and angry, the daytime air growing dark, fronds and lianas whipping past the mouth of the cave that sheltered her. Still, her heart pounded with the rhythm of it. When she heard the crashing of a fallen tree, she worried one might block the entrance to the cave and she would be trapped here with only the tunnel to the spirit world as an exit.

But finally, after what seemed a very long time, the air around the cave calmed, the light bloomed, and the whole of the brush in front of the cave sparkled with water drops, everything gilded and bright. The air was fresh, and the earth and the green of the trees were already responding to the pulse of rainwater by opening into the air. Growing. She stepped into the sunlight. She could smell the sea.

Zach

Bodies heave on the ground, and in the lull that follows the violence, Zach is sure he can hear their breathing, before realizing it is his own. He closes his mouth and forces his breath to slow. His heartbeat pounds in his ears. The ocean shushes them all. His iPhone slips in his sweaty hand, and the reflection on the screen makes it impossible to see what is in the frame. Instead, he stares directly at the action in front of him. Slowly, the players take the hands offered to them and return to their places in the circle.

Robson moves to the centre, holds his bible aloft, gazes up to the sky before bowing his head. "Let us pray."

Next to his mom, Zach's father bows his head, closes his eyes. His grandmother does the same. He's never seen them pray before, even at Dylan's funeral, where everyone but Chelsea just sort of stared straight ahead, red-eyed, dead-eyed, not seeing anything. Zach shifts, uneasy at the intimacy of his father's closed eyes in such a public place. He raises the phone between them. His mom glances at him and then away as if she can't meet his eye, can't stand to look at him. He touches his hand to his cheekbone, prods at the ghost of pain there. He hoped for a dark bruise, like some kind of badge. A warning so people would know to stay away. But there is no mark.

The sun and the heat press him into his chair.

Robson finishes his prayer and another song begins, the voices rising and falling on the air. Zach waits for his dad's eyes to open.

When the singing fades, David steps back to the centre. "What would they say to us—those who have gone on? What would our ancestors say to us if they could see us now? What should we say to them?" His voice is loud enough to carry to everyone, even though he seems to be speaking directly to Zach and his family. "Their blood, their stories, their bones, we carry them in us, and they tie us to this place, make us a part of the land, as the land is a part of us. We must honour them, for the promises they made with the planting of crops and fruit trees, the making of kastom. They whisper to us and it is our obligation to listen."

What would Dylan say to Zach if he could? Or William and Josephine?

He thinks of the mark on the stone where William died, and of his own blood left behind at the entrance to the cave. He thinks of Jacob's blood spilled across this island through all the cuts and scrapes of boyhood, and of Jacob's brother buried somewhere nearby. He remembers Dylan's blood at the lip of the pool, and the sight of his own in their sink. They leave their unintended marks wherever they go.

What would he say to them?

Zach gazes around the circle of people, searching for Jacob, and spots him standing at the far edge of the assembly, watching with feigned disinterest. Beside him, Bridely holds her belly in cupped hands and smiles up at Jacob, who doesn't seem to notice. She reminds Zach of Chelsea. He lifts his phone again and films the two of them for a few moments before turning off the camera.

"But words are only a beginning. Saying sorry, asking for forgiveness, agreeing to change and move forward together. That is not the thing in itself. Vows require action, just as our gathering here is an action. Here we name and recreate the obligations that we will carry into the world." David stares at them, as though waiting for them to do something. Zach wishes he knew what that was.

His mother stands and sways a moment in the breeze. She seems small in her billowing dress, so unlike anything he has ever seen her wear. She hesitates briefly, but then sets her shoulders and, without glancing back at any of them, steps forward to join David in the centre of the nasara.

She is walking away from him; he's being left behind again.

The night she returned, the night Dylan died, he woke up to find her in his room. She was a shadow over him. He didn't know it was her at first. He whispered his brother's name into the cold air, and there was a choked sob and then his mother was holding him close to her. They clung to each other, both weeping, but neither said anything. She held him for a long time. He needed her to tell him things would be all right. He needed her to say something. He needed her to just make it not hurt.

Instead, she squeezed him tight and left him in the dark. He realizes now she was saying goodbye.

She stands in the open space of the nasara and squints at all the people surrounding her. He has seen her talk in front of large groups before, but she looks uncertain this time even as she is compelled to speak. His stomach churns. He doesn't want to listen to what she has to say. David is right: words don't change anything.

"I'm not sure how to do this," his mom begins. "For so long William and Josephine were just a story to me. But they were real, and what they did was real. This place is real, and I am here because of them. They came here for lots of reasons, and I know they believed that what they were doing was right, that they were making things better. But why they came doesn't really matter. The fact is they brought so much pain with them, so much illness and death. And I am sorry for the hurt they caused, even while I'm grateful for the link they forged between us that has led us to meet all of you and to try to understand what happened here.

"It's hard to look at your own family and know that your ancestors committed some of the horrific actions that history is so full of, that they could be so cruel. It feels so much easier to just close your eyes, say it all happened such a long time ago. Because how do we even begin to make amends for the past? How can we ever hope to right those wrongs?

"But I want to try. I really . . . I need to try. I always thought what happened here was ancient history, but I know now that's not true. Their ghosts are all around us. I'm so sorry for the harm that William and Josephine caused. I'm sorry for the loss of your homes and your loved ones. It shouldn't have happened. You don't need our forgiveness, but I want to ask you for yours."

She stares down at the folder in her hands and pulls out a large official-looking envelope. Her expression shifts as she examines it. She smiles and gives a small nod to something only she can see before she clutches the folder to her chest and looks skyward, as though she is praying. Before she speaks again she wipes at her eyes. "We all want a better future, for our children, for ourselves. They deserve that, don't they?" Her gaze lands on Zach, and she gives him an almost-apologetic half-smile, before meeting David's eyes once more. "We would like to give you something. It was our son's. It was meant to be for Dylan's future."

He can't remember the last time she said Dylan's name. And then she stands straighter and for the first time in a long time he recognizes the certainty in her stance, recognizes his mom. He is glad to see her again; he lifts his camera to capture her there.

"I know it doesn't change anything," she continues. "It's barely even a token. But he would want you to have this. It's not a lot, but it's something—a beginning. Please accept it."

He doesn't understand what his mom is talking about, but a few seats down, past the empty space where she was sitting, his father is shaking his head. "Goddammit, Michelle," he hisses. Zach shifts the camera to his father, but when he sees his father's face, tense and red, his jaw slightly trembling, he turns the video off.

Rebecca

Rebecca doesn't watch the re-enactment. She would have gone for David's sake, but he will be so busy and distracted he is unlikely to notice her absence until it is time for her to participate, and despite her reservations, she will be there.

The songs and the sounds of the re-enactment drift through the brush to where Rebecca is sitting in a small clearing, watching Anaei and Astrid play nearby. Like the cave, this grove is a place she comes to often. It used to be peaceful, well-tended. She brought Ouben here as he was learning to crawl, the ground soft on his knees.

When David first suggested inviting the Stewarts to Iparei, he was so sure it was the right thing to do, and she wanted for something to be right. But now that she has seen them, gotten to know them, she is less certain. She's not sure they truly comprehend what they are doing here. Even if David and Robson think the exchange will please their ancestors, or God, and renew a broken relationship, she doesn't know that it will. Still, she hopes that something good will come from the ceremony, even if it has nothing to do with the Stewarts. She hopes it will bring Jacob and David back together, or David and Robson. That through ceremony some roads will be repaired.

Anaei and Astrid chatter and flit about like mourning doves, alighting on a flower, a leaf, a stone, a shell, before moving to the next. Rebecca should urge her daughter to keep her dress clean, she but can't bring herself to dampen her current joy.

She sits through the wailing and the silence that follows and imagines the scene in her head. David will speak and then Robson, perhaps Scott or Michelle. If they were from here, the Stewarts would have brought something to exchange, even if only a token, as is kastom. Not the cheap plastic that tourists bring to alleviate their guilt, not knowing what the goods are meant to symbolize, but something imbued with meaning. Rebecca hopes that they will have brought something to offer, that they understand what they are meant to be doing here, but she doubts it. Still, the ceremony will allow them to finally join both sides of the story. They are like two sides of a leaf, both always present in each other's lives, even if they weren't aware of it until now.

Rebecca tries not to imagine the grief of those parents, long dead, whose children died from the illness that was first brought to the island in the mission days. That is a connection she would rather refuse, this echo from the past. But sorrow wells up in her and she curls her fingers into her palms and then flexes them as though expelling the thought, the pain. She wants someone to blame for her loss, for theirs. She would like to run up the slope of this island and hide in the women's cave until the pain of Ouben's death recedes, but she knows she would be there forever.

Anaei laughs with Astrid.

"It's almost over," Jacob says, appearing suddenly beside her, startling her. Rebecca nods, about to call Anaei to her, but Jacob stops her. "They won't understand this," he says.

He is probably right, but the offer today is symbolic, not as it was in the old days.

"Someday you will know that children are what bring us together," she says. "You were a little boy when I first met you, when I first loved you. You made it easy to love your father. Our care for you tied us together as much as our care for each other. And now look at you." She can't help but smile at him, thinking of him as a young boy, even while noting the man he has become—how tall, how handsome, how good he is. Jacob blushes under her scrutiny. She inhales deeply. She has not spoken this much in so long. "Now you are becoming who we talked about when you were just a child. That doesn't make it easy to let you go," she adds. "You make your father so proud. Whether either of you knows it." She pauses. "Your mother is proud too."

Jacob stares at the ground and they both hold his mother here between them. Anaei and Astrid have grown quiet, are kneeling at the edge of the bush. Rebecca takes Jacob's hand and leads him to where the two girls are whispering.

"What are you doing?" Rebecca asks her daughter, kneeling down beside her. She cups her hand around her daughter's skull and then slides it down her cheek to her chin, tilting Anaei's face up to hers.

"We are leaving some gifts for Ouben and Dylan," Anaei says. "It's our ceremony, so they remember we love them and so we remember they love us too."

"We thought it would be hidden here from other kids," Astrid says, "but Dylan and Ouben will know where it is. We'll tell them when we dream about them."

The two of them smile at her, pleased with themselves. "Clever girls," she says.

"I like your necklace," Astrid says, reaching out to graze Rebecca's throat. "Like Anaei's."

"It's for Ouben," Anaei explains, and Astrid cocks her head.

"We wear them," Rebecca adds, "so that we remember him every day. When we move, we feel it against our skin, against our breath, and it reminds us to stop and hold him close, to let him know how much we love him."

"I keep this." Astrid pulls a stone out of her pocket and hands it to Rebecca. She noticed the little girl carrying it before. It is smooth and black, and does not seem to be out of place on the island. It shines like it is wet and sits heavy in Rebecca's hand as though drawn to this ground.

"It was Dylan's. He loved it. Grandpa gave it to him, and he said it came from his grandpa and that it was magic, it would keep you safe." She frowns a little, furrows her brow. "I was using it in my garden when Dylan died. I think Dylan would like it back now." She holds out her hand and Rebecca returns the stone to her. Astrid places it carefully in the space they have marked out under the vines, next to a few slices of fruit and Ouben's rattle. The rock seems to settle there.

"Come," Rebecca says, "it's time." She reaches for the children's hands.

They return to the nasara, Anaei on one side of Rebecca, Astrid on the other, each holding one of her hands, connecting them. Jacob trails behind. David steps forward as she has seen him do so many times since she arrived here. At first, every action of his was new to her, but now she anticipates them all. She knows he will lift his hands slightly from his sides before he speaks, a movement no one else is aware of, even as it focuses their attention. The air is sharp after the performance and the dance that she has heard being practised for weeks a short distance from the village. She has imagined the steps and the rhythms; she did not need to see it. But something that she didn't imagine, something unexpected, seems to have happened. There is a murmur drifting through the congregation. She glances from David to Michelle, who stands in the centre of the circle, an island alone, papers held out towards David.

Everyone seems to breathe in unison, deep shaking breaths, as though the whole island, even the sky and sea, is breathing with them. Everything hums and feels fragile, temporary. Some faces shine with tears. They are crowding close to her—Ouben and Dylan, Jacob's mother, the children who died all those years ago, Josephine. They are all here. The air is thick with their spirits.

As Rebecca leads Anaei and Astrid towards David, Michelle sees her and lifts the clutched papers in her direction. The woman gestures to her family behind her, and they rise to join her, though they stand separated from each other and do not grasp hands. David takes Anaei's other hand and reaches to take the pages from Michelle at the same time. Rebecca shoots a look at David, wondering what the pages are, but he simply passes them to Jacob who hangs back. The two families stand facing each other. They form a loose circle in the nasara, and when Astrid takes her mother's hand, she connects Michelle and Rebecca, their two families. The others, the audience and performers, all seem to lean forward in anticipation. Rebecca thinks of lines in the sand.

"In kastom," David says, "we are always striving for balance, between people, between villages, between us and the land. We live in a cycle of giving and returning of gifts. They tell us who cares for us and who we care for. When a wrong has been committed, we must acknowledge and correct it with a gift of equal value."

He turns to smile at Rebecca, reaches out to her and squeezes her hand. "Women and girls bring new life, they usher in the next generation, they are the living connection between the past and the present, carrying on the bones and souls of those who went before to pass down to those who will come after." He lets go of her hand and looks down at Anaei, then back at Michelle. "In the older days, we would make an exchange of our daughters, after battles and in marriages, because they bring new life where life has been taken. Our daughters, our children, their children are what join us all together. We exchange lost lives for the ones to come so that we may recognize our obligations."

He lets go of Anaei's hand and he and Rebecca both step behind her as she stands on the line between her parents and the Stewarts. Michelle's eyes go wide and then meet Rebecca's.

She hopes that Jacob is wrong and that they do understand.

Michelle

She is certain she doesn't understand.

David and Rebecca stand with Anaei in front of them. The little girl is beautiful in her white dress, shifting her weight from foot to foot, biting her bottom lip. Astrid goes to her, and the two girls clasp hands, giggling and whispering. Michelle almost blurts out the same words Scott hissed at her. *What the fuck?*

"I'm sorry—you want us to take her?" Scott asks. He is trying to keep his voice and face neutral as he squints in the bright air. But she knows him so well she can read the panic in his puffed-out chest and his pushed-back shoulders, so he takes up even more space than he usually does. It's the way he used to get when Dylan was on the ice and a bigger kid would come careering at him.

And for a second, Michelle can't help herself. She fantasizes about Anaei sitting in Dylan's chair, returning them to that lopsided asymmetry around their kitchen table. The idea is as absurd as it is heartbreaking. But she surprises herself with wanting to be charged with sharing responsibility for this little girl who only days ago was a stranger.

Rebecca places her hands on her daughter's shoulders and pulls Anaei to her. Astrid moves with her. "Her home is here, of course, her place is with us. But she represents the lives that were taken." Her hands wave between her family and Michelle's before they settle on Anaei's shoulders again. "She will be—"

"No," Michelle interrupts, and Rebecca shoots David a look that Michelle can't read. "I'm sorry, but you don't owe us anything," she continues. "There is nothing to make up for. William and Josephine came here, you didn't ask for that. They forced themselves into your story. You don't owe us anything," she repeats. "But we, we owe you our apologies and our care. We are the ones who have to make amends. We will provide for Anaei. She'll be like"—she glances at Scott quickly and then looks away—"our godchild. We'd be honoured."

Scott's eyes are on her, but she holds Rebecca's gaze instead. "We'll do whatever we can for her." Michelle needs Rebecca to believe that this is true. It will be a fresh start, a way to prove that she really means to change. She will be different. It has to be different. This will be her proof.

"Through her, you will not forget your connection to us again, or us to you, because we are family now," David says, and then speaks louder to include the assembled crowd. "And now we feast together and celebrate our new relationships."

Robson closes the ceremony with another prayer, another song, as the Tabés and the Stewarts stand facing one another with their two daughters in the middle. On either side of her, Michelle senses Zach and Scott both pulling away, their patience stretching to breaking between them.

The flurry of activity has settled down, and the sun is beginning to sink to the horizon. When a group of men pull the roast pig from its earth oven, they ask Scott to uncover it and he does, the smell wafting up at them. Michelle's mouth waters, her stomach growls. Something has shifted in her; the sensation is almost physical. She will be better, she can be. She will think about what Scott has said, about selling the house. She'll tell him she isn't ready yet, but she will think about it. She will be open to it. She feels more generous to her family than she has in a long time, and she keeps trying to seek them out in the crowd but is intercepted over and over, with handshakes and hugs and smiles. With welcomes.

She is certain Dylan is trailing behind her, just out of sight. She tries to catch the shape of him, tries to grasp his hand in hers.

Eventually, she takes a seat on the ground with a plate of food, and Robson sits next to her. He rubs his hands together. "Do you feel it?" he says and stretches his arms up over his head. She worries that he is going to pray again. There has been so much prayer today. "We are all free now, God's grace is smiling on us. Our grandfathers must be pleased that we have finally finished what they began."

She nods, thinking that Robson is right, they have opened up new possibilities. Sitting opposite, Jacob disagrees.

"Nothing is ever finished. Isn't that the point in kastom? That we must renew these obligations? It is an ongoing cycle. Not"—and here he puts on a kind of performance voice— "a one-time payment."

She is stung by his words. She wasn't trying to buy her way out of her responsibility. That was not what she meant to do. She tries to find the words to explain that he doesn't understand, the money is a reparation, but before she can, someone slaps Jacob on the back and he follows them to another group, where everyone takes turns embracing him.

All around her, people sit in clusters with food on leaf platters in front of them. The villagers who performed in the re-enactment are the stars of the gathering. Others congratulate them on their performances, laughing and joking with them. Everywhere there is a great deal of talk and laughter. Fires have been lit and someone has produced a couple of guitars; soon jangling chords sound across the cove.

Michelle watches Zach get up and pretend to wander nonchalantly near Jacob, who moves over slightly and invites him to sit. Zach glances over his shoulder at her and she thinks about what Jacob said. Her intention wasn't to try to buy them off, but is that what she's done? She seeks out Rebecca where she sits in a crowd of women, watching children frolic on the beach. The sun has almost disappeared into the sea. How many days have women sat here watching children in the infinite sea?

Michelle waits until the other women return to their individual conversations before leaning towards Rebecca to get her attention.

"I hope it will help," Michelle says, but Rebecca only watches her. Michelle takes in the other women nearby—Bridely, whose baby may come any day; David's mother, Numalin; and Lalim. Michelle swallows. "The money. I want it to help. Because I do care, about what happened to your baby." She gestures at Bridely. "And yours too. That's why I want you to have the money. It's a gift. I know it's not much, it's just . . . maybe it can do some good." She can feel her face flush. Why won't Rebecca say something to save her from having to explain? She wishes someone else would speak. She scoops a fistful of sand and lets it run through her fingers. She thought she understood. She thought she was doing something good.

Instead, Bridely speaks, her tone exasperated, or maybe just exhausted. "We have all given something—food, songs, a place to sleep. Rebecca has given something. We are honoured to do it because gifts are what bond us to each other. Good gifts are met with their equal."

Rebecca puts her hand on Bridely's thigh, and the younger woman sighs before speaking again.

"I know, their ways are different. But they are in our place, not the other way around."

"Of course," Michelle says, rushing to fill the silence that follows. "It is an honour to take care of Anaei, to share in her growth with you, all of you. And I am grateful for everything, for your hospitality, for what you shared with us today." She has to say something else, something to make them understand. The folder is sitting beside her on the sand. She picks it up and pulls out the old, weathered envelope. "These are Josephine's papers. She came from far away, but these came from here. Her bones are here. Maybe these should be too." But she doesn't offer them.

Instead, she opens the envelope and fans the pages out. The words of a woman trying to make sense of what she was living through, of what she had lost. Rebecca reaches out and takes them from her. Beside her, Bridely makes a kind of noise. Michelle doesn't know if she is approving or disapproving, or maybe just trying to be comfortable inside a body that Michelle knows must feel foreign to her.

Rebecca lifts the pages to her face and inhales, then looks slowly through them, examining the front and back of each page. She stops at a hand-drawn image that is fine and faded and would have been unnoticeable in the dim light of the solar lamps when the pages were circulated the other night. A drawing of a girl's face, maybe thirteen or fourteen years old if Josephine's hand is to be believed. Michelle can't believe she didn't point out the image before. She notices now that the girl looks a little like Anaei around the eyes, in the shape of her small nose, the dimple below her bottom lip. Her chin is tilted with a mature poise.

Rebecca runs her fingers over the face. She shows the image to Bridely, who passes it on to the other women, the story moving far beyond Michelle. The women confer briefly in their own language and Michelle wonders what they are saying.

"Faina," Rebecca says to her as the portrait returns to her hands. "Her name is Faina."

There is the faintest trace of a smile on Rebecca's lips. Next to her, Bridely laughs.

The women continue to pass the picture of Faina back and forth, and Michelle wonders if she is finally ready to try to heal old wounds. Maybe more is possible right now. Maybe David is right and a road has been opened up.

She finds her husband and holds out a hand to him. She is going to tell him things will be different, that she wants to see the house he talked about. As he stands, some of the other men make gentle joking comments and she remembers what it was like to sneak away from a party because they'd rather be alone together than with anyone else in the world. Maybe they can get back there.

"I'm not sure you want to talk to me right now," Scott says when they arrive at the beach.

"Of course I do," she says, reaching towards him to stop him from moving farther away. "I think things can be different now. I think—"

"Why? Because you're ready now? Because *you've* decided they will be?" She is surprised at the anger that is settled along his jawline. "I'm not going to do this anymore—be the only one not making decisions."

He isn't even looking at her. She tries to move in front of him to make him see her, but it is as though she is a ghost.

"I didn't tell you the whole of it before. I did it. I already bought the house," he says, and blood floods into her ears.

"What do you mean? You can't just buy—"

"Why not? At least I'm trying to put things right. You're so busy trying to fix something that happened hundreds of years ago instead of trying to fix what's happening right in front of you. That money doesn't change anything!"

"I think it could—"

"You just gave it away! What was it? Fifteen thousand dollars? Twenty? More? What the actual fuck, Michelle! You brought us to the other side of the world. You slapped our son! You made us responsible for someone else's child. So yes, I bought a house. With the money *we* saved, *I* bought *us* a future. I won't live there anymore—I can't. The kids can't. Jesus, Michelle, you can't live there anymore either, don't you get it? The place is haunted. Zach is throwing himself at the world without thinking, Astrid is having nightmares. We have to leave."

"You're leaving me?"

This pulls him up short. "What? No," he says and takes a step towards her, and without meaning to she steps back. His face crumbles. "No, of course I'm not leaving you. I don't want to leave you. This is for all of us."

She shakes her head. "I can't just leave him behind. How could we do that to him?"

"I'm not leaving him, Michelle. He's not there. That's what you don't seem to get. He's not the one doing the haunting." He turns slightly and his whole face is lit by the last flare of the setting sun. "Please, Michelle. Come with us."

She stands staring at him. She cannot move, cannot think.

Scott turns to look at the sea. "Right," her husband says, as if from a great distance. "Right. I get it. I understand." And he walks away.

Jacob

Jacob had to walk away during the ceremony, surprised by what he felt.

He participated in so many ceremonies growing up—gatherings with dances and songs and stories and prayers—for marriages, for harvests, for funerals, and to mark sacred days. But it has been a long time since he attended one. In the city there are few opportunities to gather for this kind of ritual purpose. Even drinking kava has become simply recreational for him, separated from the listening that his father and the other men of his home do at the end of the day. When did Jacob stop listening?

And so, while his father spoke in the nasara, Jacob strained to hear those long-ignored voices—those of his brother and mother, his grandmothers and grandfathers. He wanted his father to be right, that those who had passed would gather here for this, that this exchange would please them. More than that, Jacob realized, *he* wanted to please them. He wished his mother were here to tell him what to do, to help him find a way to stay.

He tried to find her voice in the harmony of voices but couldn't, so he left the circle of the ceremony, and in the relative quiet of the bush he listened once more. He waited and hoped, but still he didn't hear her. It was only after he returned with Rebecca to the nasara and, from his place in the circle of his people, watched as Michelle handed some papers to his father. When his father passed them to him, he thought he heard whispering. He strained to catch their words, even as Rebecca tried to explain what the exchange she was offering meant. It wasn't just his mother's voice he was hearing, there were his forefathers' too. And he finally understood: they had always been there; he was the one who had left.

Now that the ceremony is finished and the celebration is underway, Jacob seeks out his father. He wants to tell him that while he couldn't make out everything the voices said, it was the first time he has heard his ancestors speak to him in a long time. He doesn't want to lose that.

When he finds his father around the side of the bungalow, Robson is with him. They appear to be arguing, and Jacob's first thought is to walk away unnoticed, but the memory of the voices urges him forward to be part of their discussions, the future. The two men fall silent as he joins them.

"What's going on?" he asks.

"This doesn't concern you, right now," Robson says, smiling and clapping Jacob on the shoulder. "Go and eat, enjoy yourself!" Laughter and chatter drift from the nasara, as does the smell of the roasted pig mixed with the smell of the sea.

"If it concerns my father then it must concern me."

David glances at him briefly, and Jacob is sure his father is going to dismiss him, but instead David turns back to Robson. "My son is right. This concerns us all. It shouldn't be just you and me discussing this, hiding from everyone, as if it is a secret. We should discuss it as a community."

"Bah, they won't know what to do with this kind of money," Robson says, folding his arms over his chest. "What do you two suggest, that we split it up? Give everyone their share? They will spend it and then it will be gone. And on what, phone cards and kava?"

The inheritance. They're arguing over the money that the Stewarts gave them during the ceremony. Already, word about the amount of it has made its way through the community. If the rumours are correct, it is a good sum.

"What do you suggest?" David asks Robson.

"We should invest it. I know some people in Vila that could—"

"You would take the money, then?"

"And invest it."

"Like the road?"

"Bah, you don't understand. You've never understood, you always think backwards. If you let me handle it, we can make money with this money."

"What if we started a business?" Jacob interrupts. And suddenly he can see it in his head—visitors, tourists staring out at the sea, eating Rebecca's cooking. They would spend their money and learn about this place, about the blue cave and the Hot Water beach. He imagines a line of tiny bungalows backed by the jungle, perched over the sea.

He explains his idea to the men.

"So *you* would use the money and keep the profits then," Robson scoffs. "What about the rest of us?"

"No," Jacob said, thinking his way through it as he speaks. "No, the bungalows will belong to all of us. Everyone will build them together and manage them. We can run tours. People can work at the front desk." He is getting excited now. "We could have a bar where people can drink and watch the sunset." He gestures towards the sea, the spread of colours that in a moment will turn to night.

His father picks up the thread. "And we could share the profits among everyone and invest it in the community. We could set aside money for other emergencies, to buy a new water tank." He is smiling at his son. "It's a good idea, yes. But we should discuss it with everyone else. Our idea and Robson's too. And we should ask if there are other ideas. Everyone has to agree."

Robson looks as if he is about to say something but holds his tongue. Then his smile breaks through, so many white teeth, bright despite the encroaching evening. "We will all have our say. Yes, yes, of course." He puts his arm around Jacob's shoulders. "Come with me. We'll eat some of that pig together and talk more about your idea, yes?"

Jacob peers at him, remembering what his father said about Robson always looking out for himself. He slips out of the man's grip.

"Sorry, uncle. Give me a minute. I want to talk to my father."

"Let's all go," Robson says, his eyes narrowing. "There is so much for us to talk about."

"We'll catch up," Jacob insists. "Save us some!" He forces a laugh.

Robson glances back at Jacob and David as he walks away.

"I'm sorry I didn't listen to you," Jacob says to his father when they are alone. "I'm sorry I said no good would come from the ceremony. Even without their money, you did what our ancestors would have done—held the kastom in your way. That should be reason enough for me to listen."

"It sounds as though you did."

"What about him?" Jacob gestures after Robson.

"He's a good man, just short-sighted. He would never mean to hurt you. But thank you for what you said. And it is a good idea. Everyone will think so when you tell them."

Jacob pictures himself standing in front of his people in the nasara, trying to articulate the vision that has only just come to him—the bungalows, all of them working together to build something new on this place that has felt cursed for so long. His palms begin to sweat.

"I'll help you," his father says, as if he can read Jacob's mind. "We will come up with the argument together. You don't have to deliver it, but it is yours to make. I think you should."

His father drapes his arm around Jacob's shoulders, steering him back towards the sound of laughter and guitars. "Now come on, it seems that we have much to celebrate."

Zach

He doesn't remember creeping barefoot out of the bungalow, but when he turns around, there it is, sitting dark and slumbering. He knows he should go back, but then he thinks of his mother striking him, and the burn of memory flares into shame and humiliation. He thinks of her saying another of her vague *sorrys*, and how useless a word it is on its own. He wills her to appear in the doorway, to for once notice that he's gone.

The air still smells of woodsmoke and the faint trace of the pig they pulled roasted from the hot ground. The earthy taste of kava is at the back of his throat, frosted with mint toothpaste. The night is well lit, the ocean reflecting moon and stars and the whole spread of the Milky Way, and when it's clear that his mother isn't going to come after him, he crosses the sand to where the scrabble of sharp volcanic rock begins and tilts his head back to take it all in. Dylan would have loved the arced spray of the stars in the sky, would have names for the constellations that Zach can't even identify. The moon picks out tide pools of water and the slickness of just-exposed rock. He hears the skitter of crabs over the hush of the water. The waves are low on the shore; the tide must be out.

He pulls out the lighter he keeps in his pocket, a gift from Chelsea—an engraved Zippo. She'd found a piece of paper where Dylan had written his name and had them copy it onto the lighter. Someday he'll tattoo it on his forearm—a permanent scar, something that will never fade. He flicks the lighter alive and waits for the metal to get hot, then presses it to his skin where he'll scar Dylan's name.

His thoughts quiet for a brief second, but as the pain fades, his mind begins to race again. *Fuck.*

He kicks at the coral with his flip-flops and feels the familiar tug inside him, the need to move. *Fuck it, they'll never know. They never do.*

He starts off, not sure yet where he is going, letting his feet pick their way over the wet, uneven coral and rock, past tide pools of changing depths. Even though the night is bright, there is not a single light to be seen on the island. He feels like a ghost, can sense all the other ones following behind him. He glances back over his shoulder but he is utterly alone. For once, he wishes someone were with him. The idea of company makes him think of Jacob, and then Zach knows where to go. The hot spring Jacob told him about. There's no way his parents will let him go tomorrow. They'll say he has to go to church, that he has to pretend they're a loving family. So he'll go now.

Earlier Jacob described how they would follow the shore to where it becomes a flat shelf of dead coral that is exposed at low tide, covered at high, until they reached the base of a cliff. The hot spring is accessible only when the tide is out, filling the exposed tide pools with water heated by the lava, deep under the earth, that created and connected all these islands. Jacob explained how the place is used to prepare special feasts. Some of the food they ate at the ceremony was cooked there.

"Is it really that hot?" Zach asked.

"When I was little, a boy from another village slipped into one of the pools and was burned. He had scars all up his arms. Grandfather said it was because he shouldn't have been there and the ancestors were angry. At school we just thought he was clumsy."

What would that feel like? Zach wondered.

———

He has told the story so many times—to the cops, to his grandmother, to his mother, who interrogated him like it was an inquisition.

It was the yell that jarred him at first, part scream and part growl, and then the splash of something huge in the pool. Zach waited for the laugh to come, or that high-pitched shriek of Dylan's. When neither came, he looked out his bedroom window but could see only part of the pool and somebody splashing in it. After what seemed an eternity, his father surfaced, dragging something unwieldy and heavy out of the pool. Zach still thought it was a joke. It had to be a joke. Static rang in his ears.

Then his father rolled the thing over on its back and it was Dylan.

By the time Zach burst into the backyard, his father was blowing air into Dylan's lungs. Zach froze, watching his brother's stupid skinny chest rise and fall with his father's breath. When his father started to pump hard on Dylan's ribcage, he shot a look at Zach, his mouth shaping words that didn't reach Zach.

He jolted as his dad's voice smashed into him. "Dammit, Zach! Call 911! Go!"

It took him too long to understand the words, to move, to race to the kitchen and stab in the numbers. "My brother. He's . . . I think he's drowned."

There were questions. His address, who else was there. A voice telling him that he should stay on the line, that it would be okay.

Would it? He didn't know. Was Dylan dying? Loud, annoying, funny Dylan? There was no way he could just die. Zach ignored the voice and ran to the Fraziers' next door. He pounded until his fists were swollen. When the ambulance peeled around the corner, sirens blaring, he ran to the paramedics and took them around to the backyard. The double side gates always stuck, and he fumbled the catch. He was too slow. When the gate opened, the paramedics pushed past him, and he just stood there, helpless.

His father was exactly as he'd left him. Moving slower now, his body shaking, hair dripping down his face and onto the wet pavement surrounding the sharp gleam of the pool. One of the ambulance guys pulled his father away gently, held him back, while the other attended quickly to Dylan. They were fast, efficient, their actions choreographed. They didn't give any indication that Dylan was already gone.

Later, he thought of all the things he should have done. Maybe he should have stayed on the line and the dispatcher could have helped. He should have heard sooner what his father was yelling at him to do. So many *shoulds*.

They found blood on the lip of the pool, near the diving board. Dylan must have slipped, hit his head, and fallen into the pool. He shouldn't have been on the diving board. He shouldn't have been alone. Zach should have been out there already instead of sulking in his room. Zach should have been there.

———

Up ahead he can see the shadow of the island where it blots out the stars and horizon, rising up straight from the ocean. The base is outlined in white where the waves hit it. He crosses the relatively flat section that Jacob described, pools of water punched into it. The place feels alive with unseen creatures, and he catches quick movements out of the corner of his eye. He watches an eel slither through shallow water onto a rock and then dart back into the waves, disappearing with a bulging swell. His feet stumble some, and he can almost imagine the scalding water on his skin.

A delicious fear spikes in his stomach.

Zach reaches the bottom of the cliff. He can sense it more than see it towering over him. The sea crashes against the shore and shatters to foam, wearing it down over years and decades and centuries. For a moment, he imagines what it might have felt like for those long-lost ancestors to have reached this island, so far away from everything they knew. It is a little like vertigo, exhilarating and terrifying at the same time, and he feels connected to them, but the feeling is swept back out to sea as quickly as it arrives.

Now to find the hot spring. He crouches low, his hands stretched out in front of him, as though he's warming them over a fire. The waves rush up the rock and the cliff behind him, splashing him, before being sucked back into the ocean. He shuffles forward.

He wishes Dylan were here with him. Zach should have been a better brother. When Dylan was small, he was Zach's best friend for a while. He remembers the two of them leaping across the furniture, pretending the floor was lava. "'Member that?" he whispers.

The air feels warmer and Zach leans over. This is it. The heat is real, and the air moves past his hand in a convection current rushing to fill the space that the sea air vacates. He pulls his hand back from the radiating heat and flicks his lighter. A face wavers in the pool at his feet, moving and resolving itself. Dylan. He bends closer. No—it's just his own reflection. His throat clenches. He snaps the lighter closed and considers plunging his hand into the boil of water. He can almost feel the sear of pain, see the flesh scald red. He already knows it won't be enough. Maybe no pain will ever be enough to blot out what's inside him.

He pictures himself leaping into the scorching pool, feet first, the way he has dropped into Northern Ontario lakes all his life— but this time the shock and pain of it will be even greater. He steels himself for the plunge, imagines his whole body blistering. And then Dylan is calling his name.

Astrid

Her brother walks out the door.

In her dreams, Dylan is always walking out the door. He waits at the threshold for her, not looking at her, but waiting. She can tell he's waiting, but she can't get up because of the shadowy figures that will grab her if she slips out of bed. That fear keeps her locked in her body, so she can't move at all.

But somehow, she knows that the scary people aren't there anymore, that they've gone away. This time, when her brother pauses in the doorway, Astrid sits up.

She knows she's supposed to follow him. The wind whispers that she should go, or he whispers; it's hard to tell the difference. She kneels on the floor and feels around for her sandals. The coral out there hurts her feet; she knows this from walking on it earlier with her grandma. Under the cot, her hands brush something furry that chirps in the dark—the cat that snuck in under the bed. She's fantasized about hiding the kittens in her backpack and taking them home with her, but worries they would suffocate or starve on the plane. She strokes the mother quickly back to sleep, and pulls on her shoes.

Outside, the moon is bright and she calls Dylan's name. The world is blue and silver and beautiful. On one side of her the ocean dances, and on the other, the trees. She is the only thing that is still. Where did he go? She searches for him, turning around slowly, peering into the gloom before spotting him down the shore. She glances back at the little bungalow. Maybe she should get her mom or her dad? They would want to see him too. Maybe if she can get him to come back, they can all be happy again. But he's disappearing into the night, so Astrid hurries after him.

She picks her way across the hard, prickly rocks. She tries to keep her eyes on Dylan, but she has to watch her feet because there are puddles of water and holes for twisting ankles, so sometimes she loses sight of him for a few seconds. She thinks about heading back, but when she looks behind her, she can't see the bungalow anymore. She stops and hopes he'll turn around. Her heart is beating hard in her throat, so it feels a little like choking, and she worries she'll be paralyzed like in her dreams and be stuck here until daytime, when maybe Zach or her mom will find her. But then the moon spotlights Dylan again and she continues to make her way towards him.

He is fast. He's always been fast, but he used to wait for her. Why won't he wait for her?

She thinks she is getting closer when he vanishes again close to the black wall of the island. She waits, standing on a bump of rock, coral laid out around her, the ocean pushing closer. It is terrifying in the daytime, the sheer size and depth of it. In the dark it is overwhelming. She can't move. The ocean keeps coming closer. She stands still, looking from the white glow of her nightgown to the spot where she last saw him, but white blotches dance in her eyes. She rubs them until stars burst against the inside of her eyelids and then she glances around, hoping to see something she recognizes. A flash of light. Anything.

The ocean is quieter now, and she can hear the trees far away. She wishes she could hear the roosters crowing because it would mean morning was coming. She waits forever, and the sea is lapping at her toes. Then there is a flash in the distance, a tiny flicker of flame. She wants to hurry to him, but the ocean is all around her. She can see the inky movement of it everywhere where there was just rock a minute ago. She spins on her tiny bump of rock, searching for a way out. At first the water tosses up playful splashes, but then her feet are submerged and then her ankles. Her heart begins to pound, her blood surges with fear.

She yells his name into the air.

Zach

He casts around, and as he turns his head the after-image of the flame moves across the ocean and the island. Zach squeezes his eyes closed, trying to press the glow of it away.

When he opens them again, the world around him is black and swaying, shadows layered upon shadows. The moon that so plainly lit his way here has slipped behind an encroaching bank of dense cloud and now there is only the faintest smudge of its light high overhead. He hears the call of his name again—desperate now, pitched high over the water. Zach peers through the dark, trying to make out who is calling him, hoping and fearing it's Dylan.

A field's length away there is a pale smear against the boundless ocean, the same colour as the foam that dances up to it and then away, entangling the ghost there.

Zach is pinned in place by the vision, unsure of what he is seeing, even as his name reaches him on the next wave. The water swells warm over his feet; the tide is coming in. And still the ghost in the distance doesn't move.

It's impossible, and yet he's already moving before he realizes it. He yells to the figure and it lifts a hand and waves, calling him again. "Zach!"

"Astrid!"

His sister is stranded by the rising tide. He sloshes forward, and the water is at his knees, then his ankles, then his knees again as he stumbles onwards. Is he getting closer? The water begins to drag at him, keeping him back from her. He is fighting the whole weight of the ocean as it rises towards the island. He thinks he can hear her crying, even though he is still too far away. "I'm coming!" The reassurance isn't just for her; it's for himself. It's for Dylan. "Hold on. I'm coming."

The water is colder now, grasping at him. He loses a flip-flop and his foot comes down hard onto a stab of coral. He thinks of the crown-of-thorns starfish, the eel he saw hunting among the rocks, but presses on. He takes a large leap onto the next outcropping, then another. He has halved the distance between them. This time he is going to make it. He's going to save her.

Then suddenly he is being swallowed by the ocean. The sea is in his lungs and throat, filling his eyes and his nostrils, pushing air from him as the world disappears. The water is tugging him downwards, pulling him farther from the surface. He struggles and flails, thrashing at the sea, cutting himself on invisible coral, every part of him stinging and burning with exhaustion. He fights until a feeling of calm washes over him with the next swell. He stops struggling. It would be so easy to just let go.

Did Dylan feel this peace?

But then he remembers Astrid, a lone, bright spot in the vastness of the sea, and he is fighting for the surface. The air sears into him and he is coughing, retching seawater. He gulps in the thick salt air, and the white noise cracks open with Astrid's cries. His name breaks in her throat.

He calls to her, his own voice ragged. "It's okay, Ash." His body is so tired. He is scraped and bleeding into the sea from small cuts on his legs and his hands. He has lost both flip-flops, but still he staggers on, the water just above his knees now. She is only twenty feet away. He can make out the cloud of her hair tossed by the wind, the way the ocean is darkening her nightgown as the cloth wicks the water up her body. "It's okay," he says, trying to calm them both. "We're okay. I'm coming. I'm almost there." He can't see where the coral drops away to the depths, so he feels his way with his feet to avoid plunging below the surface again. He just has to go slow and then he can get them both back to shore. He can do it. His mom's face flashes in his mind. The sound of her voice. He has to do it.

"I'm almost there, Ash."

She is so close he can make out the pastel rabbits on her nightgown, but he is going too slow. Only a dozen feet separate them.

"Don't move," he says when she steps towards him. He can't watch her disappear into the waves. He can't fail her too.

Almost there. If he could swim it would be much faster, but he has to negotiate the coral one interminable step at a time, drawing closer and closer, until finally he can hold out his arms to her. They clasp each other's hands, and then his sister is in his arms, and he is holding her tight, her legs curled around his waist. She is heavier than he remembers, and he wants to fall to his knees but knows he can't. They are still so far from shore.

"What are you doing here?" he asks.

"I thought I saw Dylan, but it was you. He's not here."

"No," he says. "He's not. Let's go home, yeah?"

He looks back the way he came. The tide is rising and the shore is farther away now. The path that he took from the bungalow is cut off. They will have to make a straight line towards the island a football field away, and find a trail to the bungalow farther up shore. But the water has started to fill in more of the pools and solid ground is hard to see. He takes a single painful step forward. It would be easier if he could put Astrid down, lead her by the hand, carefully, step by step, but they would move slowly and he doesn't know how quickly the tide is coming in. Or maybe they could wait for the water to come in and then swim for it, the way he sometimes piggybacks her in the pool. But there could be an undertow, or any number of dangers. He doesn't know what to do, and they are both cold and shivering now. He has to make a decision. He has to move fast.

They are utterly alone, and it is up to him to get Astrid back safe.

"Okay," he says to his sister, says to himself, "we're just gonna go slow, but it's really uneven. I'm gonna piggyback you, okay?" He puts her down, turns around, and crouches so she can climb onto his back. The weight of her presses his scraped feet into the coral again, but for once, he doesn't want the pain as a distraction. He watches his pale feet move through the water, taking one step at a time towards the shore.

When he stumbles, Astrid tightens her arms around his neck and he murmurs that it's okay, it's okay, it's okay. The water is at his knees, his feet invisible. He doesn't look at the shore; they aren't even halfway there yet. The ocean tugs at him, tries to slip his feet out from under him.

They are in the sea forever, trapped between shores. They aren't going to make it. His body is heavy and slow, and the ocean is so much stronger than him, and rising fast. He can't do it.

"Look!" Astrid's voice is at his ear, but he just watches where his feet disappear in the dark water, tries not to imagine what is lurking there. "Zach, look!"

He worries if he stops to look, he'll never be able to start moving again. Still, he does what she says. Ahead, a small train of lights is racing along the shore, and Zach adjusts his direction slightly to head in their direction. Astrid yells, calling for their parents, and her voice clangs inside his head. His body is exhausted, but he ignores it. He has gotten used to pain. He can save her.

And then there are voices nearby and the sea froths ahead of him.

Zach almost collapses as David scoops Astrid from his back and Jacob slings Zach's arm across his shoulders, taking the weight off Zach's battered feet. Jacob helps him limp the last thirty feet to the shore, where Zach crumples to the ground, heaving from exhaustion and fear, his face wet with the ocean and his own tears.

Nearby, his mother and father are on their knees and clinging to Astrid. His grandmother grabs David and Jacob both into a hug. Zach shivers and wants so much for them to be holding him. Why aren't they racing to hug him? He wraps his arms around himself, cold and shaking, his feet both numb and scathed. His mother is whimpering into Astrid's hair, you could have been killed, you could have been killed.

He almost failed again. If David and Jacob weren't there . . .

"I'm sorry," he manages to say into the air, but it isn't enough, the word isn't even close to enough. But they are finally looking at him. "If anything had happened to her . . ." He stares at his mom. No wonder she hates him so much. "I should have been there for him, but I wasn't. I should have tried harder. Mom, please . . . I'm so sorry. It's all my fault."

Michelle

"What? Zach, no," Scott says, but Michelle can barely hear him. The world around her is murky and strange, lit by beams of moonlight piercing through cloud.

For a split second another story emerges from behind the one she knows, or thinks she does. A story in which Zach rushes down the stairs and saves the day. She clutches Astrid as she thinks of the police in their backyard, like a scene she's watched on television. Accidental drowning, they declared it. And she thinks of Zach and Astrid out there in the sea, and how she couldn't get to them, even though it was all that she wanted to do. But she couldn't. She couldn't. All she could do was watch as someone else reached them, someone else rescued them.

"Buddy," Scott says, "it wasn't your job to be there. It was an accident. A fucking awful accident, and it's not your fault." Her husband peers at her in the gloom, his face a pale blur, bruised dark where his features should be. "Right, Michelle?"

She nods but can't bring herself to speak. And in spite of Zach's pleading look, she can't help but notice how easily David pulls his son into a hug, all the tension between them evaporated by the successful rescue, at least for now. She owes them everything. She owes them her life.

"But you said . . ." Zach says, and for the first time in a long time she truly sees her son. He is drawn and distraught, his face wet with snot and tears. "You said it was my fault."

"No," she says. "No, I would never." She glances from Zach to Scott, wanting him to say something, do something. In the moonlight, the wavering flashlight beams, Scott's face is stricken.

"You said, 'Where was Zach?' I heard you say it. 'He should have been there.' And I tried. But I wasn't fast enough. I wasn't there and I was too slow and . . ." Zach's words disintegrate into choked sobs.

She is too stunned to say anything. She doesn't remember saying those words. She wouldn't have said that, would she? Those days were such a blur. Maybe she was occasionally thoughtless to Scott, but could she have been so cruel to her own son?

She passes Astrid to Scott and takes a tentative step towards Zach, still cowering on the ground, his face hidden now in the crook of his arms.

"I didn't . . . I wouldn't have . . ." and as she says it a glimmer of memory arises—she and Scott in Dylan's room. Scott was begging her to come back to bed, and she was furious, looking around at her dead son's belongings. She was so angry that no one had been there for him. And she said it. She turned on Scott—*Where were you? Where was Zach?*

Jesus. She's the one who has broken her son. It's her fault. What has she done?

She is kneeling in front of him, trying to pull his arms away from his face. "Look at me," she begs. "Zach, please." And now she is crying too. "I'm sorry. I'm sorry I said that, that I made you feel like it was your fault. I was hurt and angry. But not at you! I wasn't there. I was so stuck in my own grief, in missing him, I didn't think of anyone else. It wasn't your fault. It isn't. And I know that saying sorry isn't enough. I don't know how to make it right. But please, let me try."

She pictures the house Scott talked about, the rooms Zach and Astrid could have, the lives they could live. She thinks about the future, and she can almost see it, she can almost grasp the possibility of it. She wants to, she really does, but it is still so far away. How can she possibly get there? How can she possibly make it right? She owes them all so much.

Michelle holds Zach by the shoulders, imploring him, "When we get home, I promise, I'll try to make it right. Will you let me try?"

At first, he resists her pull, but then her son is in her arms. He is stiff for a moment, but then he collapses against her and she holds him tight, feels how much he has grown, but also how much he still needs her. How could she not have seen that? She leans back a little to look at him before squeezing him tight again.

Behind Zach, Astrid is in Scott's arms and leaning back to gaze up at the stars. "Dylan loves the stars."

Jacob nods and says, "Me too," and David gives him a gentle cuff on the back of the head.

"We can never repay you," Michelle says, and maybe now she truly understands the obligation they carry towards each other. And she is so grateful for it. Grateful for the demands of her family, grateful to owe so much, because she has been given so much.

Overhead the clouds have cleared, the moon is already dipping to the horizon. The stars spread across the whole bowl of the sky, across the immensity of the sea, and it is like seeing into the past and the future all at once. She feels Dylan there, just beyond her grasp, just out of her sight, watching them. And then he is gone. He is utterly and truly gone. She holds the pain of that close until the edges of it begin to dull. When they finally do, she stands up and extends a hand to Zach. He stares up at her and, for a second, she worries that there has been too much damage done. But he reaches up and slips his hand into hers.

VI

IV

Faina

When the story of that day was told, passed along the allied roads, versions sung and danced at the yam exchanges, it was said that the men had found William and Josephine in their garden alone. The storm was surging across the waves.

Faina was not in the story, not in the dance.

She sat at the edge of the clearing, her baby heavy in her belly. She thought they might be twins, like Louvu's lost boys. Her three-year-old daughter stamped her small feet in the outer circle of the dance, holding aloft her palm frond, even though she was too young to be a part of the dance.

Just as Faina had not been meant to be part of the story.

She did not see the seven warriors from the village go, dressed and painted for the war that they were about to wage, even though they were her curse come to life, the execution of her magic. That part of the story is never sung.

She wasn't there, so she only has the songs that have shifted over seasons. In the dance, William refused to climb aboard his boat. Louvu offered to row him to the ship himself, and when William reached for his gun, Louvu struck him with the axe that William had exchanged with him that first day. And then it was over quickly, the two missi cut down before they could call out to their father in the sky.

As the people from Middle Grove danced and sang their story for the Uplanders, Faina narrated to the baby in her belly. She murmured N-glish names and N-glish words like *ship* and *gun* and *reading* and *writing*.

The song came to an end, and the stamping of feet faded into the distant rhythm of the ocean. Faina's little girl ran back and threw herself at her mother, sticking to her with sweat from the dance.

"Did you see? I was being you." The little girl whispered the secret into Faina's ear.

While everyone gathered in groups and circles to eat, Faina snuck away and climbed to the ledge that overlooked the sea. She had not been here since she watched the *ship* sail away. The one that had held Masai and Nako, where they were cursed before they were returned. Dusk would settle on the island soon.

She cupped her hands over her swelling belly and began to tell her own story. She talked about the boy in the picture and wondered if he was still alive and whether he would know what had happened to his parents. Would they come to him in the night? She had been frightened that perhaps she would see Josephine during her nighttime walks, but she did not. In her sleep she repeated the words that she had learned from Josephine, already turning soft, settling, the way the earth had settled on all the graves that had been dug, the way the forest, it was said, had started to creep over the mission.

The nighttime was beginning to deepen. She should go back. Her husband would wonder after her, and she still wanted to ask for news of Telau, who she had heard was pregnant with her first baby now. Spirits still walked the island at night and there were so many more of them now. As she watched, fires sparked to light across the island, marking villages, marking stories being told, places of importance, tabu places. She sat and scratched the words she remembered into the dirt with her fingers. Her own name, Josephine's, Masai's, even William's. She wrote *tree* and *ground*. She wrote and spoke the words into the air, her own and theirs that matched them.

The whole of the sea stretched out in front of her to some invisible shore. Other strangers would come soon, she was certain. She watched for them.

Jacob

It has been almost five months since he was last home.

Jacob swings himself out of the bed of the pickup truck that is pushing on towards Robson's village, and thumps the back of it as it drives off. Quiet settles with the dust from the road. He didn't send word he was coming home, hasn't called or texted his father. He wants to surprise him and Rebecca, see the look on his father's face when he arrives home unexpectedly after a semester away.

The stretch of shore is different than when he left. There are new sprays of green brush as tall as he is, overlaid with tangled vines, all of it punctuated by bright blossoms. Pointing to an opening cut into the brush is a hand-painted sign complete with tiny red flowers at the start of an irregular stone walkway—*Welcome to Iparei Bungalow.* He is certain the sign is Anaei's doing.

He snaps a picture with his new phone and presses send. It buzzes in response almost immediately.

Zach: *U made it home! Sign looks great. Did Anaei make it?*

Jacob: *I think so. Just got here. Surprising my father and R. Ouben's ceremony is tomorrow.*

Zach: *Im sorry man*

Jacob: *Thx. It will be good to be together. What about you? How's the new house?*

Zach: *Good, yeah good. Mom's still staying at the old one, but A and I go over on saturdays. We all have dinner a few nights a week. She's trying. I dunno . . . Bugging them to let me come help with building in the summer! Volunteer credits for school!*

Jacob: *did you add yer video to the website?*

Zach: *yestrday. And traffic looks good!*

Jacob: *We have our first booking! Gonna check out the bunga-lows now.*

Zach: *Woo! Say hi 4 me. I'll check out the site. Oh! Ash says hi to Anaei! Latr*

Jacob: *Latr.*

Jacob makes his way down the path outlined with small, whitewashed stones towards the bungalows. So much has changed—the first year of his business program is behind him, and he feels optimistic about their future. This venture they are building together.

A few days after the earth oven was filled in, the ground sinking over it, everyone gathered in the nasara again for the first time since the ceremony. The Stewarts were gone, though all around there was evidence of them still, in the windup flash-lights that pierced the bush at night, and the brightly coloured water bottles spotted in people's hands. They were a smaller group than at the exchange, just the people from their village and Robson's. It was late afternoon and the men sat on one side, clustered in groups making a half-circle that joined the women's side. There was a lot of talk and laughter until David stood and welcomed everyone.

His father told those gathered what the Stewarts' gift entailed and let the murmur of conversation run itself out—there were those who claimed to know how large the amount was, others who scoffed at it. Some were surprised. Almost all of them could see the possibilities of the gift. David explained that everyone would have a chance to have their say, but he thought that Jacob could start them off. Jacob stood and outlined his proposal.

He had never made a case for anything in the nasara before, and after his nervousness passed he felt his chest swell and he stood taller, as though all his Fathers' Fathers were holding him up. He was rooted to this place, a part of it. He spoke easily and described how he had known immediately what he thought the community should do with the money the Stewarts had given them—Dylan's money, Michelle had explained. "It was meant for their son's future," he said, "but now it can help solidify ours." He described how they should convert David and Rebecca's old home to a guest house and build small bungalows overlooking the sea. He drew the shelters out of the air, creating a vision for his people, before returning to his place in the circle. He tried not to flush when his father clapped him on the back.

"But why should we cater to foreigners?" someone asked. "We should use the money on our own homes, or to buy better tools for our farms. Not on them."

Jacob waited for his father to answer, but when he didn't Jacob stood again. "We could do that, of course. I'm not saying that wouldn't be a good investment too. But if we do this right, it could be a business that will create jobs and bring in money over the long term."

"Bah. The cyclones will keep coming, and then what? The tourists won't want to come. How long until these new bungalows are washed away?"

David did speak then. "Nothing is without risk. And you're right, the cyclones are why we are rebuilding our own homes away from the shore. In the forest the traditional homes stand strong, shaped to take on the winds. That isn't the case on the shore where the tourists want to stay. So we will buy concrete and rebar and cinderblocks with the money. We will build the bungalows as strong as we can, and with the money they make we will be able to maintain the bungalows and our homes as well. It won't happen immediately, but we can make something that will last if we work together."

The conversation went around the circle. At certain moments Jacob was sure they were going to agree with his plan, at others he was worried they would not. Finally, they reached a consensus. The men broke away to drink kava as the sun set. Naling and Robson both praised Jacob's idea.

"When do we start building?" Jacob asked his father the next morning. He was anxious to begin, worried that the plans would fall apart, that some of the men would have thought about it overnight, found holes in his plans.

"We start, not you," David answered. "If we are to do this, then we need to do it right. So you are going to go to school. There is a program that Robson told me about, in New Zealand, a business program. He thinks that it would be good for you to learn about that side of things. We can plan the bungalows and build them. You will go study and then come back to help."

"I don't know if I believe Robson anymore."

"He wants this to work, now that he sees that this is what we are doing. And he is right. Someone needs to know this business." He paused a moment. "Unless you don't want to go?" A smile played at his father's lips.

For the first time in a long time, Jacob felt he belonged in this place. He wanted to stay, but he wanted to be able to build something that would last. He wanted to help make his people strong again.

"No, I want to go," Jacob said. "But I also want to come back."

Now he can see the work that his father and the other men have already accomplished. There are two new bungalows perched above the shore, and farther along, concrete pads have been poured for three more. They've been busy.

Jacob loops around to stand on the covered patio that has been built at the back of his father and Rebecca's old house, and gazes out at the ocean. Soon they will serve Rebecca's food here, as well as Serah's bread and cold beer, because they have bought a backup generator to run the second-hand refrigerator. They'll call the restaurant Bratas to remember Ouben and Dylan both, and to proclaim what Jacob and Zach are trying to be to each other.

Someone has been here recently—the layer of sand and crushed coral covering the floor has been neatly raked. He pulls a sign that he has carved with the restaurant's name from the duffle bag on his shoulder. He leans it against the low wall, angling it so it will not be caught by the onshore breeze, then runs his finger along the curve of letters and snaps a picture with his phone to send to Zach.

"Jacob?"

He turns to see Bridely in the doorway of the bungalow. She smiles widely at him and they hug each other close before she ushers him into the building, holding a finger to her lips and pointing. Her daughter lies on a bundle of mats, curled into sleep. Tiny and perfect.

"What's her name?" Jacob asks.

"Sari," Bridely says, "after Jimmy's aunt. But we call her Faina."

Bridely takes his hand and leads him behind a wooden desk, where there is a chalkboard listing homemade meals and drinks for purchase, alongside local coffee and fresh fruit.

"The first reservation arrives in less than two weeks," she says, showing him the calendar.

"Are we ready?"

Bridely laughs and the gap between her teeth flashes. "I hope so! But we have had more calls too. The reservation system seems to be working, as long as the mobiles work." She shrugs at this before pointing past Jacob to where his father is approaching, his arms already wide open. And then Jacob is in them and clasped hard to his father, who holds him tight in return.

"What are you doing here?"

Jacob is thrilled to hear his own language again, his father's lilting words. They warm him all the way to the bottom of his stomach.

"Would you rather I wasn't? This is my home." Jacob laughs and his father laughs with him.

"Of course! But what are you doing here right now?"

"I came to help out. I couldn't leave our first guests all to you!"

"Wow," Jacob says, as he follows his father down the last few steps of the path that leads into their ancestral dancing ground. The limbs of the banyan trees stretch over the whole of the nasara, so that the space is dappled with blinking sunlight. A shelter leans near the massive trunk of the largest tree, as wide as the truck that dropped Jacob off. In front of it, a low smoky fire burns.

There is no one around—this early in the day everyone will be in their gardens, or hard at work making canoes, or fishing, or in their cooking shelters. The children are at school. Near the brush a few chickens scratch for food, trailed by their chicks. He can hear the snuffling of several pigs.

Jacob inhales the waft of smoke, the sweet perfume of blossoms, and the rich scent of fertile earth that plucks at a memory deep inside him. His body remembers this place, belongs here. "Nowhere smells like this place."

His father laughs. "Come on, let me show you the rest of what we've built," David says before he leads him on a tour through the resurrected village, along narrow footpaths that weave between clusters of homes built in a mix of traditional and modern ways, woven walls and corrugated metal standing side by side. In one of the terraced gardens, Naling lifts a hand to them. When they join him, he carefully brushes some soil away to show them a kava root growing there. He will harvest it for his daughter's wedding.

Near another path to the nasara, his father stops Jacob with a smile. "Look at this."

David kneels next to a small wall made of layered rocks, their edges softened with age.

"What is it?"

"We think it was part of a platform where the old nakamal might have been. The Kaljoral Senta is sending some people to help us excavate it and then rebuild it. There might be more of the old place still to uncover."

Jacob runs his hands along the stones, which are warm under his palm, as though they are alive, and thinks of the men who placed them here—how the blood in his veins connects him to them. He can feel it in his own body—what it must have been like to dance in this nasara all those years ago. The men who built this wall laid the foundation for everything that he is, and everything that is still to come. He hopes he is making them proud.

He is still carrying their warmth when they arrive at his family's new home. Anaei throws herself at her brother. She is taller now, and her face presses hard into the space just below his ribs. He hauls her up with one arm, and reaches for Rebecca with the other. Her face is softer than it was when he left in December, though her eyes are still hooded and sad. She smiles at him and the smile reaches her eyes and dances there for a moment before retreating back. She lifts a palm to his cheek and holds his gaze, before patting his face playfully.

"I would have made you your favourite if I knew you were coming," she says as she pulls away. She wipes at tears in her eyes before she reaches up to retrieve woven containers from the rafters, immediately beginning to assemble a meal.

He puts Anaei down and they sit together on a woven mat.

"Anything you're cooking is my favourite," Jacob says, before turning to Anaei. "I've something to show you." He takes out his phone, scrolls to Zach's message, and hands it to his sister.

"Can I?" she asks after she reads what is there and grins.

He nods and she types in a message laden with emojis and hits send, then frowns at the phone when she realizes there is no service. "We'll make sure it goes later," he says.

Rebecca hands him a cup of fresh juice. He drinks, taking in Rebecca's new cooking hut. It is cool beneath the neat thatch roof. Tools and containers hang from the rafters, everything tidy and in its place. On one intricately woven wall he spies the photographs that used to hang in their old home by the shore—his great-great-great-grandfather standing in a group of others, the small photo of Ouben, and newer ones of Anaei and even himself that he doesn't recognize.

"Where did these come from?"

"Michelle sent them," Rebecca says.

Jacob is surprised, but also glad to hear this. "It looks like you have always lived here," he says. "I can't believe how much work has been done."

"How long are you staying?" David asks.

"Trying to get rid of me so soon?" Jacob jokes. "I'm going to stay and make sure everything is running smoothly." He slips a piece of paper out of his pocket and hands it to them. "I passed the first year. Now it's time to put the learning to work. Maybe next year I can go back for more."

"I think you should stay forever," Anaei says.

Jacob laughs again. "Me too. So long as you stay too."

He is talking to Anaei, but he means David and Rebecca as well.

And now, here they are. Even though he is so happy to be home, his throat tightens. He misses his brother.

"It's not the only reason I came," he says, and he reaches over to touch the cord at the base of his sister's throat.

Rebecca nods.

Rebecca

It has been one year since they buried Ouben, a year of harvests and exchanges, of new births and other losses. A new home that he never laughed in, a new future he should have been a part of. Now they carry his favourite foods to the smooth ground where he rests. Her boy, who she did not have enough time with to hold, but who still fills her with love.

In the quiet of the early morning, it is the four of them, she and David and their two children. Later, there will be more grieving and remembering with others in the village; they will cluster and talk about the cyclone that changed everything last March, and all that has passed since then; they will sing a new song that the song-maker has been preparing since they returned to their ancestral land. But for now, it is just them. The doves coo overhead, their feathers iridescent in the morning sun. Somewhere a cock crows.

Every day, she walks Ouben through a new story of this place. She points out the new route to her garden, which is already growing familiar. She tells him how when they reach the sandal-wood grove, the path forks, and one way leads to the church and the other to the cave. If she heads towards the church, there is a spot where the sea air creeps through the trees, letting her know she is nearly there. She can smell the sea before she can hear the calls of people and the motors of boats where the government dock has reopened in Robson's village. She walks Ouben across her new landscape so that he can find her when he needs her.

Anaei's hand fills Rebecca's. Soon her daughter's hand will be the same size as her own. Anaei likes to press her palm to her mother's and stretch her fingers, hoping they have grown. Rebecca narrates this to Ouben too—the changes she sees in Anaei, in tiny, precious Faina, in the growth of the gardens. She has only just realized that occasionally she forgets to share such changes with him, and it causes a different kind of ache in her chest.

At the grave they kneel on the ground and bow their heads. Rebecca clasps her hands and prays. She thanks God for her family next to her, and asks Him to keep those she loves safe. She asks Ouben to look after her and his sister, his brother and father, and to speak well of them to their ancestors. She hopes they are pleased. She imagines him on her own grandmother's knee, listening to the songs that Rebecca was taught as a child. She hopes someday she will be a good ancestor too, blessing her grandchildren and her great-grandchildren from the other side.

Beside her, her family is quiet, each holding their own remembrance of Ouben, holding him close for just a few minutes longer. Then Rebecca offers him a last meal: a cup of papaya juice, some laplap, and a plate of fruit cut carefully into bite-sized pieces. She lays them out on the ground for him and can't help but smile when Anaei's stomach rumbles in response. Then Rebecca takes out some of the photographs that Michelle sent her. These images will keep Ouben company. She places them one by one on the ground: a photo of Anaei smiling, of Jacob and David with their arms around each other's shoulders, one of herself she doesn't remember Zach taking, but her fingers are at her throat and so she is thinking of her son.

She turns to Anaei. "Ready?"

Anaei lifts her fingers to the cord at her throat and nods. Rebecca puts her fingers over her daughter's and together they pull until the cord snaps. It comes apart easily after a year of wear. Anaei places it on the ground in front of her and Rebecca lifts her hands to her own throat for a moment. She inhales deeply as if she's about to plunge into water, and then tugs her own cord apart. She squeezes it in her fist and whispers a small prayer, then places her palm flat on the ground, the cord hidden under it. She is still for a long time.

Eventually, David reaches for her, and then Anaei. Jacob takes his sister's other hand in his own. Together, they sit with Ouben, dreaming the past and the future.

Author's Note

At the end of 2015, while I was visiting the island of Tanna in the Oceanic archipelago of Vanuatu, I sat outside a small bungalow overlooking the Pacific and skimmed one of our hosts' well-thumbed guidebooks.

Among the many fascinating facts and anecdotes was a short paragraph about Canadian missionaries who had travelled to the islands in the 1800s. It seemed such a strange spark of a connection—other Canadians in this place so very far from home—and I briefly wondered if it might be an idea for a novel. But I quickly dismissed it, realizing both that I didn't know how to tell that story in way that hadn't already been done and that I didn't want to continue to emphasize a colonial-settler version of history.

Still, that connection, Maritime Canadians on this Oceanic island, stuck with me.

After my husband and I returned home, Vanuatu, and Tanna, in particular, occupied my thoughts. I devoured anything I could about the place and its history. Still, I never intended to write about the islands.

And then I read about a reconciliation ceremony that had taken place in 2009 on the southern Vanuatu island of Erromango, between the descendants of Erromango's Indigenous Peoples (now called ni-Vanuatu) and those of two Canadian missionaries.

This, I thought, might be a way in for me.

———

The Sea Between Two Shores is inspired by historical events.

The first missionaries began arriving on the islands of Vanuatu (then called the New Hebrides) in the 1830s. A number of these missionaries were from the Protestant Maritimes, though I do not envision the fictional characters of William and Josephine Stewart as being part of the many official missions sent to convert the Indigenous Peoples of Oceania.

The story of the Stewarts on the fictional island of Iparei is based loosely on the events surrounding the deaths of George N. Gordon and his wife, Ellen Catherine Powell, who arrived on Erromango in 1857. The year 1861 was a horrible one for Erromangans: they suffered through a terrible cyclone and, later that same year, sandalwood traders intentionally brought measles to the island, leading to the deaths of hundreds. Because of vast cosmological and cultural misunderstandings between the Gordons and the Erromangans, the Gordons' presence on the island was believed to be responsible for these calamities.

The other historical event that inspired the novel was the reconciliation ceremony held on Erromango in 2009, between the descendants of John Williams, an English missionary who was killed on the island in 1839 as a result of cultural misapprehensions, and the descendants of the Erromangans. This ceremony, which wasn't without controversy in the country, was seen as a way to seek forgiveness and repair the road that had been ruptured between the two Peoples. The event is documented in the book *No Longer Captives of the Past: The Story of a Reconciliation on Erromango* by Carol E. Mayer, Anna Naupa, and Vanessa Warri.

In recent years, I have been thinking a lot about what it means to *move forward* from past wrongs, in both systemic and personal ways. This has been driven by numerous conversations—some painful, all of them elucidating—sparked by powerful justice movements such as #MeToo, Black Lives Matter, and Land Back that we have seen rise, and the need to reckon with abuses of power and injustice in every facet of our lives. We have heard some apologies and many excuses, but what we seem to be struggling with are meaningful ways to make amends.

How do we make good?

How do *I* make good?

These are some of the questions that propelled the writing of this book.

My family, like the missionaries in both the historical record and my novel, are from the East Coast of Canada, having settled there from parts of England and Scotland. I was fascinated to learn that settlers like these had been such a driving force in the colonization of not only what is now Canada but also what we now call Oceania. My ancestors didn't go to the Pacific, but they were from the same stock, the same religious community, the same places as those who did.

I wanted to think about and interrogate how we stumble towards conciliation in public and in personal ways—with partners and parents and children; with our ancestors and our descendants; with those whose disenfranchisement and displacement I still benefit from.

It has been an education in different modes of thinking about forgiveness versus reparation, exchange versus trade; about what we owe each other and the value and gift of obligation. That initial connection—between those long-ago Canadians and the ongoing inequalities the past continues to forge—has only been reinforced for me. Each day I want to dig deeper and learn more, and I end up with more questions and, I hope, more compassion.

I thought long and hard about whose voices should appear in the novel, and different drafts contained different points of view. I initially wrote only from the Canadian family's perspective, but that left out too many voices and perspectives. And while the novel itself asks questions about whose stories get told, and how other stories are forgotten, erased, retold, and resurrected, it seemed imperative that the Tabés' voices were central to the construction of the narrative.

For the last five years, I have researched and read extensively about Vanuatu and its vast array of kastom, about Melanesia and its range of cultures, its history and concerns for the future, and about Oceania in general. Throughout the revision process, I worked with several readers and cultural consultants from across Vanuatu and Oceania, who generously read and critiqued the manuscript. Their feedback was essential to the development of the novel, and I will always be grateful for the time and consideration they each provided, answering my inquiries and challenging me as necessary. The novel has benefitted in countless ways from these exchanges.

The Sea Between Two Shores is not a novel that offers many answers, as I'll admit I am still fumbling towards them. But it is, I hope, a novel that might provoke readers to ask these kinds of questions of themselves—what do you owe and to whom?—and to see that not as a burden but as a gift.

Tanis Rideout, April 2022

Acknowledgments

I am indebted to a great many people for their help with this book.

Thanks go first to my editor, Anita Chong. Without her commitment, probing questions, and insightful challenges this book would not be what it is. Thanks also to everyone at McClelland & Stewart for their support, including Jared Bland, Kimberlee Kemp, Lisa Jager, Kim Kandravy, Gemma Wain, Kendra Ward, Ruta Liormonas, Sarah Howland, Tonia Addison, and Adrienne Tang.

I owe immense gratitude to the readers and cultural consultants from across Oceania and Vanuatu—that *sea of islands*, to use Fijian poet Epeli Hau'ofa's phrase—who were so generous with their time, knowledge, and experience: Vilsoni Hereniko, Caroline Nalo, Lora Lini, Margaret Terry, Vivian Obed, and Kaitip Kami. All mistakes and misapprehensions are my own.

In particular, I want to thank Anna Naupa, not only for her thoughtful read but also for her willingness to answer my many questions and for offering solutions. If you want to learn more about the real-life reconciliation ceremony on Erromango, please read the book *No Longer Captives of the Past*, which she co-authored and which partially inspired this novel, and follow her work. I'm grateful to Kirk Huffman and Maggie Cummings, for answering questions and pointing me in the direction of great readers; as well as Kim Arnold and the staff at the Presbyterian Church in Canada Archives.

Thanks are also due to Elizabeth Walker, Sheetal Rawal, Carolyn Smart, Tate Young, Stephanie Earp, Grace O'Connell,

Shannon Moroney, Scott Belluz, and Michael MacLennan. And to Hinahina Gray at Salt & Sage Books for her generous feedback.

And, as always, to Simon—for all the endless seasons.

———

For a list of book recommendations and resources, please visit my website: tanisrideout.com.

The epigraph from Rebecca Solnit is from *Hope in the Dark: Untold Histories, Wild Possibilities* (Haymarket Books, 2016).

The epigraph from Rainer Marie Rilke is from *The Dark Interval: Letters on Loss, Grief and Transformation* (Modern Library, 2018), translated by Ulrich Baer.

The epigraph from Christina Thompson is from *Sea People: The Puzzle of Polynesia* (HarperCollins, 2019).

The bible verse that Josephine quotes on pages 166–67 is from Mathew 18:10–14.

Robson's prayer on page 284 is from the Opening Prayer in the Book of Common Worship.

Discussion Questions for
The Sea Between Two Shores by Tanis Rideout

1. In her author's note, Tanis Rideout talks about the first sparks of this novel igniting while she was visiting the island of Tanna in the archipelago of Vanuatu. She describes dismissing the idea, initially, but gradually finding her way into the story. What do you imagine were some of the specific challenges Rideout, as a white settler in Canada, might have come up against in telling this story?

2. The novel begins during a cyclone that ultimately leads to the death of Ouben—the event that prompts the Tabé family to invite the Stewarts to the island for a reconciliation ceremony. But where does the *story* begin for the characters in the novel? For example, does it begin when Faina first visits the missi? When the missi first arrive on Iparei? Or perhaps even before that? If you were to put yourself into the minds of various characters in the book—David, Rebecca, Michelle, Zach—where might each of them think the story started?

3. In her author's note, Rideout writes, "I thought long and hard about whose voices should appear in the novel, and different drafts contained different points of view. I initially wrote only from the Canadian family's perspective, but that left out too many voices and perspectives." How do you think the story and its impact would be different if it never showed the world of the novel through the perspectives of Faina, Rebecca, David, or Jacob?

4. Which characters did you find most relatable? Which did you find more difficult to connect with or understand? How do you think your own identity influenced your experience of the characters and their perspectives?

5. Why do you think Rideout chose not to include any chapters written from Josephine's or William's perspective? What did you learn or see from reading about the past events from Faina's perspective that may not have been possible to convey from Josephine's or William's view?

6. We can infer a lot about William and Josephine through Faina's view of them. For example, we might surmise that Josephine is a somewhat unconventional Euro-Canadian woman of the nineteenth century. Yet her behaviour suggests she is very much indoctrinated in colonialist views that dehumanized and disregarded the people of Iparei, even as she is subjected to William's mistreatment of her and, in a broader context, the limitations of patriarchy. How did you feel about Josephine? Which qualities of her character are reflected in her descendants, especially Joyce and Michelle? And what has changed?

7. What is the significance of Faina's attraction to writing and recording that keeps drawing her back to the missi? How do you think gaining that knowledge changed Faina and her people? What evidence in the present day of the story suggests how that knowledge evolved on the island?

8. Zach engages in another form of recording—video, through his phone. What connections could be drawn between Josephine's drawings of the women of Iparei and Zach's viewing of the world through his phone's camera? What does the novel have to teach

us about whose stories get recorded, how stories are recorded, and how knowledge and wisdom are transmitted?

9. The first night Michelle joins the women in the nasara, having done her research about what to bring, she presents her hosts with her plastic bag of gifts—pens, notebooks, water bottles, and CN Tower flashlights. Why do you think Rebecca, Bridely, and the others are perplexed by her offering? What is suggested by Michelle's reaction to their indifference?

10. When Michelle learns that Scott wants the family to move, her resistance to the idea prompts a reflection on her life. "What has she ever wanted that she didn't get?" the narrator writes. "She has a husband, a family, a successful career, and when it all happened for her it didn't surprise her it just seemed her due . . ." Michelle attributes her previous good fortune to luck, and thinks that her luck ran out when Dylan died. What is Michelle not seeing about her so-called good fortune? How might Rebecca receive the idea that Michelle's luck had run out?

11. Michelle believes Rebecca can help her, and seems to be confounded by her host's unwillingness to absolve her of grief and guilt over Dylan's death. Why does Rebecca resist helping Michelle? What parallels might be drawn between Michelle's expectations of Rebecca and Josephine's transactions with Faina?

12. When Rebecca takes Michelle to the cave, she does so because of the changes she has seen in Anaei in preparation for the ceremony and in excitement over her friendship with Astrid. She notes that Anaei doesn't understand yet "that there is a balance to be found between sharing and protecting." What feelings came up for you in this scene, as you read about Rebecca's connection to that sacred place and watched Michelle through her eyes?

13. While they are at the cave, Rebecca gives voice to a crucial fact: that Ouben would not have died if he had been Michelle's son. Michelle is silent in response. What do you think Michelle hears and understands in that place? Are there any revelations for Rebecca?

14. We learn details about how Dylan died through the telling of the story by Scott, Michelle, and Zach at various points in the novel. And yet, still a sorrowful kind of mystery surrounds the young boy's death. In what ways does the portrayal echo experiences you might have had of grief, either personally, or in your family or community?

15. Rebecca and Michelle deal with their grief quite differently. Rebecca's cultural traditions (for example, washing Ouben's body, wearing the braided vine around her neck, and the family ceremony to mark the anniversary of his death) seem to help her integrate grief into her life and the life of her family. Michelle's grief, in comparison, seems disorganized and destructive. How do both women and their family members ultimately come to terms with their respective losses?

16. Ancestors are a recurring presence in the novel. During the reconciliation ceremony, David welcomes their ancestors and says, "They planted gardens that we might harvest them, they built roads that we might be connected. It is our duty to ensure the same is true for our children, and their children, and theirs." Rebecca, David, and their community express a living relationship with those of the past, one that affects the unfolding of life in the present. How does the Tabés's sense of obligation to their ancestors relate to their invitation to the Stewarts to the reconciliation ceremony? What do the Stewarts learn about their ancestors and obligation through their time in Iparei?

17. Many characters observe that Michelle is always saying "sorry." At the reconciliation ceremony, David talks about how "asking for forgiveness, agreeing to change and move forward together" are not the same as doing—that their gathering represents the start of action and obligations to each other to carry forward in the world. What do you think motivates Michelle's gift of Dylan's trust and her offer to provide for Anaei? Is this a moment of redemption for Michelle? Why or why not?

18. Two parent-child relationships are fractured—the one between David and Jacob, and the one between Michelle and Zach. What needs to happen for each of these characters to be able to repair the relationships?

19. It is said that there can be no reconciliation without truth first. What truths need to be accepted in this story, and by whom, before there can be reconciliation within it? In the novel, who is responsible for reconciliation, and is it achieved? What do you think is the author's view of reconciliation, and what it means for us both personally and systemically?

20. The end of the novel signals an economic future for Iparei, along with a way for Jacob to stay most meaningfully connected with his family and his ancestors through his connection to place on the island. Jacob and Zach have developed a brotherly relationship, and Anaei and Astrid's friendship continues. The novel reaches this hopeful conclusion, but where do you think this *story* ends?